BEYOND THE SUN

'I'm not proud of what I'm doing. And I searched desperately for another way. I'm not going to lie to you. I do feel responsible for bringing Errol here. For bringing all of them here. But I will do what I have to do to keep them alive.'

Do what I have to do. If the words did not make sense, the meaning behind them was clear. 'That's a threat, isn't it?'

'Maybe.'

'Maybe.' He wanted to laugh, but all he could manage was a grim smile. 'You're worse than the Sunless. At least they aren't hippocrites. At least they are willing to accept who they are.'

'Please!'

He shook his head, a weight lifting from his shoulders. He felt free for the first time in the year since the spaceships had come and brought terror and chains to his world. 'You're going to have to kill me, Bernice Summerfield,' he said. 'Nothing else is within your power.'

THE NEW
ADVENTURES

BEYOND THE SUN

Matthew Jones

First published in Great Britain in 1997 by
Virgin Publishing Ltd
332 Ladbroke Grove
London W10 5AH

Bernice Summerfield originally created by Paul Cornell

Cover illustration by Mark Salwowski

ISBN 0 426 20511 1

Typeset by Galleon Typesetting, Ipswich
Printed and bound in Great Britain by
Mackays of Chatham PLC

For Marsha, Alan and Emma,
names that mine fits so well beside,
with so much love.

CONVERSATIONS WITH THE ENEMY

Kitzinger slipped down to the deep pools in the basement of the university. The shadowed subterranean chamber was empty of people. With no swimmers to disturb it, the water was dark and still. The surface appeared solid, like clear resin.

Through the water, Kitzinger could see the Blooms nestled at the bottom of the pools like clamshells on a seabed, their huge, dark, ribbed surfaces lit by the underwater spotlights.

Kitzinger stripped off her clothes and waded down the gentle slope on the near side of the pool. The liquid the Blooms produced was soaked in oxygen: there wasn't any need for breathing equipment. The water was thick and felt creamy next to her skin. She looked down at her naked body in the low lighting in the room. Her fifty-year-old legs were muscular, but hadn't escaped the ravages of time and cellulite. It had been years since she had done anything but tend to the Blooms. She would take some exercise, she told herself as she did at least three times a month – maybe involve herself in a new project, something more physical than caring for the children that grew like sea anemones in the bottom of the pool.

She paused when the water reached her mouth. Her body tensed as she allowed the water to lap over her tongue. She forced herself to open her throat and breathe in the sweet liquid. She tensed as she felt herself start to gag; some

1

instinctive part of her mind refused to allow her to drown herself. But her body relaxed as her lungs drew the oxygen out of the liquid. The water closed over her head and the sound of the chamber disappeared, replaced by the intense quietness of the pool. With no air in her lungs to give her buoyancy, Kitzinger began to sink slowly to the bottom of the pool. She rested on the sloping floor for a moment, staring up at the lights of the chamber above her, distorted by the water. When she felt comfortable breathing in the thick liquid, she swam down the underwater slope towards the deepest part of the pool.

The Blooms were slightly open, like mussels after boiling. A leviathan marine creature sieving the sea for food. She swam up to the lip of the shadowed bulk: a middle-aged woman kissing a whale.

As Kitzinger slipped through the metre-high gap, she experienced a childlike fear that the Bloom might suddenly snap closed, breaking her in two or else trapping her inside for ever. It was ridiculous of course. The Blooms weren't sentient, not according to every test and examination. There was certainly nothing that could be described as a brain dwelling inside them. In fact, they had more in common with a chunk of crystal than an oyster, belonging to that small group of silicon life forms scattered throughout the galaxy.

They were artificial, that much was known, although no knowledge about their creators existed. The enormous cloning machines were all that were left of yet another lost civilization in the universe, found lying among the debris of a long-collapsed society.

The spiralling ribbed tunnels inside the Blooms had been lit with electric lights fed by cables, which had been stapled to their curved fleshy walls. However, despite what the scientists had said, swimming through the gloomy tunnels still felt unnervingly like being inside a giant's nervous system.

Kitzinger visited the children who floated in the nearest tunnels. The children were completely unaware of her care and attention of course. There was little to do for the sleepers now except wait for the umbilical cords of the human children to wither and tear and for the others to hatch out of their eggs.

Sometimes it was necessary to guide a newborn out of the tunnels; on other occasions the newly woken child would find its own way. And Kitzinger would be startled by their breaking the surface of the pool, coughing the liquid out of their lungs, eager to take their first desperate gasp of air.

There were over four hundred families of eight growing in this Bloom. Eight was the Ursulan family unit. One child to represent each of the eight species on Ursu.

An Oolian girl was curled in a transparent rubbery sac. There was a tear in the bottom of the thick bubble, and one of her thin, scrawny legs was poking through. The pink leg was scrabbling to get a purchase on the edge of the bubble in order to climb back inside. It was a comical sight and Kitzinger was forced to stop herself laughing as she began to hiccup the liquid in her lungs.

She dived underneath the soft egg and, cradling the child's foot in her arms, explored the tear in the surface of the sac. If it had torn prematurely it would be necessary to tuck the child's leg back inside and seal it so that the child's development could continue without further discomfort. Kitzinger peered through the transparent wall of the egg. The child's skin was pink. The wiry red veins that had been visible until a few weeks ago had now disappeared and her wings had grown their first feathers. The girl looked as fit and strong as any four-year-old. Her eyes were screwed up tightly above her hooked beak. Her brow was heavy and tensed, a grumpy Neanderthal expression on her face. Kitzinger smiled in welcome at the little brutish face before her.

The split frayed and widened in her fingers. The egg was decaying naturally, its job done. The child's awkward unconscious movements were freeing her from her first home. The little girl kicked out as Kitzinger ran a hand over her leg. Kitzinger recoiled in the water.

My, this child is strong, she told herself.

The small tear split wide open and, without warning, the

3

girl dropped out of the sac and into a startled Kitzinger's arms. It all happened so quickly that the girl had wrapped herself around Kitzinger before she had realized what had happened. The little girl's wings opened suddenly, blocking out the light, their span wide for such a tiny creature. Kitzinger felt a thrill of emotion rush through her with the simple pleasure of being present at the birth of another person. She let out a small cry of emotion, the sound echoing around her head.

They floated in the dark, ribbed tunnels for a few minutes. Kitzinger could feel the child's heart pounding against her chest, and she waited until it began to slow as the child adjusted to this new environment and to her first contact with another.

Slowly, and with some regret, Kitzinger made her way out of the dark Bloom and up towards the surface of the pool. She swam slowly, one-handed, holding on to the child with the other. It would be necessary to leave the girl in the shallows so that Kitzinger could attend to the remaining children in the Eight. It was important that the children should begin their lives in each other's company and not form a relationship with her.

Kitzinger saw the dark figures lining the poolside from a few metres below the surface. She frowned, her body tensing without her knowing why. The figures were motionless against the tiled wall of the chamber. They weren't the familiar outlines of the other people who came to care for the Blooms. Who else would come down here? As she neared the surface, she saw that they were humans. Tall and white-skinned.

She broke the surface of the pool and was instantly forced to retch up the fluid in her lungs. She was out of her depth and had to tread water with her feet and one hand until her lungs cleared and she had coughed the last of the fluid out of her throat. She felt disorientated and swam until her feet touched the floor, and then she began to walk up the sloping bank of the pool, the warm body of the newborn in her arms.

There were ten humans standing at the top of the slope. Their heads had been shaved, only a dusting of stubble remaining.

Strangely, they were all wearing identical clothes: loose, one-piece, charcoal-grey outfits made from some durable-looking material. The clothes looked weathered and worn, like the wearers themselves.

Their ashen faces were drawn tightly over their cheekbones, their lips bloodless, making them appear gaunt and quite striking. However, something about their appearance disturbed Kitzinger greatly: their expressionless faces bore a leukaemic glaze – as if they weren't really there at all. Ghosts. Ten pairs of expressionless eyes stared at her from their sharp, angular faces. Dull, industrial-grey eyes. Their eyes disturbed her more than anything else about them.

Kitzinger saw her naked fifty-year-old body reflected in those mercury eyes.

She had seen eyes like those once before . . .

They stood silently, watching her. The tension in the chamber was palpable. Everything about the strange people suggested violence and aggressive behaviour. They were clearly some kind of warrior or – Kitzinger searched for the word – soldier. That was it, people trained to fight and kill. However, for the moment, they seemed to be content just to appraise her with their cold eyes.

She was distracted by the newborn in her arms. The child folded her wings with a wet flapping sound and then opened her beak and vomited Bloom liquid over Kitzinger's shoulder. It ran down her back, hot from being inside the tiny body.

She set the child down in the ankle-deep water, and wiped the thick liquid from her own face and shook it out of her short, white hair. The little girl wobbled unsteadily, flapping her wings and crouching like a gargoyle in order to keep her balance. Like a foal, she stumbled on her matchstick legs. It took all of her concentration to prevent herself from toppling over.

Kitzinger turned to look at the silent, menacing figures; they must have sensed this as their attention shifted from the Oolian child, and their dark eyes came to rest on her. They weren't Ursulans, that was for sure. The idea of their being off-worlders didn't disturb her half as much as the fact that they were all wearing identical clothes.

Uniforms.

These, and their shorn scalps, were a symbol of subservience to something or someone. Kitzinger felt a chill of fear for the first time since she had set eyes upon them. People who didn't make their own decisions, who just followed orders, were inflexible and dangerous.

Her own brightly coloured clothes were still in an untidy pile where she had stepped out of them. The silent figures were in the way. Her nakedness suddenly began to trouble her. She shivered, feeling vulnerable. 'Are you just going to stand there or what?' she demanded, surprised by how frightened her voice sounded.

The nearest figure, a broad-shouldered female, cocked its head for a second as if it were trying to understand Kitzinger's words. Later, Kitzinger would wonder whether this had in fact been a signal to the others, because immediately afterwards they began to move.

Fast.

Too fast for Kitzinger to protect herself. Two of them launched themselves forward, knocking her over backwards into the shallow water.

Kitzinger heard herself grunt as the wind was knocked out of her. The water closed over her head. She was struggling to the surface when one of them pressed its knee to her chest.

Hard.

Her head connected with the bottom of the pool. Panic coursed through her just as pain shuddered through her body.

They were trying to drown her!

A dark shape was visible through the water. Emotionless eyes staring down at her. Her lungs flooded with the thick water. She tried to struggle against the figure above her in the water, but she couldn't get any leverage. The grey-suited figure was strong. Not like flesh and blood at all, but like a machine. She relaxed, playing dead, keeping her breathing shallow. She forced herself not to blink – perhaps they would leave her alone. Through the water she could see its pale face staring impassively down at her. Patiently waiting for her to asphyxiate.

Even through the thick liquid she could see that its face was quite beautiful. After what felt an age the weight on her chest lifted slightly and then was gone. The dark shape hovered above her for a moment and then moved away. She exhaled slowly, breathing in the thick oxygen-rich liquid. Her attacker hadn't known about the property of the Bloom water. They'd left her for dead.

She lay in the water wondering how long she should wait before daring to lift her head up. After what felt like an hour, but could only have been a minute or possibly two, she broke the surface quietly.

Too soon.

The grey figures were still in the room, although, fortunately for her, they all had their backs to her. One of them – the female – dropped a small flapping bundle into the shallows near her. It floated on the surface, a ragbag of spindly, pink limbs. It was a moment before Kitzinger realized that it was the body of the newborn child.

Not caring about drawing attention to herself, she splashed over to the little girl. The Oolian child's wings were open behind her in the water. Her beak was cracked and a dark-red mark ran across her broken neck. Her eyes were still closed. They had never opened.

Wouldn't ever open now.

Kitzinger knelt over the child, shivering with cold and shaking with fury. A shadow fell across her. She looked up into the grey face of the female. Metal eyes staring out of its thin pale face. It began to speak, its face convulsing with the effort, as if it were not accustomed to doing so.

'You . . .' it stuttered, its voice scratchy and hoarse, 'are our prisoner.' Its teeth were thin and sharp. White triangles against the darkness of its mouth.

Kitzinger stared at it in confusion and horror. 'Prisoner?' she said. 'What does that mean?'

1

AN INDOOR BOY

Emile Mars-Smith made his way down four levels of business class before he found the floor where the economy cabins were. His hands were full of greasy food cartons, so he'd jammed his boarding card with his cabin number on between his teeth. He tried to peer down his nose at the card, but the large black numbers were a blur, and the effort sent him uncomfortably cross-eyed. Sighing, he set the strawberry yassi and the masala dosa he'd just purchased from the Kwik Kurry kiosk in the passenger lounge down on the floor and checked the number on the now damp card. Coconut sauce had dripped out of the paper-thin dosa and was spreading down his arm. He licked the line of green sauce. It was surprisingly good. He found his cabin number.

14L. Should be about three corridors down.

His cabin was a few doors beyond a group of adolescent Vilmurians who were crawling about in the corridor, snapping abuse at each other and flicking their thick tails in irritation. They had marbled eyes and long crocodile mouths. These three wore razor-sharp black suits and were surrounded by empty bubblejack cans. Emile whispered apologetic excuse-me's as he stepped over their scaly tails. The corridors of the ship were full of people looking for somewhere to sleep or to party. Passengers who hadn't paid for cabins were supposed to sleep on the recliners in the lounges, but the snores of people from a couple of dozen different races led most travellers to search out more private places to set up camp for the long journey.

One of the Vilmurians tugged at Emile's trouser leg, and he looked down at the rows of sharp yellow teeth on display.

'Hey mate, you got a room?' the Vilmurian hissed, and then gestured at the crate of cans with the point of his thickly scaled tail. He offered Emile a share in them if he let them have a party in his room. They'd sold their cabin tickets to buy the bubblejack. Emile had seen Vilmurians only on the small screen and found them disconcerting. No, that was another lie. They were terrifying. This one's eyes were completely dilated from the bubblejack. A half-remembered documentary popped into his head. Didn't they eat their enemies alive? Or was that the Vendurians?

He muttered something about his cabin being full and tried to slip past. The nearest one made a lunge for him, its mouth snapping loudly. It shouted a string of curses as he dodged its long jaws and shot down the corridor, spilling his yassi down his overcoat in the process.

'Lightweight!' the Vilmurian called after him. An empty pink can whistled past Emile's ear and bounced on the pastel-coloured walls of the passenger liner.

Emile collapsed into the tiny windowless cabin, thumbed the lock control, chucked his holdall on to one of the two bunks and then sank down on to the floor, leaning heavily against the door. There was a strawberry-coloured smear down the front of his coat. He mopped it up with the edge of his hand and licked his sticky fingers. Maybe if he rationed his masala dosa he could spend the whole trip in his cabin. He wished that he hadn't spilt his yassi. Was he going to be like one of those crash survivors, forced to drink his own pee in order to survive?

Maybe not.

You're getting hysterical, Emile, he told himself. But he still felt reassured when he had checked that the cabin had an *en-suite*.

He put what remained of the yassi on a small moulded-plastic shelf which formed part of the headboard of the bed

9

and wiped his mouth on the cuff of his heavy coat.

He was sweating, so he tugged himself out of his overcoat and climbed into the bathroom, which was a tiny white plastic cell three feet square. He washed his hands and face and then examined his reflection in the mirror. The fluorescent light turned his pale skin a sick green and transformed his carefully bleached flat-top pus-yellow. He frowned at the two spots he had picked that morning, which were now standing out angrily on his chin.

Sexy.

He stared into his large brown eyes and wondered what he was doing here. College life wasn't turning out quite like he'd imagined. The trip to St Oscar's from the relay station had been horrendous enough, but he'd been at the university only a week before he'd been told that he was to meet his tutor at a dig site two systems away. Two systems! How many light years was that? Shit, at least ten million, I'll bet, he guessed. Ten million! That was more zeros than he'd got in his last maths test.

When he asked the department secretary which member of staff was going to accompany him on the trip, the matronly woman had only smiled apologetically and muttered something about a timetable mix-up and handed him his ticket. 'Well, you made it here in one piece didn't you, my dear? You're a grown man – I'm sure you'll be fine.'

He pulled a face at his fifteen-year-old reflection and it pulled it right back. Emile Mars-Smith, you are a dirty stinking liar, he told himself. When he had begun this lie about his age he'd only ever worried that he wouldn't be able to pass it off. It hadn't occurred to him that people would actually treat him as if he really were eighteen. And that wasn't the only lie he'd been spinning to the universe. He turned away from the mirror, suddenly unwilling or unable to look at himself. Some things were harder to come clean about. Even to himself.

Especially himself.

He felt a gentle rumbling as the passenger ship began to lift itself away from the ground. No going back now. Then he gasped in horror as someone started rattling the door handle in the other room.

Oh my God, the Vilmurians were coming for him! He imagined their long snouts snapping around his ankles. He looked around for a panic button or a puter terminal but there was nothing.

Someone outside swore and threw their weight against the door. There was an unhealthy splintering sound and the door buckled in its frame. Emile dived out of the *en-suite* and put his back against the cabin door. 'We're full!' he squealed. 'Wrong cabin!'

The person on the other side of the door said something that might have been 'Stinking lightweight' and stopped pushing. Emile waited for a full minute, listening carefully for signs of life in the corridor. No easy task over the sound of his own heart pounding frantically in his chest.

'Please let them be gone,' he whispered to himself in terror. He was going to be stuck in the tiny cabin for ever. Just like when Demona, the most powerful woman in the universe, finally beat Comrade 7 and trapped her in a black hole.

But that was in a comic and Comrade 7 had managed to get out – although he couldn't remember exactly how.

Maybe he hadn't bought that issue.

He put his head in his hands and swallowed down panic. Yeah, but I bet she didn't have to face crocodile men, out of their snouts on bubblejack!

The door suddenly crashed open, cracking against his head. He was too surprised to try to hold it closed. He tumbled to the floor, protecting his face with his hand, too scared to open his eyes. 'Don't eat me!' he yelled, curling up into a foetal position in the middle of the floor.

When sharp teeth failed to bite into the soft flesh of his calves, he took a peek through his fingers.

A young woman stood in the doorway. A human woman. Despite her heavily made-up face, Emile could tell she was Hispanic. She had long, raven-black hair and thick, dark eyebrows that almost met in the middle. She was dressed entirely in black. Thick leggings, miniskirt, leather jacket. Emile recognized the style as Vampire Chic – the news pages of the fashion glossies were only just reporting it. The woman held a hard matt-black suitcase out in front of her like a battering ram. She was peering at him over a pair of goggle-shaped black shades, an expression of annoyance on her heavily powdered face. However, the more she stared at him the more her hostility melted into surprise and amusement.

'Eat you?' She raised a painted black eyebrow. 'I don't think so, little boyee.' Her voice was surprisingly low, almost gruff. 'I mean, like, *dream* on.'

The young woman stepped over him and laid her suitcase down on the empty bunk. Her long black hair slipped around her face like silk on marble. He found himself staring at a pair of genuine Titañon pro-wrestling lace-ups. Wow!

'If we're going to share this cabin, you're going to have to stop trying to lock me out – my luggage won't take that kind of abuse. That's rule number one in a series of several thousand.' She frowned down at him from behind her shades. She was a striking woman, although Emile thought her features were probably too sharp for her to be a model. Her nose was as straight as a laser, and she had the kind of cheekbones that could cut paper.

She sighed in exasperation. 'Can you even understand what I'm saying, boyee?'

And then Emile realized who she was. Tameka Vito was in his year at St Oscar's. He was suddenly very aware that he was lying, cringing, on the floor. He started to feel very foolish indeed.

Like him, Tameka had been at St Oscar's for only a week, but unlike him everyone in his year already knew her name. She was just *smotheringly* cool. She was the only undergraduate who wore *haute couture* for starters, and she sort of just glided around the campus like Blake's Tyger, only in black Lycra. He'd seen her lounging in the sun with her boyfriend, a purple-skinned Jeillo with thighs like a lion's. Emile had spent twenty minutes watching them from a window in the library. Tameka had been reading under a black parasol in the driver's seat of her custom speeder, wearing her corpse-like foundation and studiously avoiding getting a tan. The Jeillo had been sprawled in the back seat wearing only a pair of obscenely skimpy Speedos, lavishly smearing his intricately ridged abdominal muscles with Coppertone Xeno, his skin slowly turning from indigo to violet in the hot afternoon light. The Jeillo had caught sight of Emile staring down at him, grabbed hold of the front of his trunks, and grinned lewdly. Emile had blushed beetroot and leapt away from the window, almost knocking over a bookshelf in the process.

People talked about Tameka. In fact, they never seemed to stop talking about her. There were all kinds of rumours going around the first-year common room. Like Emile, she had been awarded a Krytell scholarship. Although, unlike Emile, she probably hadn't copied her essay out of an obscure study guide. Despite being on a scholarship, she dressed for a New Paris catwalk, which only fanned the flames of gossip. She was variously reported to have made her money from drug-dealing, prostituting herself for her Jeillo pimp – Emile had even heard someone whisper that she was the Cat's Paw, the intergalactic thief who was terrorizing the art world. The rumours were the twisted and cruel words of the jealous. But if the sly comments bothered Tameka she didn't show it.

He watched her activate the lock on her case and it opened with an expensive sigh. She pulled out a carton of orange juice, a neat Krytell Stowaway with detachable speakers, a well-thumbed hardback called *Down Among the Dead Men* and a huge bottle of duty-free tequila. And then she turned to where Emile was still lying on the floor and pushed her sunglasses up on to her forehead. Her eyes were *paradise* blue. The colour of tropical sea in phoney touched-up holiday simulations. They had to be retinal stains. Nature just couldn't produce colours like that.

Particularly not for Hispanic girls.

'Hey, don't I know you from somewhere?' Tameka asked in her husky voice.

'Er' was all he could manage. He climbed awkwardly to his feet, adjusting his waistcoat a bit self-consciously. Next to her, his carefully chosen clothes looked like Share Wear.

'Ernie, isn't it?'

'Emile,' he said, completely devastated.

'Emile. Right. We shared a desk in that introductory lecture. Have some tequila.'

He shook his head. 'I'm not supposed to drink.'

'Jeez, are you in rehab already? You're so *young*.'

'I'm not young!' he blurted out, feeling foolish again. He wasn't really sure what she meant. 'I'm not in rehab. At least, I don't think I am.'

She seemed to find this funny for some reason, laughing warmly. He noticed that some of her scarlet lipstick had stuck to her perfect teeth. 'Somehow I don't think you are either, Emile.' She poured two generous measures and then added the tiniest amount of juice. 'Here's to our first field trip. To Emile, Tameka and Bernice.'

'Who's Bernice?'

She rolled her heavily made-up eyes. 'Hoo boy! Did you come down with the last shower or what?' She tossed the book over to him. He spilt half of his tequila trying to catch it, which was maybe just as well because the fiery liquid was already burning a hole in his throat.

The name on the dust jacket was Bernice Summerfield, Ph.D.

'She's only our *tutor*. Didn't you read the First-Year Handbook?'

'Does anyone?'

Tameka shook her head. 'Sheesh, I don't know why guys like you bother going to college.' She leant over and directed his attention to the back flap of the jacket. There was a photograph of the author and a short biog. The woman in the picture was in her early thirties, attractive in an awkward, angular kind of way. Her hair was dark and short, and she wore large hooped silver earrings that Emile knew for a fact had not been fashionable for at least five years. However, the most striking thing about the picture was the woman's expression. Unlike most academic portraits, which radiated dignity and dustiness, Professor Bernice Summerfield was

14

staring madly out of hers, grinning from ear to ear like a woman possessed.

Emile liked her immediately.

'Is it any good?' he asked, not bothering to open the book. He knew he wouldn't understand a word of it anyway. Academic books were full of words with more syllables than centipedes had legs. The thought of having to read one scared him almost as much as the Vilmurians did. Or was it the Vendurians? The threat posed by the crocodile men didn't seem quite real now that Tameka was here.

He was just very glad not to be alone.

'I've got some reservations about her book – she ain't no Howard Carter, that's for sure. But then she's no faker like that Kryptosa guy.'

Emile had never heard of Howard Carter. Although the name was sort of familiar. He was probably one of the other lecturers at St Oscar's. But Emile didn't need to be told who Kryptosa was. Franz Kryptosa was an explorer who had vanished about a hundred years ago. Now he really had been famous – his own programmes, major product endorsement, everything! The networks still repeated his old shows when they had a gap to fill in the weekday lunchtime schedules. Emile always associated the glamorous documentaries with being home from school with a fever or just bunking off.

Father hated Kryptosa of course. Said he was unscientific, irresponsible. There wasn't much room for explorers or for glamour among the community on the relay station. Father said that it wasn't right for a man to wander the stars. A man's place was at the head of his family. That was the Natural Path, after all. You'll understand when you have a family of your own, Father would say. Emile had never known how to reply to this. In the old days, Mother would rescue him, changing the subject, telling him to go and clean up for dinner. And as he washed his hands, he would listen to Father's muffled shouts, feeling sick with the knowledge that the anger Mother was enduring was somehow all his fault.

But Mother was dead and gone. Leaving him alone with

Father. And without Mother he had been left to face the Natural Path without an ally. At classes, the mentor had read about the true natures of men and women and how they had become distorted by technology and the dilution of humans out among the stars. Emile would listen but they didn't seem to be talking about him. It was as if he didn't quite fit, but he wasn't exactly sure why.

He was reminded of the day he had left the relay station, and he swallowed uncomfortably.

Tameka was rattling on about Bernice Summerfield in her throaty growl. 'She's got this like *obsession* with the twentieth century. Goes on about it page after page.'

Emile was dragged out of his memories. The twentieth century? Did anything special happen then? He didn't think so. 'Was that the one with Big War Four in?' he asked, tentatively, not wanting to show his ignorance.

'Yeah, maybe,' Tameka said, pausing for breath. 'I dunno. Anyway she keeps going on about cancer and capitalism, space shuttles and safer sex, you know?'

Emile didn't. But he nodded anyway.

'But she writes well, doesn't try to bamboozle you with jargon, and tells you about the little things. The details. Ordinary people, not just emperors and generals and crap like that.'

Emile thought about this. 'You mean as if she really might have actually been there?'

Tameka laughed. 'What *are* you talking 'bout, boyee. If she'd actually experienced all the things in this book, she'd have been dead and buried *years* ago, I'm telling you.'

Emile blushed. 'Yeah, course. I knew that.'

2

BURIED TREASURE

'OK, I admit it, Bernice. This archaeology business has got me *beaten*.'

Her tutor raised an eyebrow and let out an exasperated sigh. 'What is it this time, Tameka?'

'I'm telling you. It's time to throw in the trowel.'

Professor Bernice Summerfield PhD wagged a weary finger at her. 'You are not the first to make that joke.'

Tameka dropped her trowel to the floor of the muddy trench as if it were a tasteless Christmas gift.

Enough was, like, *enough*.

'I'm serious, Bernice. This is just not fun.' She was shivering in the spitting, greasy rain. 'I'm up to my . . . my *armpits* in stinking mud. I'm cold. I'm wet. And I'm just plain *bored*.'

'Be patient,' Bernice said, resting her hands on her hips. 'Urnst didn't find Sakkrat in a day.'

Tameka gave Bernice her best scowl. 'I've read that book. Urnst never found Sakkrat at all. And anyway, at least he was in with a chance of finding something interesting. Admit it, Bernice, there's nothing here but bits of broken parasite pottery.'

'Well –'

'This place is a joke. I'm telling you. I've had it.'

The whole thing reminded Tameka of chemistry lessons when she was twelve. She'd quickly lost interest in the subject after she'd excitedly reported to her teacher that her tiny strip of amber paper had turned pink when she'd touched it to the piece of lemon. What do you mean, you know that lemon turns the paper pink? she'd demanded of him after he'd failed to display the required enthusiasm for her import-ant discovery. Her twelve-year-old self hadn't been able to comprehend the point of doing the experiment if everyone already knew the answer.

This Chelonian site was the same. When she'd read about the Chelonians in Bernice's book, the giant warlike turtles had caught her imagination. But since they had begun work at the site, it was becoming abundantly clear that she had as much chance of finding anything remotely new or interesting about them by unearthing the millionth slave dwelling as Emile did of getting married.

Archaeology was not turning out the way she had expected.

Bernice was speaking. 'OK, I accept we're unlikely to uncover any examples which have not been recorded before. But this place isn't a joke, Tameka.' Benny gestured around at the dismal site. 'Far from it. Just try to imagine what this place must have been like.'

Tameka sighed. The site was enormous, a vast plain stretching between two low rises of hills. A network of cordoned-off pits marked the foundations of the tiny slave dwellings. Above the site, spindly beige trees with long, rakish leaves stretched away into the hillside. Grey mud, the consistency of wet sand, was everywhere.

The only thing she found herself imagining was the trip home.

'These buildings were packed with people from a dozen or so races, huddled together, cold and afraid, at the mercy of the Chelonian guards. No, we won't find any treasure or anything completely new. But we might find clues to how the *parasites* struggled to survive.'

'Yeah, yeah, I know,' Tameka conceded. Bernice was right of course. As she invariably was. Since its discovery twenty years ago, the site of the slave camp on Apollox 4 had become more than just archaeological interest. It had come to signify and represent human struggle against alien domination. Extremist groups used the existence of the camps to justify a position of intense xenophobia. The less radical claimed them as a testament to human courage and survival.

It was still cold and wet and boring though.

A plastic sheet covered the edge of the excavation pit. Tameka sat down heavily upon it. Too heavily. She felt the wall give a little and then it completely collapsed under her weight, and she slid ungraciously into a puddle at the bottom of the trench, pulling with her the plastic sheet and several of the recovered artefacts that had been carefully laid out.

A stream of curses flowed from her mouth. She glared furiously at Bernice and Emile, daring them to laugh at her. A clump of her sodden hair slapped her in her face and she grimaced. It was going to take a month of intensive hot-oil treatment to salvage the knotted mess.

She had a suspicion that Bernice was stifling a smile. Emile bit his cheeks and then turned away and started to giggle.

'Right! That's it,' she stormed, clambering angrily to her feet and wiping the slimy grey mud from her backside. 'That's absolutely it! I'm booking myself on the next flight out of here. I'm telling you, anything is better than this.'

She was annoyed to see that Bernice had stopped listening to her protests. In fact she wasn't paying her any attention at all. Tameka tried to see what had so arrested Bernice's attention – without letting on that she was at all interested.

Glancing behind her, she noticed that a circular pipe was protruding from the gouge in the new bank that she had inadvertently created. 'Pipe' was an exaggeration. It was little more than a dark circle etched in the mud wall. Most of it had crumbled into the surrounding earth.

Bernice was speaking rapidly to herself under her breath. 'Probably a water pipe, built to bring fresh water to the Chelonian slave dwelling from the reservoir further up the hill – although the diameter of the pipe is rather large for a water pipe.'

Continuing to completely ignore Tameka's complaints,

Bernice knelt down to examine it further, her knees sinking into the soft mud. 'This is no water pipe . . .'

Bernice turned to Emile. 'Go to the Excavation Director's office,' she started, unable to keep the excitement from her voice. 'Tell them we need a coprolite analyst down here at the double. Hurry.'

'Coprolite analyst,' Emile repeated, carefully committing the words to memory. 'OK, Professor S,' he added, and nodded obediently before clambering out of the pit, levering himself up on one knee.

He hadn't been that bothered about wearing one of the brightly coloured cagoules that were standard issue at the archaeological site. His was bright yellow and made him look like a giant jelly bean.

Tameka did her best to remove the worst of the mud from the back of her skirt and all down her woollen leggings. She suspected that the skirt was ruined. She almost regretted not having put on one of the waterproofs. But a promise was a promise. She'd made a solemn vow when she arrived on Apollox 4 that she would never put on one of the hideous fluorescent suits that most of the diggers wore. She was no fashion victim – not like the zero brains at St Oscar's – but there were levels to which she was unwilling to descend.

Despite her earlier outburst, she couldn't stop herself from feeling intrigued by Bernice's sudden interest in the site wall. 'What? What have you found?' she asked, trying without success to shake off the slimy grey mud that clung to her hands and embedded itself behind her black-painted fingernails.

'Correction,' Bernice smiled, wagging a finger at her. 'What *you've* found.' She traced the dark circle with a brush. 'This could be really important.'

'Yeah, but what is it?'

Bernice was too busy with her own thoughts to answer. Which, Tameka already knew from spending a week in her company, was typical of the young professor. In many ways Bernice was a typical academic. She was completely absent-minded, often distracted, and sometimes she was almost embarrassingly awkward in social situations. But she was also warm, funny and didn't ever use her expertise to put you down. It was as if it mattered to her whether you understood the subject. She was the first teacher Tameka had ever had who treated her students like . . . well, like *people*.

Tameka looked at the skinny woman, crouching in the mud in her battered combat trousers and cheap shirt. It had to be said, though, that the woman did not know how to dress.

'This pipe must run down to the main system,' Bernice muttered, completely lost in her investigation. 'It's rare to find them still intact. The Chelonians didn't build their slave dwellings to last. In a good waterlogged site like this one, there's a chance that we might find some actual coprolites. That's if we're really lucky.'

'Coprolites?' Tameka had never heard of them before. 'Are they valuable?'

Bernice began to loosen the mud packed inside the pipe with the tip of her trowel. 'Well, no, not in themselves.' She seemed to find something slightly amusing. 'Not financially anyway. But from an archaeological point of view, they're invaluable. They can help us form real insight about the lives of the people who lived here.'

'Oh right.' Tameka began to lose interest. 'They're not worth anything, then?'

'If you want to find buried treasure, buy a metal detector,' Bernice scolded. 'This is archaeology, not beachcombing.'

'OK, OK, I know. You don't have to give me the lecture.' Not again. 'I was just wondering, that's all.'

Bernice popped her head up from her work and winked. 'I know you were, Tameka, I know you were.' Her tone was gentle and affectionate. Bernice's approval swept over Tameka like a warm breeze.

Bernice's attention returned to her work. 'Do you know, I think we're in business here.'

Tameka watched over Bernice's shoulder as she began to loosen a long, charcoal-grey object which was embedded in the soil in the bottom of the pipe. To Tameka's untutored eye it looked like a thin, gnarled branch. Either that or a –

'You there,' a new voice demanded. 'Stand away. Immediately.'

Two middle-aged men had hopped down into the pit and were scurrying towards them. The speaker was tall and lanky, with a superior air about him. The second was short, fat and visibly sweating despite the cold and rain. His waterproof suit was tied around his thick waist with a piece of knotted string. Emile brought up the rear, panting in his cagoule. Tameka scowled at him and he averted his gaze. She still hadn't forgiven him for laughing at her.

Tameka had seen the two men before, wandering rather aimlessly around the site, although she didn't know that they were 'coprolite analysts' – whatever that turned out to be. They seemed to spend most of their time alone. It wasn't that the other archaeologists ignored them, but they weren't exactly welcoming either. Most people were polite but maintained a discreet distance.

The short, sweaty one bustled up to Bernice, pushing her out of the way in his eagerness to examine the discovery. 'A marvellous example,' he cooed. 'How long has it been exposed to the air?'

Bernice, still recovering from his rudeness, muttered something unintelligible.

'There's no time to waste,' the tall analyst interrupted in a disapproving tone. 'We need to get this into a chemical solution. Now.' He produced a small transparent plastic box from beneath his waterproofs. The first analyst lifted the object out of the pipe and, as if he were holding something unbelievably precious, carefully transferred the small item into the container. Tameka was surprised when, just before he closed and sealed the lid, the smaller coprolite analyst leant over the box and took a deep sniff.

'I think we've got something really special here,' he confided to his companion, a satisfied smile spreading across his face.

'Now Anton,' the other chided, 'you know we won't be able to detect anything until we've treated the coprolite. Come along now, we've got a busy afternoon ahead of us.'

As the two men prepared to leave, Tameka turned to Bernice and asked, 'What do they think they're gonna find?'

'After they've treated it, the coprolite will regain its original form, texture and smell. It's a mucky business but it provides the most direct evidence for what was actually eaten.'

'You don't mean –'

Bernice started to laugh. 'I'm afraid so. Coprolite is fossil faeces. You discovered a piece of the sewage system that hadn't disintegrated and a piece of a Chelonian slave's faeces was lodged inside.'

'Ergh!' Tameka screwed her face up. 'That is the single most disgusting thing I have ever heard.' The two ill-matched men turned and stared at her, looking affronted. Tameka pulled a face at them. 'I just hope you wash your hands, that's all.'

'Coprolite analysis is a serious business,' Bernice continued, having missed the exchange. 'There's a specialist at St Oscar's who claims to be able to recognize some foodstuffs in treated coprolites from odour alone. Liquorice, apparently, is particularly easy to identify by smell.'

'Sniffing ancient poo?' Tameka screwed up her face. 'Hoo boy! That is *no* way for a grown person to earn a living, I'm telling you. It's just so . . .' Words couldn't really describe it. 'Icky,' she managed eventually.

'Your tutor is referring to Professor S'Cat, Chair of Coprolite Studies at St Oscar's, young woman.' The tall, snooty man had been listening in. 'You should show some respect. He is, after all, the foremost authority on coprolite analysis in this sector of space.' Satisfied with their attempts to secure their prize, the two men explained that they would inform Bernice of any developments and then moved off, giving Tameka their most disapproving looks as they did so.

'Although it must be said that on the whole they're an odd bunch,' Bernice murmured when they were out of earshot.

'You're telling me.' Tameka turned her attention to her muddied clothes. Most of the mud was gone now, leaving a wet greasy stain behind. She sighed. The slimy grey mud had already ruined half of her wardrobe since she'd arrived on the planet.

'Well, if you'd listened to me and worn your cagoule...' Bernice raised an eyebrow and indicated the little Day-Glo yellow parcel which sat discarded and still in its wrapper.

'Oh don't start!' Bernice was going to make a prize-winning mother one day.

Bernice glanced at her own waterproof, which was a vibrant shade of lilac. 'I think they're rather fetching. I did ask, but they don't do them in black.'

'You're such a comedian.'

Bernice sighed and adopted a singsong voice. 'And anyway kids, it's what's on the inside that...' she started, and then her voice trailed away. She was looking past Tameka, her eyes widening in horror. She cursed, using one of her ancient expletives that Tameka always found rather endearing, and then began to struggle out of her cagoule. 'I don't bloody believe it,' she hissed.

Tameka was shocked by the sudden transformation in her professor. Bernice's casual confidence had vanished and she looked worried and nervous. Edgy. Tameka thought all of this in the tiny moment before she spun around, eager to see what or who could have such an effect on her tutor.

The enormous ancient Chelonian site had been divided up into rectangular digs, each marked off with coloured line and flags. A figure was approaching along one of the muddy trenches between two digs. He was tall and loped a little as he walked. He wore a heavy dark overcoat with the collar turned against the rain. The bottom of the coat was splashed with mud. Tameka failed to find anything remarkable or threatening about him at all. Nothing that might have created such a reaction in Bernice. His hair was an unremarkable dirty blond and he was unshaven. He was attractive in a traditional sort of way. Laddish. Not her sort of bloke at all. Well, she thought, grinning to herself, he wasn't purple to start with.

This man was frowning against the weather, and was clearly looking for someone. He stopped and asked a couple of cagouled diggers who were dragging a wheelbarrow of soil towards a spoil heap. In their baggy pink and orange outfits the diggers looked like giant jelly babies. One of them pointed over towards the St Oscar's site and then they continued to drag the wheelbarrow along the narrow path.

'Bugger!' Bernice exclaimed again, as the man headed towards them.

Tameka stared in astonishment at her tutor. Bernice had climbed out of her cagoule and was tucking her denim shirt into her combat trousers. 'Trouble?' Tameka asked.

'Big trouble,' Bernice growled.

Tameka had never seen Bernice so rattled. 'Who is he?' The man had seen them now and was hurrying over, waving a little self-consciously. Tameka looked around for something to hit him with. The best she could come up with was a muddy trowel.

'Should I run and get someone?' Emile piped up, fearfully.

'Like who?' Tameka snapped. There weren't any security guards or police at the site. Tameka knew that the tutors and professors kept an eye on the more raucous students, taking it in turns to drink in the bars where the trouble occasionally erupted. She turned to Bernice. 'Is he dangerous?'

'Dangerous?' Bernice asked herself rhetorically as the man approached.

He came to an awkward stop at the lip of the dig. She looked up at him, squinting against the greasy rain. 'Is he dangerous?' she repeated, this time for the man's benefit. She made a show of considering this. 'You could say that, Tameka.'

'Hello, Benny,' the man ventured. There was a cautious tone in his voice.

Benny? Tameka had never heard Bernice called this before.

Bernice ignored the man and turned to Tameka. 'This is Jason Kane. As in Kane-Summerfield. He's my husband. That is my *ex*-husband.'

This was the last thing Tameka had been expecting to hear. She didn't even know that Bernice was married. 'Oh, hello,' she managed. 'Nice to meet you.'

'Well I wouldn't jump to any conclusions on that score, Tameka,' Bernice muttered and introduced Emile, who was staring up at the newcomer and smiling openly.

She turned back to her ex-husband. 'So, what can I do for you? Money, I suppose? Or have you just travelled six hundred years and God knows how many parsecs to humiliate me again?'

The man, Jason, frowned at the bitterness in her tone. Tameka had never heard Bernice so angry. It was a shock to see her so tense, so obviously out of control.

'A chat. In private. Please, Benny, it's important.'

Bernice sighed. 'You'll have to be quick. I've got a pipe full of fossilized excrement to excavate and, appealing as you are, if it's a choice between spending time with you or digging up an ancient toilet, I'm afraid the toilet wins every time.'

She raised her hand to him and after staring at it for a moment as if it might bite, he took hold of it and pulled her gently up and out of the pit. Bernice let go of his hand quickly when she reached the top as if touching him were painful. She turned back to Tameka. 'Cover our discovery with a tarpaulin and then call it a day, all right? Go and get some food and I'll see you in the morning. Usual time.' She nodded goodbye to Emile and then left.

Tameka watched them make their way towards one of the tractors that were waiting to ferry diggers from the site to the student village. She found herself wondering what they were talking about.

She noticed that Emile was staring at the retreating figures, still smiling absently. Benny's husband had clearly made an impression on the boy.

'Tameka calling Emile, come in, Emile.'

'Huh.'

'Could you, like, put your tongue *back* in your mouth and help me clear up.'

'Wha– I wasn't . . . I mean . . . er . . . Sure.'

She rolled her eyes and waited for Emile to finish blushing. 'So you want a beer or what?'

* * *

26

Apollox 4 had become the number-one destination for inexperienced archaeology students from a hundred or so universities, colleges and private institutes in this sector of space. The reasons were obvious. For one thing, it was close to the major travel routes, and secondly it had an abundance of ancient sites, which, thirdly and most importantly of all, no longer held any significant academic archaeological value whatsoever.

The last thing archaeology professors wanted were marauding gangs of undergraduates trampling over new sites which might yet yield valuable information.

Bernice led Jason away from the noise and bustle of the student village. 'Village' was one of those optimistic descriptions for which, Bernice had long since decided, marketing directors and image consultants should be shot.

It looked nothing like a village and smelt nothing like a village. It looked like a camp site and smelt like a music festival. Tents of all sizes and shapes littered the plain. Some of the recently pitched tents were still brightly coloured, little ridged structures of red and green. However, most had been here long enough to be coated with the grey mud that seemed to get everywhere. Little thought or planning appeared to have been given to where the tents were placed. They were just littered across the landscape, loosely erected around the buildings that contained washing facilities and several of the worst eateries on the continent. These establishments, which Bernice shuddered at calling restaurants, provided a steady stream of deep-fried meat, a fried potato-like vegetable and a rough beer that the locals studiously avoided. Needless to say, the thirty thousand archaeology students who were to be found in the 'village' at any one time adored the brew, drinking their fill every night before trying to find their tent or a better one.

Whenever Bernice came to Apollox 4, which was as rarely as possible, she made sure that she pitched her tent as far away from the main thoroughfares as she could. The first night she had stayed on the planet, a drunken couple had tripped over her guy ropes and ended up on top of her.

They'd been too full of beer and passion to notice that they were sharing their impromptu bed with her. After trying and failing to attract their attention, Bernice had crawled out from under her collapsed tent and slept in the wash house.

Tonight, they ate in a quiet restaurant away from the town centre where the students partied away every evening. Bernice rarely ventured into the cobbled streets of the old town, a small group of stone buildings which cluttered up the hillside behind the student village. If the camp site was the students' territory, the old town belonged to the academic staff. Despite the horrendous food, Bernice preferred to eat with Tameka and Emile in the cheap cafeterias in the student village – just as she slept in a ridge tent rather than in one of the small hotels in which most of the tutors stayed. It was a token gesture of equality, but one she rather suspected her two students were secretly terribly pleased about.

Bernice had eaten at this restaurant only once before: a dull evening spent listening to a couple of professors enviously criticizing the work of their more productive colleagues. She had selected it tonight in order to keep her discussion with Jason private, and, if she were completely honest, to give her the opportunity to scream and shout at him without it becoming the subject of student gossip the next day. As they took their seats at a table in a small covered courtyard built on to the main restaurant building, Bernice began to regret the decision. She would much rather have faced Jason on her own territory, somewhere familiar, where she felt that she had the advantage.

Christ! When had she started treating their relationship as a battle of wits? She closed her eyes for a moment and tried to relax, but with little success. The drumming of the rain on the glass roof of the conservatory only echoed her dark mood.

Jason wasn't helping. He was chatting amiably with the owner, a small grey-speckled reptilian creature who was giving him an animated description of the day's specials. Jason had a curious ability to get on with anyone, anywhere. It was as if he just assumed that he would be liked and welcome wherever he went. It was an act, of course. She'd never met a man so insecure, so haunted by feelings of complete unworthiness. But she couldn't help envying him the ability to put up such a useful façade.

The waiter left them alone with a bottle of wine and some small pastries. Their eyes met and Jason shifted uneasily. 'You're looking really well, Benny.'

She knew that tone: he wanted something. She'd been expecting as much, but she was still surprised by how deflated she felt by the realization that he hadn't come to beg her forgiveness, declare what a mistake the divorce was, or, at the very least, apologize.

She leant forward and poked him with her dessert spoon. 'If you try and pretend that this is a social visit, husband, it will be very grim. Trust me on this. Just ask me what you want, allow me to refuse triumphantly and then we can get on with the rest of the evening. All right?' The last words came out more sharply than she had intended. Bernice was a little shocked by just how irritated Jason made her feel. She took a deep breath. They were inches away from a blazing row.

He flinched from her anger. 'I . . . oh, never mind.'

The first course arrived. They sat in embarrassed silence as the waiter arranged the food on the table, smiling curtly when he was done. Bernice picked at her food, barely tasting it. She was annoyed that she could still be so affected by Jason's presence. She'd been kidding herself that she was over him and their short marriage. She remembered watching him walk away from the divorce ceremony, shoulders hunched, leaning forward. She'd thought then that she was never going to see him again. She'd thought that she never wanted to. She'd been very wrong on both counts.

He hadn't changed much in the months since then. His hair was a little longer: the dirty blond locks now hung down over his eyes, forcing him to brush it back with his fingers every time he looked up. He wasn't looking up now. He was staring down at his food. Bernice knew that he was quite capable of sulking for the rest of the meal. The rest of the night. Possibly for ever. She sighed with exasperation. 'Well?'

He looked up and immediately had to attend to a stray strand of hair. 'Well, what?' he asked, all innocence, but there was hope in his eyes.

She was going to regret this. 'I presume that you didn't come all this way just to see how I am. What's this trouble that you've got yourself into?'

'I thought you said –'

'Never mind what I said – just tell me.'

He set his knife and fork down and ran his fingers through his hair. Again. Bernice felt her stomach tense. If he did it once more she was going to be forced to throttle him.

'I need you to look after something for me. Something precious.'

Something stolen, Bernice thought. 'What kind of something?'

He twisted around to rummage through the pockets of his overcoat, which he'd slung over the back of his chair. 'It's right up your street, actually.' He pulled out a smallish uneven package: brown paper tied up with string. He pushed it across the table towards her. Bernice lifted it cautiously, glancing at him as she turned it over in her hands. It was heavy, but not uncomfortably so, she guessed stone or maybe crystal. She cut through the string with her dinner knife, too intrigued to bother about hygiene or table manners.

The artefact was wrapped in a thick cloth. The cloth itself was covered with tiny etched symbols. If it was a written language, it wasn't one with which Bernice was familiar. The artefact itself was a humanoid figurine, vaguely female in form, crudely sculpted from a dull, opaque crystal. Bernice found herself feeling a little disappointed.

'Have you seen anything like this before?' Jason asked.

Bernice held the figurine out in front of her. 'Yes and no. I've never seen this particular type of crystal before, although it doesn't look exceptional. I suppose the figurine could be old, but equally, it might be something knocked up for tourists last week. Who knows?'

It was Jason's turn to look deflated. 'Oh . . . I see.'

'You sound as if you were expecting a different answer.'

'I'd been led to believe that it was important, that's all.'

'Oh dear,' Bernice managed, trying to suppress a smile. '*Ching!* I think Phineas T. Barnum just rang up another sale.'

He shook his head, a little impatiently. 'No, no, I didn't buy it. I was trying to stop it from falling into the wrong hands.'

'The wrong hands? Do you mean the rightful owners?' Bernice bit her lip when she saw that he had been genuinely hurt by her remark.

'Thanks,' he snapped, retrieving the figurine and carefully wrapping it in the paper. 'You're right. I did come here for your help. And, yeah, it's trouble. And yeah, I'm in over my head. But I had thought that maybe . . . No, never mind.' He stood up and prepared to leave. 'I'm sorry. I made a mistake coming here. I'm just upsetting you.'

Bernice stared at him open-mouthed. 'Who's upset?'

He stuffed the package in one of the pockets of his heavy coat. 'You are. You're all tensed up and you can't stop insulting me.'

Bernice blinked. Twice. 'That's not upset. That's just . . . Any reasonable person would respond to you like that.'

'See, you're doing it again.' He was infuriatingly calm.

She was about to launch into a tirade of abuse, when she realized that he might just have a point. 'All right, I'm upset. It's just that you disappear, I don't hear from you in months and then when you do show up, it's only because I'm the one person in the universe who might just possibly harbour enough good will to do you a favour. Frankly, it makes me feel a little used.'

He looked away for a moment, frowning. 'Ouch.'

She shrugged. 'Well, it's the truth.'

The waiter had seen them get up, and now hurried over waving the bill in one of its three-fingered claws. 'You're leaving so soon. Is there a problem with the meal?' the little grey creature began, trying to guide them back to their seats. Bernice assured him that it wasn't the food. The speckled reptile placed the bill on the table in front of Jason, who looked at it, opened his mouth, closed it, and then stole a glance at Bernice.

She rolled her eyes. 'Some things don't seem to change

though.' She reached for her wallet.

Jason smiled sheepishly. 'Sorry. Thanks.'

They walked back towards the main part of town. The rain had stopped and Bernice could hear the distant sound of relentless dance music from the nightclubs.

'I went to St Oscar's looking for you. The Dean said you were here. Seemed to think that it was amusing.'

'Did he indeed? Somehow that doesn't surprise me. There was a mix-up in Admissions. Two scholarship students missed the first field trip of term, so someone had to take them on a special trip. I pulled the short straw. Personally I think the Dean fixed it. Trying to get me out of the way while he cuts the budget again. I'm really the only person in the department who puts up any kind of fight. So I ended up here, digging up the four million and seventy-second Chelonian slave dwelling and finding exactly the same pitiful items that were found in the four million and seventy-first. Tameka's right: it's really a waste of time.'

'I thought you liked getting your hands dirty. Or have you become an armchair theorist in your old age?'

'Me? Never!' Bernice exclaimed, and found herself smiling without really knowing why. No, that wasn't true. She did know why. It was reassuring to be in the company of someone who knew her so well. Jason was a miserable, self-obsessed, arrogant git, but he still knew her better than anyone else in the universe. When he was around she didn't have to put on a show. Didn't have to play Super Benny for the crowds. She missed that.

Jason paused at a junction of two muddy roads. 'My hotel is this way.'

'Really? Are you going to walk me to my tent or am I going to be murdered on my own?'

'I never realized that archaeology students were so dangerous.' He paused, as if he were uncertain whether to proceed. 'I'd be happy to walk you to your tent.'

She fixed him with a hard stare. 'Just a walk home, all right?'

He managed to look wronged. Which was something that he hadn't had a great deal of practice at. 'Of course, just a walk, all right?'

Benny felt an irresistible urge to tease him. To tease him and something else. She made a show of frowning at him, resting one hand on her hip. 'What, no sex when we get there?' The words had slipped out even before she was aware that she wanted him.

She almost burst out laughing at the range of expressions that fought their way across his face. 'Well, if . . . um . . . you insist,' he spluttered.

And then she really did burst out laughing. 'I'd forgotten how much I love winding you up.' She was going to regret this in the morning, but . . . 'Let's go back to your place. I've got a reputation to maintain around here.'

3

FRANTIC

From the diary of Bernice Summerfield

I woke to find myself being slowly throttled by my ex-husband. Not deliberately, of course. Jason was still fast asleep. One of his many infuriating habits was hanging on to me fiercely throughout the night. It was an act of desperation. Often he would cry out in his sleep, like a hurt child. However hard I had tried, I had never been able to make out any of the words. His stubble was scratching painfully into the back of my neck. I arched myself away from him and loosened his grip on my throat. Once free of the neck-lock, I twisted over and stared at him for a whole minute. I must admit to being more than a little shocked by how attractive I still found him. I found myself thinking of ways that I could accidentally wake him so we could have sex again.

I ran a finger down the side of his face and he shuddered and wrinkled his nose as if trying to discourage an insect. And then he turned on to his back and began to snore loudly.

No sex then.

I swung my legs out of the bed and headed for the bathroom. My lips looked a little red and puffy in the mirror from kissing his stubbly face. I grimaced and my reflection grimaced back at me. It was going to be terribly obvious to everyone what I had been doing all night.

At the time I remember thinking that it probably hadn't

been a very good idea to have had sex with Jason. He was probably going to walk back out of my life, leaving the deep wounds from our marriage open to the elements again.

I was hit by a vague feeling of unease. Something about my students. I'd arranged to meet Tameka and Emile at the site at nine. I finally found my watch where I had discarded it in my drunken hurry to be naked last night.

10.37 a.m.

Damn. I hated being late for my students. Probably because it was such a frequent occurrence. I leapt into the shower, shrieking as the hot water hit me, and I made a desperate grab for the cold tap. I was shampooing my hair when there was a knock at the hotel room door.

I have gone over what happened next a thousand times in my mind. I have fantasized a hundred alternative possibilities and outcomes. Most of them involved me being suitably heroic and all of them ended with Jason in my arms.

'Husband,' I bellowed, 'get that, can't you?'

I didn't hear anything further and had assumed that he'd answered the door, when the knock came again. I popped my head out of the shower curtain and shouted, 'I said –' And then Jason interrupted me.

'I heard,' he grunted back, sounding groggy with sleep.

I listened for a few moments before clambering back in to the shower. I heard the hotel room door open. There were voices and then a muffled thumping sound as the door was rudely slammed shut.

Ha! I thought at the time, assuming that Jason hadn't been pleased to have been woken. I pitied the poor porter who'd knocked on the door.

I took what now feels like an agonizingly long time towel-drying myself and then strolled naked into the bedroom. Only then did I suspect that something might be wrong.

I ducked back into the bathroom when I saw that the door to the corridor was still wide open. 'Jason!' I hissed. 'Close the bloody door!' But Jason hadn't returned to bed. The hotel room was empty.

Jason had gone.

Alarm bells were ringing in my head. I wrapped the towel into an impromptu minidress and glanced out into the long, shadowed hallway. The only natural light came from a small window at one end of the corridor. The small hotel was built out of the same grey stone as all the other buildings in this part of the town. The hallway looked dark and unfriendly. Suddenly it had become unknown territory. Jason wasn't in sight. Why would he have left the door open if he had been called away? And why would he leave without telling me where he was going? His clothes were still scattered over the floor. It seemed unlikely that he would wander off naked or just in a dressing gown.

The elderly creature at reception was too flustered by my semi-nudity to make much sense. It took me a few desperate minutes to extract the information that Jason had left the hotel in the company of two humans.

'They were different from you,' the creature began uncertainly, when I demanded a description.

'Do you mean they were men?'

The creature retracted its snout a little and grimaced. A gesture which, several field trips to Apollox 4 had taught me, meant that the Apolloxian was confused.

'Men,' I repeated. 'The male of the human species. Often taller, broader, facial hair, no sense of fair play or monogamy.'

'I was going to say that they were different from you in that they kept themselves covered with . . . fabric.'

'Well that narrows the field,' I muttered. 'Damn.' I slapped the reception desk in frustration. The noise shocked the little creature and it retreated hurriedly into the private quarters behind the desk.

I ran out on to the street, which was still busy with early-morning traffic. I heard the screech of tyres and I turned just in time to glimpse a dark ground car disappearing around a corner further down the narrow road. I was about to head out into the rain when I remembered that I was barefoot and only wearing a towel. Reluctantly I turned on my heel and hurried back upstairs to dress.

The bloody crystal figurine was sitting on Jason's bedside

table staring sightlessly at me when I returned to his room. I pulled on my combat trousers and was about to hurry back out of the room when I caught sight of the stain on the carpet by the open door.

Blood. Fresh. And there seemed an awful lot of it.

I fought down a wave of nausea, struggled into my boots, picked up the figurine and then set off at a dead run.

Extract ends

Bernice was hurrying towards them, looking ruffled in yesterday's clothes. Tameka grinned inwardly: clearly, relations between Bernice and her ex-husband were no longer as estranged as they had been the day before. She shot Emile a look which said: Told you!

'Bernice, listen, this is important,' she started, wanting to say what she needed to before Bernice could interrupt and try to persuade her to stay. 'It's nothing personal, right, but I've decided to leave. I mean I'm just not cut out for this place and this mud is destroying my wardrobe. It's OK. I mean I can just transfer my ticket and make my own way home . . . and . . . Bernice?'

'Hello. Yes?' Her tutor was completely distracted, looking around this dig, patting her hands anxiously on her combat trousers as if she were looking for something. 'Absolutely. Whatever.' Her gaze returned to Tameka and she smiled awkwardly. 'Er, how long do you think it would take for you to tidy up and pack?'

Tameka had been expecting a *little* bit of resistance. 'Sorry?'

'I'm afraid I'm going to have to bring this trip to a premature end. I know that must be disappointing for you both, your first dig and everything, but . . . it's just . . . well, the truth is . . .' Bernice sighed, as if this was embarrassing to say. 'I rather suspect that my husband has been kidnapped.'

Tameka was so annoyed that Bernice clearly hadn't heard a word of what she'd said that she almost missed the content of her tutor's remark. 'Oh,' Tameka managed finally, when the news had sunk in. Her earlier anger dissipated. 'I'm . . . er . . .

sorry,' she finished, rather lamely. 'Kidnapped?'

'Yes. Don't look so worried. It's not as if it hasn't happened before. Twice in fact, if memory serves.'

It would have been funny except that Bernice didn't look amused. She looked like she was cracking up.

Bernice pulled a wrapped parcel from the bulging side pocket of her combat trousers. 'I think it must have something to do with this.' She unwrapped a piece of crystal which had been sculpted into a crude female humanoid shape.

Tameka was about to give voice to the millions of questions that were forming in her head, when Emile scurried over.

'Hey, you guys,' he whispered conspiratorially and pointing behind them. 'We've got trouble.'

'That, my dear boy, is the understatement of the decade,' Bernice muttered, her attention focused on the small figurine. 'Not only has my husband been kidnapped, but I rather suspect that whoever was after him was after this. Which, seeing as I am now the holder of the artefact, puts me in a rather delicate position.'

Tameka looked up. Two men were standing on the edge of the dig. They wore dark suits and overcoats, and were probably the only two people wearing ties in the surrounding five kilometres. One of them was carefully wiping away some mud which had splattered up the side of his shiny black shoes, a pained expression on his face. The other was staring down at them, holding a warrant card out in front of him.

'Professor Bernice Kane-Summerfield?' His voice was clipped and formal.

Bernice waved him away without bothering to look up. 'You can drop the Kane bit, I did. Not now, eh? I'm a little busy.'

'No, you're not,' he said with such calm authority that Bernice was forced to look up at him. 'As of now you're under arrest.'

*   *   *

'I think you should know that this is the most humiliating experience of my life.'

'Being arrested?'

'No no no. Good heavens, I've been arrested hundreds of times. It's being arrested in front of my students that I find particularly embarrassing.' Bernice stopped pacing the small dimly lit room and settled down opposite the man who had identified himself as a Trans-System detective. She couldn't remember whether he'd actually offered his name. Events had been moving rather too quickly this morning. 'It hardly sets a good example, does it? And I am supposed to be responsible for them. You know, *in loco parentis* and all that?'

The detective poured coffee into disposable cups from a metal flask and pushed one in front of her. He was in his early forties, muscular, with short dark hair that was gracefully receding. Colonist ancestry, she guessed. He had deep brown eyes and looked intelligent and serious. Bernice found his calm confidence unnerving.

'Sugar?' he asked, his voice calm and polite. She couldn't place his accent.

Bernice shook her head and watched as he sorrowfully allowed himself half a spoonful. 'Trying to keep trim,' he explained and almost smiled.

'Really? Er . . . good for you,' Bernice said, not quite knowing what to do with this random piece of personal information. She'd been here for what felt like hours. It was a small holding cell at the spaceport: dull, grey, metal walls and a plastic bench in the corner. 'Why don't you ask me some questions or something?'

'Is there anything in particular that you would like me to ask you about, Professor?'

'We could begin with the kidnapping of Jason.'

'Your husband?'

'Ex-husband. But yes, that would be a start.'

'I want to be honest with you, Professor Summerfield. I've listened to your account of his disappearance and I don't believe that your husband – sorry, your ex-husband – has been kidnapped. I'm afraid that it just doesn't quite ring true.'

'It doesn't? Oh and why exactly is that?'

The detective lifted the disposable cup to his lips and was about to take a sip before he paused. 'To begin with I would like to know what you were doing in his hotel room at such an hour.'

'That's not really any of your business.'

'Well . . .'

Bernice noted that the detective had the good grace to look pained at this. He took a sip of his coffee and winced at the heat. 'I'm afraid it is, Professor. You see, I don't believe you when you say that last night was the first time you had seen Jason Kane in almost . . .' He made a show of checking the date in the statement in front of him. 'What is it, eight months? I am only made more suspicious by you describing him as your ex-husband when it is clear that you returned to his hotel room last night in his company and engaged in sexual intercourse with him.'

Bernice felt caught out. She reached automatically for her coffee cup and took a sip. The coffee was strong and smelt rich and expensive and burnt the roof of her mouth. 'And I suppose you were there, were you? Were you hiding in the *en-suite* or did you just bug the room?'

'No,' the detective replied, his voice remaining even, brown eyes blinking slowly. 'I arrived on the planet this morning. The receptionist at the hotel reported that you had returned with Mr Kane last night. You have a slight inflammation around your mouth which I guessed was the result of you kissing your husband – sorry, *ex*-husband.' He scrolled through the file in front of him until he found a holo. 'The unshaven gentleman is your Mr Kane, I take it.'

Bernice stared at the image and nodded. It looked as if it had been taken from a distance with some kind of telescopic equipment. Jason, in evening dress, was escorting a young woman into an expensive-looking restaurant. The woman was strikingly attractive, with bright red hair. The holo could have been taken for a society publication. They looked like a young aristocratic couple in love. Bernice adjusted her crumpled denim shirt, and tried to hold down the sick feeling in her stomach.

When she looked up, the detective was observing her attentively. 'We believe the young woman to be his accomplice.'

'Accomplice?' Bloody hell! What had he got himself involved in? Suddenly Bernice just wanted the interview to be over. 'Look, can you explain to me what it is that you think Jason has done? I've really told you all that I know. He arrived yesterday suggesting that he was in trouble, asking me to look after a small artefact. The figurine that you took from me. This morning he disappeared. That's really all I know.'

'Professor Summerfield, this is a very serious matter. We suspect that your husband has been involved in the sale of arms in this sector. We have information which links him –' The detective broke off as his partner entered the room, carrying the small crystal figurine and a sheaf of hard copy. They moved to a corner of the room and conversed for a few minutes before the detective returned, placing the female figurine on the table in front of her. Bernice stared at its crude face, before looking up at the detective's solemn one. He seemed disappointed about something. 'It seems you're free to leave.'

Bernice blinked. 'I'm sorry?'

'We had assumed that the statue contained some kind of encrypted data related to the sale of arms. It seems it doesn't. We have no reason to keep you. You're free to leave. If your husband makes any attempt to contact you, I would very much appreciate that you contact me.' He handed her his puter address.

'Have you been listening to a word I've been saying? Jason has been kidnapped. For all I know he could have been murdered. I very much doubt that he's going to be in a position to give me a ring or drop in for a chat.' She leant forward. 'If you're so interested in speaking to him, why don't you try and find him?'

The detective shrugged and began to close down his puter

terminal. 'I was operating on information I received concerning this artefact. I haven't been able to find any evidence which directly links your husband to arms dealings. I have no reason to authorize the expenditure for a search.'

'No reason? I've just told you that he's been bloody kidnapped!'

He shrugged. 'Then inform the local police. It's hardly a Trans-System matter.'

'Thanks. So it's a Trans-System matter if he's dealing weapons, but not if his life's in danger, is that it?'

Bernice could tell that the detective was tiring of this conversation.

He nodded. 'If you like, Professor Summerfield. You're an intelligent woman. Why don't you search for him yourself? You're far more likely to be successful than we are, anyway.'

'Thanks for the vote of confidence.'

The detective got up and made to leave. 'I was merely suggesting that you probably have a good idea as to where to begin such a search. Thank you for your time, Professor.'

'Look, just tell me one thing: what did you suspect you'd find encoded in the figurine?'

The detective hesitated for a moment. 'You really don't know, do you?'

'Well, I'd hardly bother asking if I did, would I?'

'Very well. A lot of hardware went unaccounted for during the war. Military hardware. There's a lot of money to be made in its recovery. For the last year, we've been hearing rumours about a powerful weapon being assembled. Several of these rumours have mentioned your ex-husband and his accomplice. Apparently they've spent much of the last year travelling across the galaxy searching for it. We received a tip-off that the activation codes for the weapon were being carried by your husband and his accomplice in that artefact.' He pointed at the figurine and shrugged. 'We tried every kind of test we've got, but found nothing. Legally, I'm obliged to return it to you.'

Bernice still couldn't believe that Jason was involved in

the arms trade. 'Just how powerful is this weapon supposed to be?'

The detective opened the holding cell door and gestured for Bernice to leave. 'The information we received was that the weapon had powers beyond that of a sun.'

4

Object

The harsh blue light of the scanner traced the rough contours of the little figurine which stood in the centre of the table. As the scanner completed its task, a three-dimensional image of the crude sculpture appeared on a nearby puter screen. The image spun silently, tiny measurements of its dimensions appearing around it.

'Neat,' Tameka said as she strode into the room, black hair flailing behind her, and caught sight of the image. 'Except the cops have already done all of this, right?'

Emile shuffled in after her and closed the door. He wandered over and crouched so that he was at eye level with the statuette. The blue light of the scan turned his bleached hair ultraviolet, and picked out the whites of his eyes and the dandruff on his shoulders. 'What's it supposed to do, anyway?'

Bernice looked up from the screen. 'I'll tell you when the scan's complete. How did you get on?'

Tameka shrugged. 'No joy. There are no flights back to Dellah until the end of the week. My credit's good. I could charter a flight, but I may as well wait for the one that me and Emile are already booked on.' She paused and then said, 'Unless . . . well, Bernice, I was thinking . . .'

'No. You can't come with me.' Bernice didn't even want to begin this conversation. The sooner her students were back on Dellah, the sooner she could be after Jason. There was no way she was taking them with her.

Tameka looked affronted. 'Oh. That simple, is it?'

Bernice nodded. 'That simple.' The puter buzzed, distracting her. 'Aha!'

'Found something?' Emile asked. 'I thought you said that the police couldn't find anything inside it. No secret codes or anything.'

'Secret codes?' Bernice laughed. Emile's face was full of the excitement of being brought up on a diet of cheap holos and comic strips. 'Oh come on.'

Emile looked embarrassed, which, she had learnt over the last week, was a semipermanent state of affairs for the boy. He was shorter than Tameka, still encumbered by puppy fat. He kept his home-bleached hair gelled stiffly in a short flat top with a tiny quiff at the front. Tiny silver rings ran up the edge of one ear, reminding Bernice of a reporter's notepad. Under his overcoat, he wore a patterned waistcoat over a brightly coloured shirt and cheap synthetic trousers (but dyed Day-Glo orange) rolled high over a pair of chunky service boots. Rings adorned his fingers and he wore a beaded necklace bearing a religious icon Bernice didn't recognize. The clothes were a carefully coordinated mishmash: thrift-shop cool.

He did his best to smile. 'What are you doing all this for then, Professor S?'

Probably gay, she thought. Probably doesn't know it. Bernice grinned back at him, suddenly extremely glad that she was never going to be a teenager again.

'The police have been investigating our friend here,' she said, tapping the figurine, 'thinking of her as a possible container of secret information, dangerous information.'

'Ignoring the container itself,' Tameka chimed in. Thankfully the young woman appeared to be too interested in what was going on to sulk.

'That's right.' Bernice turned back to the puter. 'I'm hoping the context and origin of the artefact itself will provide a clue as to what Jason was up to. And where he may have been taken.'

'What have you got?' Emile asked. 'Do you know where it came from?'

'It's a match from a series of company records.' Bernice looked closer at the screen. 'Old records. Very old. These predate the Galactic War.'

'I didn't know that much was left over from then.'

'There isn't. Have you heard of the Butler Project?'

Both Emile and Tameka shook their heads. 'No.'

'It's a massive attempt to collate and index the records of the companies that went bankrupt during the war. This information comes from the archive of the Piercy Corporation.'

'Never heard of it.'

'You wouldn't have. It went out of business years ago. According to the biog provided by the Butler Project, the Piercy Corporation was a small outfit which specialized in deep-space exploration. Its ships were commandeered for the war effort, and it didn't last long after that. No ships, no exploration. No exploration, no rich pickings. No rich pickings, no profit.'

'No profit, no company?'

'Tameka,' said Bernice, grinning, 'you are on the wrong course.'

Tameka picked up the figurine. Bernice saw that she had won the girl back. 'And does it tell you where our little friend came from?' Tameka asked, now absorbed in the problem at hand.

'I can't tell yet. Butler are a wily bunch. They're only letting me see the company biog at the moment and telling me that there's a match. I'm going to have to pay for the information before they'll let me see any more. Which is going to be expensive.'

'How expensive?'

Bernice eyed the screen. 'About a month's salary. I'm trying to work out whether he's worth it.'

'Who?'

'Jason, of course.'

'You're not serious? You wouldn't really leave him in the hands of kidnappers, would you?'

Bernice could tell that Tameka was shocked that she appeared to be even considering leaving Jason to suffer his fate. 'No, unfortunately.' No one had been more surprised than Bernice to learn that she still harboured strong feelings for her ex-husband. Perhaps she was still in love with him in some perverse and cruelly unfair way. Best not to think about it. She'd deal with all of that when she found him.

If she found him.

She cursed him under her breath as she authorized the transfer of funds from her account on Dellah to the Butler Project. As ever, Jason was costing her an enormous amount of money. She grimaced as she glimpsed the heights to which her overdraft soared as the transaction took place. There would be angry correspondence from her bank waiting for her when she returned home. She smiled grimly. No change there then.

There was a short pause as the Butler Project acknowledged the receipt of her payment and then transmitted her newly purchased information. The screen of the puter filled with text and images. Bernice recognized it as fragments of a planetary survey report. Whoever had compiled the report had been thorough. Most of it was geological information. Bernice frowned, unable to make much headway with it. She was probably going to have to find a specialist, which would mean more money.

The search took her directly to the match it had found. The symbols on the cloth, which she had scanned into the puter, were placed next to a series of images which had been included as part of the survey. The images were holos of a large stone disc buried in the ground within a dark chamber. The surface of the stone was covered in the thin, angular symbols. The same symbols that adorned the cloth. There were two rectangular trenches cut into the surface of the disc. The pits reminded Bernice of –

'Graves!' Tameka exclaimed, looking over Bernice's shoulder. 'Hey, that's so cool! Where are the bodies? Have they been robbed?'

'Don't leap to conclusions,' Bernice admonished. 'First rule of archaeology. For all we know the people who built your "graves" weren't even humanoid.'

'What planet is it? Where is it?'

'There's only a system code listed here.' Bernice was still searching through the fragments of the report. 'I can't find any planetary coordinates listed at all. If I had the whole report it would be a different story. I fear that I may have just blown my wages on nothing. According to the tag, the report was initially purchased by the Ursu Group way back before the war. They sponsored several more. And according to this, there was an expedition too. But it doesn't say who the Ursu group were.'

'What system is it?' Tameka asked.

'I've only got the code. V15.'

'V15?' Emile said.

Bernice nodded. 'That's right. Does that mean something to you?'

'When we were looking for flights out of here, a private ship left for the V15 system. I stopped to watch it leave.'

'Bingo!' Bernice cheered, clapping her hands together.

'I'm sorry?' Emile spluttered. 'What's Bingo?'

'Never mind.'

'But you think this is where Jason has been taken?'

'It would make sense. If he did steal that artefact, perhaps someone from that system wants it back. Perhaps the Ursu Group or rather their descendants? Who knows?' Bernice was aware that she was telling her students more than she really wanted them to know. It wasn't going to do her reputation at St Oscar's any good for them to hear her suspicions that her husband was a thief. She tapped the puter screen. 'We need to check this information against any of the other destinations of ships, but I find it difficult to believe that this is just coincidence. Thanks Emile, that was really useful. We're in business,' she caught herself. 'Or at least, I am.'

'Bernice . . .' Tameka began.

'The answer's still no, I'm afraid.'

'Oh.'

V15 turned out to be a forgotten system which sat midway between Apollox 4 and Dellah. Bernice couldn't believe her luck when she discovered that tucked away in its planetary system was a world listed as Ursu. However, her luck was not to last. For the large desert planet was a prohibited world. This was not good news. Prohibited worlds were usually off limits because they were prison colonies, reported sites of new diseases or local war zones. According to the available information, no one had travelled to Ursu since before the Galactic War. It was one of several hundred planets with which contact of any kind had been lost during the conflict. In the years since the war had ended, governments and companies were working hard to re-establish communications with these lost worlds. It was a slow process – leading the societies back out into the light after so many years in the darkness of isolation. Many of the worlds had fallen back into a new barbarism. Bernice had heard the stories. Ugly stories.

However, the injunction around Ursu had been in existence since way before the war. Although the reason for its being struck off the trade routes was now lost. Prison? Disease? Local conflict?

Oh, I'm really looking forward to this, Bernice thought to herself.

There was a tiny moment after the gravity of Apollox 4 had let go of them and before the artificial gravity of the ship kicked in, when everything in the passenger room of the ancient haulage ship weighed absolutely nothing. All of the scattered papers, food cartons and other debris lifted gently away from the floor and the furniture and started to glide about the room. Bernice had to bat away a curry carton which was heading towards her and got a streak of cold curry sauce in her hair for her troubles. The artificial gravity in the ship began to tug at her and then the air was no longer filled with cartons, papers and cutlery. The debris rained down on the floor with the clatter of a sudden hailstorm.

Relieved that she wasn't going to go floating off, Bernice unclipped the harness and slipped down from the couch, picking her way carefully across the room.

'Can we talk about personal hygiene?' Tameka growled as

she glanced around the rest area. She'd already released herself from her hammock and was inspecting the only communal space in the whole of the ship. Bernice grimaced inwardly as she looked around the living space. The room was dimly lit from a series of thin glass tubes which snaked across the extremely low ceiling. She kept banging her head on the tubes, which were surprisingly hot. The air was warm and smelt of oil. It made the back of Bernice's throat dry and she found herself swallowing frequently and uncomfortably. Probably due to a cheap recycling unit, she thought to herself. The whole experience was like being shut up in a poorly maintained ventilation system.

'You'll get used to it in a couple of days,' Errol had muttered, when he'd noticed her discomfort. His welcome aboard had consisted of pushing a stack of import/export documents on to the floor to create some sitting space in the tiny common room. 'Best thing is to try and not move around too much.' He chuckled to himself and ducked to avoid a light fitting. 'It's not as though there's anywhere to go.'

Errol was right. The living quarters of the ship consisted of three main rooms, of which the common room was the largest. The 'bridge' was a tiny transparent bubble which protruded from the front of the vessel, with barely enough room for two people to sit at the pilot and navigator stations. Errol's stateroom was nearby, but had, thankfully, not been included in the tour. Bernice had shuddered when she had glimpsed the sanitary facilities: they were not good. The rest of the ship was inaccessible during space flight, and was made up of a series of large, unpressurized, cold-storage bays.

As well as owning the ship, Errol was the pilot, navigator and engineer. Bernice had met people like him before. Sometimes it seemed that the frontier was made up of people like Errol, making ends meet by living in isolation, far away from cities, culture and life. Errol himself seemed content with his three-room life. He was a tall, thickset man in his late forties. He kept his head shaved, and was dark-skinned, although he still managed to look sickly pale – the effect of spending so much time under artificial light or behind the shielded glass of the bridge? Bernice wondered. One side of his face was pitted with a smattering of pockmarks, as if his head were a moon displaying the impact strikes of a shower of meteors. Bernice tried to guess at their origin. Some strange frontier infection perhaps? The pushing back of the frontier had resulted in people stumbling across new diseases and bacteria.

Errol seemed entirely unselfconscious about this disfigurement. Despite his height, he moved with a crablike grace through the low passageways of his ship. Bernice had enjoyed watching him make the preparations for the journey. Despite the clutter and mess, there was a kind of crazy method to his madness.

Tameka slumped down into a low couch and began to reapply her eyeliner, carving thick black lines beneath her eyes, continuing them past the edge of her eye and up towards her eyebrow. She worked slowly and carefully, her whole attention focused on the task. Bernice smiled warmly as she watched her student. There was something ridiculous about putting on make-up while locked up in here for the three-day voyage. But then Tameka's make-up wasn't about looking attractive. It was part of who she was. As important to her as her name. Bernice remembered a series of disastrous hairstyles from her own youth and grimaced.

Bernice heard Emile moan. 'Ah, I'm bleeding.'

The acceleration of lift-off had given him a nosebleed. Bernice handed him her handkerchief and he looked at it blankly for a moment before gingerly dabbing at his nose.

'I've got blood on my shirt.'

She ran her hand through his bleached blond hair. His dark roots were well established. 'All right?' she asked.

He nodded. 'I'll survive.'

'Good show.' The sooner she got the two of them back to Dellah and the safe, cloistered walls of St Oscar's University the better.

Emile's necklace was twisted around the collar of his shirt, its small wooden beads digging into his fleshy neck. She

51

unknotted it and examined the small image of an oak tree which hung from it. It was unfamiliar to her, although something about the necklace suggested religion. That was it: it reminded her of a rosary.

'The Natural Path,' Emile whispered and looked a bit embarrassed.

'Right,' Bernice said and let the necklace drop back on to his chest. There were millions of religions scattered across the galaxy. From those that offered a bit of reassurance and meaning in all this uncertainty to those that claimed that they alone knew the secret truth about life. Emile didn't seem to want to talk about it, so she smiled and left him.

Bernice had long ago decided that the secret of life was that there was no secret. All that you needed to know about life was there for you to see. All you had to do was open your eyes and recognize what you already knew.

She thought about Jason. It was the opening-your-eyes part that was usually the hardest.

Feeling a little disheartened, Bernice made her way to the bridge, cautiously ducking around the piping and light fixtures which threatened to knock her brains out. Errol was sitting upright in the high-backed pilot's chair, silhouetted against the starscape visible through the glass bubble of the bridge. Bernice caught her breath at the beauty of it.

A window on to space.

Errol was reading something in his lap, one foot idly swinging to and fro. When he saw Bernice coming he smiled and dropped the puter terminal on to an instrument bank and turned and nodded a welcome.

'Everyone survive take-off?'

Bernice paused in the entrance to the bridge. There was barely enough room for two in the glass sphere. She decided not to enter. 'Nothing a clean hanky couldn't cure.' Errol looked puzzled so Bernice explained.

'You get used to it. This isn't a liner. I can't afford acceleration buffers.' He swung around in his chair and attended to a series of small instruments which buzzed for his attention. 'I've hooked some extra cargo that was waiting in orbit. We're going to be in hyperspace for about thirty hours. We'll emerge in the V15 system, not too far from Ursu. I'll stay in orbit long enough for you to do a single instrument sweep and then we'll jump all the way to Dellah.'

Behind him she watched Apollox 4 recede until it became a small white disc, the size of a coin, and then was swallowed completely by blackness. 'Great. You'll get the rest of the payment when we get back to St Oscar's.'

He looked at her seriously for a moment, as if he were wondering whether he could trust her. 'Yeah, I'm sure I will, Professor Summerfield.'

'Please, call me Bernice. The only person who calls me Professor is my bank manager.'

'Bernice it is.' He paused. 'So, you're really planning to return to Ursu, to go down there?'

'You must think I'm crazy – I think I'm incurably insane – but yes.' She gestured in the direction of the living quarters. 'Once I've got those two safely home, and studied the results of the orbital scan, I'll come back.' She felt the weight of the task for the first time.

Errol turned away from her and looked out at the stars. 'You're a braver person than I am, Bernice Summerfield. You wouldn't catch me touching down on a prohibited world.'

Thanks, she thought. And why not try to undermine my confidence while you're at it? 'Well, it's probably not that bad,' she said, mostly to reassure herself, but the words sounded feeble.

Errol flashed her an incredulous look.

She shrugged. 'OK, it probably *is* that bad, but I really don't have a choice. Someone important to me is in trouble and I'm fairly sure they're in trouble on Ursu.'

'Ah, I thought it might be something like that,' Errol replied, still staring out into space.

After they'd made the jump into hyperspace, Errol had joined them in the cramped living space. The seventy-two hours dragged by like a wounded animal. Bernice sat slumped on one of the low couches, playing travel chess with Emile. His beating her five games to nil had done nothing to improve her mood. By the end of the journey she had convinced herself that the already sluggish life-support system was grinding to a complete stop. She felt like she was suffocating.

Bernice was relieved when the violent, shuddering turbulence hit the ship, indicating that they were shifting between the dimensions, dropping back into normal space. Her relief was short-lived. First, in her haste to catch sight of the planet where in all probability Jason was being held hostage, she had leapt to her feet and smashed her forehead on a hot plastic light fitting. Being burnt and concussed in the same moment didn't feel like an accident: it felt like a conspiracy. And as she was stomping back from the MedSys bay, which Errol hadn't bothered to service and now was off line, she had glimpsed through a porthole the large black spaceships bearing down on them.

She had just enough time to call Errol's name before they started their attack in earnest.

5

SMALL+FIRE+IN+CABIN+ONE+

Emile had been lying in Errol's cabin when the first attack came. He was lying quietly on the floor, using his holdall as a pillow and trying not to draw attention to himself. He'd never shared a room with anyone before. Errol had suggested that they both sleep on the bunk, lying head to toe. But Emile, not knowing how to refuse, had just sunk down on to the floor and shaken his head. Errol had shrugged. 'Suit yourself,' he'd said, and then climbed into bed.

By closing his eyes and concentrating, Emile could block out Errol's snores and imagine that he was back home. Back in his room on the relay station.

And that was when the attack came and the world was turned upside down. Errol swore loudly. The floor beneath Emile lurched dangerously and Errol rolled off his bunk, and landed on top of him, cursing loudly. He was so close that Emile could smell his breath. Spicy food and alcohol. Emile's first reaction was to try to push the older man away, but then the ship lurched again and Emile heard the spluttering sound of an electrical fire starting somewhere nearby.

'Get out of my way, kid,' Errol yelled as he clambered past him and made a grab for the door.

'What's going on?' Emile climbed out from under the bedclothes, which had fallen on him, grabbed hold of his bag and then staggered out of the tiny cabin after Errol. The pilot shouted something that Emile couldn't hear as he hurtled away.

The low corridors of the ship were full of smoke and steam. A pipe half buried in the wall shattered, spraying the corridor with hot, oily mist. Emile shrieked as he was scalded under a shower of spitting grease. He threw himself forward and then screwed his eyes tightly shut and groped his way to the bridge.

Bernice and Tameka were already standing in the doorway shouting at Errol, who'd climbed into the pilot's chair.

'Can't you take evasive action?' Tameka was yelling.

'Evasive what?' Errol looked at her in astonishment. 'What do you think this is, a battleship? It takes fifteen minutes to make a forty-five-degree turn.'

Emile looked beyond them. The stars were being blocked by something. Something big. 'Trouble,' he told himself as he saw the grotesque ships ahead of them in the darkness.

'Weapons?'

'No.'

'Force fields? Shields? Anything defensive?'

Errol frowned. 'You're kidding, right?'

'I see. That good, eh? What about ordinary equipment which can be imaginatively used as a weapon or disguise or something.' Bernice was, she had to admit, clutching at straws.

'You mean like confusing their targeting systems by ejecting the cargo? Fill the space between us with a million tons of rice grains, that sort of thing?'

Bernice felt the first ray of hope. 'Yes!' she exclaimed, wagging a finger. 'Precisely that sort of thing. Can you do it?'

Errol shook his head. 'No. You can't access the cargo holds from here. This is a haulage vessel, Bernice. I can take off, land, and . . . and that's about it. The best I could do is uncouple this section from the cargo bins. It wasn't built for anything like this.' Another volley of shots glanced off the side of the vessel. 'Somebody really doesn't like you, Bernice, you know that?'

'I'm afraid being shot at has become a bit of an occupational hazard.'

Errol looked bemused. 'I thought you said you were an archaeologist?'

'Yeah . . . well, academics can be the harshest critics.'

One of the lead ships let loose another barrage. The space outside the bubble glowed brilliant white for an instant – Bernice had to turn away and cover her eyes – and then they were knocked off their feet as the ship was hit. Metal groaned, grating in Bernice's head, as the hull was pushed past its tolerance. Somewhere far below them, there was a shrieking sound as thick metal was torn. The deck they stood on lurched sickeningly.

Bernice staggered to her feet. Her vision was blurred and full of dark spots. Despite this she managed to get hold of both Tameka and Emile by the wrists and hung on tightly to them. 'Errol, where are the lifeboats?'

Bernice blinked hard, willing her vision to return to normal. An outline of the bridge interior formed with infuriating slowness in front of her. One of the equipment banks had exploded, erupting hot plastic and warped metal over the floor and, she could now make out, over Errol. He'd fallen from the pilot's chair, blood running freely from a cut on his forehead. Bernice winced. Hot plastic had splattered against his face, coating one eye like a mask. One of his legs was trapped under a smouldering sheet of metal.

'Lifeboats?' she demanded.

'Bernice!' he shouted. He didn't seem to be able to see her. 'Don't leave me,' his voice sounded thin and reedy. A boy's voice, not his usual mature baritone. He tried to free his leg, but the metal burnt his hand. He howled.

Jesus, Bernice thought, God only knew what state his leg was in beneath that lot.

'Errol, I need to know where the lifeboats are.'

He said something she couldn't make out. Behind him, she could now see the shape of one of the ships moving relentlessly towards them. It looked ugly. A huge black insect, six legs curled under its length. It filled the entire window. For a moment she just stared at it.

She felt someone tug at her arm. 'I know where the escape pods are located,' Emile said.

Bernice nodded. 'Right . . . right then, come on.'

She moved off after Emile, pulling Tameka along behind her. The young woman was making a low rasping noise that might have been crying. As they turned the end of the corridor, Bernice heard Errol call out her name again and then it was drowned out by a series of small explosions.

'Here,' Emile called to her and pointed to two hatches cut into the wall close to the deck. She hurriedly made sense of the simple procedure, thumbed one of the controls and the first hatch slid open after a few seconds, which felt like hours. There was a coffin-sized space clearly designed for one.

'Get in, both of you.'

Tameka pulled her arm free. 'I won't be a minute,' she promised and disappeared in the direction of the living quarters. Bernice stared after her, speechless. Emile climbed into the small space, still hugging his holdall.

'You won't need that,' she told him and tried to lift it out of his arms but he hung on fiercely.

'No,' he muttered. 'I can't leave it. It's all I've got.'

It was ridiculous. 'Emile, listen, this is no time to argue. You can't take that with you. We need to make the lifeboat as light as possible. It's already way over capacity.' Emile didn't appear to be listening to her – he just turned away and was staring defiantly at the far wall.

Great.

Tameka returned moments later carrying a small black drawstring bag. 'Overnight bag,' she said brightly. 'Well I'm not going anywhere without at least a change of clothes and an eyeliner pencil.' Her mascara had run down her face in long spikes, betraying her cool expression. She climbed in after Emile. Somehow, there was just enough room.

Bernice felt a wave of anger rise over her. 'You stupid little . . .' she started, before realizing that she was just wasting time. 'Stay near the pod when it lands, we'll follow you down.' She closed the door and hit the controls that would activate the pod. There was a slight tremor as the pod was loosed and the control panel glowed green and buzzed cheerily.

'Bombs away,' Bernice muttered to herself. She couldn't believe that girl. She'd almost killed herself over a bag of make-up! She remembered hearing a story of two women returning to a factory after a fire alarm to retrieve their handbags. They hadn't come out again.

Bernice glanced at the second hatch for a moment. No. It was tempting. But no. She wasn't going to leave without Errol. She made her way carefully back to the bridge. It was almost impossible to see her hands in front of her face in the smoke. The air was hot. Several of the sprinklers had activated and were spraying jets of unpleasantly warm foam throughout the ship.

Errol was slipping in and out of consciousness. Part of one of the control panels had torn into the side of his thigh as it exploded. It was now embedded in his leg. There was a lot of blood and the sweet smell of burning flesh. She took off her shirt and wrapped it around her hands before pulling the torn metal sheet out of his thigh.

The metal was ragged and misshapen. It sliced into his leg as she pulled it free, making the wound longer. He shrieked – a high and desperate sound. Blood flooded out of the wound and over her hands. Bernice knew that she was making the injury worse by removing the metal, which had probably been keeping a severed artery sealed. But she had to free him from the wreckage or he would certainly die when the ship blew. She used the sleeve of her denim shirt as a tourniquet, tying it above the wound.

She grimaced. She was breaking a first-aid rule with her every action. Never mind, she could sort it all out later. If she got a chance.

'We have to leave, Errol. We have to leave now.'

'How?' he murmured. God, his face looked bad.

'What do you mean: how? The second lifeboat, of course. Emile and Tameka have gone in the first.'

He opened his one good eye and grimaced at the mess of his leg. 'The other pod hasn't worked in years. There never seemed any point in getting it fixed. Bernice,' he added, after a moment. 'I can't open my right eye. Feels strange.'

'Ah,' Bernice said, because she couldn't think of anything else to say. Her adrenaline-fuelled energy abandoned her. She slumped on to the floor and rested her back against the wall. Electrical fires flickered around her. Acrid smoke billowed through the cabin. It was getting hard to take a breath. She suddenly felt very tired. Exhausted.

Bloody Jason. All your fault.

They were now directly below one of the ships. Through the bubble she could see its underbelly. It was made up of irregular grey piping, which was scorched with dark streaks. It looked unfinished, as if the whole ship had been put together with little thought as to the final result. Bernice thought she recognized parts of the design – hadn't she seen something like that recently? It might just have been her imagination. She couldn't be sure. Didn't care.

For a few moments she was content to watch the ship pass over them until she began to be aware that they were moving away from it. The grey underbelly was getting further away. Bernice frowned, trying to keep her head clear. There was a lot of smoke now. She could feel it trying to clog her lungs and pull her down into unconsciousness.

Down.

The view of the huge ship began to twist in front of her. The small haulage vessel was being dragged into a spin. Dragged down. Bernice opened her eyes wide, suddenly alert. They were being dragged down by something. She leant forward and saw the huge orange disc of Ursu directly below them. It was rising to meet them like a sunrise. Gravity. The planet was reaching for them.

Bernice pulled herself up into the pilot's chair. She glanced at the ship above them. It no longer blocked the whole of the view from the bubble, and had stopped firing at them. For now. She fastened herself into the pilot's harness, and felt reassured by its embrace. She paused, realizing that she had no idea what she was about to do, except try to stay alive.

The navigation instruments were missing, the jump-drive monitors were melted and she had removed most of the engineering station from Errol's thigh. The puter kept displaying the words, SMALL + FIRE + IN + CABIN + ONE. DESIGNATED + FIRE + OFFICER + PLEASE + ATTEND and repeating them in an infuriatingly calm feminine voice. Bernice tried to tell it to shut up but broke into fits of coughing instead.

Not a good sign, she told herself.

There was no information on three of the main cargo holds. She assumed that they had taken direct hits. Despite the puter's gross underestimation of the problem, angry warnings kept flashing up on the screens in front of her, registering the sites of fires throughout the ship. The sub-light drive instruments kept displaying messages about things she didn't understand. Most of the ship was now open to space. Only the cabin containing the living quarters and the bridge had integrity. No wonder the ships had stopped firing: the old haulage vessel was breaking up. Even if it managed to hold together, it would shortly burn up when it came into contact with the atmosphere of Ursu.

Exactly how had she got herself into this mess?

Bernice was about to curse her husband again when she was distracted by movement out of the corner of her eye. Errol was awake and had leant forward to the edge of the glass and was now staring down at the planet below. He glanced up at her, his left eye blinking rapidly to keep the blood from the cut on his forehead from running into it. He didn't speak.

'I'm open to suggestions,' Bernice informed him and burst out coughing again. He said something that she couldn't make out over the calm but loud puter warning. 'You'll have to speak up.' Her throat was on fire.

He grimaced. 'I said,' he managed, wincing with the effort, 'uncouple the cabin and try to make a landfall. The fuel's going to go up. I'm surprised it hasn't already.'

'Right.' Bernice glanced at the controls and then swung

back around at him. 'Er, how do I do that – uncouple the cabin from the rest of the ship, I mean?'

'I'll talk you through the whole thing. All the way down.'

Bernice rolled her eyes. 'I think I've seen this movie. Look, I can get us safely through the atmosphere. I just need to know how to uncouple the cabin from the cargo hold and the engines.'

A rumbling shudder gripped the ship, followed by a booming explosion. Their eyes met, wide with fear.

The image of the cabin of the haulage ship hitting the atmosphere was fuzzy and distant. In monochrome, the bottom edge of the cabin burnt a grainy white for a few seconds as it cut through the top layers of the atmosphere and then disappeared. On board the first of the three ships, neat lines of pale figures watched the fate of the tiny vessel with lifeless metallic grey eyes.

6

THE DRAGON BOY

Scott woke shivering and wet with sweat. He was breathing hard and lay on the mattress for a few minutes to catch his breath. He felt his heartbeat slow and tried to shake the dream out of his mind.

It was still dark outside the large room. Everyone else was asleep. He could hear one of his sisters snoring loudly a few beds down. The person lying in bed with him responded to his movement, twitching, grunting and finally turning over. He peeled back the sheets to discover the identity of the person he was sharing with. Beneath a mass of long hair, twisted by sleep, was a young woman who often maintained farm equipment in this village and the next. Her face was smudged with streaks of oil and her fingernails were ingrained with the greasy dirt of old engines. Scott watched her sleeping for a moment, trying without success to remember her name. She must have entered the dorm late; he had seen a group trying to kick-start a reluctant harvester which had slid into a ditch earlier in the evening.

No one paid much attention to the curfew this far from the cities.

Scott slipped out of the bed and padded naked to the washroom at the end of the dorm. He splashed himself with cold water and leant against the cold stone wall. Its coolness was a pleasure after the distressful dream.

When he closed his eyes he could still see the huge

expanse of red sun rising to meet him. He was falling between the stars, falling towards the fire. He felt the first flames lick at his skin and then a blinding agony for a tiny moment as he hit the red giant's aura and his body flared like a match. His hand burnt to the bone in front of his eyes and then he was nothing but dust.

He felt a deep ache in his stomach, like a longing or regret. He opened his eyes to discover that he was hugging himself tightly. Fresh sweat had broken out on his brow and upper lip.

The dreams were coming more frequently now. The rest of his family were also plagued by them. Some more than others. When the dreams had first started they had talked of little else, but when no answer or meaning became readily apparent they had tired of the endless speculation and drifted back to their separate lives.

He was distracted by something in the night sky visible through the open door to the washroom. A scarlet light had streaked across the blackness for a second – a tiny red tear in the night. At first, Scott wondered if it was an after-effect of the dream, but the accompanying faint high-pitched whistle assured him that it was real.

He ran out into the darkness, searching for any sign of it. It must have been some kind of plane or ship. A muffled sound echoed through the plain. He thought he felt a tiny tremor through his bare feet although he might have imagined it. The sound reminded him of thunder heard from indoors.

Whatever it was, it wasn't like an Ursu airship at all, which meant that it probably belonged to them, to the Sunless. Scott stood in the dust outside the dorm, straining to hear anything else. The night had cooled the sun-baked ground. He massaged the soft dry sand between his toes. It hadn't looked like a ship travelling through the air – it was more like something falling out of the sky.

He heard voices talking and giggling somewhere behind him. Ben and Felice emerged out of the trees behind the dorm. Scott frowned. For some reason, he was annoyed by their arrival, as if they were interrupting something private, something meant just for him. He considered keeping quiet about what he had witnessed and then changed his mind. That would be childish and stupid.

Their faces were flushed and their eyes glistened. Ben's feathers were all ruffled and Felice's long golden hair was full of tiny twigs and bits of leaf. They looked embarrassed to have been caught outside after curfew. Felice said they'd been walking through the woods and fallen asleep, which was such an obvious lie that Scott had a sudden urge to slap her. Felice actually apologized to him, as if Scott's approval might matter.

'Your choice,' he told her. They were both a little younger than he was, only a few years out of childhood. And it was the young who had been most affected by the arrival of the Sunless.

He asked them if they'd heard anything but they said they hadn't. When he told them that he'd seen something fall out of the sky, they looked concerned. The Sunless didn't usually travel far from the cities, but there were always stories.

'It didn't look like one of their ships, unless it was one crashing.'

'I wish,' Felice said with feeling.

'I think it hit the reservoir. It sounded like it struck water.' When he told them that he was going to look for the ship, neither of them showed any interest in accompanying him. Scott understood. Sneaking out to the trees behind the dorm was one thing: taking a trip to the reservoir after curfew was quite another.

As they were making their way inside, Ben turned, grinning, and said, 'Oh, dragon boy, if you're thinking of going chasing after the Sunless, I'd put some clothes on if I were you.'

And then they were gone, giggling as they disappeared inside the shadowed doorway of the dorm. Scott looked down at his near nakedness and gave a rueful grin. There was a pile of uniforms in an untidy heap by the door. He tugged the greasy canvas overall on over his brightly coloured shorts. He smelt the stale odour of many people's bodies. The uniforms were rarely washed – it was one of many small rituals of resistance against the Sunless.

The uniform felt stiff and clammy. It bore three wide yellow stripes across the chest: the number of stripes denoted the wearer's place in the new hierarchy; the colour identified the wearer with a region. Yellow for the outlying villages in the three valleys, blue for the two smaller cities and as far as the mountains, and red for the city of Anarray and the coast. People kept in their place by nothing more than numbers and the colours on a randomly divided map. An absurd arbitrary decision which no one would have even remembered if it hadn't been enforced with the threat of being beaten or killed.

It took almost an hour to walk out to the reservoir. Scott moved quietly across the dusty forest floor. He knew he was unlikely to come face to face with the Sunless, but if he met a patrol of collaborators they would almost certainly report him.

The surface of the lake was almost still, disturbed only by tiny ripples that made no noise as they rushed to greet him in the darkness. Scott walked out to its edge from under the canopy of the forest. A long concrete bank sloped down gently to the water. He used to swim here with his brothers, Michael and Leon, on the really hot days a few summers ago, splashing in the water before soaking up the sun on the slope. It seemed like a long time ago now, although it had been only two or three years. He looked up and caught sight of the thick overhanging branch of an ancient tree which they used to swing from and tumble into the water. Michael had once fallen and crushed his knee on the steep bank. Scott and Leon had carried the big man back to the village, with him howling in pain all the way. Michael was still troubled by the injury.

Michael lived in the city now. Red Zone. Travel between zones was forbidden. Scott hadn't seen him in . . . too long.

The hard slope was wet under his feet, turning the dust between his toes into a film of thin mud. Ursu had been a very different place then. Another world. A better one.

He shivered: the air by the reservoir was cold. The chill

reminded him why he had made the journey. If a ship had crashed into the lake there wasn't any trace of it now. Staring out across the quiet waters, Scott wondered if perhaps it really had just been the dream preying on his mind. He was about to leave, feeling as if the trip had been a mistake. But there was something troubling him, something different about the place, which was just at the very periphery of awareness. He walked down to the edge of the reservoir to wash his feet – and then it hit him.

The concrete bank was wet but there were no waves or wind. Nothing to have caused the water to travel this far up the slope. He walked back up the gentle bank. The water stain ended close to the top. It would have taken a colossal wave to have caused the water to reach this far. He remembered the muffled thunder he had heard. A ship hitting the water? He stared back at the lake, imagining a tidal wave crashing down on the bank.

And then he saw something floating in the centre of the reservoir. A small rounded curve on top of the flat water. It hadn't been there a moment before. He watched the little rounded platform bobbing in the lake for a few minutes before his curiosity got the better of him. Scott tugged off the uniform and waded into the water a little way, in just his shorts, before diving in and swimming towards the object. He was a strong swimmer and cut through the dark water with sharp, clean strokes. It took only a few minutes to reach the object. It was a thick circle of metal, two metres across, slightly domed, like a piece of a giant eggshell.

The metal was warm under his fingers. The water was chilling. His teeth chattered as he traced the edge of the platform, treading water as he moved around it. The curved metal was part of a machine of some kind. There were instruments built into its surface. A small red light blinked on and off, and the edge was filled with indentations. He pulled himself up on his elbows to examine the surface of the strange object, his legs still dangling in the water. There was a series of symbols etched into the metal. Scott was surprised to discover that he recognized the words: EMERGENCY HATCH 3.

Something cold nudged his foot in the water. Cold and hard. He gasped, gripped by fear and terrible childhood images of sea monsters and tentacles. Instinctively, he tried to swing his legs on to the platform. As he did so a huge, unyielding hand closed around his ankle and pulled. There was nothing to grip on to on the surface of the airlock hatch and his fingers squealed against the metal as he was drawn violently down into the water. He caught his head painfully on the edge of the platform as he went over the edge and yelped, inadvertently swallowing a mouthful of foul-tasting water as the reservoir closed over his head.

Tameka stood by the smoking capsule, smoking one of her last cigarettes in the darkness. There were three creased cigarettes left in the packet. She'd left her other packet in the living quarters of the ship. The idea of going without cigarettes was almost as terrifying as the idea of being stranded on a prohibited world with only Emile for company.

The boy was still in the capsule messing about with the puter. Probably playing games. She was about to take another drag when she realized that in the darkness she had already smoked the cigarette down past the filter. Reluctantly, she dropped it into the cracked earth and ground it out with a booted foot.

The lifeboat had come down in a field. It was neatly bordered with scrawny bushes. The night air was hot and sucked the moisture out of her mouth. The earth was dry and dusty. The crop, which looked like a weed, clearly struggled to grow to maturity in these conditions. The capsule had carved a deep furrow through the field, destroying a significant proportion of the crop. Whoever intended to harvest the spindly plant wasn't going to be pleased with them. There hadn't been any sign of a farmer so far, but it was only a matter of time. Still, the chances were good that Bernice would find them first.

Emile swore suddenly.

'Say again?' she demanded as she stumbled down the bank created by the crash to where he lay inside the capsule, a puter on his lap. He was leaning on the console in front of him, turning one of his earrings with his fingers.

'We've got trouble.'

She looked from his anxious brown eyes to the puter screen, which was scrolling through technical data. The ship's logo winked on and off in the corner of the screen. It didn't mean anything to her. 'What?'

'Other lifeboat didn't launch.' Emile's chubby face shone sickly green with the light from the small screen. Beads of sweat lined his upper lip.

Tameka swallowed. The implication of what he was saying was too terrible to contemplate. 'What? Are you psychic? We left before them, so how could you know what happened?'

He gave a small shrug. 'Our capsule's still linked to the ship. Or at least was while the ship was in one piece. The second capsule was, too. Never launched. It couldn't – there was a malfunction in the locking device. It was still attached to the ship when the communication systems went off line, which is probably when the rest of the ship disintegrated.'

Out of the corner of her eye, Tameka could see that Emile was staring at her, waiting for her to say something. Tameka didn't want to meet his gaze, so she locked her eyes on to the scrolling screen. Finally she turned away from him and sank down on to her haunches. She felt giddy and needed to steady herself on the edge of the open escape hatch. Bernice wasn't going to get here before the farmer chased them away. Bernice wasn't going to get here at all. Ever.

'What do we do now?' Emile asked.

Tameka realized that she had no idea at all.

Conversations With The Enemy

Kitzinger had learnt the meaning of 'prisoner' in the year that she had spent among the ashen-faced aliens. It had been a difficult and brutal lesson.

For the first few weeks she had been repeatedly beaten for failing to understand or follow her captors' instructions. She was so unused to people attempting to dominate others by means of threats that it had taken her several days to realize that there was a connection between the orders, her refusal to comply and the following violence.

Slowly, over the long months that she had been kept 'prisoner', she had learnt to follow orders. She was all too aware of the process of conditioning that was taking place. It felt as if her very personhood was being whittled away along with her autonomy and self-esteem. In trying to predict the actions of her violent captors and then placate them she was turning herself into their servant. She was turning herself into a slave.

By her own calculations it had been eleven and a half months since she had woken on the floor of the ice cavern surrounded by the grey-suited figures. Her head had been affected by the drugs they had given her but she had still felt the intense cold. She had known immediately that she was no longer on her own world. There was nowhere on the dusty, orange bulk of Ursu that was as cold as the cavern. Someone had strapped a respirator mask on her face. She could hear the small compressor inside it wheezing as it made the hostile atmosphere more tolerable to her frail human body.

She had been outraged that she had been fed drugs against her will, that she had been lifted from her home and carried off into space. And when she had clambered to her feet and given voice to her outrage, one of the grey-suited figures had walked over to her and broken two of her ribs and three of the fingers on her left hand.

'Don't speak,' it had said. But Kitzinger hadn't understood about orders. She had tried to ask it what it meant. But even as the first words had left her mouth, it had smashed its elbow into her face, loosening a few of her teeth. Red spots had dripped on to the ice-covered floor. Her blood.

She knew how to follow orders now. Oh yes. She was an expert at doing exactly as she was told. All of her senses were finely tuned to detecting what her captors required of her. To do whatever was necessary to avoid another beating.

One of her captors was walking towards her now and she stepped away from the wall she was working at before it reached her. When she had first started to work in the chamber, her captors had physically pushed her away from the ancient machinery to inform her that her work shift was at an end. Now they only had to take a few steps in her direction and Kitzinger would abandon whatever she was working on. Head bowed, eyes averted; ever the obedient slave.

She hated herself. No, she hated what she had become. They had made her into something less than a person. Something pitiful and ugly.

She carefully packed away her tools and shuffled quietly across the huge white chamber to the pressurized quarters which were tucked away in the corner of the room. The reflective metal structure was little more than a foil-covered box, ten metres square.

Her captors did not use respirators or pressurized environments. They appeared to require less oxygen than she or Aric did. It occurred to her that they might not be flesh and blood at all but some kind of human-shaped machine.

She could see her fellow prisoner now. Aric had stepped

out from behind one of the giant shell-shaped Blooms where he had been working. The young man was slightly bent over and kept his arms tightly at his sides, as if he were trying to make himself smaller. Perhaps trying to make himself so small that he might disappear altogether.

They stepped into the airlock of the small cabin together and stood in silence as the cubicle slowly pressurized. Aric peeled off his respirator and chucked it carelessly into the locker. She managed to stop herself from berating him for not looking after his equipment – but not before she had ruefully noted that she had started to give the young man instructions just as their captors gave them to her.

It was as if oppression was a contagious disease. Maybe it was. She certainly felt infected by it. Corrupted. On her homeworld, Ursu, it was widely believed that free people had by nature an instinct, an incentive, which always encouraged them towards virtuous acts. Well Kitzinger was no longer free and her imprisonment was a cancer eating into the cells of her body. Changing them. Changing her. Permanently.

The inner door hissed and opened slightly – the magnet lock was automatically released when the pressure in the airlock equalized with the interior of the little metal hut. Aric caught her eye and smiled, a little uncertainly, before pushing his way inside.

They had not been getting on at all well recently. She knew that she had been taking out her feelings of frustration and helplessness on him. And now he was having to negotiate her moods just as she had to negotiate their captors' violence. He was having to placate her.

Aric began to prepare what little food they had. Their captors hadn't brought them food for several weeks now and there was enough for only two more meals, three if they reduced their rations again.

She watched Aric for a few moments as he carefully, sorrowfully, divided up the food. He was a thin, good-looking man in his late twenties. His face had been pleasantly angular, but a year under the rule of their captors had made him gaunt. He wore a hunted expression. His hair was short, dark curls, his eyes a sad brown. She had known him on Ursu, although that seemed like a lifetime ago now. He had been studying at the university, part of a group of friends conducting research into the crystalline structure of the Blooms. He was bright, although terribly insecure with it. One moment arrogantly proclaiming the radical nature and importance of his ideas, desperately searching for re-assurance the next. He was not someone she would have chosen to make a friend of back on Ursu. Here, all they had was each other.

'I'm sorry for yesterday,' she started. 'I was rude and thoughtless. You do so much in the hut as it is. It was unfair of me to have shouted at you.'

'Doesn't matter.' His eyes didn't leave the small cooking equipment as he carefully heated up the basic rations their captors had provided. Kitzinger knew that she had really hurt his feelings.

'It does matter, Aric. It matters to me. And I think it matters to you, too.'

He looked at her for a second and then turned back to his work. He nodded, almost imperceptibly.

She rested her hands on his shoulders and began to knead the hard, corded muscles. 'However hard it is, we've got to remain honest. If we start bottling things up we'll end up resenting each other. We'll be dividing ourselves.' She nodded towards the chamber, which was visible through the transparent section of the wall. 'We'll just be doing their work for them.'

He handed her a little dish of rehydrated and heated food. 'I know. I just . . . I'm just finding it harder and harder . . . just to go on.'

'I know. I know you are.'

They ate in silence. Food was so scarce that their meals were taking on an almost sacred quality. After they had finished their meagre dinner, she slipped her arms around him and pulled him into her lap. He twisted and slipped an arm around her, burying his face in her neck. They sat like that for a little while. Kitzinger closed her eyes and rested her

73

chin on his head. They had run out of conversation months ago – their life histories recounted, favourite stories told, songs sung. Kitzinger made a point of keeping in physical contact with Aric in the evenings. If they could no longer distract each other with sparkling wit and exciting anecdotes, then they could offer each other at least the basic comfort of a hug.

Aric shifted in her arms, struggling to sit up. She opened her eyes and saw the reason for his movement. There were three dark shadows standing patiently in the airlock, waiting for the air to equalize.

They had visitors.

Aric slipped out of her embrace and quickly scuttled over to the far side of the hut, staring anxiously over at the airlock. He tucked his arms around his knees as, heralded with a hiss, the door began to open.

As ever, Nikolas was accompanied by two of the ashen-faced humanoids. Nikolas called them the Sunless, but not, Kitzinger noted, when they were nearby. He pulled off his respirator and nodded an empty welcome to her. Despite his wearing one of their charcoal-coloured uniforms, there was no way that Nikolas could have been mistaken for one of the aliens. His face was long and narrow, his nose and forehead particularly so. His dark red hair curled at the nape of his neck, and his mouth was continually caught up in a sneer. He didn't look any older than eighteen. His eyes were large and prominent, and were the same industrial grey of the invaders. Pools of mercury staring coldly back at her.

Kitzinger had often wondered if he was somehow related to them. But there was no doubt that he was an Ursulan. One of her own people. If he was the age he looked then she had probably birthed him from the Blooms herself. If she hadn't ever met him then she would have never believed that an Ursulan could have behaved as he did.

There were dark rings under his eyes and he was unshaven. Nikolas looked tired – perhaps the cold affected him as much as it did her. Despite his tiredness, he was smiling at her, lewdly. It made her feel sick.

'If I'd known you were . . . busy I would have come back later,' he lied.

Kitzinger didn't say anything. She didn't want to provoke him. Instead she just shrugged her shoulders noncommittally. He had once instructed one of the Sunless to beat her when she had ignored him.

He wandered over to a small collapsible table on which a puter sat. He ran a finger across the top of the frame of the screen as if he were checking for dust. 'You have compiled an update?'

Kitzinger nodded at the puter. 'A complete record of all of our work is recorded there. You could have accessed it from –'

He raised an eyebrow. 'Don't you want me to come and visit you?' he interrupted, a smile flickering across his thin mouth.

Kitzinger froze. She could feel beads of cold sweat between her shoulder blades. He was teasing her. She was dangerously close to a beating. 'Yes. Yes I do want you to come here.'

Nikolas shot Aric a look of mock surprise – the first time he had acknowledged the other man's presence since he had entered the hut that evening. Aric only flinched in reply. 'Aric, my friend, I didn't realize I was so popular, did you? If I had known I was so welcome I might have come more often.'

Kitzinger swallowed. She had once received a sharp kick in the kneecap for trying to flatter him. 'You're not popular here. Not with me, I mean. I can't speak for Aric. But I do want you to come, because I hope that one day you will come to tell me that I am to go home.'

Nikolas stared at her neutrally for a moment, appraising her. Deciding what he wanted to do with her. 'So honest,' he commented. 'So principled. You're a model for us all,' and then he grinned. 'You will go back to Ursu, of course you will. But only when the work is finished here. Not before.'

Kitzinger swallowed. He was lying of course. He always grinned when he said something that was an out-and-out lie. Like most teenagers, he couldn't disguise his body language, which was quite easy to read. But she didn't need to pick up non-verbal cues to know that he had no intention of making good his promise. Why would he go to the trouble of arranging for the two of them to be taken several light years across the galaxy? It would be so much easier just to kill them both. The promise of a return home was just to ensure her complicity. Preying on her hope, on her desire to live, on her willingness to accept the tiniest chance of a reprieve from this hellish place.

And it worked. Oh, how it worked.

'I don't have time to read the report now,' he said dismissively. 'Tell me, what progress have you made now that the device is almost complete, now we have replaced the equipment that was removed?'

He was referring to the Blooms. It didn't really surprise her that he didn't like to mention their name. A month after she had been brought to the ice planet, Kitzinger had been woken by the sound of heavy machinery. She had stood at the plastic window of the hut, open-mouthed as she had watched the Blooms being lowered into the chamber. She had never seen them out of water before. They were like enormous clams, their ribbed, fan-shaped bodies blocking out the deep-red sunlight that invaded the crystal chamber as they descended towards her.

Like all Ursulans, Kitzinger and Aric – and even Nikolas – had been born from the Blooms. For as long as she could remember they had nestled at the bottom of the pools in the university on Ursu. Her whole society depended upon them – no, more than that, the Blooms were the foundations upon which Ursulan society was built. Without them no children could be born and Ursu would surely die.

And Nikolas had scooped them out of the water and brought them here, destroying her whole culture with one casual theft. It was horrifying that one of her own people was capable of such a betrayal.

Nikolas was speaking. She looked up at him and saw that he was impatiently waiting for a reply from her. 'Well?' he said.

The threat of violence in his voice stirred her out of her musings. Well what? What had he been talking about? She'd been so caught up in her thoughts that she'd stopped listening to him. She felt a sinking feeling in her stomach as the likelihood of another beating loomed. Filling her voice with as much confidence as she could, she guessed, and said, 'The Blooms are now connected to the rest of the artefacts in the chamber.'

He raised an eyebrow. 'You've made a lot of progress since I was last here.'

She'd guessed correctly. She was tempted to take the credit for the work but it would be dangerous to actually lie to Nikolas. He would probably kill her.

'No. I didn't connect the Blooms to the chamber . . .' she began, hesitantly.

He nodded to where Aric cowered. 'Don't say that what's-his-name did it.'

Aric knotted himself into a tighter ball as Nikolas directed his attention towards him.

'No,' Kitzinger replied. She still wasn't absolutely sure what had happened herself. 'They just sort of did it by themselves.'

Nikolas stared at her, suddenly very interested. 'Go on,' he said, after a moment.

'I don't know how or why, but as soon as they were lowered on to the floor of the chamber, they began . . . taking root. I only discovered it recently when I was drilling down for samples.' She remembered the coils of thick tentacles pushing their way through the ice-packed ground, attaching themselves to the foundations of the ancient structure.

'Taking root? Are they . . . alive?' he asked, his bulging eyes full of excitement and wonder.

She shrugged, her fear of him temporarily forgotten. 'I don't know. Not in a conventional sense, I'm sure.' She found herself giving voice to an idea that had been nagging at her for a few weeks now. 'They . . . belong here, don't they?'

He looked amused. As if she was a student who had just grasped a basic but fundamental point. 'Oh yes, they are the

77

key to this place. The heart of its power.'

'I've told you before, Nikolas. There isn't any power here. There aren't even any residual energy readings. I've tried every scan I know of. As far as I can tell, there never has been anything here but ice and rock. That's the truth.'

'You're wrong,' he said wearily. 'This structure is here for a purpose. I don't need your science to know that there is energy here, just out of sight, just out of our reach. I can practically taste it on my tongue.' He signalled his readiness to leave to the two ashen-faced humanoids who waited patiently by the door, turning his back on her as he did so.

It was only then that Kitzinger realized that the Sunless had been listening attentively to the conversation. Quietly watching the proceedings with their dull, lifeless eyes.

'Bring them food, enough for another two weeks.' Nikolas paused for a moment, before adding, 'Then we'll see.'

He seemed to delight in being vindictive. There was a melodramatic campness to his threats, as if they were carefully rehearsed. He probably practised the routine in the mirror, Kitzinger told herself, feeling a little more rebellious now he had gone.

She joined Aric at the back of the hut. He was rocking gently back and forth, his eyes staring straight out in front of him. He looked an awful lot older than his twenty-eight years. She placed her hand on his shoulder. 'We've won another reprieve.'

He didn't say anything. Kitzinger thought he looked almost disappointed, as if he would have preferred the ordeal to be over at any cost, even if it meant dying.

That was what being a 'prisoner' did to you. It chipped away at your self-determination. While they were here, there was no way that they could stop the process continuing. They couldn't fight back. They'd tried that and learnt just how physically powerful their captors were. They could only ever be dominated, only ever be slaves. There wasn't any other position to take, besides that of suicidal martyr – and Kitzinger wasn't ready to die for her beliefs, not when she might yet find a way to live for them. Perhaps they should think

78

again about trying to find a way of leaving this place, of stopping being prisoners. They needed to leave here without permission. There was a word for that, dusty with lack of use.

Escape. That was it. Perhaps they could escape.

7

DEEP WATER

Blackness. Panic overtook him and he lashed out wildly in the water. The weight of it absorbed the power of his blows. Scott kicked at the icy grip on his ankle with the heel of his free foot. It wasn't a human hand, far too big even for the Sunless. He imagined it as a grey metal fist wrapped around him. Was this some creature of the Sunless? Or even a giant version of one of those cold-hearted warriors?

He felt his lungs begin to ache and he redoubled his efforts. A second huge cold hand was trying to grab hold of his free leg. He kicked down at the grip around his ankles and missed. His foot travelled further down in the water and struck something else – the creature's head?

The effect was dramatic. The grip on his ankle loosened and then disappeared altogether. He turned and struck out for the surface, his lungs burning. He surfaced with a yell of fear, and had clambered on to the floating hatch before he was even aware of thinking of doing so. He stood shivering in the darkness, keeping his legs apart to maintain balance on the platform, eyes scouring the surface of the water for any sign of the horrific creature.

The shore suddenly seemed kilometres away, the line of the trees just visible against the night sky. Only minutes ago, he'd been standing safely on the sloping bank, under those trees. Now he was going to die in the lake. He realized that he was cursing desperately and continually through his chattering teeth.

He heard something break the surface of the water behind him. Here it comes, he thought. A huge head had appeared out of the water. It was more than twice the size of a human's: dark and perfectly spherical. There was a faint hissing sound, like air escaping, and the entire front of the blank head slid back. A woman's face was revealed beneath. Scott was astonished, the 'head' was a helmet, the dark blank 'face' only a visor.

'Er, good evening,' the woman said, and smiled awkwardly. 'If this is your planet then I'm really very sorry for crashing on it. I didn't have much choice. Some rather mean black spaceships took a dislike to me in orbit.'

Scott was so relieved that he forgot for a moment that the woman had tried to drown him and started to giggle, almost upsetting the platform in the process.

The woman must have thought that she'd scared him, because she lifted a large, gloved hand out of the water and pointed at herself. 'There's no need to be afraid: friend.'

'I'm not afraid. Not now.' He suddenly became aware of how cold he was and hugged himself tightly. 'Anyway, what kind of friend are you? You tried to kill me!'

'Ah, we can converse. That's a relief. Actually, I thought you were a sea monster trying to kill me. I panicked. Sorry. It's been one of those days. Death, disaster, leaving home without deodorant. You wouldn't mind helping me with my friend, would you?'

'What friend?'

As if on cue, a second similarly attired figure surfaced next to her, bobbing lifelessly on its back in the water. The woman doggy-paddled over to it, the torch on top of her suit cutting a beam in the darkness. She began to tug the prone figure towards the platform. 'He's in a bad way. You don't happen to be a doctor, do you?'

Scott shook his head in puzzlement. Doctor?

'That's a shame. My skills don't go much beyond administering aspirin and patting people on the head. How's your first aid?'

Scott didn't realize that the woman had been making a joke until he'd replied that he could dress a wound, resuscitate a heart and splint a broken limb. The woman looked at him bemused but impressed. 'I bet they loved you in the cub scouts.'

Bernice watched the boy attend to Errol, who lay on the bank drifting in and out of consciousness. Actually 'boy' didn't quite describe him. He was humanoid, tall and slender with pale skin and shoulder-length hair that looked black in the darkness. He was probably a few years older than Emile, maybe eighteen. Her attention was arrested by the smattering of tiny, reptilian scales over his back, shoulders and arms. Droplets of water glimmered on them in the torch light. As she approached him she saw that his hair wasn't black, but dark green in the artificial light from her suit helmet. The irises of his eyes were a metallic grey colour which Bernice had never seen before. Crouched over Errol, he looked like a creature from a fairy story. An elf or a sprite. Despite his otherworldliness, he appeared to be wearing a pair of very ordinary, brightly patterned boxer shorts.

He examined the wound on Errol's thigh, flicking the loose end of the tourniquet with his fingers. 'Did you do this?' His tone was neither disapproving nor approving.

'If you mean did I dress the wound, then yes. He was injured when our ship was attacked.'

'The wound won't heal like this. You've cut off the blood supply to his leg.'

Bernice felt a wave of irritation at this remark. She was too exhausted to take criticism easily and was about to tell this strange boy that he should try doing first aid under combat conditions but bit her tongue. It wouldn't be a good idea to alienate her rescuer. The young man continued his examination and Bernice was given the impression that he had been merely making an observation about the tourniquet rather than making a judgment of her skills.

She began to unfasten the clasps that ran down one side of her suit. Out of the water it was enormously heavy and she was finding it difficult to move about in. The suit clattered as it hit the ground. Concrete – she was standing on something concrete. The lake wasn't a natural phenomenon. A reservoir, then. Which – along with the clothes the boy had retrieved from the bank – suggested an industrial society at the very least. Maybe this prohibited world would have medical facilities.

'I'm Bernice,' she said. 'What's your name?' She nodded when he told her. Scott was an old Earth name. It wasn't what she had been expecting at all.

'Have you come because of the Sunless?' he asked, not looking up as he tore the yellow strips from his overall and used them to bind the wound. He seemed to take pleasure in tearing the outfit apart.

'Sunless? Er, no. At least, I don't think so. I was actually looking for my husband.'

'Husband? What's a husband?'

Bernice grinned. Ah, this prohibited world was civilized indeed. 'Scott, I think I must have died and gone to heaven.'

It took them over an hour to carry Errol through the forest. He was awake now, sobbing quietly because of the pain. Crimson blossoms had already spread across the yellow bandages around his thigh. Scott directed them through a forest of tall trees, which reminded Bernice of giant pines. The trees gave off a sweet scent and left a slight stickiness on her bare arms as she brushed past them in the darkness.

The other side of the forest opened out on to cultivated land. Scott led them to a small barn in the corner of a field, full of old equipment covered in dust sheets. It didn't look as if the barn had been in use for a long time.

The journey had been hard on Errol, who seemed to relax a little when he was laid on the barn floor. She found a couple of empty sacks and made a pillow out of them. His bald head was slippery with cold sweat. He offered Bernice a brave smile but she could see the agony in his one good eye. The plastic which had splattered against the side of his face had hardened into a half-mask. The flesh around it was blistered and red raw. He needed proper medical attention.

The boy – Scott – had lit a small stacked stove which stood in the corner of the barn. Bernice walked over and watched the flames burn the kindling visible in the small window at the front of the stove. Scott was wearing his torn clothes, having draped his wet underwear on top of the stove, where it gently began to steam. His grey eyes glinted like metal in the firelight. There was something incredibly self-contained about his behaviour. He approached every task methodically, whether it was treating Errol's injuries or merely filling the stove with wood. His thoughtfulness didn't seem appropriate to someone his age. Bernice reminded herself that he wasn't human and she was only project-ing her own cultural perspective on to him. A classic but unavoidable problem in all social science, as she so often told her students.

She tucked her shirt into her combat trousers. 'Thank you, Scott,' she said, and cleared her throat. 'You've been very kind. I'm not sure what I would have done on my own.' She realized as she spoke that they'd barely exchanged a word on their journey through the forest.

The boy shrugged and sat down, leaning against one of the covered machines in the barn.

'Is it OK to stay here tonight?' she asked. 'Errol really needs a doctor or a hospital. Is there one nearby? Would it be all right to take him there?'

Scott didn't seem to understand. 'All right?' he repeated, frowning. 'There's a woman who lives in the village. She was in the hospital in Anarray for a year. She's good at helping the injured. I'll ask her to come in the morning. I think he will be "all right" enough until then.'

Bernice felt some of the tension leave her. 'Thank you. Again. I have to find two more of my friends. They came down in an escape pod. I followed their flight path down. I couldn't get exact coordinates, but they shouldn't be too far away. There's tracking equipment built into my suit. I can look for them tomorrow. With any luck they'll have stayed near the capsule.' She heard what she was saying and groaned inwardly. Staying in one place was going to be the last thing Tameka would do.

Scott looked up at her, meeting her gaze for the first time since they had entered the barn. 'Where do they come from?'

'My friends?'

'No. The Sunless, of course.'

'Ah,' Bernice said, puzzled. She shook her head. 'Who are they, then?'

The village was made up of a few stone buildings, which nestled in the sticky trees. From here among the trees, Bernice couldn't see any design to the village or uniformity to the buildings. They looked as if they had been hastily dropped on to the landscape. The architecture was both exciting and naive, and definitely amateur – some of it was already crumbling. Bernice was reminded of one of the art degree shows back at St Oscar's on Dellah – fired-up talent with little experience to support it. One of the buildings looked like a stone igloo, with spiralling designs carved into its rounded walls. Another was rectangular, built of huge stone blocks, each of which had been painted a bright colour. Bernice imagined a huge toddler appearing over the tops of the trees to reclaim their building bricks.

The streets were full of people. Humans living alongside a handful of alien races, some of whom Bernice recognized from her travels. Others were new to her. Strange and beautiful in their novelty. The humans weren't particularly beautiful. They had large hands and feet, thin limbs and flat bellies. No one else shared Scott's curious ancestry. The street was busy with voices of greeting, laughter and argument. Children of a half-dozen races scampered in the dust, playing the complicated games children always seemed to invent for themselves. Games that always seemed to involve lots of shouting and pointing and thumping.

Surprisingly, all of the adults were dressed in the same type of rough coveralls as Scott wore. Three yellow bands across the chest of an otherwise grey outfit. This one example of conformity in the midst of so much diversity was strange.

She was about to ask Scott about it, when he began to speak: 'I'll go and speak with my friend. I'll come back with a uniform for you.'

'Can't I come with you?'

'No, it would be best if you stay among the trees, out of sight.'

Bernice had a bad feeling about this. 'May I ask why?'

'Don't you know?' he started, averting his gaze. It was a moment before Bernice realized that Scott was embarrassed. It was the first time that he'd appeared unsure of himself. His practical, straightforwardness had disappeared beneath blushes. 'You're not supposed to be here. The treaty says . . . Well, there's a . . . a rule about it.'

'I thought as much. This is a prohibited world, right?' Something about the way he had pronounced the word 'rule' nagged at her, but she pressed on, 'Why do I get the feeling that this isn't going to be one of those friendly, civilized rules like free milk for all schoolchildren or an equal age of consent?'

He moved off, talking over his shoulder. 'No off-worlders. Not alive ones anyway. Stay here.'

Bernice sat down and leant against a tree. She'd been half expecting something like this, of course. Well, you don't go crashing on a prohibited world and expect yourself to be welcomed with open arms. If Jason was here, then he would be facing similar dangers. Jason and her students. Tameka and Emile were somewhere on this world. Probably somewhere nearby.

She watched Scott wander into the crowds, where a few of the inhabitants welcomed him, slapping him on the back or kissing him on the cheek. Bernice thought they looked friendly enough, until an elderly woman who walked with a stick became agitated when she saw that the yellow stripes were missing from the front of his uniform. She hit him around the head and swore at him. Scott didn't fight back, but only protected his head. He looked outraged that she had hit him. No, not outraged. Shocked. Two people nearby immediately dragged the woman away from him. They didn't even hesitate before they involved themselves in the conflict.

People started to congregate around the scene. Bernice moved forward to the edge of the wood, until she was as close as she could be while remaining under cover of the trees.

Voices were raised in indignation and anger. The older woman, who had now been released, was still shouting at him and was waving her stick threateningly. Bernice could only hear fragments of her conversation. Picking out strange terms of what sounded like abuse. Other voices quickly joined in, siding either with Scott or with the woman.

Everyone who had stopped, and that included almost all of the people on the street, was actively taking part in the scene. Some appeared to have taken the role of mediators, shushing those who interrupted and making sure Scott wasn't hit again. Others were loudly shouting their views. It took Bernice a moment to realize that there were no bystanders to the conflict at all. It was so different from life on Dellah. If a fight broke out on the streets there, most people would just hurry past, pretending that they hadn't seen anything or, worse, move to a safe distance to watch.

It was frustrating not knowing what the argument was about. Bernice was itching to get closer, but she kept her curiosity on a tight leash. She wasn't going to be any use to Errol if she managed to get herself locked up in a police cell. Locked up or executed.

The crowd began to disperse. The woman with the stick had moved off with a group of supporters. Scott was standing with a taller reptilian humanoid who appeared to be comforting him. Bernice wondered if they were somehow related. She had met several reptilian races, and while she was sure that their biologies were not compatible with humans, that didn't rule out *all* such cross-species breeding. Apart from a slight paunch around the waist, the tall reptile man's body was slender and covered with the same kind of dark-green scales which coated Scott's shoulders and upper arms. His head was bulbous, with large oval eyes and two dark vertical slits for a nose. Long thin arms tapered away to three thin claws. Despite the loose-fitting grey uniform, it was obvious that his legs were back-jointed like a bird's. His ankles were lower than a human's, located behind the foot rather than above it. He walked with a gentle, bobbing movement, reminding Bernice of a chicken. It occurred to Bernice that the dispute might have been racially motivated.

She was lost in her thoughts and was only aware of the two newcomers as Scott and his companion turned to look at them. Bernice's heart sank as she saw Tameka and Emile wandering down the dusty road, looking like tourists who had become separated from their tour party. They were the only two people in the street not wearing uniforms and were attracting attention; a tall feathered male had walked over and was staring at them intently.

Bernice had already broken cover of the trees and was heading towards them when Scott waved her back. She was left hovering near the roadside, unsure of what to do.

'What are you looking at?'

The bird man who was doing the staring seemed surprised at her remark. 'You, of course,' he said, as if the answer was obvious.

Tameka was momentarily taken aback. 'Oh, well don't, all right?'

He tilted his feathered head to one side: Tameka was reminded of a parrot her mother had kept in a cage.

'You're not wearing a uniform. Are you a friend of Scott's?'

'No,' she said, defiantly. She didn't have any idea what he was talking about and kept getting distracted by his thin grey tongue, which slithered around in his beak. 'Maybe I just don't like yellow stripes, OK?'

A crowd started to gather around them. She reached out for Emile's arm and pulled him closer to her; his hand slipped gratefully into hers.

'Look, just leave us alone, will you? We don't want any trouble.'

An elderly woman using a gnarled stick to support her shrieked when she caught sight of them. 'More of them!' She spat curses as she hobbled across the dusty road to where they were standing. 'You're putting everyone's lives in danger just to make a point. It's the sort of thing I've come to expect from that half-breed, but not from a woman. They're in the village as well – you know that? They catch you dressed like that and who knows what they'll do? Don't you care at all?'

Tameka started to back away, having no idea how to respond to the old woman. The woman's face was crumpled and deeply lined. Her few teeth were blackened. Tameka just wanted to keep some distance between them.

The woman pointed her stick at her and kept demanding that she explain herself.

They were becoming the focus of attention in the street. There were too many people gathered around them, a closed circle of angry, interested and bemused faces.

Time to get out of here. Gripping Emile's hand tightly, she turned away from the woman and began to push her way through the crowd. 'Let us through, all right?'

Thankfully, no one tried to grab hold of them, but they didn't step out of their way either. A few people shouted questions and accused her of things she didn't understand.

She came face to face with a boy as she struggled through the crowd. She was given the impression that he'd been looking for her.

'Tameka?' he asked.

She stared at him. His hair was long and fine and *green*. It shone like emerald silk against his pale skin. His eyes were the colour of mercury: she saw the panic on her powdered face reflected in them. 'How do –'

'Doesn't matter now. Come on, I know someone who wants to see you.'

His was the first friendly face she'd seen since they'd crashed on the planet. She let him drag her through the tightly knit crowd. However, they didn't get far. His presence only angered more of the people around them. The people around them became more aggressive, pushing them back into the middle of the crowd.

'I knew it!' The elderly woman cried when she saw them together. 'I knew she was one of the dragon boy's friends.'

'Oh get lost, Margaret,' the green-haired boy shouted. Tameka was shocked by the anger in his voice. 'Keep your ugly face out of my life. Haven't you got anything better to do than poke it in where it isn't wanted?'

'Why won't you think about the implications of what you're doing? They'll kill us all if they see us out of their stinking uniforms. You know that. Why do you insist on provoking them?'

The argument reminded Tameka of her mother, who'd never approved of the way she dressed. She'd called her a slut for putting soap in her hair. Tameka was relieved that the focus of the present argument had moved away from her. Now she just needed to get herself and the kid away from here. Somewhere she could get her thoughts together. Work out a plan for getting them off this weird planet and back to Dellah. Get Emile back to the university and call up her boyfriend and get a lift home. She'd had enough.

The green-haired 'dragon boy' was screaming something at the woman, but Tameka wasn't paying any attention. She didn't want to have to get involved. Where was Bernice? She should be dealing with this – not leaving it all to her. She remembered the destruction of the haulage ship and felt her guts twist. As she stared at the angry faces shouting around her, she suddenly felt like screaming at them all.

I don't want to have to deal with this! she thought. This doesn't have anything to do with me. I don't belong here with these crazies. This isn't fair. She glanced at Emile, who was standing close to her. He was trying to look brave, but it was obvious that he was scared half to death. He was twisting his wooden beads in his fingers and chewing on his lip.

Someone on the other side of the crowd started yelling frantically to get off the streets. She heard the word 'sunless' repeated over and over again as if it were a warning of some kind. Maybe it was.

And then she was grabbed roughly from behind, and almost pulled off balance. This was the last straw. 'Leave me alone, *asshole*!' she screamed and turned around and smacked them in the face.

The woman who had manhandled her fell back on to the floor, yelping and cradling her bloody nose. 'Tameka!' the woman yelled. 'That hurt!'

Tameka stared down at the woman in shock. It was her tutor. It was Bernice.

8

THE LAND OF DO AS YOU PLEASE?

'They're here,' the reptile man whispered.

Standing next to him at one of the low windows of the stone igloo, Bernice tried to follow his gaze. She kept being distracted by the pain in her nose. 'Where?'

'At the far end of the street.'

'What do they look like? Wait, I think I see them.' The street had emptied. Most people had hurried inside after the arrival of the Sunless had been announced. Bernice caught sight of a few figures who weren't wearing the now familiar wasp-stripe outfits.

At first glance, in their dark-grey combat fatigues and tough black boots, they reminded Bernice of mercenaries. Their hair was crew-cut, but carelessly so. Their heads were almost skeletal: snow-white skin drawn tightly over their skulls. Their features were sharp and quite striking, almost beautiful.

Angels of death.

Bernice became aware of cold sweat trickling down the middle of her back.

Their movements were coordinated, like machines running smoothly. Their lifeless eyes scanned the faces of the crowds. Evidently they were searching for something or someone.

It occurred to Bernice that if they had followed the flight of the haulage ship then they would know that it had made planet-fall in this region.

The people remaining on the street moved aside to let the grey figures past, careful to avoid eye contact. Only the children stared openly at them and pointed. The Sunless ignored the attention of the children. They seemed oblivious to the effect they had on the people around them, which only made them appear more frightening. There was no trace of arrogance in their manner and they didn't seem to take pleasure in the dramatic effect they had on the population.

Not stupid, then.

'They don't usually come out this far,' the lizard man beside her whispered.

The group of Sunless reached the far end of the village and disappeared through the trees. Bernice let out a sigh when they had gone, realizing only as she did so that she'd been holding her breath.

'They're probably looking for us,' Bernice replied, feeling responsible. She turned away from the window. The tall reptilian humanoid was staring at her with his bulbous eyes. They were so wide in proportion to his thin face that he looked to Bernice as if he were perpetually surprised. 'I'm sorry if we've brought them to your town,' she said, quietly.

She was surprised when his eyes opened further. 'What have you got to be sorry about? You didn't make them come here.'

'Didn't she?' A new voice demanded angrily. Bernice turned around and saw the old human woman who'd fought with Scott on the street. Margaret was staring defiantly at her, her knuckles white where they gripped her walking stick. 'Well what other reason have they got for coming out this far? That's what I want to know.' Bernice met the woman's gaze, but didn't say anything. She wasn't sure what to say. For all she knew the woman was right.

The large stone igloo was full of people who'd hurried off the streets. Large dark pots were bubbling over an open fire, which burnt in the middle of the room. Tameka and Emile were sitting at one of the nearby benches, watching the scene closely. Tameka hadn't taken her eyes off Bernice since they'd been reunited. They hadn't had a chance to speak since Tameka had hit her. Bernice was too pleased that they were both alive to feel angry.

'Well?' Margaret demanded. 'Can't you answer me?'

Bernice hadn't realized that the old woman was expecting an answer to her question. 'Oh, I'm sorry. I don't know why they've come to your village. But, yes, I should think it is at least possible that they are looking for us. I think it must have been them who shot our ship down from orbit last night.'

'I didn't think you were Ursulan. What were you doing in orbit anyway? This is a closed world: a treaty prohibits contact with us.'

Bernice started to feel frustrated with the woman. 'Well if I'd known that my arrival was going to upset you so much I would have tried to crash somewhere else.'

'You can make jokes about it, but your arrival may well cause people to die. The Sunless have burnt villages to the ground because people wouldn't wear their uniforms. All of my brothers and sisters among them. I'm the only one left of my Eight.'

Bernice was suddenly aware that the whole room was listening to their conversation. 'I'm sorry.'

The woman slammed her stick against the stone floor. 'I don't want a stranger's sorrow. What use is that to me? I want the people I care about to stay alive. *I* want to stay alive. You being here puts us all in danger.'

'Well, my friend will die unless he gets medical help. I appreciate that we've broken your laws by coming here and I'll answer to whoever's in charge if I have to. But we didn't mean any . . . harm.' Her voice trailed away as she realized that people in the room were talking over her. A few people were looking at her as if she were saying something they couldn't quite understand; others were shaking their heads and laughing.

'What? What have I said?'

The tall reptilian, who had been standing behind her during her confrontation with Margaret, rested a claw on her shoulder. 'You won't convince anyone of your intentions if you talk like a subject.'

'A subject?' She could feel his breath against her neck. It was cool and fresh. 'I'm not sure that I know what you mean.'

'That is very clear, Bernice Summerfield. My suggestion to you is to stop talking and take some food to your friends. You're just digging yourself deeper into shit here.'

'What about Margaret?' Bernice said, nodding towards the elderly woman, who was still staring malevolently at her.

'What about her?'

'I get the feeling that she isn't going to leave me alone.'

'I think you're right. What do you want to do?'

Bernice laughed hollowly. 'Tell her to shove that stick where the sun don't shine.'

The reptilian made a cooing noise, which Bernice guessed was laughter. 'Then do it.'

The idea was tempting but she decided against it. Partly because she could tell that Margaret was hurting beneath her anger; partly because she wasn't yet sure that she could trust the softly spoken reptile man; but mostly because she didn't want to add to the scene she had created. She'd had the eyes of these people on her for far longer than felt comfortable. So she told Margaret that she was too tired to talk to her now and was going to sit down. Bernice was surprised when the old woman let her go with a dismissive shrug.

Her new friend directed her over to the cooking area. Strips of vegetable were being roasted over part of the fire. At the reptile's invitation, Bernice picked off several strips using wooden tongs which were quite hot to the touch. There was a selection of what looked like sauces or dips nearby, but Bernice wasn't sure whether it would be the done thing to carry one of the bowls to the table. Several of the people in the room were still staring at her and she didn't want to appear selfish or greedy. She was aware of her new friend filling a plate with vegetables next to her. She was glad of his presence beside her.

Scott had taken an Ursulan girl, Yvonne, and a stretcher to retrieve Errol and, while she was extremely grateful for this, Bernice had missed the familiar presence of the young man.

Emile and Tameka, brought up no doubt on a diet of Kwik Kurry and McSwine burgers, took one look at the curled-up strips of dried vegetable and simultaneously screwed their noses up.

'Just don't start, all right?' Bernice whispered. 'We're in enough trouble as it is. First rule of field trips: eat what's offered and look grateful.'

'Benny, you should meet my mother,' Tameka said, picking up a strip of what looked like aubergine between finger and thumb. 'You'd get on like a house on fire, I'm telling you.' She bit into the strip and chewed slowly, making no attempt to hide her displeasure. 'So, who's your friend?' she added, nodding towards the reptile man.

'This is . . .' Bernice began.

'Leon,' he finished, and pushed a bowl of white sauce that looked a little like yogurt towards Tameka. 'Try it. Those vegetables can be a bit dry on their own.'

'Cheers, Leon,' Tameka said and dipped her vegetable strip. Inexplicably she began to giggle. 'Leon the lizard! I just got it. Hoo boy, I'm not even going to touch that one.'

Bernice closed her eyes, suddenly wanting the ground to swallow her up. She was about to apologize for her students – again – but Leon spoke first.

'You people are so strange,' he said in his gentle, almost melodic voice. If he'd been offended by Tameka's comment, he didn't show it. 'Scott said that you were from the companies. Is that right? Are you corporate people? Profiteers?'

Emile was staring at Leon, trying to work out what he was saying. 'My father works for Krytell,' he said. When Leon looked blank, he explained. 'It's one of the biggest companies in the sector. In our sector, that is. My dad's a communications engineer. I lived with him on an X-boat relay station. That's a sort of artificial satellite, only smaller.'

Leon looked puzzled, but intrigued. 'And he works for this Krytell company and is paid for his labour in return, is that right?'

'He gets a salary, if that's what you mean. Quite a decent one.'

'And works late and ignores his son and thinks more about machines than he does about his wife,' Tameka butted in as she reached over to wipe up some sauce with a strip of the aubergine-like vegetable. 'Just like all the other company robots. Selling their soul for a few stupid shillings.'

Leon cooed with humour again, and Bernice was startled to see a thin forked tongue flicker around the edge of his mouth. 'Ah, do I detect a voice of dissidence?'

'Detect what you like, mate. You wouldn't catch me working for Krytell. They're as corrupt as the church.'

The conversation between Leon and Tameka became more animated as Leon suggested that all companies were corrupt by definition. Bernice noticed that Emile had slumped back in his seat a little, his shoulders sagging. Tameka's earlier comment seemed to have deflated him somehow and he suddenly looked like a little boy. 'Are you all right, Emile?' Bernice asked.

He met her gaze for a moment and smiled weakly. He wiped his nose on the back of his hand. 'Yeah, I'm all right. You don't have to worry about me, Professor S. I was just thinking about my dad, that's all.'

She reached over and stroked his cheek with the back of her fingers. 'I know I don't *have* to worry about you, Emile. I just like worrying about you.'

His smile grew a little. Poor kid. His colourful clothes were covered with the dry orange dust of the planet, and he'd lost an earring since he'd baled out of the haulage ship. His usually neat bleached hair was sticking up all over the place, and was dusted with grit. He looked like he'd just walked away from a space crash, and then Bernice remembered that this was precisely what he had just done. 'Missing home?' she asked.

He shook his head and then took a deep breath as if he were struggling to control a powerful feeling. He distracted himself by refilling his plate. 'No, not really. Just wish I'd left on better terms.'

'Ah, I see. Parents not pleased to see you go?'

'Something like that.'

He seemed uneasy and Bernice wondered if he was afraid that he wasn't going to see his family again. You're just being nosy, she reprimanded herself. She tried to think of something to say that might reassure him, but everything that came to mind sounded trite given their circumstances. She realized that she wasn't sure that they would get off this planet alive. Their ship was destroyed, no one knew that they were here, and the planet was in the grip of an invasion. The odds were definitely not in their favour. She bit into a strip of vegetable – Tameka was right: it tasted filthy.

Eat it and be grateful, Summerfield.

Emile had turned to listen to Tameka and Leon, his large brown eyes glistening as he followed their animated discussion. She'd obviously touched a delicate spot. Bernice didn't know whether her students had met on Dellah before the dig, but there certainly existed a strong bond of friendship between them now. Emile was watching Tameka closely, always nodding at whatever she said and laughing along with her barbed comments.

Tameka wasn't paying Emile any attention at the moment. She was waving her heavily braceleted arms in front of her and swearing at Leon, telling him that he was a dickhead. Bernice shuddered. Was the girl completely oblivious to the precarious nature of their situation? However, the tall reptile appeared to be taking her insults with his characteristic good humour.

'If you think they're wrong,' he was saying, 'if you think that they shouldn't be operating in the way that they are, why don't you do something about it?'

'Don't be an asshole all your life, Leon. Have you got scales for brains or what? You can't fight the corporations. They've got it all sewn up. You try and fight a company and pretty soon you'll wake up with a smoking blaster hole in your chest. It's the same all over. There's nothing you can do to change it.' She shrugged. 'That's just, like, how it is: shit happens, you know?'

'Shit never just happens. People cause shit to happen. It is not like that here. If you don't like the situation, you *change* it.'

This was the first time Leon had raised his voice in the discussion. His gentle warmth had been replaced with a calm passion. 'That's the first duty of every Ursulan. First and last.'

'Oh yeah? I don't see you taking on the baldies from outer space. I've met politicos like you before. It's just words.'

Leon looked a little flustered at this. 'We *are* fighting the Sunless but . . . it is hard. They are so very cruel. So quick to violence and indiscriminate with it. In the year since they arrived almost half of the population has been killed. It was a massacre. Many died opposing the Sunless's rule; more were executed.'

'Hey, I'm, like, sorry.'

He smiled at her, his gentler manner returning. 'I am sorry too. In the face of such terror, people have given up their choices. Where there is authority there is no freedom.'

Bernice remembered what Leon had said to her earlier. About telling the old woman what she thought of her, about not being a subject. She was going to ask Leon more about his society, but at that moment Scott entered the stone building and joined them at the table. He'd changed into an undamaged uniform. He patted Leon on the back and Bernice was reminded once again of the physical similarities between them.

'Have you been trying to convert our new friends to the cause?' Scott asked playfully.

Leon made his cooing noise, his forked tongue vibrating with what Bernice assumed was pleasure. He waved a claw at Tameka. 'I don't think we need to convert this one.'

'Convert me into what? Get real! I think you're all brain-dead.'

Bernice wanted to know about Errol. 'How is he? Did you manage to get him back here all right?'

Scott slipped on to the bench next to her. Bernice noticed that both Tameka and Emile turned to look at him. He nodded a hurried welcome at them and turned to face Bernice, clearly missing their symmetrical expressions of interest.

There's going to be trouble there, Bernice thought to herself before focusing on what Scott was saying.

'The Sunless were moving towards the reservoir but we dodged them. They're fast, but they're not trackers and they don't seem to be able to get used to the climate. Yvonne is with him now.'

'Is he going to be all right?'

'No, I don't think so,' he said. That straightforwardness again. 'He'll die in the next few days unless we can get him to a hospital. He's lost a great deal of blood. Yvonne suspects that some of his injuries may be internal. He's asked to see you.'

Bernice cradled her head in her hands and stared at the wooden table top. This wasn't what she wanted to hear. Her plan had been to steal a ship or at least stow away on one and get back into space. There could be no question of that with Errol severely injured. They were going to be forced to stay here until he was well enough to travel. If he was that fortunate. If they all were.

'Thanks, Scott. I'll come and see him now if that's OK. And then tomorrow perhaps you could tell me the best way to a hospital.'

'The nearest hospital is in Anarray. That's only about fifty kilometres away from here. But it will be difficult to get there. The Sunless don't allow us to travel freely. Special documents are needed to travel between zones.'

'Somehow I didn't think it was going to be easy,' Bernice said, getting up to leave.

9

SUNLESS RISING

'Emile,' a woman's voice whispered. For a tiny blissful moment he thought it was his mother. 'You have to wake up. Wake up now.'

He opened his eyes and saw that Bernice was kneeling over him. Reality intruded like the sunlight which flickered through the gaps in the shutters, streaking across the floor of the dorm.

He looked up at his tutor, feeling a familiar pang of loss. Emile noticed for the first time that her eyes were framed with lines. Somehow he'd imagined that she was too young for that. Maybe it was the way she behaved.

She stroked his hair and smiled, but Emile could tell that she was tense – her smile was a little too fixed on her face. Her expression looked brittle, as if it might suddenly crack. 'We have to leave now.'

'Trouble?'

She nodded and then turned to Tameka, who was still fast asleep next to him, drooling on the pillow like a toddler. He lifted himself up on to his elbow. The dormitory was full of sleeping figures. He could hear the sound of men and women snoring. Scott was sitting on the edge of the mattress opposite, shaking himself awake. He was wearing only a pair of brightly patterned boxer shorts. Emile could see that his scales ran all the way down his back, making a dark V shape against his pale skin. The tail of the scales disappeared beneath the elastic of his underwear.

Leon was standing over Scott, pulling on one of the wasp-stripe uniforms. The lizard man was naked and Emile could see that his scales covered his entire body. They were paler and looked softer on his bulging stomach. He didn't appear to have any nipples or genitals at all. Just completely smooth like a snake. He was beautiful in a nonsexual way. Emile found his eyes wandering back to Scott. He wondered what Scott's scales would feel like under his fingers. Leon caught him looking at Scott and cocked his head in puzzlement. Emile turned away blushing.

Tameka was awake now. She was half-heartedly rooting through her make-up bag, but Emile could tell that she was taking sneaky looks at Scott as he dressed. Scott looked across at them, nodded good morning and then smiled at Tameka. Emile felt a sinking feeling in his stomach he didn't have a name for.

He dressed in the uniform Bernice had handed to him. It was the familiar grey one-piece, but with two white stripes across the chest rather than yellow. When he was done, he joined Bernice by Errol, who was lying on a stretcher which had been laid on top of one of the mattresses near the door. He was whispering something to Bernice. Errol's bald head was covered in sweat, his black skin accentuated by the white sheets. The lines on his face looked deep and craggy. His lips were swollen. The sheets which covered him were littered with dry bloodstains. He didn't look at all well. Emile was surprised by the speed of the man's decline. He swallowed and looked away.

'We're leaving,' Bernice informed him.

'I guessed. The Sunless?'

She gestured for him to keep his voice down. 'Leon says that about thirty of them came through the village this morning. There are more of them in the fields. They've taken equipment to the reservoir. From what it sounds like I think it must be underwater gear.' She nodded towards the front of the building. 'Keep an eye on the door, would you? We'll be leaving out of the back way and then going cross country, but I don't want to be surprised by the Sunless.'

'So what do I do if I see one?'

'Whistle.'

'I can't whistle, but if you hear someone scream you'll know who it'll be.' He was about to leave when he turned back to Bernice. 'How come you're so calm about all of this?'

'What do you mean?'

'You just seem to be taking all this in your stride. Falling out of the sky and being hunted and everything. Like you're used to it or something. You're not, like, in the Dellah Auxiliaries in your spare time or something are you?'

'No.' She winked at him. 'Just practice, that's all.'

Emile stepped out on to the veranda of the dormitory and collided with someone coming in. Their heads connected sharply, and Emile stumbled backward, falling over into the doorway.

He yelped as a sharp pain filled his head. He must have hit his head harder than he thought because when he looked up all he could see was a skull framed by fire. And then he realized this was the head of the person he had collided with, leaning over him and blocking out the early-morning sun. The face came closer for a moment. Its skin was dry and looked dusty, tiny wrinkles etched around its eyes and mouth. Emile felt his heart trip a beat as he realized that he was looking up into the face of one of the Sunless.

He froze, his mouth open, unable even to take a breath. The face moved closer. He could feel its breath against his face. Its eyes were the same dark metal colour of Scott's. But the Sunless's were dark and sightless. Like a shark's. It smelt bad. The pungent smell of neglected animals.

He pursed his lips and tried to whistle, but only managed to let out a noise that sounded like a tiny puncture in a tyre. It looked him up and down slowly, taking in his uniform. He noticed that the top of its shorn head was terribly blistered and sunburnt, as if its skin had no resistance to the bright orange Ursulan sunlight. It snorted loudly, as if it were dismissing him and then it stepped over him, stalked across the veranda, down the other side, and was gone across the dusty street.

He heard a clear note and wondered for a tiny moment where it was coming from, before he realized that it was escaping from his own mouth. He stopped whistling and clambered on to his hands and knees, feeling too nauseous to stand. Only then did he realize that the creature was not on its own. There were Sunless all over the street. There must have been at least two hundred of them. Emile turned and half staggered, half fell back inside the dormitory.

'Emile, I thought I asked you to –' Bernice started and then caught sight of the expression on his face and said, 'Company?'

They left through the washrooms at the back of the dormitory and made a detour through the trees to cover their tracks before setting off in the direction of Anarray. Emile didn't see any more Sunless, but he didn't stop looking over his shoulder.

He and Tameka took turns carrying Errol with Bernice and Scott. Leon always walked ahead, making sure their path was clear and safe. The stretcher was heavy and, as they walked in the morning sun, Emile felt the back of his neck begin to warm uncomfortably. He was sweating in the rough uniform, which chafed the inside of his thighs. Flies circled his head, buzzing noisily and preventing him drifting off into his thoughts and pleasant fantasies of being back in his room on the relay station.

They trudged through fields of a rape-coloured crop which Scott said formed the staple diet of people in the area. Thin but sturdy fruit trees were planted along the side of the fields, drooping with wormy fruit. Emile watched Scott pull off a few fruits and take a bite of one before offering it to Tameka. They came to an awkward stop at the corner of a field while Tameka, whose hands were occupied holding the front end of the stretcher, ate the fruit out of his hand. She laughed as the juice splashed down her chin. Emile watched silently from the back, feeling a now familiar discomfort.

He was brought out of his private world by Bernice, who was holding another of the fruit in her hand. He took a bite. The skin was quite thick and mottled, although the sweet flavour of the flesh inside was surprising and delicious. But it failed to dull the ache in his chest and left his lips sticky and greasy.

'Enough?' Bernice asked, and he nodded, not meeting her gaze. She was too good at sensing his mood and he didn't want to have to explain himself. Particularly not this, particularly not to his lecturer. He lifted his shoulder to wipe his face on the collar of the suit, and nudged the stretcher forward, a little harder than he had really meant to.

Tameka looked over her shoulder. 'All right, all right,' she scolded, a frown cutting across her powdered face. 'What's the hurry, boyee?' She swung a thick clump of her hair out of her eyes and shook her head at him wearily, but she started to move forward all the same. Scott waved at him for a moment and Emile managed a weak smile.

He started to feel guilty for pushing Tameka. He was being really childish. In fact that was exactly how he felt – like a little kid. Left behind with his bloody mum while everyone else got on with the interesting stuff. He resolved immediately to be really cool and fine about the situation. If Tameka got it together with Scott, that was going to be all right with him. Out of the corner of his eye, he became aware of Bernice looking at him thoughtfully.

'So,' she said brightly, 'are you up for the sixty-million-dollar question?'

He almost lost his footing in reaction to this. 'Wha– What do you mean? What question?'

'Hey, take it easy, I was only going to ask why you chose archaeology as a degree.' She paused. 'Why, what did you think I was going to ask?'

He let out a breath. 'Nothing. Doesn't matter.' He hoisted the stretcher in his hands. He could feel sore patches developing on his palms. 'Do you really want to know, Professor S?'

'Well if I didn't want to know the answer . . .'

'I mean it probably doesn't matter now anyway,' he

sighed. 'I mean you can't exactly give me detention, can you?' He paused for a moment to collect his thoughts. 'Tameka was right – about my dad I mean. He never had very much time for me or my mum when she was alive. And after, well he just locked himself away. I wouldn't see him for days – weeks sometimes. I just wanted to get away from home and I was pretty sure that going to college was the only way I was going to be able to do it. Well, I didn't really know what course to do, so I just . . . well . . .'

Bernice stopped walking and slapped her hand against her forehead. 'Signed yourself up for the first course listed alphabetically in the brochure. I don't believe that someone actually did that!'

He shrugged, feeling a bit embarrassed. 'Sorry.'

The airship lifted above the small huts and drifted away from the mountainside. Below them on the ground, they could see the tiny shape of Leon, waving up at them. His plan had worked like a dream. They were posing as a group of healers returning to the hospital at Anarray from the out-lying villages with a cargo of important patients. Leon had managed to persuade a group of genuine healers to toss down their travel documents once they had boarded the dirigible. Although the collaborator had questioned Scott for what felt like an eternity about their vaccination tour of the outer reaches of the yellow region, they had all been ushered on board shortly before takeoff.

'Is this a good time to mention that I get airsick?' Emile said to Scott. There was a drop of at least two hundred metres to a horseshoe-shaped plain. The view was breathtaking: a city was visible on the plain below them and beyond that the shore of an ocean. In the distance the tiny metallic shape of a spaceship lifted away from the city and darted off through the clouds.

'It's a shame he's not coming,' Emile said, leaning on the rail and waving at Leon. 'I liked him.'

Scott rested a hand on Emile's shoulder. 'He's a man of passion.'

'Is he . . . is he your best friend or something?'

'Best friend? Leon's my brother.'

'Brother . . .' Emile's eyes came to rest on the scales which were just visible above the collar of Scott's uniform. 'Oh, half-brother, right?'

Scott looked surprised and amused. 'How could someone be only half a brother? Best? Half? Why do you try and measure people all the time? It's so crazy. People just are. A person is either your brother or not. Leon's right, you are really weird.'

'I'm not weird!' Emile exclaimed, remembering the look Leon had given him that morning in the dorm.

'All of you. You profiteers, none of what you say makes any kind of sense.'

'Oh, I see.' Emile turned back to the large glass window which made up the wall of the airship's cabin. They didn't speak for a while. The engines of the airship drummed noisily, and the rail that Emile was leaning against vibrated to the rhythm of the sound.

They were high over the orange plain now, gliding quickly over the land. The city was a sprawling patch of grey in the distance. Some of the other passengers in the cabin had joined them at the window and were pointing out towns and villages as they passed over them. Emile discreetly listened to their conversations. Simple stories about family and friends who lived in the places below them. The conversations were so ordinary that it was hard to believe that the planet was in the grip of an invasion.

The airship began to descend as it entered the airspace over the edge of the city. As it did so it was caught in the rush of powerful air currents. The cabin lurched and rolled on to its side. Suddenly the floor he was standing on became the wall. Emile felt his stomach turn over. He lost his grip on the rail and tumbled over it.

For a second all he could see was the distant ground beneath as he fell towards it, and then he hit the thick glass of the window. His face was squashed up to the glass. A wisp of cloud passed beneath him.

Beneath him!

He could see the grey tarmac of a spaceport. Battered black ships lined up like toys. All that was preventing him from falling down on top of one was the plate of glass under him. How thick was it?

There was a cracking sound and he felt something shift beneath him. In his mind's eye he saw himself fall through the ribbon of cloud and hit the hull of one of the black spaceships below. 'Help!' he squealed.

'I've got you.' Strong hands gripped his wrists and he was pulled up and over the rail. Emile allowed himself to be held in Scott's arms for a moment. The young man's long emerald hair tickled his nose. Emile had never been this close to Scott before. Never actually touched him. Emile was vaguely aware that the Ursulan smelt of cheap soap and old sweat beneath that. He had an urge to tell the boy that he needed to invest in some cologne, but didn't dare speak because he didn't trust his voice not to crack.

After a moment Emile lifted one of his hands in front of his face. It was trembling violently.

The airship was still shaking as if it were struggling in turbulence. Scott guided Emile away from the window to where the rest of the passengers were huddled in the centre of the room. The pilot's voice came over the intercom, trying to reassure the passengers.

'Nice flying,' Tameka replied. 'When's his second lesson?'

'I don't think we can blame the pilot.' Scott pointed to the window at the other side of the cabin.

'Oh my God!' Emile exclaimed. A huge black ship was rising up past the dirigible. It reminded Emile of a giant hornet. Whoever was piloting the ship obviously hadn't cared about the effect it was having on the airship, which was tiny and inconsequential next to it. The black vessel was so close that Emile could make out every detail. The surface of the ship was rough and unfinished. There was much evidence of hurried repairs and welded sheets of dark-grey metal.

The ship hovered next to them for a moment, and then

banked towards the huge orange sun, before shooting away in a blaze of white light, which left Emile's eyes watering.

After a moment, the dirigible pilot's voice came over the speaker again. He sounded terrified. 'We'll be making landfall in Anarray shortly. Weather and Sunless permitting, that is.'

10

CITY OF ANGELS

It took Bernice a little while to realize what made the city so different from any of the hundreds that she had visited before. She began to notice the differences when she tried to cross a road and looked without success for symbols or pedestrian lights. There were no instructions at all. No Give Way. No Stop. No Walk. No Don't Walk. No lines on the road. No police. No traffic officers or parking meters. But then there were no cars to park on the roads. Only ancient buses trundled through the dusty streets, their steam-powered engines hissing and spewing clouds of vapour as they carried their uniformed passengers through the bustling, twisting roads.

None of the low-rise buildings bore signs, although most were elaborately decorated. There were no shops. If there had been a town planner, which Bernice rather doubted, then they must have been easily distracted and had the attention span of a toddler. Architectural themes lasted for a few streets, sometimes only a few buildings, before bleeding into new styles. Most of the buildings were single-storey, although some bore signs of aborted attempts at more levels. This, presumably, explained why the city sprawled, was so ungainly.

The people on the streets were of the same races as Bernice had seen in the village. Birds, reptiles, mammals. All wore the same style of grey uniform, but with bands of red around the chest, instead of yellow. There were few of the Sunless creatures on the streets, but Bernice had seen several Ursulans wearing the plain charcoal-grey uniforms of the Sunless. These were the collaborators, she'd learnt. They were always in groups, and Bernice imagined that she could see fear in their faces as they walked among the people they had betrayed. The tension when the collaborators were present was palpable. The rest of the people on the streets avoided eye contact with them. Occasionally they were shouted at, but only from a distance. Scott had spat on the ground when he had seen them.

The atmosphere of the city was full of tension as if it might erupt into violence at any moment. It felt as if they were sitting on a tinderbox.

Bernice tried to imagine what life in the city must have been like before the Sunless came, before there had been collaborators, before there had been uniforms. It wasn't easy to do, and time travelling was something Bernice had a great deal of experience at. All archaeologists did. Piecing together the past with the fragments that had survived was the business of her profession. In her imagination, she saw the people of the city dressed with the same individuality with which they decorated their buildings. Clashes of bright colours instead of the drab grey and disciplined hierarchy of stripes. It would have been chaotic, but she realized that she would have liked to have visited the city then.

Scott had a brother who lived in a large dormitory near the hospital. It was one of few multistorey buildings in the city. Unlike the single-room dormitory in the village, this one was made up of smaller rooms which contained a few double and single mattresses each. Once again there were few possessions to be seen, although all of the rooms had been painted with brightly coloured murals. The murals were amateurishly executed and covered with graffiti. Bernice thought of her carefully chosen prints in her cluttered rooms back at the university. It felt like a lifetime since she had been in her study and she felt an ache of homesickness.

Since she had arrived on the planet she had lost almost all of her possessions, salvaging only a few precious items which could fit in the pouch of the spacesuit. She'd exchanged her own clothes for the stiff uniform that she had now been wearing for what felt like days. It was so much harder to keep a hold on who you were without the accessories of your identity. But that was what uniforms were for, after all: to whittle away your uniqueness and individuality. To mortify your personal self.

Bernice stood staring out over the city from the window of the room in the dormitory, her eyes lingering over the irregular shapes of the buildings.

She could hear Emile and Tameka arguing about something. Something stupid and inconsequential no doubt. Arguing while Errol lay on a mattress next to them, dying. They had carried Errol there from the airport. No one had questioned them as they carried the injured man through the streets. Errol was lost in feverish delusions, murmuring and sobbing quietly under his breath.

She could feel herself becoming increasingly angry with her students, but she knew her anger only hid her own helplessness and her fear of being stuck on this strange, forgotten world for ever. Keeping Errol alive was proving a full-time occupation. She'd barely given a thought to anything else since they had crashed on the planet. She'd hardly thought about Jason. For all she knew he wasn't even on this crazy world.

However, she couldn't shake the feeling that there was something going on here, that someone was playing a game with her. She pulled out the small crystal statue. Its blank eyes stared back at her. Jason had said that it was important, dangerous. And then he had been abducted. She'd followed him and been attacked, forced down on to the planet. The haulage ship had been a sitting target: they could have shot her out of the skies, but they hadn't. And then Scott had said that the Sunless had brought diving equipment to the reservoir. That couldn't all be coincidence or an accident, could it? But then, if that were true, then all this fuss really was about this one tiny artefact. That didn't seem at all likely. Perhaps someone was trying to get to her. Get at her?

Ahem, Bernice, you're getting just a little paranoid, my

dear, she told herself, forcing a smile. Calm down, take a deep breath, and let the universe throw its worst at you.

She made herself useful by changing Errol's dressings, noticing that his wounds were becoming increasingly inflamed. The beginnings of infection. She mopped his brow and let the water from the cloth trickle into the corners of his dry mouth. His face looked painfully swollen. The pockmarks on the side of his hairless head seemed more pronounced.

She was surprised when he licked the moisture from his thick chapped lips and opened his one good eye. 'You look terrible, Summerfield,' he said in a croaky whisper.

'Welcome back,' she replied.

She saw him try to lift his head to take in his surroundings. 'Hospital?' he asked.

She swallowed. 'Not yet, but I'm working on it.'

He looked at her closely for a moment. 'How am I doing? How are *we* doing?'

'All right.'

'That bad, huh?'

'Not good.' She wasn't going to lie to him.

'Uh, just do what you can, OK?' There was fear beneath the modest request.

She nodded and sat for a while holding one of his large hands in hers. Gently stroking the rough patches of skin on his palms.

She was feeling a little more confident, or at least more composed, when Scott appeared at the door with his brother Michael in tow. Like Scott, Michael had mixed ancestry. He was tall, broad-shouldered, almost hulking. His skin was the deepest purple. He had a full, rounded face, heavily lidded eyes, and would have looked completely Jeillo except for the soft down of white, silken feathers on his hands and shoulders. Bernice guessed that he was part Oolian, just as Scott was part Saurian. Neither fish nor fowl. The idea of their being brothers seemed absurd as they couldn't have been more unalike.

There was an air of tension between them and Michael only nodded quickly at her before looking away. Bernice wondered if there was bad feeling between them. Was Michael annoyed that Scott had brought off-worlders to his home? She couldn't really blame him.

Scott hurried over and Bernice guided him to the window – away from Errol. She wanted to know what Scott had to say before she let Errol in on the conversation. The look on Scott's face did not inspire confidence. 'Well?'

When he spoke his voice was full of suppressed anger. 'The hospital is in the hands of the collaborators. There are guards checking the identification papers of patients. I would have been questioned but for this,' he said, indicating the white stripes of his medical uniform. 'Bernice, I didn't realize that things were this bad. People no longer have access to medicines. Not unless the collaborators decide that what they're doing is essential work.' He spat out the words. 'People are just being left to die around the hospital buildings.'

Bernice cursed, using words she usually avoided. 'We can't leave it any longer. Errol isn't going –' She stopped herself, glancing over to the mattress. In a quieter voice, she said, 'We need to get Errol to a surgeon today.'

'I know, I know we do,' Scott murmured.

Bernice noticed that his mannerisms became more angular, more reptile-like, the more angry he became.

He sighed and then said, 'We could try and smuggle him into the hospital. Although I'm not sure that I know how.'

Bernice shook her head. 'I don't like the idea of trying to sneak in carrying a stretcher. We'd be bound to lose him if we had to make a run for it.' As she spoke it was becoming clear to her that the only viable option was going to involve bringing a surgeon to Errol.

Scott didn't agree. 'Paranoia is rife as it is. There were people in the village who suspected that you were in league with the Sunless. It's going to be ten times worse here. No one is going to help off-worlders when they're not even allowed to help their own people.'

'I can be very persuasive.'

Scott must have heard the threat in her voice because he

looked at her in alarm. 'What do you mean, persuasive? I won't use violence, not against another Ursulan.'

'I'm not talking about violence. Only . . . kidnapping.'

'Kidnapping?' he said, pronouncing each syllable carefully. 'I haven't heard that word before. What does it mean?'

The room next to Michael's was empty and Emile had quietly slipped inside. One of the walls was decorated with a mural of a middle-aged white man standing on a rough lunar landscape, holding his empty hands out in front of him. It wasn't a very accomplished picture. It reminded Emile of a cheap book illustration. He didn't like it.

Two mattresses lay on the floor covered in grubby white sheets. Emile closed the door behind him. The privacy and peace were as delicious as ice cream. On the relay station, Emile had spent almost all of his time alone and he wasn't used to being in company for such a long period. After his mother had died, his father would permit Emile to join him only for Sunday lunch – formal silent affairs which dragged on uncomfortably. Emile had never been particularly close to his father, a cold man who had always lacked any kind of vocabulary for his feelings. The distance between them had telescoped since the funeral. He'd never once seen his dad cry.

Emile was neatly folding his grey-and-white uniform over the back of a rickety wooden chair when Scott stormed into the room. Emile made a clumsy dive under the sheets, not wanting the beautiful young man to see him in his underpants.

'Jesus, Scott! I mean don't, like, try and respect anyone's privacy or anything!' He pulled the sheet up over his flabby chest. He needn't have bothered: Scott hadn't once glanced over in his direction.

'I don't understand you profiteers at all!' Scott exclaimed. 'I mean, what's the point in trying to save lives if all you're going to do is subjugate others?'

Emile had no idea what he was talking about. 'Have you had a row with Bernice or something?'

'I don't understand her. I thought I did. But I can't believe

115

what she is proposing to do. I've been so stupid. Just because you look like some of us and share our language, I thought that you were like us. But I was really wrong. You're more like the Sunless than an Ursulan.'

Emile stared at Scott in silence, not really sure what to say. He wanted to defend Bernice, say that Scott was wrong. But he didn't really understand what Scott was actually criticizing Bernice for. In the end he said, 'I'm not like the Sunless.'

Emile's quiet words had a profound effect on Scott. He stopped pacing and sat down on the edge of the bed and ran his fingers through his fine emerald hair. He looked away, and chewed an already heavily bitten fingernail. 'I know you're not, Emile,' he said after a moment. 'I know you're not like them.' Scott reached over and squeezed Emile's thigh through the bedclothes. 'I'm just angry, that's all. When I first met Bernice it was so clear to me that I wanted to assist you. I wanted to be the good Ursulan helping the profiteers who had fallen out of the sky. I think I wanted to prove to you that even with the threat of the Sunless hanging over us, Ursu is special. That what we have here is better than what you have with your wealth and technology.' He sighed. 'Margaret's right, I am an egoizing idiot.'

Emile stared down at Scott's hand, at the long square-tipped fingers which gripped his leg. His mind was completely frozen. He couldn't take in what Scott was saying; he couldn't think at all. He could just stare at that hand and feel the warmth of Scott's palm through the thin white sheet. Scott was still talking and Emile had to wrench his attention away from the hand in order to listen. The scale-covered boy was staring at Emile intensely, his strange metal eyes full of curiosity.

'But if you're not like the Sunless, what *are* you like, Emile? You're so quiet. Sometimes it's like you're not even here. What *do* you believe in? What matters to you?'

'Well, I . . .' Emile wasn't sure. What did he believe in? He didn't know really. He'd never thought about it.

He felt uncomfortable, as if he were being tested by Scott, scrutinized by him. He knew that he didn't want to fail the test somehow or seem stupid, but he didn't really have an answer. Politics had always seemed very boring and remote from his life. He'd always switch the news off, unless it was about a serial killer or the latest audacious crime by the Cat's Paw or something exciting like that. There were so many political factions and interests vying for control in his sector that he knew he would never be able to keep up with it all even if he tried. It seemed that every day a war broke out on some backwater planet that he'd never heard of. He used to spend his days watching holos of pop concerts he could only dream of attending. Pop concerts and old movies.

He looked up to see that Scott was still staring at him with his shiny mercury eyes. 'I'm not really sure I can say what I believe in just like that. I mean, what do you believe in?'

Scott pulled a thin chain from around his neck and handed it to Emile. A small, dull, metal ring hung from it. The ring was warm from being around the young man's neck. Etched into the band were words. Emile peered at them closely.

> *Any rule is tyranny.*
> *My one duty is to accept no rule.*

'That's it? That's what you believe in? No rules?' It didn't make any sense to Emile.

Scott nodded. 'That's it. Everyone has their own code. Almost everyone that is. Some people choose not to. The idea is that it is based on your learning from being in your Eight. But our codes change as our lives change.'

'Eight?'

'My family. Leon and Michael. Eight brothers and sisters. Representing the different species who came to Ursu to get away from the profiteers.'

'What? Don't you have mothers or fathers?'

'You can't be free if you're someone's son or someone's father. Or if you're carrying a baby inside of you. All Ursulan children are born from the Blooms. We are all born as half-grown children. We bring ourselves up together. For a reason that no one understands – not even Kitzinger, and no one knew more about the Blooms than her – there were ten children born in my Eight. Two extra humans. Our Eight became a bit of a melting pot: Michael got some of Yvonne's feathers and I got some of Leon's scales.'

'Yeah?'

'Michael's even got tiny white wings growing from his shoulders.'

'Wow! Like a purple angel?'

Scott looked puzzled. 'Angel?'

'Doesn't matter.' Emile was impressed. 'So there's no one else like you on the entire planet?'

'I'm the only "dragon boy". It's hard. People can be cruel and superstitious. Particularly since the Sunless came.'

'And your eyes, you have their eyes.'

Scott removed his hand from Emile's leg. Emile shifted uncomfortably under the sheets. He wondered if he'd said the wrong thing. 'I didn't mean to –'

'No, it's all right. I know it's because we're different and people are scared. Well, in my head, I know, but in my heart . . .'

There was a pause – Emile wanted to change the subject. He realized that he was still fingering the small metal ring between his fingers. 'And do you? Accept no rule, I mean?'

Scott got off the bed and began to tug off the uniform. 'We all did before the Sunless came. "Do what you will" – that was Michael's code.'

Emile noticed that Scott frowned a little when he spoke about Michael.

'I think he may have changed it now,' he added, after a moment. 'He seems so affected by the presence of the Sunless. So frightened. I've always lived in the country where they've really left us alone. The city is so changed. So tense. Fear everywhere.'

Emile was going to ask him what Michael had changed his code to, but was distracted by an increasingly familiar feeling of discomfort as Scott casually started to undress.

Scott seemed completely oblivious to the effect he was having on Emile, caught up with his remembrances of his brothers and sisters. 'Leon's code is, "I am able to respond to you and you to me". He's a great one for response ability is Leon.'

Emile smiled to himself. It sounded just like something the tall reptile man would say. He liked the tone of the phrase. It wasn't as bold as Michael's, which, to Emile, just sounded selfish.

'But if everyone did as they pleased, well, surely, everything would just fall apart. I mean what's to stop someone stealing or something?'

'So speaks a true profiteer!' Scott laughed with pleasure and Emile remembered how much Scott and Leon had enjoyed debating with each other on the journey to the airship. 'There's nothing to steal on Ursu, Emile. Nothing at all.' And then he said something that sounded like it might have been a quotation. 'And possessing nothing, we are free.'

'Oh come on, that's bollocks!' Emile exclaimed. He curled his fingers tightly around Scott's metal ring and chain and held them tightly in his palm. 'What if I don't give your ring back? What are you going to do then?'

'Emile, that's only a couple of bits of metal. A bit of an old washer from a harvester. The chain is from a broken sewing machine. I made it a few weeks ago. It's the words that are important and you can hardly steal those. Like everything of value, the harder you try to grasp it for your own, the quicker it will slip through your fingers.'

Emile didn't know what to say to this. He knew that Scott was wrong but he couldn't quite work out how to point this out to him. Tameka would be able to, though. There was no way she was going to accept any of this nonsense. You had to have rules.

His life had been full of them back on the relay station. The Natural Path was full of laws governing the behaviour of men and women. The mentor had instructed the class of boys in the Natural Path to manhood. The old man had read them stories about different men – the hero, the lover and the guide. Emile had learnt the lessons by rote. Lessons designed to make them all good, strong fathers and mates. But it had never meant anything to him. Emile had kept waiting for the meaning to fall into place, but at the same time he knew that it never would. He wasn't ever going to be like the men in the stories. Wasn't ever going to be like his father.

'I don't really want your chain, Scott,' he said suddenly. 'Here, take it back.'

'It's not mine, it's just bits of scrappy metal.'

'Take it! Please!'

'OK,' Scott said and did so, before sauntering over to the window. He grinned and then gently tossed the chain out into the night.

'Hey! You didn't have to do that just to make your stupid point! I would have kept it if you didn't want it.'

'It was worth it just to see your face. I've never seen anyone so worried about things,' Scott laughed. He closed the shutters over the window and then, without warning, stepped out of his boxer shorts, and threw them casually over the back of the chair where earlier Emile had neatly folded his uniform.

Emile glimpsed the curve of Scott's backside, before he forced himself to turn away, his cheeks burning hotly. Scott turned the light off and Emile felt rather than saw Scott climb into bed next to him.

Next to him!

Next to him, when there was an empty bed on the other side of the room. What did he intend? Emile panicked, caught between desire for something to happen and a blind terror that it actually might. He sat bolt upright. 'Scott, what do you think you are doing?'

'What do you mean?' Scott's voice sounded confused in the darkness. 'Going to bed.'

'What? Here?'

'Where else would I?'

'Scott!' Emile pulled the sheet up to his neck, covering himself even in the dark. 'Well in your own bed, of course! Don't you know what the word "privacy" means?'

'Umm . . . I think so.'

Privacy turned out to be yet another of those basic concepts that Scott seemed to struggle with.

'It means to disconnect from others, doesn't it?' Scott said. 'Ursulans sleep where we fall. Together. Why would I sleep over there alone and cold, when I could sleep next to you and keep warm?'

'Because . . . because . . .' Emile didn't actually have an answer for this. Not an honest one anyway. As the feelings of acute embarrassment and fear receded, he was suddenly aware of an enormous incongruence between what he was asking for and what he really wanted. A faint but urgent voice in his head was whispering that it would be the most fantastic thing for Scott to slip his arm around him and keep him warm through the night.

Words tumbled out in an effort to drown out that little voice.

'I just want to sleep on my *own*. In my *own* bed,' Emile lied, 'and if that makes me a profiteer or a bloody Sunless or something then I don't care, all right?'

Scott was silent for a moment, and then said, 'You can do whatever you want, Emile. If you really want to sleep alone – fine. Go sleep over there. I'm comfortable where I am. And anyway . . .'

'What?'

'I thought you might want to have sex with me.'

'Scott!' Emile squeaked. 'Are you crazy? I mean what gave you that idea?'

Emile felt Scott shift his weight on the mattress as he lifted himself up on to one slender elbow. 'Just something Leon said.'

'What did he say?' Emile immediately regretted the question: he wasn't sure that he wanted to hear this. He stared into the darkness, feeling desperately sick. The world was careering wildly out of control.

Scott laughed, gently. 'Just that you can't keep your hungry little eyes off me.'

'Oh yeah, sure. I mean, what does Leon know? Tameka's right: he's got scales for brains.'

121

Silence.

Emile immediately regretted saying what he had said. What had he gone and insulted Leon for? He liked Leon and he'd probably offended Scott now. The words had just tumbled out of him as if he had no control over his mouth.

'OK, OK,' Scott said, gently. 'I guess Leon must have got it wrong. And I guess that I must have too.'

Emile was shocked when Scott leant over and kissed him lightly on the forehead.

'Sleep well, Emile,' Scott whispered and then turned over. A few minutes later he had fallen asleep.

Emile lay in the darkness, wide awake, listening to the sound of Scott's regular breathing. The panic he felt subsided and he felt relieved that he was no longer exposed by Scott's dangerous words. But beneath that feeling of relief was something else.

He spent the night lying motionless, his head dizzy with questions and accusations. It was a relief when dawn came and finally he drifted off to sleep.

11

SHE WHO FIGHTS WITH MONSTERS . . .

Jock stood by one of the large windows of the hospital, staring across at the figures huddled around the small campfires in the grounds. There was no wind that morning. The thin plumes of smoke from the dying fires trailed vertically into the sky like threads of cotton. The area around the hospital was becoming more like a refugee camp or a war zone with each passing day. Despite the hospital being off limits to the general population, people still made their way here when they were sick, or brought their injured friends or siblings.

When the Sunless had come, hospitals were among their first targets. And when the new collaborating administration had taken over, a group of healers had immediately begun to resist. Small but important gains had been made. Antibiotics were being smuggled out and dispersed to those who did not qualify for treatment. A network of children were distributing and administering vaccines to their younger friends.

Several healers in the hospital resistance had been caught and all of them without exception had been killed. The Sunless would enter the hospital and without a word of warning set upon the person and beat them to death in front of whoever happened to be there.

They had just beaten people to death with their bare hands.

Twice Jock had seen it happen. And when the Sunless were finished they would remain for a whole minute staring at the witnesses with their dead eyes as if daring them to respond, before stalking out of the hospital, with their smooth matching strides. They walked as if the world was theirs. And it was.

Twice Jock had been witness to the violence and twice he had not dared intervene. He had just stood by and let it happen. Angela, a woman he had worked with for twenty-five years, had screamed at him in terror. He could see her now, kneeling on the floor as the Sunless stood around her pummelling her with their fists. She had been screaming for his help. He remembered her spectacles cracked and lopsided on her bloody face. He had allowed people he knew to die, let his friends die even as they had cried out his name.

Despite all his efforts in the resistance, Jock still felt that he had become a bystander. His fear of the Sunless had made him somehow only half a person. Something in him had died, something he didn't even know he had until it had been extinguished. Something important. Even if some miracle led to the Sunless disappearing from the face of the planet, he didn't think Ursu would ever be the same again. He knew that he wouldn't be the same.

He was joined at the window by a young Saurian healer who had just spent a sleepless night sneaking out through the kitchens to tend to the injured outside. She was enthusiastic and brave, and if Jock had been ten years younger he might have flirted with her. Well, maybe twenty years younger.

The young healer told him in a breathless whisper that she had managed to splint a broken leg and tend to two infected wounds during her secret patrol of the campfires. He saw the idealism in her large diamond-shaped eyes and felt curiously moved by it. He could almost believe that the principles of Ursulan society were still intact beneath the oppression of the invaders.

A frozen seed biding its time beneath a hard winter's snow.

A little cheered by her valour, Jock decided to take a tour

of the injured inside the hospital. As he moved through the still, quiet wards he heard footsteps behind him. For a moment he thought that it was the Saurian female returning, but when he turned he saw that it was a human woman. She was in her teens, with long dark hair tied back in a pony tail. Although she could have been no more than eighteen, she walked with the calm authority of someone much older. Her uniform bore a single white stripe, which was strange because he hadn't heard that there were new people with medical skills being brought in.

'Hey, are you, like, a surgeon?' she asked. Her accent and phrasing were strange. It was rare to hear himself described *as* something. He was Jock, and he conducted surgery. But he nodded despite himself. 'Yes, I suppose that is what I am now, for I have done little else since they came.'

'Cool.'

He didn't understand what she meant by this, but she hurried forward, seeming pleased. As she stepped into the faint morning sunlight which leaked in through the window, he was intrigued to notice that she was wearing pale make-up. He hadn't seen a man or woman wear make-up since the theatres had been closed. It somehow didn't belong to this new world at all.

'Could you do me a favour and come with me? It's really important.'

He allowed himself to be led along the corridor by the hand. 'I haven't seen you around the hospital, have I?'

She grinned, disarmingly. 'I am so new, I'm still shrink-wrapped. Hey, you don't have a cigarette, do you?'

He shook his head, struggling to follow her unfamiliar words. Was she a collaborator? She wasn't wearing a plain grey uniform. But if she was, it would be dangerous to refuse her anything. Yet Jock was still an Ursulan – he wasn't going to just passively follow her instructions. 'Where are you taking me?'

'To see a patient. Special case. Very serious. Like life or death, you know what I'm saying?'

He nodded. 'That I *do* understand.'

She led him to a small room in intensive care, which had been empty the previous day. One of the beds in the room was occupied. Two figures stood next to the bed; both wore white stripes, although again he had never seen either of them before. One was an attractive woman with dark hair and a serious, intelligent face. The other was a young man with grey eyes and green hair. The woman and the young man exchanged glances as Jock walked over to the bed. There was an atmosphere of tension and anticipation between them.

He turned to the girl who had brought him here, but she only nodded towards the bed. The occupant of the bed was a boy of no more than sixteen. His face still bore the puppy fat of youth. His eyes were closed, although Jock thought it was unlikely that he was sleeping, because his breathing was exaggerated and rapid. His short hair had been dyed white, although the roots were showing. The edge of one ear was stapled with tiny rings.

Everything about this was wrong. Jock's unease began to spiral into panic. What was going on here? Who were these strangely dressed people? He rested a hand on the boy's forehead. No temperature. He could see that the boy's eyes were moving beneath their closed lids. He was alert and awake.

Jock looked at the woman standing opposite him. He decided that the less he said the better. 'Well?'

The older woman had a sad expression on her face, as if she were troubled about something. 'Perhaps you have already guessed that he's not your patient.'

The boy opened his eyes and stared up at him. Jock was rather surprised when the boy smiled at him. It was an open smile, not malicious, as if the boy had been enjoying playing a harmless game with him.

'Then what do you want of me?'

'A friend of mine, of ours, is hurt. I need you to come with us and treat him.'

Jock took a step back from the bedside, narrowing his eyes. Was this some complicated test designed by the collaborating administration to trap him? It struck him as a

126

rather clumsy way of attempting to trick him into revealing his sympathies. However, the idea that he was now suspected of resisting terrified him. Would the Sunless be coming for him next? Would he be the next person screaming in vain for help to the mute witnesses that had once been his friends?

He decided to brazen it out. 'If your friend is hurt, bring him to the hospital where his need for medical assistance can be assessed. If he is worth treating, he will be.'

The green-haired boy moved towards him angrily. 'How can you measure people's value?' he began, clearly ready to argue. The woman pulled him back and he fell silent, biting on his anger.

'Look, we don't have time for this. A man is dying. Take it from me, he won't qualify for treatment here. Will you please help us?'

The strange thing was he almost believed her. 'Look out of that window and you will see a hundred people who need access to the facilities here. In case you haven't noticed, we are no longer a free people. People do not live for long in cages. It is you who are measuring people. Valuing your friend over the lives of those others and over my life. By coming here you endanger us all. Please leave.'

'Is that your last word?'

Last word. What a strange idea. Where were these people from? He frowned. 'I do not wish to continue speaking with you.'

'Then I'm sorry,' the woman said. 'Tameka?' she added, gesturing to someone – the pretty girl? – behind him.

He whirled around just in time to glimpse the young woman who had led him to the room push him forcefully towards the bed. She kicked his legs out from under him and he fell forward, his face buried in the sheets. He felt her grip hold of his hands and then felt rough cord against his wrists.

They were trying to bind his hands together! Bind him like an animal.

He began to struggle, scraping his shoes down the front of her shins. He heard the girl curse, and then pain lit up the back of his head as she struck him. Someone, he didn't know who, yelled at her. He managed to wriggle one arm free and lashed out with it. The girl with the painted face cried out. He felt several other people hold him down and his legs and arms were tied. She swore angrily and then someone hit him again and he didn't remember anything else after that.

Bernice sat in the passenger seat of the ambulance as Tameka concentrated furiously on driving the unwieldy, steam-powered vehicle through the busy streets. Her long dark hair was tousled from the fight and she was chewing slowly on her bottom lip. Bernice had screamed at the girl for hitting the surgeon.

The silence sat between them like an accusation.

The cab of the ambulance was open to the back. She could see Emile and Scott sitting next to each other in silence. Emile was peering out of the back window absently watching the city go by. Scott was staring straight ahead. She couldn't read the expression on his face.

They had bound the old man on to a trolley in the end. The surgeon was glaring defiantly at Scott. Suddenly Bernice understood why Scott's face was so fixed. He was studiously avoiding catching their prisoner's eye.

Tameka cursed and slowed the ambulance to a crawl. The street ahead ended in a junction with a main road. Uniformed crowds were lining this street, completely blocking the road they were travelling on.

'Stay here,' Bernice ordered Tameka and hurried out of the vehicle. Away from the engine noise Bernice quickly realized that the crowds were entirely silent. The presence of so many people standing together without speaking was powerful. They were all looking in the opposite direction, towards the main street. She stepped between them, slipping through the loosely packed crowd, until she could see what they were all staring at.

A convoy of military vehicles was winding its way through the streets. The vehicles were low and matt-black. Chunky blocks of armoured metal. Figures stood motionless on the flat roofs, staring straight ahead. Bernice didn't have any trouble recognizing the now familiar sight of the Sunless. The road curved away in both directions, so she couldn't see either end of the convoy, but she lost count after fifty vehicles. All she could hear was the breathing of the crowd and the low growl from the vehicles' engines. It was a harsher, more aggressive sound than the spluttering hiss of the steam-power ambulance. She imagined the line of vehicles twisting through the city like a snake in short grass. The threat was so tangible she could almost taste it in the air.

A middle-aged woman standing next to her in a single red-striped uniform began silently to cry. In other circumstances Bernice would have gone over to her, comforted her, perhaps made a friend, but the fight at the hospital and the argument with Tameka had left her feeling unsettled and disconnected.

The final few vehicles carried Ursulan members of the collaborating administration. And it was only then that Bernice realized that this wasn't only a convoy but a parade. She noticed that there were no Saurians or Oolians or Jeillos among the humans who had sided with the invaders. She wondered whether that was their choice, or whether the Sunless allowed only humans to work for them. The collaborators, who wore the plain uniforms of the Sunless, looked healthy and well. As ever, those who had climbed on to the top of the heap were doing all right for themselves.

The mood of the crowd changed as the people on the streets recognized the collaborators. A few people began to jeer and spit on the roadside. They were quickly joined by others. The people on the floats suddenly looked scared, huddling together in the middle of the armoured vehicles.

A male collaborator was struck by a half-brick, and he was knocked from the vehicle and fell into the road. The crowd sensed their moment and surged towards him.

Bernice was jostled by people as they tried to get to the part of the road where he had fallen. Bernice turned and tried to push her way back against the tide of tired, bitter and angry faces. She slipped and fell, and for a moment all she could see around her were uniformed grey legs and dusty boots stumbling towards her. Someone stood on her hand and she yelped.

She had suddenly fallen into the middle of a nightmare.

Get up, get out of here, Benny. Get away. She didn't want to be on the street if a full-blown riot started. She forced herself up on to her feet. As she was struggling through the crowds she caught sight of a familiar face.

A red-haired woman in a collaborator's uniform was staring down at her from the roof of one of the vehicles. It took a moment for Bernice to remember where she had seen the woman before. It was a shock to recognize a face on a planet full of strangers, and when she did remember she felt a little queasy.

It was the woman who had been on Jason's arm in the holo the Trans-System detective had pushed under her nose back on Apollox 4. How had the detective described her? His accomplice? But how had this woman come to be here, on a prohibited world? A collaborator?

Bernice desperately wanted to speak to the woman. Maybe she knew where Jason was. If anyone on this planet knew it was going to be her. But there were more than a hundred people between them. Even as Bernice started to make her first steps towards the woman, she saw the smooth coordinated movement of Sunless heading towards the disturbance. She saw the young woman climb down through a circular hatch into the belly of the vehicle and then she was gone.

There could be no doubt that it was her. Benny knew that she had to find her. Find her, find Jason. And then get everyone back home.

The crowd around her started to back away as the Sunless arrived. Anger turned to panic and fear. Feeling frustrated, Bernice turned and fled the scene.

The man was dying. Jock didn't need to have spent a lifetime healing the sick to tell that. The skin on the man's face had been terribly burnt by some kind of hot liquid plastic, which now hardened into a half mask. It would be difficult to remove. The eye beneath had probably been destroyed by the heat. The wounds on his legs were deep and infected. He'd lost a lot of blood. Several of his ribs were broken. It was likely that one of his lungs was grazed, possibly punctured.

Jock had explained all of this quietly to his captor, the woman who had introduced herself as Bernice Summerfield. She had pointed over at two boxes of medical equipment they must have brought with them from the hospital. 'Please,' was all that she had said.

Her use of the word was obscene. The captor imploring the captive. A year ago he wouldn't have even understood what being captive meant, but since the Sunless had come, it had become a way of life.

He had wondered whether he might be able to surprise her, overpower her quickly and be gone before her accomplices in the other room realized anything was wrong. But he was an old man and she was young and looked strong. He wasn't going to be able to assert himself physically.

'I . . .' He coughed for a moment, his throat still dry after being gagged. She offered him some water, which he refused. 'I will do nothing for you while you treat me like an animal.'

'All you have to do is treat him, then I promise that you will be free to leave.'

'Do not think to tell me when I will be free!' He saw her recoil from his anger and felt some small satisfaction. He pursued this advantage. 'Who are you? You don't look like members of the collaborating administration.'

'No, we're not collaborators. We're travellers.'

And then he knew. Their mannerisms, their words, their funny hair and jewellery. 'You're from the companies, aren't you?' He gestured to the ceiling. 'From the stars.'

The woman nodded. 'We're not company people. But we are from another world.'

He sensed her embarrassment and seized upon it. 'Of course you're company people. Look at your behaviour.'

'I'm an academic. I work for a university. We came here by accident searching for my ex-husband.' She must have seen his incomprehension because she quickly added, 'My partner, the person I made a commitment to.' She paused for a moment. 'The man I love.'

He struggled to understand her. Despite his fear, he was intrigued by her. All of his life he had heard stories of the profiteers but never had he thought that one would be standing in front of him. She shared his language but her words were so bizarre and their meaning absurd. She said she wasn't a profiteer, but she called her lover her *partner*? Did they run every aspect of their lives with contracts and promises? And how could you love only one person? How could one person provide you with all the love you needed?

The woman gestured to the man in the bed. 'This man is called Errol. He is a freighter pilot. I hired him to bring me to your world to help me find my husband. He's innocent, not involved in any of this. I can understand you being angry with me but please don't vent your anger at him. He didn't sign up for this.'

'I think I understand the situation. You paid him to bring you here and here you both are. Now you feel guilty because the task will cost him his life. Can you afford to pay him for such a sacrifice, I wonder?'

She just stared at him. And for a moment she looked so vulnerable that he almost felt sorry for her. Almost. The harsh light of the single bulb in the dormitory picked out the tiny lines around her eyes. He could see now that she was older than he had first thought. At least ten years older than the girl who had beaten and bound him. Perhaps fifteen years older. This woman looked a little weathered, as if she had had to struggle in her life.

'I'm not proud of what I'm doing. And I searched desperately for another way. I'm not going to lie to you. I do feel responsible for bringing Errol here. For bringing all of them here. But I will do what I have to do to keep him alive.'

Do what I have to do. Jock wasn't surprised that the profiteers had to resort to speaking nonsense in order to justify their acts. If the words did not make sense, the meaning behind them was clear. 'That is a threat, isn't it?'

'Maybe.'

'Maybe.' He wanted to laugh, but all he could manage was a grim smile. 'You're worse than the Sunless. At least they aren't hypocrites. At least they are willing to accept who they are.'

'Please!'

He shook his head, a weight lifting from his shoulders. He felt free for the first time in the year since the spaceships had come and brought terror and chains to his world. 'You're going to have to kill me, Bernice Summerfield,' he said. 'Nothing else is within your power.'

Tameka put her ear to the door. 'Bernice is shouting at him now.'

'You should stop eavesdropping,' Emile called over from where he lay on the bed. They'd been stuck in the dormitory room for what felt like hours. Scott had gone off somewhere in a black mood, so Emile had been left alone with Tameka, who had stalked around the small room like a jaguar in a cage. Full of bottled-up energy and anger after Bernice had screamed at her.

'Well, *sorreee*,' Tameka drawled, sarcastically. 'Hey! You can't tell me what to do – I can do what I like. No rules, right? No laws to break. What is the matter with that old man anyway? Why doesn't he just get on with it? Doesn't he like being a doctor or something?'

'He probably didn't like being hit,' Emile snapped, realizing only as the words came out that he was saying too much.

'You little shit!' Suddenly Tameka was on top of him, slapping him around the head. 'Just shut your stupid fat face, all right?' The blows stung him more than they hurt. The words wounded him more. He protected his face with his hands, only catching glimpses of Tameka's face, which was full of fury.

'I got him here, didn't I?' she kept yelling at him.

They rolled off the bed and on to the floor, wrestling desperately. She was much stronger than he was and he had to continually wriggle across the floor to stop her from pinning him down. He snagged one of his earrings in her

133

long hair and yelped when she jerked her head back and it was torn from his ear.

She pushed him against the floor and his head slammed against the bare concrete. Her face was centimetres away from his own. He could feel her hot breath on his face.

'Queer!' She swore and let him go.

'Leave off! Leave off me!' he yelled, and scrambled away from her. When he'd put a few feet between them, he touched his ear and his fingers came away with little traces of blood on them. 'Look what you've done! You could have ripped my ear off!'

They sat in silence for a few moments, Tameka with her head in her hands. Scott and Michael chose that moment to return, each carrying a parcel of food. They stared at the mess. There was bed linen everywhere and the mattress was crumpled where it had been pushed up against the wall. It must have been obvious that there had been a fight.

The two Ursulans stood silently in the doorway. Scott looked between Emile and Tameka, bemused. Michael's face was set into a disapproving frown.

Tameka was still curled up, staring into her lap. Her black hair was wild around her head. She hadn't seen Michael or Scott arrive. 'I'm sorry, Emile,' she said, very quietly.

The room was incredibly still for a moment. Like it was a holo and not real at all. Emile just stared at the wall. He began to smell roasted vegetables coming from the parcels the young men carried.

'I didn't mean . . .' she started. 'I don't believe all that old Jeillo shit. I'm sorry I called you queer.'

Emile caught Scott's eye and then looked away. 'Nice one, Tameka,' he whispered.

She looked up. Two jagged black tears of mascara had run down her cheeks. On seeing that they had company she wiped her runny nose. She grinned sheepishly at him. 'Oops.'

Without knowing why, Emile started to giggle.

'I am just an old man, unarmed, alone. And very afraid. But I won't be your slave, so you will have to take my life, Bernice

Summerfield. As you can see,' he added, stretching out his rough hands, 'it's all I have.'

The surgeon was red-faced, framed by a shock of white hair and watery, light-blue eyes. He stood with a slight hunch, probably from a lifetime of leaning over hospital beds. Bernice swallowed and turned away, his words ringing in her head.

They were too familiar. She had a growing suspicion that she had somehow slipped on to the wrong side of the argument. It was usually her standing in front of the captors, laughing at them or pitying them.

She liked to think of herself as the one with the flowers and champagne.

She walked slowly over to the window, half hoping that the old man would try to escape. She didn't even know his name. It was getting late. Dark clouds had covered the setting sun like a fire blanket. The air was thick and warm. There was going to be a storm.

She didn't need anyone else to tell her that kidnapping was wrong. But then the only law of this planet – that off-worlders were to be killed – was hardly the most just rule she'd ever encountered. She told herself that she had just been practical, that there hadn't been time to consider ethics, but she wasn't reassured. She wished that she hadn't brought the surgeon here in the first place. And immediately told herself that the alternative would have been to let Errol die. And she wasn't exactly happy with that either.

But she was stuck with her decision now. If she let him go, he could come back with his friends, or with collaborators, or even the Sunless. Her head filled up with regrets. It was too late to go back.

It's never too late to be what you might have been.

The old quotation had popped unbidden into her head. The author was an old Earth novelist, from an earlier period than Benny's twentieth-century specialism. The woman's name eluded Benny for the moment. It was something Jason had said to her when she had moaned on about never having completed her doctorate. About not being a real professor. He'd whispered it to her in bed on their honeymoon. He'd been so obliging, agreeing to exchange their luxurious hotel room for a tent on the forgotten planet Youkali where she had begun her field work again. She remembered how proud he'd looked when he'd attended her graduation ceremony.

She had been so sure then that the marriage would last. So sure that they would grow old together. Now she wasn't sure about anything.

The door to the room wasn't locked – there were no locked doors on Ursu – but she opened it anyway, before turning to the old man. 'If you tell anyone where we are then we will very probably be killed.'

He just stared at her as if he hadn't actually understood her words. Bernice found it difficult to meet his gaze. 'Please. I won't try to stop you. Just go.'

She began to tend to Errol, wiping the sweat from his face with a cool cloth and lighting the tiny steam ring to boil some water to treat his wounds. Errol had been unconscious for hours. Bernice suspected that he wasn't going to wake up again. He was very near death.

She heard the door close behind her. She closed her eyes and felt more alone than she had in years.

She almost jumped out of her skin when a wrinkled hand gently touched her shoulder. 'I think we can do a little better than boiled water and tender loving care, Bernice,' the surgeon said, ushering her out of the chair.

Bernice was dazed. Then she saw that Scott was standing in the corner of the room. The sound of the door had been his entering, not the surgeon's leaving. 'I don't understand,' she started. 'I thought you were . . .'

The surgeon had his back to her. He was already peeling back the bandages on Errol's leg, and indicating to Scott to bring over one of the boxes of equipment. Without looking at her, he said, 'I have no intention of leaving.'

Bernice was flabbergasted. A cautionary part of her was telling her to shut up, not to do anything that might change his mind, but she was too intrigued to pay it any attention.

136

'But . . . I thought that . . . Oh Christ,' she swore as the realization hit her. 'You mean you put me through all of this to make a point?'

He turned at this remark, glaring at her over the hygiene mask he had just fixed over his mouth. 'I didn't put you through anything!' he barked. 'My freedom is all I have, all that I own. You can't separate me from it. It *is* me. Now either help, shut up or leave. It's your choice. Be grateful that *you* have one.'

There was a long pause.

'I'd like to help.'

For a moment, Benny thought she saw the flicker of a smile stretch the elastic of his mask. 'Then come over here and do what you are told.'

Scott hummed to himself as he stood over the sink, washing the blood from his hands and arms. He had enjoyed helping the healer, of course. He had always been interested in medicine despite never having learnt more than basic life-saving skills. But most of all he had been relieved that Bernice had changed her mind. The day had been a tremendous struggle for him. Twice he had almost intervened and defended the healer against Bernice. He knew that if Bernice had attempted to kill the old man he would have physically fought her off.

But she *had* changed her mind. She had been faced with true choice and she had chosen well. He had always believed that people chose well if they were free. It felt that, despite the invaders having brought his world to its knees, the principles of Ursulan life were still alive, growing like weeds beneath concrete. In the face of true choice, even these profiteers with their pettiness and love of property couldn't help but shine.

His two new friends were lying asleep on the double mattress in the smaller dormitory room. Tameka had her arm draped protectively over Emile. Both were fully clothed and the remains of their meal still lay on the floor by the bed.

They were probably used to servants or slaves cleaning up

after them. He imagined them living in huge palaces surrounded by piles of clothes and presents. Or perhaps they had been the slaves, days filled with mindless drudgery just to have enough food to eat and a place to sleep.

He wondered what they had been fighting about earlier. Property, probably – the boy certainly liked things. Emile was like a magpie – one eye always on what glittered. Scott found himself wondering what it would be like to have sex with someone who wanted to own you, to make you theirs. It sounded both exciting and unsettling. Almost perverse.

Lightning flickered outside and was quickly followed by a roll of thunder. The storm was near and getting closer.

The young woman, Tameka, lifted her head off the pillow. 'Oh, it's you. Hello, dragon boy. What time is it?'

'It's late.'

'How is it next door? Are they still going at it?'

'It's over. Your friend is going to live.'

'Hoo boy, did the old man come to his senses or did Benny have to kick his ass up and down the stairs?'

Scott, for once, wasn't in the mood for a debate.

They stepped out on to the small balcony beyond the window, closing the shutters behind them so they could watch the storm alone. Neither of them wanted to wake Emile, who was snoring quietly and drooling on to his pillow. There was no rail on the balcony and they sat with their legs dangling over the edge. The sky was a deep orange colour and the lightning which flickered across it was a brilliant yellow. There was no sign of rain.

He watched her closely, as if he might physically see the differences in their lives if he looked long enough. He couldn't see them. Just a beautiful girl watching a storm, her eyes widening with wonder as the clouds flickered with electric light. Her dark make-up was smudged from the pillow. He licked his finger and wiped it away from her eyes.

She raised an eyebrow but didn't object. 'You're confident.'

He didn't understand the meaning behind her words but the smile was universal.

'I'd like to have sex with you. Are you interested?' he asked.

'Last of the romantics, I see.' She reached out and pulled him towards her. Her lips tasted of make-up and he stopped kissing and asked her to wipe it off.

She sighed and wiped her mouth on her sleeve. 'You sure know how to spoil a moment, don't you, dragon boy?'

They had sex on the balcony while the lightning flickered over the irregular outline of the city. The sex was as strange as he thought it was going to be, but not in the way he had imagined. She didn't try to control him or force him to do what she wanted. She didn't actually ask him to do anything for her, but instead seemed to expect him to guess what she might enjoy, rewarding him with whispered sighs when he guessed correctly. It was enjoyable, but it also felt like a game that had fixed rules or a ritual of some kind. He was beginning to tire of it, when she pushed him over on to his back and climbed on top of him. They began to move rhythmically, gently at first. He looked up at her face, which was almost completely silhouetted against the orange sky. Her head was a grey shadow. He could just see that her eyes were closed and she was breathing quickly.

Afterwards, they lay on the cold concrete of the balcony, as the night retreated, showing the very first sign of a lemon dawn. Tameka rested her head on his chest. She ran her hand down his side, tracing the line where his scales merged into his pale human skin.

'Your skin is so strange, so beautiful,' she whispered.

He shrugged, a bit annoyed. 'They're just my scales. They're not strange.'

He felt uncomfortable with her gaze on him. He slipped out of the embrace and retrieved a sheet from the room and wrapped it around them.

She fell asleep before he did.

Emile woke up feeling uncomfortable. His body was twisted up inside his creased uniform and he was busting for a pee. He felt the disorientation of waking in a strange place and didn't notice at first that he was alone in the room. He didn't want to wake Errol or Bernice next door so he decided to go out on to the balcony to relieve himself.

He stood for a full minute, staring at Scott and Tameka asleep in each other's arms. Then he closed the shutter quietly and crept back to bed, where he lay awake until morning. The sun was already bright when he heard Scott and Tameka stir. Scott cried out, shouting words Emile still couldn't make out. The young man seemed to be troubled by nightmares most nights. Then Emile heard Tameka's voice soothing him.

He heard them move to open the shutters. Without knowing why, Emile turned over and pretended to be asleep. They opened the shutters and came in, flooding the room with light. He heard them whisper something to each other and then Tameka climbed into bed next to him and Scott left the room.

He lay silently next to her, his heart pounding in his head, his bladder aching painfully, and feeling lots of things he didn't have names for.

CONVERSATIONS WITH THE ENEMY

They squeezed through the cracks in the side of the crystal structure and half slid, half stumbled down on to the rocky ground. Kitzinger's eyes watered behind her goggles. She had lived the last year under artificial light and the few chinks of thin sunlight which leaked into the crystal structure. It was the first time she had seen the sun.

It was a huge pale-pink disc eating up the sky. Clouds of black dust covered its bloated surface. It was so large that she felt dizzy staring up at it; a childlike part of her feared that it might roll into the planet or swallow it whole.

It was a red giant, a dying sun. And as it died, the planet around her was also dying, the aged sun incapable of providing the planet with the heat it needed to thrive. The bloated sun was still capable of soaking the landscape in deep crimson light, making the glaciers appear as if they were frozen blood. The world was beautiful, but sinister – dangerous. It was like standing on the very edge of chaos.

She'd never seen anything so barren, so lifeless. The surface was a desert of ice and rocky stone. A blizzard of ice tore across the expanse, raking up stones and small rocks. The tiny hailstones rattled noisily against the glass of her goggles.

Aric hadn't stopped to admire the scenery. He had blindly stumbled into the blizzard, shielding his masked face with his hands. Kitzinger set off after him, pushing hard against the wind which threatened to knock her off her feet. Even as she ran she knew it was hopeless. There wasn't anywhere for them to 'escape' to. Just kilometres of scarlet tundra stretching out before them. Once their captors realized they were gone they would find them easily.

The thought made her shudder. Nikolas would kill them for sure. She felt a cold sweat prickle beneath her suit. Why hadn't she just done what she was told? Been a good, obedient slave? Swearing continually into her respirator, she forced her way through the icy wind after Aric.

The blizzards became heavier and she lost both Aric and her sense of direction. A rocky ridge appeared through the clouds of sharp ice, which tore at her body. She made her way towards it, clambering up its loose surface on her hands and knees, hoping to spy Aric from the top.

She couldn't see him, just the harsh surface of the planet and the outline of the crystal structure from which she had fled. Despite having lived inside it for almost a year she had never seen it from the outside. From this distance it looked like a city of thin geometric towers. Each side of the long crystal spires reflected a different shade of the scarlet light. They soared above the landscape as if they were reaching up to the weak sun. The ice structure looked organic as if, rather than having been built, it had somehow sprouted from the ice-packed ground like a lesion.

What had she been living in for the last year? What kind of society could have produced such a thing? Certainly not the Sunless, that was for sure. Then who?

A dull roaring began to compete with the sound of the wind. Kitzinger screamed and almost lost her footing as a huge, dark shape cut through the storm clouds above her, like the shadow of a shark moving below the surface of a grey sea.

Some kind of ship, she thought, her ears deafened by the noise of its engines as it raced on through the sky. Searchlights swept over the ridge. For a tiny moment she was caught in one of the beams and she cringed beneath its blinding intensity. And then it moved on, lighting up the icy plain in front of her.

Moments later the searchlight picked out a tiny running figure on the blood-coloured ice below her. It was Aric. He was like a stick figure against the dark ice. She saw him desperately try to evade the beam, but it was hopeless. The ship, a functional black object with curled legs, buzzed around him like a hornet before settling down on the ice beside him.

Moments later she heard Nikolas's amplified voice. 'I know you can hear me, Kitzinger. There's nowhere to go. Nowhere at all.'

All hope of escape died with his voice. She guessed that he was on the ship. Kitzinger stood on the ridge, unsure of what to do. If she stayed out here, she would die when her respirator failed. If she went back, Nikolas would kill her. He'd enjoy it, too.

She sat down on the slope of rock and hugged her thick legs defiantly. She wasn't going to give him the pleasure. She'd sit here until the blizzards and the cold did their work. Let them find her sitting frozen to death on her backside!

She could see other figures in the searchlight now. Nikolas's voice came again. 'Don't be stupid, Kitzinger,' he called. She could tell that he was really angry. Her feet were beginning to go numb in her thick boots. 'I'll give you five minutes to find your way here or we'll kill your young friend. Your choice.'

She couldn't believe what she was hearing. What kind of warped logic was that? How could she be responsible for what Nikolas was going to do to Aric? What kind of Ursulan was he? How had he become so changed? Whatever had happened to him, she was still an Ursulan, responsible to all of her people, but not for them.

She remembered her code. *I am responsible for myself and responsible to others.*

And then she heard Aric's screams amplified a hundred times, echoing through the snow. His pain merging with the howl of the wind until she couldn't tell where his screams ended and the storm began. Before she had consciously come to a decision she had staggered down the loose slope and was running towards the motionless searchlight.

The light was fixed on to the side of the insect-like black craft and directed downward. Aric was kneeling on the hard ground in the middle of the beam, one of the Sunless standing behind him. They looked like they were standing on a stage.

The Sunless didn't seem to need respirators to breathe the rarefied atmosphere. It occurred to Kitzinger that they were almost certainly natives of this world. As cold and as unwelcoming as their home.

Reluctantly she turned her gaze towards Aric. He was bent over, clutching his jaw. Blood, black in the harsh light, leaked out from between his fingers. Kitzinger winced. She wasn't sure what they had done to him. Broken his jaw? Torn out a tooth? His eyes were wide open and desperate – imploring her.

Nikolas appeared from inside the vehicle, casually walking down the ramp as if he were making an entrance at a party. He was wearing a respirator mask, which covered his entire face, but she knew it was him by the affected nonchalance of his walk. She was grateful that he at least had to wear a respirator out in the open. She would be spared having to listen to his arrogant young voice before he had her killed.

She stood her ground – there wasn't any point in deferring to him now.

He made a show of nodding a greeting at her and then made a quick gesture to the motionless uniformed figure standing over Aric. Suddenly Kitzinger knew exactly what was going to happen next.

The ashen-faced humanoid slipped one of its hands around Aric's neck and then leant backwards violently jerking its arm. Aric twisted and fell on to his back and was still, one leg caught under his body.

Kitzinger made a wordless cry under her mask and then turned to flee, but grey figures were already running out of the blizzard towards her.

12

VERY WISE WITH MY HIPS

Extract from the diary of Bernice Summerfield

Errol is getting stronger by the hour. The last couple of days he's been sitting up in bed watching us rehearse, looking restless and impatient. He keeps talking about suing the university (and me!) for the loss of his ship. I told him that if we get out of this alive I'll be his star witness. He's looking more like a human being and less like someone could fax him to his grave. This has to be a good sign.

And I feel more like a human being. I feel like me again. Another good sign, I think. I hope. I can't excuse what I did, but I can try to understand it. Maybe the more our lives become about just surviving, the harsher we become. Until suddenly I'm standing there in a jackboot uniform holding someone's life in my hands. I always thought a chasm separated me from being a soldier. And then I look around and realize that I've become one of the monsters. I'm the one in the figure-hugging patent-leather catsuit. I think, for the moment at least, we can put that particular costume back on the rail.

Which is very wise with my hips.

The kids are in strange moods. The usual banter between Emile and Tameka is conspicuous by its absence, the upside of which is that our communal life in the dorm is quieter. Tameka is being curiously polite to the boy, which is very suspect in itself. Yesterday she even gave him a haircut, cutting the blond out of his hair. She's no longer wearing her Gothic make-up – she looks more Mexican – and they are both starting to look like Ursulans. More natural, somehow, which seems strange, because the society is artificial, so deliberately designed and manufactured. Tameka is also spending more time with Scott, who, it has to be said, seems a little uneasy with the attention.

Idealistic boy meets cynical girl: damage estimated at ten thousand shillings.

In rehearsals, Emile is enthusiastic and full of energy. He's practically choreographed the whole show. Mind you, he's had plenty of practice. Well, what else is there for a young boy to do on an artificial satellite but lip-synch in the mirror to disco anthems with a hairbrush for a microphone? Outside rehearsals Emile is quiet and withdrawn. I'm intrigued by what is going on, but I also feel a bit like a mum who is prying into affairs which don't really concern her. An over-protective parent who doesn't know when to let her babies get on with it.

I think I may be taking this *loco parentis* lark a bit too far. Please don't let me be getting broody. Not again.

I spent a whole day with Scott's brother Michael for the first time yesterday. We went searching for costumes for the show. He took me to a boarded-up theatre on the other side of the city. We had to break in through a back window. The stage looked like it had been abandoned mid-rehearsal. Dusty scripts and food cartons were scattered on the wooden boards. There were old bloodstains on the floor of the auditorium.

The Sunless do not patronize the arts.

Michael was so nervous, fretting that we would be caught in the theatre or that someone would ask for our identification papers on the streets. He couldn't be more different from Leon and Scott. They are a rather unique family. His shoulders and hands are covered in tiny soft white feathers, which look astonishing against his dark purple Jeillo skin. Scott said that he actually has vestigial wings growing out of his shoulders. He's the nearest thing I've seen to an angel. We found some brilliant frocks which are definitely going to be included in the show. Strapless with about a million blue sequins apiece.

Very me.

I had a hunch that Emile wouldn't have any objections to dragging up, but I wasn't sure how Tameka would take to the idea. I was surprised by her enthusiasm. Fortunately for me, Tameka's Krytell Stowaway has an extensive archive. My favourite era, the late twentieth century is particularly well represented. We're doing 'I Lost My Heart To A Starship Trooper', 'We Are Family', 'Sisters Are Doing It For Themselves', and finishing with 'I Will Survive'. It's not going to be the most original drag cabaret set the universe has ever known but at least I already know the words.

We go over the top tomorrow.

Perhaps I should rephrase that.

We spent the evening having a bit of a celebration, drinking some rough fruit wine and trying out the costumes. We did a final run-through in front of Jock, Scott, Michael and Errol. They were impressed.

At least I think they were impressed. It might have been shock.

After that, I got a bit drunk and listened as Jock told us stories about Ursu before the Sunless came. Tameka remains extremely cynical about the possibility of a society without laws and took every opportunity to argue with Scott about it. It was that kind of teasing that people exhibit when they really fancy someone.

Made me think about Jason. I can't stop wondering if we're sleeping under the same moon.

Scott, true to form, started a debate about the ethics of profiteers, and we ended up following a sort of Ursulan tradition by writing down a sentence which defined our moral code. Apparently it's important that we keep them close to us (although of course Tameka was quick to point out that she didn't have to do anything). They take this sort of thing very seriously. Jock rummaged through the medical supplies and produced small plastic capsules on thin chains for us to use to keep our codes in. They're usually used by patients at the hospital to carry daily doses of medicine. I stared at my blank square of paper for a few minutes before I suddenly knew exactly what I wanted to write. When I read back what I had written I felt tearful without knowing why.

I sat on the balcony on my own for a little while, toying with my strange new necklace, trying to prepare myself for tomorrow night. Emile followed me out a little later and lay with his head on my lap. In other circumstances his close crop would be cute. But looking at him in his grey uniform and big clumpy boots, I can't help thinking of the news coverage I saw of the liberation of the death camps after the Galactic War. Emile looks like an entirely different person from the boy I met on Apollox 4. His carefully chosen clothes are lost, his bleached hair is gone, a line of tiny puncture marks are all that's left of his earrings. I know these things are only on the surface, only superficial, but they make such a difference.

They're the symbols of who we are.

I held his hand in mine – his fingernails are bitten down to the quick. I found myself wondering if that's a recent bad habit. The back of his neck has caught the sun. The skin there is the colour of golden syrup. His complexion is completely unblemished. It's as if he'd never been outside before.

An indoor boy.

If he is eighteen, I am Catwoman. And, as I believe we have already established, the Eartha Kitt one-piece is not mine.

Extract ends

13

FROCK TERRORISM

We don't have guns, we don't have knives, we don't have identification papers, Bernice thought. We have three posh frocks, padded busts (well, Emile and, um, I do), twentieth-century disco music and more slap than Arlon Jardolz's Big Night Out.

'We are going to die,' she whispered to herself. *But at least we are going to do it in sequins*.

Below her, she heard Michael put the old and empty bus into gear. Standing on the roof, Bernice, Emile and Tameka were forced to hang on tightly as it shuddered and then moved off. Tameka hit the play button on her Stowaway, which they'd wired up to the bus's PA system, and the opening strains of 'I Lost My Heart To A Starship Trooper' began to belt out into the evening. The flashing lights Jock had strung along the side of the bus began to pulse. Not actually in time to the music – but then you can't have everything.

The spotlights made her blink and the world beyond her was plunged into darkness. Bernice tried to imagine what they must have looked like: three bewigged, electric-blue-sequined figures, dresses shimmering in the white lights, dancing in time on the top of the balloon-strewn coach.

Attracting attention was not going to be a problem.

'You wouldn't believe I spent the seventies in a punk-rock band, would you?' Bernice shouted to Tameka. Bernice waved to a young Ursulan man who was staring up at them, his bald head creased into a frown of incomprehension. Confidence was going to be their greatest ally.

'What's punk?' Emile asked, from between them, already slightly out of breath beneath his blonde wig.

'Dance to disco, Emile,' Bernice laughed, waving away his question. 'Trust me, you wouldn't like rock.'

Emile looked quizzically at her, but then was forced to concentrate on a neat twist and a twirl. He was rather good at this, Bernice thought, and he certainly had better legs. She desperately tried to remember her steps, failed completely, and lost her place in the music. She bobbed up and down as best she could in her bright-red wig, but was terribly aware that she was not the strongest dancer in the trio. Tameka moved with the easy confidence of a girl who had spent her teenage years in discos and nightclubs, walking through the dance steps and clapping her hands with panache. Emile was really enjoying himself. Knees slightly bent, grinding his young hips to the stomping disco beat and giving little yelps of pleasure.

Bernice's hips weren't quite so young and didn't so much grind as lurch. Still, she had other things to worry about. As the bus moved slowly down the long street, the guards behind the gates of the New Administration building started moving forward. Bernice did not fail to notice that they were carrying long black truncheons.

Bernice carefully counted herself in and began to dance. After a fashion.

The building of the New Administration was squat and functional, with narrow windows irregularly spaced along its grey front. It was as if the architect had anticipated that it would need to be defended. It was lit from below with hundreds of orange lights. Spotlights swept across it. Bernice wasn't sure if they were a security measure or just part of the celebrations.

The streets were thick with Ursulans in their grey, red-striped uniforms. They stood in silent protest outside the high metal fence that surrounded the building. There must have been at least two thousand people standing motionless. Once again Bernice was struck by such a powerful demonstration of their unity. Denied the right to define themselves with their words or clothes or acts, the Ursulans still refused to speak as slaves. Silence was their last defence.

This silence was rudely interrupted by the sound of Sarah Brightman and Hot Gossip asking if they were like a droid, devoid of emotion.

Any moment now they are going to start throwing bricks at us, Bernice told herself, feeling rather reassured. But they didn't. Instead the people in the crowds began to clap and cheer them on. Tameka and Bernice exchanged worried glances as they danced. This was disastrous. The people in the crowds appeared to think that they were some kind of brave and no doubt suicidal protest against the Sunless.

This was not the plan.

Tameka had realized the consequences of their being thought of as protesters. Emile was, for the moment, oblivious to it all, skipping excitedly through routines like he was attending his first youth-club disco. And maybe – in a bizarre sort of way – he was. Tameka stopped dancing and began to shout down at the crowd, her words lost beneath Sarah Brightman's amplified voice.

Bernice left Emile dancing and scrambled gracelessly over in her high heels to where Tameka was standing. She turned the music off and suddenly the crowds could hear Tameka's voice clearly.

'Up the Sunless!' Tameka was screaming. 'More rules!' Her curly brown wig had slipped back on her head and she was hanging on to it with one hand. 'Collaborate and survive!'

An ugly murmur swept through the crowd. They clearly hadn't been expecting this.

Bernice joined in. 'Sunless and Ursu together for a bright new future!' She glimpsed the faces in the crowd – bemused and increasingly angry faces. The young bald-headed man she had spotted earlier, who had been running alongside the bus, had stopped clapping and was now shouting something at her which she couldn't hear.

'Wear more grey!' Bernice screamed. 'Support your local coup!'

A window on the bus shattered noisily. That's more like it, Bernice congratulated herself. The crowd surged around them. People were thumping violently on the metal panels on the side of the coach. Even Emile had got the idea now and was stamping his feet and shouting slogans at the top of his voice.

Michael pulled the bus parallel with the gates, and they toured past the guards. Tameka and Emile began, on cue, to scream for the guard's assistance. Bernice waved frantically at the uniformed figures. The guards tracked the coach, keeping themselves between it and the building. Bernice almost lost her footing as Michael accelerated, leaving the hordes of protesting Ursulans in their wake.

The service gates at the back of the building were less ornate than those at the front, but no less sturdy. They were also closed. As the coach headed towards them, guards in collaborators' uniforms waved them back. Behind them, a crowd of Ursulans chased the bus, while others stopped to lob stones at them.

Michael leant out of the coach and waved his identification papers at the guards. 'They're after us! Open the gates!' he cried.

'The building's closed for the party,' the nearest guard yelled.

'We're supposed to be in there,' Bernice yelled from the roof. 'We're the entertainment!'

The fastest protesters were almost at the back of the bus. The two guards on duty at the gate saw them and their faces lit up with fear. Michael had climbed down from the driver's booth and had handed his papers through the gate. The nearest guard glanced at them, frowned as if he was uncertain of something and then nodded. He looked up at Bernice. 'Where are yours?'

Bernice pointed downwards. 'In the bus.' She made a show of looking behind her. 'But . . . there isn't time.'

And that was when the crowd reached them. Sticks rattled against the side of the bus. More glass was smashed. A few people started to climb up the sides. A young woman made a lunge for Emile's foot and he cried out, hoisted up his skirts and scampered down the centre of the coach.

Bernice stared at the angry hordes who surrounded them. If this didn't work they were going to be lynched.

'They're after me,' Emile squealed and leapt from the front of the bus, landing on the top of the gates. 'Save me from the enemies of the New Administration!'

That boy had a whole new career in amateur dramatics just waiting for him.

'Hey, you shouldn't be . . .' The guard yelled, staring up at Emile who had already straddled the gate. 'Get down from there!'

Tameka followed Emile's example. Bernice was trying to pluck up the courage to leap across, when she saw an old woman running towards the bus with a flaming bottle in her hand.

Oh no.

The home-made bomb hit the back of the bus. A sea of burning liquid swept towards her along the roof. She somehow doubted that her dress was flameproof.

'Frocks away!' she screamed, her dress billowing around her as she leapt through the air, landing on the top of the metal gate. She had scrambled over before she knew what she was doing, landing next to Emile and Tameka and the two guards.

'Thank you! Thank you so much!' she cried, breathlessly, neatly stepping in front of her students. 'They were going to kill us!' She straightened her dress. 'Now we're probably running a little late. If you could just point us in the direction of our dressing rooms . . .'

The guards were distracted by several protesters who had decided to breach the gates in all the excitement. Their grey bodies flickered with orange light from the burning coach as they climbed.

'Wait here,' the guards ordered and hurried towards the gates, waving their truncheons.

Bernice, Tameka and Emile were left unguarded. The building was only a few metres ahead of them.

'Well, I don't know about you,' Bernice said, 'but I, for one, am rather impressed.'

Scott was woken by the sound of someone returning to the dormitory. He was curled up on the single bed, his stomach still tense from the dream. His head still ringing with his own screams.

His skin blistering into nothing as the dying red sun flickered and then ignited with white fire.

Michael appeared by his side. Scott wondered if he had been crying out in his sleep again. Tameka said that he did. 'How did it go?' he asked his brother.

'All right.' Michael shrugged his broad shoulders. 'They got in. Whether they get out again is another matter.'

Scott was relieved. He padded out of the room to the bathroom. Michael followed him and stood scrutinizing him while he splashed his face.

'It's the dream, isn't it?' Michael said.

Scott nodded. 'Yeah, it's getting stronger. More real. Do you still get it?'

Michael nodded, but didn't say anything else.

Scott dried his face on his shirt. 'The profiteers believe that our dreams are messages to our waking minds. Tameka told me.'

Michael frowned. 'Messages from where?'

'From another part of ourselves. From a part of our mind which is shadowed and hidden.'

Michael snorted. 'They're so full of shit. I don't understand why you've involved yourself with them.'

'Are you saying that you want them to leave?'

'Look, Scott, the Sunless are going to find them eventually. It's just a matter of time. Eventually someone is going to ask them for their papers. If they find out that you've helped them, they'll kill you too.'

'So what should I do, turn them in?'

There was silence for a moment, before Michael said, 'We

154

could just leave. Tonight. Go back to the village. I haven't seen Leon in years.' He must have seen the expression on Scott's face, because his voice trailed away.

'Michael, where are your principles? Do you think they deserve to be killed? Just because their heads have been filled with a load of crap doesn't mean that they're not people.'

'They're profiteers! They're not supposed to be here. There's a rule about it.'

'Since when did that bother you?'

Silence.

'I don't want to talk about it any more. I'm going to bed.'

But Scott wasn't prepared to let it go. He followed Michael into the smaller room, watching as his brother sullenly began to undress. Michael was about to pull off his shirt when he became aware of Scott's eyes on him and suddenly stopped. He climbed self-consciously into bed still wearing his shirt.

'What?' Scott frowned. 'Why are you wearing a shirt in bed?'

'No reason,' Michael snapped. The lie was so obvious even he looked embarrassed about it.

'Take your shirt off.'

'No.'

'Do it.'

'*Do it*?' Michael repeated, a sneer forming across his face. 'Who is the profiteer now?'

Scott leapt on to the bed, straddled his brother and began to pull at his shirt. Michael was a much larger man than Scott and would have easily overpowered his brother, but Scott knew his vulnerabilities. He landed a kick on Michael's injured knee and the large Jeillo collapsed on to the bed grimacing. Scott twisted his brother on to his back and pulled his shirt up.

The long feathers which had always grown on Michael's shoulders had been removed. Scott felt his brother give up his struggle under him. Scott gently caressed the stubble of hollow feather shafts which protruded from his brother's purple back.

'Did *they* do this to you?'

Michael shook his head, burying his face in a pillow.

155

'*You* did it?' Scott felt sick. 'Oh, Michael, you've clipped your wings?'

'Just leave me alone.' Michael said and pushed Scott off him.

Scott let him go, unable to believe what his brother had done. 'What has happened to you?'

'I'm sick of being different from everybody else. Sick of it!' He got up, made a grab for his clothes and stalked out of the room.

Scott lay back on the bed and closed his eyes. How had the world become so insane? Suddenly he just wanted his nine brothers and sisters around him. He wanted the comfort and protection of his 'Eight'. He whispered their names, as if that might magically summon them to his side: Leon, Michael, Emma, Yvonne, Nikolas, Melanie, Azaro, Iain, Iranda.

Eventually he slept. The dream rose to greet him eagerly. For once he welcomed the fire from the dark-red sun, for it overwhelmed the hurt he felt inside.

Walking into the party was an uncomfortable homecoming. Suddenly Bernice had stepped into a world she knew all too well. The frugal, uniformed life outside quickly faded in the face of a whirlwind of colour and music. But it was the excess that reminded her of her own society. After the emptiness of Scott, Michael and Leon's frugal lives, she was suddenly surrounded by an excess of *things*.

They had emerged into a courtyard, which must have been a central pivot around which the rest of the building was erected. It was wide and high, several storeys up to a covered glass roof. Heavy dance music blared, and costumed dancers spun around a fountain which dominated the centre of the room. There were people everywhere. Dancing, eating and drinking on the ground floor, fanning themselves while spectating from the balconies, which were strewn with exotic flowering vines.

The room stank. Stank of rich food and perfume. So powerful it made Bernice feel a little nauseous. The party was a shock to her senses after the usual dull smells of vegetables and sweat. She realized that she hadn't eaten any gourmet food since she had arrived on Ursu. Scott seemed to survive on a diet of roasted vegetables and dairy products. Here there were tables laden with the golden and glistening carcasses of large birds and even whole herd animals. Meat, pastries and huge desserts that looked like miniature buildings. She was reminded of her own wedding.

Bernice slowly walked down a few steps into the noisy courtyard, aware of Emile and Tameka keeping pace at her side. She wanted to reach out and take their hands, partly to reassure them, but also for her own support. She held herself back.

'None of them are wearing uniforms,' Emile whispered from her side.

Bernice had nodded before she realized that this wasn't wholly true. The people who were serving the food wore the plain grey uniform of collaboration.

Servants, that's what they were. It was the first time she had seen a waiter or an attendant since she had crashed on the planet.

The guests at the party wore brightly coloured, sensual clothes. Designed not for work but for showing off their healthy, tanned bodies. Many of the men and women wore make-up. Their eyes looked too big somehow, too dark and unreal. Their scarlet mouths were threatening, as if they had been dipped in blood. Bloody mouths laughing and shouting and kissing and biting into the greasy animal flesh. The drunken revellers looked lawless but Bernice knew that this wasn't freedom. This was indulgence. The land not of do as you please, but of snatch what you can. The land of I'm all right and sod the others.

It was horrible and it was home. Or at least the closest she had felt to her life since she had crashed on the planet.

Bernice walked through the noise and laughter, feeling like a lowly peasant in the court of a king. She felt as if she were not really there at all, as if she were walking in a children's story or through a lucid dream.

Tameka leant over. 'Can you see her?'

'What? Oh –' Bernice was about to shake her head when she glimpsed a flash of red hair crossing the dance floor. 'Wait. Yes, I do. Stay by the stage, I'll catch up with you there.'

The red-haired woman was small and slight. Bernice almost lost sight of her as she squeezed her way across the busy dance floor. The young woman hurried up a set of stairs tucked away in an alcove at the edge of the room. Bernice followed her up to the second floor and watched her as she crossed to a large set of impressive double doors. The woman moved confidently as if she owned the building. And for all Bernice knew, she did. Bernice hitched up her dress and entered the room.

Bernice closed the doors behind her and rested against them for a moment. The sound of the party was immediately dulled. Only the heavy bass beat of the music still vibrated through the floor.

The room was large, tall and long – clearly designed to impress a visitor. The young red-haired woman was perched on the edge of a desk, speaking earnestly into a handset. She looked tiny in the huge, austere room.

There were framed pictures on the wall and objects under glass. The room smelt like a museum. It was the first room Bernice had been in on Ursu that felt cluttered. Most of the buildings that she had been in in the city and in the village contained basic items of battered furniture. Crappy art slapped on the walls with loads of enthusiasm but little skill.

When the woman caught sight of Bernice she quickly finished her conversation and replaced the receiver. 'Can I help you?' she asked. Her voice was soft and a little girlish.

Bernice stared at her for a moment, unsure how she should best approach this conversation. Butterfly feelings fluttered in her stomach. Had this woman been Jason's lover? Was she still? Bernice was furious at herself for feeling so bloody jealous.

The young woman walked slowly towards Bernice, who was blocking the only exit to the room.

Bernice took a deep breath. 'Can you help me? I'm not sure. I hope so.'

This was the closest Bernice had been to the woman. Her

curly auburn hair was cut into a short bob. Her features were small and childlike. Button nose, thin lips. The photograph hadn't done her justice: she was strikingly beautiful but delicate, almost fragile, like a china doll. Bernice noticed that the young woman's eyes were the same mercury grey as she had seen in Scott's family. Not unlike the Sunless.

The woman stopped in front of her. She seemed to find something amusing. 'I think you'll find that the stage is downstairs.'

'I'm sorry?' Bernice was suddenly acutely aware that she was in bad drag and wearing a comedy wig. This wasn't the outfit she would have chosen to confront the woman in. She felt like wiping away her garish make-up, and had to force herself not to. 'Oh I see,' she began. 'No, I know where the stage is. I followed you up here to speak with you.'

'Oh?' The woman frowned, but the amused expression remained on her face. 'I can't imagine what we might have to talk about, but go on. You have my full attention. For the moment.'

Bernice came straight to the point. 'I'm looking for Jason Kane. I believe you know him.'

The woman's composure collapsed. Her jaw dropped open. 'How could you ... Jason Kane? How could you possibly know Jason?'

'He is . . . I mean he *was* my husband.'

The woman leant forward, trying to see past all Bernice's make-up. 'I don't believe it,' she whispered, shaking her petite head. 'You're Bernice Summerfield, aren't you?'

Benny managed to hide her surprise at being recognized. 'I see my reputation precedes me,' she said, maintaining a cool façade while desperately wondering what Jason might have told this woman.

'How did you get to Ursu?'

'With great difficulty.'

'I'm not surprised to hear that.' The woman turned and walked back into the centre of the room. Her confident manner had evaporated. She was chewing on a nail. 'This is very embarrassing.'

159

Bernice decided to be very adult about this. 'You don't have to be embarrassed. I think he's in trouble. Do you know where he is?'

The woman seemed to respond to Bernice's matter-of-fact approach. She shook her head. 'No. No, I don't. I haven't the faintest idea.' She was looking at Bernice, an expression of intense interest upon her face. 'You've travelled all the way to Ursu to find him? I'd heard about the obsessive love that profiteers sometimes share, but I didn't realize that it could be so all-consuming.'

Bernice was barely listening. She swallowed uncomfortably, feeling her chance of finding Jason diminishing. This woman had been her last hope. She leant back against the desk and covered her mouth with her hand. 'How did you meet him? Did he come here?'

'To Ursu? No. There haven't been any off-worlders here since the Galactic War. Excluding the Sunless and, of course, you and your little friends.'

'I didn't realize that Ursulans had travelled into space.'

'They haven't. At least only very few of us have. The Sunless have been trying to reclaim various items of equipment which were stolen from their world. They needed people to negotiate with governments and private individuals. Their homeworld was plundered of its ancient artefacts and technologies by several companies before the Galactic War. Now the Sunless are powerful enough, they've come to take back what is theirs. They invaded Ursu to reclaim the Blooms, but obviously they couldn't invade the entire galaxy. They've been forced to negotiate for the return of some of their legacy. As you can imagine, they aren't the most skilled diplomats.'

'And I suppose you were happy to sell out Ursu to them?'

The woman shrugged, ignoring the judgmental tone in Bernice's voice. 'I happened to be in the right place at the right time, so I took up their offer. I met Jason on Denaria 7. I needed someone with experience of different cultures to help me in my work.' She paused before adding, 'And he was amusing to have around.'

Bernice took a deep breath. Why was she so freaked

out that he was having sex with other people? They were divorced, for heaven's sake! She'd had sex with other people. All right, she'd almost had sex with other people. She had wanted to. She was reminded of her rather unethical flirtations with Doran. But she hadn't done the deed, and by the sounds of things Jason had. Somehow that was more of a final severance than their decree absolute.

She forced the painful thoughts out of her mind and tried to concentrate on the present conversation. 'And Jason? He didn't return with you?'

'I woke up one morning and he'd gone.' Bernice must have looked worried because the woman added, 'Oh, nothing sinister. He left a note and everything.'

'What was his reason for leaving?'

'I think his conscience got to him. He wasn't keen on getting involved with weapons.'

Bernice frowned. 'Hang on, what have weapons got to do with it? I thought you said that the Sunless were trying to reclaim their heritage?'

The woman laughed. 'Their heritage *is* weapons. You don't think that the Sunless would go tearing across space to try and reclaim a few works of art, do you? Their ancestors were great militarists. The companies took it all. Now the Sunless want it back.'

Bernice sighed, remembering her conversation with the Trans-System detective. *A weapon with powers beyond the sun.* But that had to be silly nonsense. She'd been an archaeologist long enough to know that lost alien civilizations did not go around leaving their powerful weapons lying around for any old nutter to find. I mean, they don't, do they? No, of course not. The whole idea was preposterous.

She explained that Jason had come looking for her, although she didn't mention why. The woman seemed genuinely surprised, although not particularly concerned to hear of Jason's abduction.

The woman began to fidget. Bernice could sense that the conversation was drawing to a close. She tried another tack. 'I don't understand why you are helping the Sunless become

161

more powerful. Why help them destroy your world?'

The woman gave a dry chuckle. 'You've been listening to Ursulans for too long. They've got their heads in the clouds. Since the Sunless arrived at least there is enough food to go around.'

Bernice snorted. 'Hardly surprising since the population has been halved.'

'I think you've been the victim of anti-Sunless propaganda. Before they came, Ursu was becoming completely unviable. I mean it was all right while everyone lived in small communities, but as the society grew and cities developed it was starting to fall apart. Important jobs were left undone, vital duties unattended. You can't live in a world where people just give up their jobs when they get bored. Industrialization requires a division of labour and a division of labour creates inequality. The old Ursu was just a romantic dream. The indulgence of a group of bored, wealthy colonists before the war. Nothing more.'

Bernice thought of Leon and Scott and felt that she was failing them somehow by being unable to defend their beliefs. But what this woman was saying was all too plausible.

She felt the door open behind her. A middle-aged man stood in the doorway in a scarlet robe with gold trimming. His face was red and his eyes glassy. He stood swaying gently from side to side. 'Iranda, dear,' he slurred, 'aren't you coming back to the party? You did say that you weren't going to be long.'

'Run along, Samuel, I'll join you in a minute.'

The man mumbled something unintelligible before retreating.

Iranda waited patiently until the door was closed before she turned impatiently to Bernice. 'Samuel's a leading figure in the New Administration. Thick as pig shit, but he's well connected. Listen to me, Bernice Summerfield, I've been honest with you. But if you try and cause me any trouble, I won't have any qualms about handing you and your friends over to the Sunless. I don't want to see or hear from you ever again. Is that clear?'

Bernice sighed with resignation. Short of torturing the woman, there wasn't anything she could do.

The drunken collaborator chose that moment to poke his head around the door for a second time. 'Iranda,' he pleaded, in a little boy's voice.

Iranda gave Bernice a look of long sufferance. 'All right!'

The drunken man seemed hurt by the harshness in her voice. 'Please come down. I think that the next act is about to begin.'

Iranda turned to Bernice and took a moment to appraise her outfit. 'That's your cue, I believe.'

14

WE ARE FAMILY

Scott was dozing when Jock shouted for him to join him in the other room. Errol was taking his first tentative steps after his ordeal. The tall man had his arms tightly around Jock's shoulders. His legs looked like matchsticks, trembling violently as he put one bare foot in front of the other.

Scott forced a smile. 'Hey, that's amazing.'

Errol laughed breathlessly. 'Feels weird.' Sweat was breaking out across his bald head, discolouring the bandage which covered his right eye. 'But I'll let you into a secret: I have done this before.' He winked at Scott and then grimaced with the effort of taking a few short steps. 'Just not for a while. But, yeah, kid, it's good to be back on my feet. Never realized the ground could be so far away.'

He lurched as he tried to take another step, and Jock steadied him. 'It's OK, I've got you. Maybe you should rest.'

Errol nodded, looking relieved. 'Yeah, only a fool argues with his doctor.'

Jock smiled. 'All my patients argue with me.'

'Sounds like you need to learn to assert yo' authority, Doc.'

Jock laughed. 'I don't think it's your legs I should be worrying about, but your mind.'

In order to celebrate Errol's achievement, Scott and Jock made a light supper. They sat around Errol's bed, talking and drinking tea. Errol, exhausted by his exertions, quickly dozed off, snoring gently, a satisfied expression on his heavily lined face.

When Errol fell asleep, the two Ursulans switched from tea to wine. They talked generally for a while and then Jock asked where Michael had gone. Scott paused before answering. He gave an account of their argument, although for some reason he didn't mention Michael's cruel self-inflicted surgery.

'So Michael doesn't like the profiteers,' Jock concluded. 'What about you?'

'I think they threaten him, somehow. I can sort of understand. I have had second thoughts about them, particularly after what Bernice did to you.' The wine had clouded his head and he shook himself as if this might clear his thoughts. 'They're just so very different.'

Jock took a sip of his wine. 'And difference can be unsettling.'

'Yes. It's like the woman, Tameka.'

'Ah,' Jock murmured, and looked into his glass. 'You've become intimate.'

'I like her. We've had sex a couple of times. But something's really changed now. Not big things, just subtleties of language. She looks at me as if she expects something of me. Almost like . . . like an answer to something. The boy's the same.' Scott chuckled a little hollowly as he remembered the other night. 'No, actually he's *worse*. Emile can't even acknowledge what he wants – even to himself. He's caught up in this elaborate fiction about himself. It's ridiculous.'

Jock put his glass down. 'But?'

Scott caught the older man's eye and smiled, shyly. 'Yes, you're right. There is a but, and I don't feel so good about this. But to feel so wanted, so desired, to be everything a person needs – even if they are hopelessly deluded – is . . . seductive. Exciting. Makes me feel . . . I don't know.'

'Special? Unique?'

'Yes! Yes, exactly that! It's an illusion, but the illusion is powerful, intoxicating.' Scott suddenly felt that he had said a little more than he had meant to. Maybe it was the wine. He felt a bit embarrassed, a bit guilty for being so caught up in such arrogant notions. 'I'm egoizing madly, I know,' he said quickly, aware that he was just passing judgement on himself before Jock did.

However, Jock only shrugged. 'It's what you feel.'

'But if you set up expectations like that, how can people do anything but fail each other?' Scott shook his head, aware that he was a bit drunk now. 'They really *are* crazy, aren't they?'

Jock rested a hand on Scott's shoulder. 'Crazy and seductive.'

'My head feels like it's spinning. I'm lost in all this.'

'How could you not be?' Jock said, and smiled kindly. 'There's no logic to their behaviour. And so there's no map to these feelings you are exploring.' Jock finished his wine and set it down beside him with a little sigh. 'No map and a compass wouldn't help at all.'

They sat in silence, listening to Errol's rasping breathing. Eventually Jock fell asleep in his chair. Scott clambered to his feet and shook the cramp out of his legs. He wandered through the rooms, humming an old song that Leon had taught him. Emile and Tameka's filthy uniforms were lying on the floor where they had been thrown. He stood a little unsteadily on the balcony and listened to the insects buzzing in the shrubs below him. He stared out at the stars and tried to imagine them full of profiteers and planets and companies and corruption, but they just looked like tiny dots of light in the orange shadows.

His foot nudged something which clinked. He looked down and saw that Bernice had left her glass on the balcony from the previous night. The strange little sculpture she had shown him was sitting beside it. He picked up the little figurine and examined it for a moment.

Bloody profiteers and their bloody things! On a drunken whim he tossed it out into the night and heard it land in the scrub with a satisfying thump.

Bernice followed Iranda out of the large office on to the

balcony. The noise of the music rushed up to greet her out of the well of the courtyard. Over in one corner she could see a spotlight being tested against a small curtained stage. She couldn't see Tameka or Emile, which was simultaneously worrying and typical. The red-haired woman had taken the arm of her partner and was about to descend. Sensing her options running out, Bernice called her back.

Iranda looked impatient. 'What now?'

Bernice bit her lip. She deliberately hadn't mentioned the artefact Jason had entrusted to her. He had wanted her to keep it safe. It was still the most likely reason why he had been kidnapped. But she had come up against a blank wall. 'Before Jason disappeared, he left something with me.'

Iranda looked at Bernice with new interest. 'Go on.'

Bernice watched the interest in the woman's face drain away as she described the figurine. It obviously wasn't what she had been hoping or expecting to hear.

'Goodbye, Bernice,' she said firmly and descended into the party. Bernice watched her go, aware that with her went the possibility of finding Jason. Bernice was distracted by the opening bars of a twentieth-century disco classic. A few playful descending piano notes, a thumping base, funky guitar, and a stomping disco beat.

It could mean only one thing.

She looked over the balcony. Two tiny blue-sequined figures were moving in time to the gentle shuffle of the introductory bars. Tameka and Emile were making a bid for their fifteen minutes of fame.

By the time she had reached the dance floor, Emile and Tameka were lip-synching the repeated refrain of the chorus. Tameka caught her eye and winked. Emile executed a perfect twirl and then waved excitedly. At first Bernice had to push her way through the crowds, but as people began to notice her outfit they moved aside. A path opened out in front of her leading up to the stage. The revellers clapped along with the song. Aware of every eye upon her, Bernice did her best to strut confidently towards the bright spotlights. She mounted the stage just as the first verse came around.

Turning to face the audience, she gestured melodramatically at the swishing, blue-sequined figures on either side of her and lip-synched:

'Everyone can see we're together . . .'

Scott picked up Emile and Tameka's uniforms, which they had left strewn across the floor of the room. The profiteers didn't take care of the clothes they wore. Perhaps, Scott thought, because they weren't their own. Weren't theirs to keep, and so not of value.

Scott was rooting through a pile of clothes when he pulled out a grey uniform which had been stuffed at the bottom. Plain grey. It was a moment before he realized what he was holding in his hands. A moment before he felt the first prickle of fear.

Someone in the building was a collaborator.

They went down a storm. Bernice's coordination didn't get any better but the audience assumed her wooden feet were part of the act and laughed along with her as she kept missing her cues. The partying collaborators quickly succumbed to the pleasures of ancient American disco music.

As they danced, Bernice was aware of more grey-uniformed figures appearing in between the revellers in the audience. She was ready to make a hasty exit as the last notes of 'I Will Survive' faded out and the audience roared with approval.

The applause didn't die, but instead turned into chanting. Emile grabbed hold of Bernice's hand as she teetered down the steps at the side of the stage in her heels. His round face was flushed with the excitement beneath his blonde wig. 'Listen to them: they're *begging* for it. Can't we do an encore?'

Typical. They were in the lair of the enemy and all the boy could think about was pushing his fifteen minutes of fame into half an hour.

Tameka clattered down the steps two at a time, clutching her bulky Krytell Stowaway in one hand and her wig in the other. Her long dark hair had been pinned back to her head with grips. 'You're gonna have to wait till the talent contest at the freshers' ball, boyee. That's if we ever get back to St Oscar's.' She nodded towards the main doors, where a group of uniformed collaborators stood. 'And I spotted some of our pale friends loitering in the hall.'

Bernice had a sneaking feeling that Iranda had decided not to make good on her promise.

They were spotted as they tried to slip out of the building through the kitchens. The three friends simultaneously kicked off their heels, hitched up their skirts and made a dash for it.

'Keep together,' Bernice ordered as they emerged into the large, newly landscaped gardens at the back of the building. Holding hands, they jumped over a low wall and dropped down on to the edge of a neatly mown lawn, landing softly. For a moment they crouched quietly in the darkness. The moonlight turned the grass a soft silvery grey. It was cool and wet beneath their stockinged feet. There was no sound apart from their heavy breathing and the distant thump of music.

'Bernice, look,' Tameka hissed, pointing to a tarmacked area on the other side of the lawn. A line of low dark vehicles were parked under a canopy of trees.

Sunless armoured vehicles.

'What do you think?'

'I'm trying not to,' Bernice sighed. 'You think you could drive one of those things?'

Tameka grinned. 'I've been itching to have a go ever since we got here.'

They broke into a run across the lawn, leaving dark footprints behind them in the wet grass. Somebody started shouting in the distance, and for a disorientating moment Bernice couldn't tell if it was ahead of them or back near the house.

The Sunless armoured car was made of thick plates of metal and was about two metres high. Its huge wheels were almost the same height as the vehicle itself. There was one hatch on the roof and another at the back. A large cannon-sized weapon sat in a turret towards the back. The vehicle looked strong and solid, like a mobile strongbox. A thick slab of violence.

Tameka swung herself nimbly up on to the roof.

Bernice saw her thumb a control and the rounded hatch opened with a soft hiss. Bernice couldn't see Tameka's face in the darkness but she heard her giggle.

Oh dear, Bernice thought. She's actually looking forward to this.

'Let me just say now that I *know* I am going to regret this,' Bernice told Emile as she clambered on to the roof and dropped down into the belly of the car. Tameka had already buckled herself into the driving seat and was familiarizing herself with the instruments.

'No keys?' Bernice asked.

'Keys?' Tameka made a face. 'This is an armoured car, Bernice. We are not trying to unlock your bicycle. The ignition is protected by a voice recognition system.'

'Oh,' Bernice said. 'Right.'

'Will it recognize us?' Emile said.

Tameka just shot him a look.

'Sorry, stupid question.'

'I reckon I can hot-wire this. But it'll take a minute. Maybe two.'

Through one of the narrow window slots in the side of the car, Bernice caught sight of a group of uniformed figures moving across the lawn towards them. They ran in perfect time, their shaven heads visible in the moonlight. 'Tameka, you've got about thirty seconds.'

Tameka glanced up from her work. 'Guess who,' she said in her husky tone. She pulled a pin from her hair and used it to connect two terminals. The vehicle's engine roared once and then died. She popped her head up for a moment. 'This may take a little longer than I thought.'

'They know where we are!' Emile cried from the barred window. Keeping his head low, he scuttled off into the depths of the vehicle.

Emile was right. The Sunless were heading in their direction, making no sound as they ran in the soft grass. There were four of them, rushing silently towards the armoured car. They ran gracefully, taking long strides. Despite their feet hitting the ground together they made no sound. Their cropped hair looked like a coating of dust in the moonlight. In a few more moments they would reach the vehicle.

The engine powered up, but Bernice's relief was short-lived as the motor noise spluttered and then faded. Tameka swore colourfully. 'The safety keeps cutting in. I've almost got it.'

'I think it's a little too late for that.' Bernice launched herself out of her seat, urgently gesturing for Tameka to do the same. 'They'll be in here in a moment. Come on, there's a hatch at the back – we'll have to make a run for it.'

Tameka was still half under the dashboard. 'Hang on, I think I've got it.'

A series of light footfalls sounded above them: the Sunless landing on the vehicle's roof. Bernice looked up at the ceiling, her heart pounding in her chest.

She made a lunge for the hatch's locking mechanism. Too late. The circular lid had already begun to lift up and swing open. A sliver of dark sky was revealed beyond it.

Something moved in the darkness.

'Tameka!' Bernice hissed. They had to get out of here. They had to get out of here right now. Bernice looked around for Emile. Where the hell had that child run off to now?

A volley of blaster fire answered her question. Something screamed in pain. Something that didn't sound quite human. There was a second burst of fire; the scream cut off suddenly and was immediately followed by the sound of a dead weight hitting the roof. The hatch clattered back into place.

'Emile!' Bernice yelled. Oh my God, the boy was operating the weapon.

'Yes!' Tameka exclaimed as the engine powered up and then settled into a steady growl. 'Are we in business or what?' She slid up into her seat, pulling the harness down over her. 'You better tell psychotrannie to strap his chubby ass down, Benny, because we are out of here.'

Tameka threw the armoured car into gear and it lurched forward, knocking Bernice off her feet. Lying on the vibrating floor, Bernice was terribly aware that the situation was entirely out of her control.

'Hey! Who are you calling chubby?' A young voice complained from the rear of the vehicle.

The armoured car tore through the gates, wrenching them from their hinges and scattering the crowds of protesters.

'Coming through!' Tameka yelled out of the window gleefully as she accelerated out on to the streets of the city. 'Lady with a baby!'

She noticed that Bernice was staring at her open-mouthed. Tameka shrugged, 'I've always wanted to say that.'

A small monochrome monitor to her left displayed the view from the rear of the vehicle. There wasn't enough light for her to see more than just the outline of the road. There were a series of small controls next to the screen. A few were labelled with strange spiky symbols which Tameka didn't recognize. She twiddled a few at random and the screen flickered and then flared into infrared.

'Hey, something goes my way!'

Three bright blobs were keeping pace behind her. They had company. From the size of the heat traces they had to be Sunless vehicles. Tameka was distracted by Bernice leaning over her to examine the symbols on the instruments. 'You know, these have some grammatical similarities with the letters on the cloth the artefact was wrapped in.' Bernice looked up at Tameka as if she expected her to be interested or impressed or something.

Hoo boy! They were being chased by the Sunless and Bernice was playing professor. 'Bernice, trust me. This is not the time for a tutorial.'

There was a communications headset hanging down to her right-hand side. Tameka tugged it on. ''Meel?' she asked, adjusting the microphone which was attached to the headphones. 'Can you hear me?'

Nothing.

172

'Benny, go see if Emile's got his headset on. The gunner position should have one.' She tapped the three bright blurs on the monitor. 'We're going to need to coordinate our efforts if we're going to shake this lot off our tail.' Bernice stared at her for a moment. Tameka thought she might have had a disapproving look on her face. But she nodded and moved away.

A moment later, the headphones crackled. 'Emile to Tameka, do you copy? Over.'

Tameka raised an eyebrow. *Over*? 'Who the hell is this? Comrade 7?'

There was a burst of blaster fire from up above her and Emile's tinny voice came through full of excitement. 'You bet your sorry ass, it is!' he quipped in a put-on accent. *Her* accent.

Tameka broke out in a grin. 'Was that supposed to be an impression? 'Meel, am I gonna *whip* your ass!'

'Promises. Promises,' came the tinny reply.

The three pursuing vehicles were still behind her on the wide road. The infrared monitor flared suddenly and she heard blaster fire. The smile slipped from her face as the vehicle shuddered beneath her and lurched into a sickening skid. Her headphones were suddenly full of eardrum-piercing static. She wrestled the car back under her control. They weren't going to survive too many of those. Which was particularly worrying as she had no idea how she was going to deal with their pursuers.

'Is everyone all right,' she yelled as she hurtled around a corner.

Emile said something she couldn't make out. Bernice appeared at her side and strapped herself into the navigator's seat. Benny accidentally brushed a control on the arm of the chair and the seat quickly reclined until it was completely horizontal.

Bernice was suddenly staring up at the ceiling.

'Mind the controls, Benny.'

'Ah, I see my relationship with technology continues apace. Er, Tameka, how do I get vertical?'

An idea dropped neatly into Tameka's head. It was crazy and suicidal and she didn't like it at all. 'Don't you move a muscle, Bernice.'

Bernice looked up at her out of the corner of her eye. 'Are you serious?'

'You bet. That's a crash position. Avoids whiplash and getting thrown out of the windscreen. Which control did you hit?'

'Top left on the panel, I think. Tameka, I just want you to know that crashing was high on my list of things to avoid.'

'Is Emile's chair the same?'

'Yes, I think so.' Bernice wagged a finger in the air above her. 'Why do you ask?'

Tameka adjusted the microphone. 'Emile?'

'What can I do for you, ma'am?' Comrade 7 replied in a husky whisper.

'Top left switch on your chair. Press it.'

'OK, ma'am,' he said in his put-on butch voice.

Bernice frowned, 'I thought Comrade 7 was a girl super-hero.'

A moment later Emile gave a high-pitched yelp of surprise.

Tameka covered the microphone on her headset with her hand. 'You were saying.' Then she told Emile to stay lying down.

'If you wanted me on my back you only had to ask,' came the tinny reply.

'Who is he kidding?'

They hurtled through an empty square and out on to a wide stretch of road. They were speeding through the edge of the city now. The buildings on either side of the road were generously spaced. The driving was easy – there were few vehicles, only the odd bus which was easily dodged. Tameka glanced at the rear-view monitor. The three vehicles behind her fanned out and began to accelerate. One of the cars was directly behind them, the other two flanking the first. The gap between their car and lead vehicle began to close.

'Keep your legs bent or your femur will be driven through your knee joints. Oh, and try to relax!' Tameka added, as an afterthought.

And then she did an emergency stop in the middle of the road.

There was a vicious squeal of brakes and suddenly they were stationary. Tameka moved her seat into a crash position. The engine stalled and died. For a few seconds there was a terrible silence.

The car in the middle had nowhere to go. The driver tried to avoid them but only succeeded in colliding with the vehicle on its right, which careered off into a low building and exploded.

From her prone position, Tameka glimpsed the middle glowing blob hurtling towards them on the rear-view monitor. The vehicle was completely out of control. For a second she thought it might miss them but then she saw that it was going to clip their rear wing.

She closed her eyes.

The impact smacked into her and she felt every joint in her body shudder as their car was pushed violently off the road in a crazy arc. The harness bit painfully into her armpits and groin. She tried to estimate how far away the nearest buildings were but her head filled up with bright painful light.

She felt the car slide sickenly to a halt with a muffled crumping sound. She allowed herself to stay lying down for a few seconds. She didn't have much choice. When she opened her eyes all she could see was the ceiling lurching gently above her like a cheap virtual image.

Tameka clicked her seat upright. She was thrown against her harness and for a moment she thought she was going to throw up. Paisley spots swirled before her eyes.

'You all right, Bernice?' she managed.

'Can we go back to the driving centre, please, Ms Vito.'

'Did I pass?'

Bernice muttered something under her breath which Tameka didn't quite catch. Well at least she was still in one piece. Tameka adjusted her microphone. ''Meel, you OK?'

Static.

Shit.

'Emile?'

Nothing.

Come on. Come on.

After what felt like an age her headphones crackled. 'I feel sick,' a tinny voice said weakly.

Tameka relaxed. The spots stopped rushing in front of her eyes. Outside she could see the rear end of the first car protruding out of the front of a one-storey, flat-roofed building. Orange flames billowed up into the night.

No one could have survived that. Not even the Sunless.

The second car, the one that had collided with them, was closer. The whole front was crumpled. The driver was pumping the accelerator, but the engine only whined impotently. It wasn't going anywhere.

The third car – the one that hadn't been involved in the collision – must have sped on past the crash site. Tameka peered out through one of the thin, vertical windows. Turning her head made her feel nauseous. The vehicle wasn't anywhere in sight. For the moment. She didn't doubt for one minute that they'd be back.

Tameka had to struggle to get the vehicle into reverse mode and it shunted sluggishly back on to the road. The crash had done some serious damage. The accelerator pedal was loose under her foot. She put her foot down to the floor but the car only limped forward, barely reaching cruising speed. Most of the lights on the control console were flashing but Tameka didn't have any idea what they meant so she decided to ignore them.

'Where did you learn to drive like that?' Bernice asked from beside her.

'Speeder races in the Jeillo Quarter back on Hoppers 5.'

'Well it was insanely dangerous.' Bernice ruffled Tameka's hair. 'But I think you just saved all of our lives.'

Tameka shrugged. She was about to say something modest about how any really cool person would have done the same, when she heard the third Sunless vehicle accelerating to meet them. The view screens were all out, but the lights from the vehicle pierced the thin windows, spotlighting the low-tech

176

industrial equipment in the armoured car. 'We're not out of this yet.'

The undamaged armoured vehicle glided alongside them, effortlessly matching their limping speed. The top hatch on the other vehicle lifted up and a grey-suited figure climbed out, crouching against the wind.

'Emile!'

Crackle. 'I'm on it.'

'Forget the Sunless. Aim for the wheels.'

She glanced out of the window. Emile's first attempt went wide. Volleys of magnesium-white lightning chased each other over the roof of the car, bleaching out the face of the Sunless on the roof. The grey-suited figure didn't react at all to being shot at – it was as if it hadn't even seen the blaster fire.

Who the hell were these people? *What* the hell were they?

The Sunless driver closed the gap between the two vehicles. The lone figure leapt across the gap for a second before it disappeared above her.

'We have company, guys.'

Without having to be told, Bernice unbuckled herself and moved to the hatch, pulling hard on the locking handle. 'I can't secure it. We don't have the codes.'

'Well just hang on.'

The creature began to pull at the hatch. Bernice wrapped one hand around the wheel and another around a fitting on the wall. Tameka could see that Bernice wasn't going to be able to keep the hatch closed for long.

Tameka felt helpless. While she was concentrating on driving there wasn't anything that she could do to help Bernice. They were going to be in real trouble if one of those cold-hearted bastards got in here.

She glanced out of the window. The last remaining Sunless vehicle was right alongside them now. She could almost see inside the cabin through the thin window slits. Further down the body of the armoured vehicle, the long dark barrel of its weapon turned smoothly towards them.

Brilliant. If the one on the roof didn't manage to break in

and tear them apart then they were probably going to get shot off the road.

'Come on, Emile,' she barked into her microphone. 'What are you doing up there?'

The barrel of the enemy weapon was pointing directly at her. No, not directly at the cabin. The Sunless were targeting their turret. Taking aim at Emile's position. At this range, he didn't stand a chance.

'Emile!'

'Hang on, I'm having trouble with the sights . . . almost there.'

'No! Just get out of there! Get out of there now!' She put her foot to the floor, but the armoured car barely responded.

'Wha– 'S OK, I've got it.'

'Emile!'

There was an exchange of fire. At almost exactly the same time as the front wheels of the third vehicle exploded in hot flame, Tameka was jolted back in her seat as their car also took a hit. She heard a wrenching of metal. Emile started screaming in the back of the vehicle. And then she smelt burning plastic and the unmistakable tang of an electrical fire. The air in the vehicle clouded up with thick, acrid smoke.

Tameka was suddenly driving completely blind. She hit the brakes. Nothing happened.

Hoo boy!

The car shot on through the darkness.

15

JUST DO IT

Bernice called Emile's name – no response. She couldn't see anything through the smoke behind her. There was nothing she could do for the kid at the moment. She returned her attention to the hatch. Her arms felt as if they were on fire. She was sweating heavily in her frock. Her heavy stage make-up had run uncomfortably into her eyes, and her grip on the locking mechanism was wet and beginning to slip.

She felt the creature on the roof put its weight against her again. It was impossibly strong. This time the hatch lifted out of its frame for a moment and Bernice felt a powerful rush of clear night air against her face.

'No . . . you . . . don't,' she hissed through gritted teeth as she tried to force the hatch back down. The Sunless on the other side must have released its grip for a second, because suddenly there was no resistance and the hatch clanged loudly home. Bernice felt a jarring shock run down her arm and she inadvertently let go of her grip for a moment.

The Sunless didn't miss the opportunity. The hatch was wrenched open and the uniformed figure was revealed above it, staring down at her.

Moving quickly – too quickly – it reached down and groped for Bernice's neck. Before she could react, its cold hands were around her throat, its fingers digging painfully into her. It began to lift her towards itself.

Throughout its attack, its face had remained completely

179

expressionless, its dark metal eyes dead. Its facial muscles seemed relaxed beneath its thin corpse-white skin. It was as if it wasn't really there at all.

Bernice's feet left the floor and she kicked out helplessly.

It pulled her further towards itself as it hung half into the vehicle. It opened its mouth, revealing rows of tiny white teeth. Impossibly sharp triangles glinting against the darkness of its mouth.

She would have screamed but her throat was being crushed.

From where Emile lay on the floor, with what felt like half a ton of blaster cannon lying on top of him, he saw Benny's feet lift off the ground and disappear upward.

The creature had got her! He'd seen it leap agilely across from the pursuing car to land on the roof. He'd tried to shoot it as it had moved towards the hatch, but he must have accidentally activated some kind of safety restraint, because the targeting mechanism wouldn't permit him to fire upon their own vehicle.

He tried to call after Bernice but his voice only cracked painfully.

Something was burning. It was probably him. His ears were still ringing from the explosion. His right arm was twisted behind him and was stinging sharply. He moved a little so that he could see over his shoulder. An angry scarlet burn mark ran from his elbow to his wrist. Seeing the injury only made the pain worse.

He wriggled out from beneath the wreckage, sniffling. His legs, arms and shoulders were covered with tiny cuts where they hadn't been protected by the sequined frock. The dress was a write-off.

The weapon turret had collapsed down into the narrow gangway which linked the front and the rear of the vehicle. Access to the front of the vehicle was now completely blocked. There was no way he could get near Bernice and her attacker. He was cut off.

She wasn't going to last long in the hands of the Sunless.

The only way out of the armoured car was the door at the back. He hit the control and the ramp slid down revealing the road stretching out behind the moving vehicle.

The car was lurching from one side of the street to the other. It hit the kerb with a thump, bounced off and then hurtled on down the middle of the road. Emile had to grip the sides of the doorway to prevent himself from being thrown out on to the road.

What the hell did Tameka think she was doing? Was she driving with her eyes closed or something?

Metal bars ran up the back of the armoured car; a long thin cage to protect the lights. If he could climb up on to the roof, then maybe he could surprise the Sunless. Maybe he could save Bernice.

Wincing against the wind, which made the angry wound on his arm burn ferociously, Emile grabbed hold of the nearest bar and edged out on to the corner of the vehicle. Slowly he began to climb up the side of the car. The bars were twisted and crushed from the impact of the crash. One of them came away in his hand as he climbed and he almost fell on to the road as it sped past him. A chill of fear shot up his spine, leaving him breathless. He stared at the ground racing beneath him for a moment before closing his eyes and clutching the side of the vehicle.

When he'd recovered, Emile found that he was still holding the bar. He hefted it in his hand. Could he use it as a weapon? Step by step, he clambered up on to the roof, the remains of his frock flapping wildly around him in the wind.

The top of the car was devastated – a massive hole was all that was left of the turret. Smoke belched from it as if from a factory chimney. The car wasn't travelling very fast, and the wind wasn't as strong as he'd imagined it would be. However, he was still forced to crawl on his hands and knees across its roof.

The Sunless had pulled Bernice half out of the hatch. It was kneeling on her chest, a patient expression on its face as it throttled the life out of her.

The look of quiet concentration on the grey-suited figure

filled Emile with rage. It would have been easier to cope with, to understand, if it had been laughing demoniacally or screaming or something. Anything. That it could look upon Bernice's traumatized face and just dispassionately kill her was the most outrageous thing he had witnessed in his whole life.

Bernice's eyes were huge, bulging horribly out of her make-up-streaked face. She was staring at him as he scuttled towards her. Imploring him? He wasn't sure. Her face was so distorted that he couldn't tell whether she could see him at all.

He scrambled to his feet, more scared than he ever remembered being. He knew that if he paused – gave himself the smallest amount of thinking space – his anger would fade and he would be overcome by terror.

Don't think about what you're doing, he told himself.

Just do it.

Emile charged the last few metres of the metal roof, pushing himself against the wind.

The Sunless must have heard the sound of his footsteps clanging against the roof because it began to twist around, showing neither surprise nor concern at his sudden appearance. This Sunless was obviously male, but somehow that wasn't enough to make Emile think of it as having a gender. In the moonlight, its face was as pale as Tameka's Vampire Chic make-up. Dark shadows highlighted its sharp cheekbones. Its glinting metal eyes stared up at him, its hands still firmly around Bernice's throat.

Despite his anger, he was vaguely unsettled to be attacking such a beautiful, calm creature.

It didn't seem to think of him as a threat at all.

And then, keeping one hand around Bernice's neck, the creature began to reach out for him. Emile swung the iron bar down against the Sunless's expressionless face. The impact jarred his wrist and made him cry out. His words were eaten by the wind.

The Sunless's head was flung back and it lost its grip on Bernice's throat. Its eyes closed for a second, its forehead creasing slightly. This slight frown was its only response to the assault. Its eyes blinked open, staring coolly up at Emile. Dark blood dripped from a wound on its shaved head. The shiny inhuman eyes filled Emile's heart with terror. Its long powerful fingers reached for his face.

Emile recovered his wits and struck it with the metal bar a second time. Then he hit it and hit it and hit it again. Rage fuelled each blow. The last time the bar smacked into its face he felt something give. Bone cracked and he felt the bar sink into softness. The Sunless stopped resisting his attacks. It tumbled over backward on to the roof of the car. The smooth shape of its skull was broken. Its face was just a bloody mess.

His rage subsided. He had done that. He had killed it. Oh my God!

Emile kicked it off the armoured vehicle and it bounced once on the road and then flopped into the gutter.

The car moved on. The body of the Sunless was eaten by the shadows and then Emile couldn't see it at all.

The smoke in the cabin began to clear and Tameka saw Bernice suddenly drop down on to the floor, landing in a crumpled heap. She was rasping and coughing and looked surprised to be alive. Emile swung down next to her, a metal bar in his hand.

'It's gone,' he said through gasps for breath. 'It's gone.'

Tameka stared at the boy for a moment. There was blood on the metal bar.

Tameka finally brought the car to a standstill by forcing it down through its drive modes. After the grinding roar of the damaged engine the quiet was tangible. They sat in the darkness for a little while saying nothing. Her ears were full of high-pitched whines and the back of her mouth was raw from swallowing bile.

Bernice didn't seem to be able to speak. She tried to give Tameka what was obviously meant to be a reassuring smile but just looked scared witless. Tameka thought that it was typical of Bernice to try to look after them when it was so obviously she who needed to be taken care of.

Every muscle in Tameka's body ached from being tensed up. She climbed out of the vehicle and shook her limbs. She assessed the damage to the vehicle to distract herself from her dizziness. The braking system was damaged but Tameka was able to do a lash-up job, salvaging parts from what remained of the weapons gear. The work took about an hour.

Occasionally Emile would stand and watch her. He didn't say anything, though. He'd wiped the make-up from his face, but was still in the ragged remains of his frock. She was so used to seeing him in the dress now that he didn't look dragged up. Just looked like Emile.

With the vehicle fixed, she drove out of the city, towards the orange ocean. She wanted to see the sea. The coastal road was completely clear and the car cruised alŏngside the beach. The smell of salt was strong in the air and she felt the skin on her face tighten as the salty air pressed against her face.

She could taste the sea on her dry lips and suddenly felt like laughing. She was alive. The feeling was strong. It felt like triumph but it was probably only shock.

They sat on the beach for a while, watching as lemon-coloured light began to trace a line along the horizon. Bernice watched her students paddling in the calm ocean, splashing each other and chasing waves. They looked exuberant, but there was an edge to their play. They were laughing a little too loudly, teasing each other hard. A release, she supposed.

She remembered Emile standing over the Sunless – a wild, uncontrolled expression on his chubby face. Hate and fear and determination. That look scared her almost as much as the blank expression of the Sunless.

Tameka and Emile were just standing in the ocean now, the remains of their dresses trailing in the water. Tameka was standing behind Emile, her arms around his shoulders. They were staring at the cool dawn light, not talking. Bernice remembered the first time she had met them on Apollox 4 – how different they had looked. She remembered how Tameka had taken charge in the armoured car. They weren't her students any more and she wasn't their tutor. They were friends – no, maybe not friends: friendship suggested choice, and they hadn't chosen each other. They probably wouldn't have chosen each other in other circumstances. But they were companions in this terrifying adventure. She found herself wondering whether they would remain as close when they got home.

If they got home.

Emile explored the armoured car as they drove back towards the town. He found a pile of Sunless uniforms stowed in a locker in the vehicle. They were plain grey and rough to the touch. He gave Bernice a set and brought an outfit for himself and one for Tameka up to the front of the vehicle. He peeled himself out of the remains of his frock and reached for the charcoal fatigues. He was totally naked, his backside freezing against the cold plastic of the navigator's seat.

'Hey,' he exclaimed, searching through the pile of clothes. 'Don't these uniforms come with jockstraps?'

He noticed Tameka glance down at his crotch as she drove. 'Honey, trust me, you don't need one.'

They abandoned the vehicle on the edge of the city and made their way back into the centre as the morning light crept slowly over the jumble of buildings.

They didn't see any sign of the Sunless or collaborators, but Ursulans in red-striped uniforms were starting to fill the streets by the time they reached the dormitory where Michael lived.

Bernice first sensed something was wrong when she saw the bedding strewn in the corridor outside the rooms. The whole building appeared to be deserted. Emile didn't appear to have noticed anything, chattering on about something inane. Tameka knew something was different. They exchanged worried glances as they stepped into the room.

Bernice's first thought was that it had been snowing in the room. It took her a few seconds to realize that it was the stuffing from the mattress. All the furniture had been

185

savagely ripped apart. The chairs and tables had been broken into sticks of wood.

There were red stains in the white cotton stuffing. Smears on the walls.

Blood.

Emile's voice died away. Bernice swallowed, barely feeling the pain in her throat.

She found Errol lying half under his bed. There was a long pencil-thin gash in one of his arms. The wound was dark against the pale brown skin under his forearm. It was a few inches long, running from his wrist up to his elbow. Bernice stared at it, unable to make sense of it for a moment. And then she realized the wound was where the intravenous life-support equipment had been linked to his veins. Someone had torn the needle from his arm, ripping out part of the vein as they had done so.

Errol was lying on his back, his eyes closed. He looked peaceful. She caressed his head. The stubble where he hadn't shaved grazed her fingers. The pockmarks on the side of his face looked deeper than ever. She couldn't see any other signs of injury, but judging by his cool temperature he was a few hours dead.

Tameka found the doctor half under a mattress. There was blood on the front of Jock's uniform. His eyes were wide open, his mouth lipstick-red with blood. There was a small hole in the centre of his chest. Bernice traced the edge of the ragged wound. Not a knife attack. Something blunt. And then she knew.

A finger.

'The Sunless did this,' she said very softly.

She was vaguely aware of Emile turning away.

'Scott,' Tameka whispered urgently, 'he isn't here.'

Michael was also missing. There was no sign him. Of either of them.

CONVERSATIONS WITH THE ENEMY

Kitzinger's respirator had finally given up on her, so she was forced to use Aric's to continue her work. He wouldn't be needing it any more. The first time she had fingered his mask she had seen that there was a tiny crack in the durable plastic, like a thick dark hair. She could feel it threaten to widen and split whenever she pulled it over her face. Every time she put the mask on she was reminded of Aric and the way she had chided him for his careless attitude to the equipment.

It had been six days since Aric had been murdered. Much to her surprise, Nikolas hadn't ordered her to be beaten. He'd just told her to go back to the hut and continue working. And she had obeyed without question, without a word.

Kitzinger was sitting at her terminal, chewing slowly on her rations when she heard Nikolas arriving. Without thinking, she tucked the parcel of food away in a pocket of her thick clothes, fearful of having it taken from her. She caught herself doing this. Once she would have felt angry – now she was infinitely weary.

She watched his shadow in the airlock. He hadn't visited her since the abortive escape attempt. Perhaps he had come to administer her punishment. Perhaps he had finally come to kill her. She retreated to the other side of the small shelter and waited for him to enter.

'I take it that you have recovered from all the excitement,' Nikolas said pleasantly when he entered and had pulled off his respirator. Ice crystals had formed on the stubble on his young face.

Excitement? Kitzinger just stared at him. He made Aric's murder sound like a street party or a Bloomday. She had no idea what to say to him. Couldn't even begin to understand him. 'What do you want of me, Nikolas?' she blurted.

He shrugged off his heavy coat and sat down in front of her. He grinned his young man's grin. 'Only for you to continue to work. To uncover the secrets of this place for me and –' he nodded to the two motionless Sunless he had brought with him '– for our hosts here.'

Kitzinger had never really considered the possibility that Nikolas was in the service of the silent pale figures. Always assuming that they were some kind of thoughtless creature he had enslaved.

'I have told you before that there are no secrets here. Just ice and rock.'

He grinned. 'Where is your imagination? You've read the inscriptions. You translated most of them. It is recorded that there is great power here.' He leant back and pulled a flask out of his heavy fur coat. 'Come, have a drink with me.'

He twisted the top off the metal flask and Kitzinger smelt coffee. *Coffee!* The richness of the smell threatened to overwhelm her. She remembered her life back on Ursu with a sudden clarity. Somehow the smell unlocked memories which she hadn't realized she still had. Lovers, friends, projects, studying, being a child in her Eight. Images were tumbling into her mind even as she was reaching out a shaking hand to accept the proffered cup.

'Why? Why are you doing this?'

Nikolas made a show of looking nonplussed. 'Doing what?'

She indicated the cup. 'All this.'

'Perhaps I like to be unpredictable. Perhaps because I don't need to threaten you any more. There is no one left for you to conspire with and, as you have seen, there is nowhere for you to go. Finish the work here and you will live, that's all.'

'Unless you choose to be unpredictable again.'

He nodded. 'Unless.' There was a long pause. 'Tell me, how goes the work?'

Kitzinger wasn't going to let herself be seduced by his sudden generosity. 'More slowly since you killed Aric,' she said, letting out some of the bitterness she felt.

Nikolas only grinned. Kitzinger was reminded of how transparent his emotions were. His smile was deeply unauthentic. He was embarrassed, maybe ashamed for what he had done. No, that wasn't right. That was just a projection – what she wanted him to feel. But she suspected that he regretted killing Aric.

'Well, I suppose that's only to be expected, but we are on a tight schedule here, Kitzinger,' he said. 'Our friends won't wait for ever.'

Kitzinger glanced over at the two silent figures in the corner of the room. If they were aware of being talked about they showed no sign of it. Was this the real reason why Nikolas was being so pleasant? Was he under pressure from the grey humanoids?

'Kitzinger? What of the Blooms?'

She turned to face him, searching for a sign of worry or fear on his face. She couldn't tell. 'The Blooms have . . . connected themselves fully to the structure. I don't understand how or why they have done that. They never showed any signs of taking root in all the time they were below the university on Ursu.'

'Well that's only to be expected, isn't it?'

'It is?'

He gestured around him. 'Well yes. This is their home after all. This is where they belong.'

Kitzinger was surprised by this suggestion. 'What makes you think that the Blooms are from this place?'

'Simply because this is the world upon which they were found.'

Kitzinger was unsettled by his suggestion. That's impossible! You're an Ursulan. You must know our history. A corporation found the Blooms abandoned on a dead world and removed them.'

'No, not a dead world,' he interrupted. 'A dying one. This is that world. The Piercy Corporation stole the Blooms from the Sunless. I'm only helping our grey friends to reclaim what is theirs.'

'I find it very hard to believe that the Sunless created something as complicated as the Blooms.'

'Created? Oh no. I should think that the Blooms predate the Sunless. I suspect that they are the descendants of the race which built the Blooms. I've managed to piece together a little of what happened, but they're not the greatest of conversationalists and they don't write history books. A party of Sunless found the permanent research base the Piercy Corporation had set up here. After learning that they had removed the Blooms, the Sunless killed the profiteers and used their spaceships as a template for a fleet of their own.'

'That would have taken decades.'

'Oh, centuries, I would have thought. But the Sunless were determined to retrieve their newly discovered ancestors' legacy.'

'And then they came to Ursu to reclaim the Blooms?'

'Not only the Blooms. The Piercy Corporation picked this place clean. We've spent the last year tracking down all of the equipment which was removed. It's been quite a task.'

'But why do this for them? You're an Ursulan. I can't believe that you're interested in profit or war.'

'No. We're not interested in money.'

'Are you intending to enslave Ursu? Dominate the world with your will?'

'Don't be ridiculous. We're not interested in that stupid little playground world. We're going to unleash the power of a sun. Now that the Sunless have learnt that they are not alone and that there are others in the universe they want the power their ancestors buried for them here. And with that we're going to be able . . . well, to do whatever we want!'

'But the Blooms are here and nothing has happened. No power. Nothing. If there ever was anything like that here it is long gone.'

190

Nikolas disagreed. 'The power only needs to be unlocked.'

'Unlocked?'

He pulled a package from his pocket. Delicately he unwrapped it and produced a small figurine. 'Key,' he said, simply.

Kitzinger was interested despite herself. 'There's no mention of any keys in the writing we've translated,' she said sceptically, as she turned the small crystal statue in her hands.

Nikolas was undeterred, quoting excitedly from the translations she had provided for him. 'The power will be unleashed by the visionaries.'

She held up the little sculpture in front of her. 'You think this is what they meant by visionary? Do you have any evidence for your suggestion? I mean at all? The writing attributes agency to the visionaries. I had rather imagined that they were people. And, anyway, there are meant to be two of them.'

'This is only half of the key.'

'So where is the other visionary then?'

'The second visionary was harder to locate, but it is being brought here as we speak.'

16

SOUR TIMES

Extract from the diary of Bernice Summerfield

We walked the streets of Anarray in silence. Nobody spoke. I don't remember where we went or for how long. We couldn't have stayed in the dormitory even if we had wanted to. The Sunless were bound to return at some point.

No one knew what to say. I was grateful that my throat was too sore to allow me to say much at all. Tameka and Emile were concerned for Scott, but were too frightened to give voice to their fears. Turning it into words would only make it more real.

Whoever had alerted the Sunless to our existence was after the artefact. Nothing else was taken, although almost all our possessions were destroyed. Which meant that Iranda was lying about its value. I had no idea what it mattered or what I could have done about it.

I didn't really care.

I watched Tameka as she picked through the remains of her belongings, salvaging her shattered make-up compacts. Emile just stood in the corner with his arms wrapped around himself looking pale. Their distress was palpable. I just wanted to take them away, magic them home.

We probably walked for miles. I was aware that my feet were hurting, but that was probably only from a night spent in stilettos. Eventually, we stopped in a small city garden and

192

sat on the grass, not looking at each other. The garden appeared to have been abandoned for quite a while, probably at the start of the Sunless occupation. The flower beds had all been left to run wild. I don't think the Ursulans bothered with their environment once they had lost their freedom.

Some kids caught sight of us in our plain Sunless uniforms and, thinking that we were collaborators, threw stones at us and called us names. Tameka tried to chase the children away but the whole thing turned into a bizarre game. The kids ran just out of her reach but didn't actually leave. Shouting and screaming with naughty pleasure. An Oolian girl kept hovering in the air above her, flapping her wings and trying to spit on Tameka, cawing excitedly like a manic crow. A short, wiry, purple-skinned Jeillo boy with no front teeth kept sticking his lilac tongue out at me and calling me a 'dirty bastard'.

There were eight children. All different colours, sizes, genders, species. They're what the Ursulans imaginatively call an Eight, a family of peers. The idealism of this society felt so pathetic, so feeble next to the violence we had witnessed. That we had experienced.

I must admit that I had been seduced by the idea of a society without rules. Until I saw the ease with which the Sunless had strolled in and killed half of the population. I just felt so incredibly angry that the Ursulans could have ever been so trusting. So naive.

In the centre of the city garden there was a notice board. It was a huge thing, black in a metal frame. Its surface was covered in messages. Some had been sent electronically, others were on paper, pinned to it with tacks. There must have been at least three hundred messages. All of them were over a year old. The electronic part of the board no longer functioned. Some messages were personal, some offering skills. Most were requests for assistance. Ursulans didn't seem to use concepts like work and play, but there were many invitations to become involved in 'projects'. Some of them sounded interesting. There were also requests for people to help with 'drudgery' – work which seemed to involve little reward and required few skills: sewer maintenance, road cleaning. But even these didn't sound so terrible as they were accompanied by other, more creative activities. A group of singers planned to write an operetta as they searched for a breach in a water pipe to an outlying village.

Emile pointed to an electronic request for adults to assist with two new Eights which were about to be birthed. The project offered to introduce Ursulans to midwifery, childcare, genetic engineering and underwater swimming. The request had been made by someone called Kitzinger. There was an address for the university.

University! The word could have spelt home. If there was one place I wanted to be on this world it was there.

It was relatively easy to find. When we entered the low sprawling buildings, we quickly saw that the Sunless had made their mark here. Half of the site had been abandoned. All the arts, humanities and social-science departments had been closed down. There were huge black scorch marks on the concrete walkways.

Book burnings. History repeating itself across time and space.

The engineering and natural-sciences departments were occupied by Ursulans in collaborators' uniforms. They didn't pay us any attention in our grey garb. We managed to break into the social-science department without being seen and set up camp in the library. The windows in the higher floors of the building were still intact. The holo equipment had all been removed, but there were still a couple of puters and even a few books strewn across the floor – spines broken, pages torn. Made me shudder. We used a few for pillows. That night, in the archaeology aisle, I wrapped my arms around Emile and Tameka and waited for them to fall asleep.

Emile had disappeared when I woke up the following morning. He didn't show up until lunchtime. Turned out he'd gone back to the dormitory looking for some jewellery of all things. Tameka said, rather dryly, that he was only conforming to type, but I didn't think Emile got the joke. It turned out to be a necklace of Scott's. Something to do with his ethical code. Apparently Scott had thrown it out of the dorm window for some reason. When I told Emile that going back for it was a crazy thing to have done, he just shrugged and looked sullen, saying that he wanted it.

'I found this,' he said, and handed me the artefact that had brought us here in the first place. I stared at it, my mind racing. It was still wrapped up in the same inscribed cloth. He said that he'd found the figurine lying outside on the scrubland when he'd been searching for the necklace. Quite how it had come to be there I could not guess.

Was this really what the Sunless had been looking for when they came? Was this really why they had killed Jock and Errol? Why they had taken Scott and Michael? Probably killed them too. Its tiny carved-out eyes stared impassively back at me, as empty and dark as those of the Sunless themselves.

The symbols on the cloth were of a similar style to those I had seen in the armoured car. None of the symbols were identical but they clearly shared a heritage. I don't know whether I was trying to run away from the horror of yesterday or try to make some meaning out of it, but I found myself sketching out a plan for a thorough investigation of the artefact. If it really was important, if the Sunless really wanted it, then I wanted to know why.

Emile managed to access the university mainframe and I used linguistic software to make a detailed translation of the spiky figures on the cloth. I must admit to being disappointed to discover that it was only the usual doomsday stuff which characterizes so many religions across the galaxy. According to the translation, the figurine represents a seer or prophet of some kind. Special sight, gift of the gods, visionary thing – that sort of stuff.

The vision of the male and the female will lead us out of the night.

The text went on like this for quite a while. Which is all very well if you're interested in doing a discourse analysis of compulsory heterosexuality in religious texts (and let me make it clear that this is one feminist who was born to deconstruct!), but less useful if you're trying to establish why someone might be willing to kill you to get their hands on the ugly little bugger.

The visionaries will give themselves up to release the power beyond the sun.

Yeah, right. Implausible as it all sounds, the translation is uncomfortably close to what Jason's girlfriend had said. But I refuse to believe this kind of tosh. I did not spend my doctoral studies tentatively exploring the possible grounds for the interpretation of cultural artefacts to then start taking hurried puter-generated translations at face value.

One thing is very clear, though. I was completely wrong about the artefact originating on this world. It must belong to the invaders. To the Sunless. I am horrified that this all may turn out to be a wild-goose chase, like that time

Extract interrupted

Bernice looked up from the few sheets of paper she was using for a journal, her pen still touching the page. The light from the small lamp barely stretched beyond the makeshift bed. Their bed of curtains was an illuminated island in the darkness of the library. The sound came again, a quiet crunching noise. Glass under foot.

Emile and Tameka were asleep beside her – no one else knew they were there. There wasn't anyone else alive to know.

And yet someone was definitely climbing up the staircase of the library.

Bernice placed her journal silently on to the floor beside her and slipped out of the bed, careful not to disturb Emile and Tameka. She trod over the tattered library books which were scattered around them, and edged towards the top of the stairwell. She could hear footsteps clearly now. They were trying to move quietly, obviously not wanting to be heard.

Bernice leant through the open door and peered down into the darkness. She saw nothing, although she imagined a whole host of terrors. She glanced back over to the glow of their camp. Had someone in the other occupied buildings seen their light and raised the alarm?

She picked up a heavy bound volume from the floor and weighed it in her hand. The footsteps reached the top of the stairs. She was preparing to smash it into the face of whoever came up the stairs when she heard Tameka's voice calling her name. Distracted, Bernice delayed her attack. By the time she had recovered her wits, the figure had already entered the library. She was struggling to lift the book above her head when a man's voice said:

'Bernice?'

Michael was standing beside her, his wide purple face almost black in the low light. He was staring anxiously up at the book she was holding.

'Michael! I thought you were dead?'

'What were you doing, making sure?'

'What?' Bernice was suddenly aware that she was still holding the weighty hardback above her head. 'Oh, I see. Sorry. I thought you might have been . . . Oh never mind. I'm just pleased that you're alive.'

Tameka had hurried over, still in her bra and knickers, she began urgently to question Michael about Scott. Emile followed her a moment later wrapped up in one of the dusty green curtains he had been sleeping beneath. Bernice led them back to their den in the archaeology aisle.

In the light of the small lamp, Michael looked tired. His heavily lidded eyes were sunken and there were dark rings beneath them. 'The Sunless were already at the dormitory by the time I got back from the gates. I saw Scott being carried out.'

'Carried?' Tameka said. 'Was he alive?'

Michael nodded. 'Yeah. I wasn't sure at first. They took him to the spaceport.'

'The spaceport?'

'He's on one of their ships. It's leaving tomorrow. Only I don't know where it's going.'

Tameka turned to Bernice. 'We've got to get him off it.'

17

WHAT TOOK YOU SO LONG?

The canvas-covered truck hissed, vapour erupting from its valve as it trundled to a stop at the high metal fence of the spaceport. Its headlights lit up the white metal gate which barred the entrance.

'This is the one?' Bernice asked from where they had hidden themselves in the shadows on the other side of the road. She shivered, which was only partly due to the chilly Ursu evening.

Michael nodded. 'It's full of sensor equipment. It's being loaded tonight.'

Bernice waited until the driver was engrossed with the female collaborator at the gate, and then she turned to Emile and Tameka, who were crouched beside her. 'Go!'

They hurried across the road, Emile a little behind Tameka. Tameka clambered up the tailgate of the truck and then helped Emile up. He tumbled gracelessly over the top and then disappeared inside.

'Now you,' Bernice said to Michael. He nodded and ran lightly across the road.

Bernice was about to set off after him when the driver appeared around the side of the truck. She held her breath as the driver checked several of the clips on the canvas cover, before returning to the cab. He hadn't seen Michael.

Bernice began to sprint across the road just as the steam truck began to power up. It clanked and hissed into gear and began to lurch forward. Bernice increased her pace and managed to grab hold of the tailgate. The truck was moving very slowly, but it was still an effort for her to match its pace on foot.

If the collaborator on the gate turned now she wouldn't be able to avoid seeing her. Bernice realized that there was no way she was going to be able to lift herself into the truck while it was moving. She just couldn't get any leverage. She glanced sideways at the yellow light which streamed out of the gate hut. Oh God, she was in full bloody view.

And then Michael reached down and lifted her up with one hand. She collapsed into the welcome darkness of the truck.

She lay there listening for the sounds of alarms and booted feet, but they didn't come.

Bernice opened the lid of the crate and peeped out. There were no people in the cargo bay, no Sunless either. Telling her companions to stay put, she eased out of the metal box and began to explore the ship. The corridors were rusty metal. The air was filled with the smell of old grease and sweat. Michael appeared at her side. 'I thought you were going to stay with Emile and Tameka.'

'Two of us have more chance of finding him than one.'

'And twice as much chance of getting caught.'

All the rooms they checked on the transport were empty. Most of them were quarters for the Sunless being brought to Ursu.

First-class accommodation it wasn't.

The smell was worse here. The whole place stank. Stank like the zoo or concentrated essence of teenage boy. The smell was so strong Bernice could almost taste it on the inside of her mouth as if it were a vapour. Sweet and rank on her tongue. She hadn't seen any sanitary facilities – maybe the Sunless didn't wash. There was no sign of Scott.

She heard the sounds of boots in the corridor. Sunless. Heading in their direction.

'Quick, hide,' she hissed to . . . no one at all. Michael was no longer at her side. He'd completely disappeared. Cursing silently, she moved back into the corridor.

The Sunless were very close now. If Michael was in the corridor there wasn't anything she could do to help him.

She looked around for somewhere to hide. The room was metal and bare except for the hexagonal bunks which were drilled into the walls of the rooms. To Bernice it looked like banks of human-sized honeycomb, reminding her of crawl-in hotel rooms back on the heavily populated cities on Earth. Or a morgue. Thankfully they were all empty. It occurred to her that the hexagonal slots might have been some kind of suspended-animation device for long journeys.

She climbed up to one of the top bunks and crawled in. It contained a thin mattress and a small shelf for food. She heard movement in the room. No speaking but more shuffling than you'd expect for a person alone. Which meant that there were two, possibly three, Sunless in the room with her.

She almost yelled in fear when she heard the Sunless begin to climb up the tubes towards her. They must have heard her. Perhaps known all along that she was there! She pushed her way to the back of the long tube, pressing her back to the wall. She glanced around the tiny space, but there was nothing she could use to defend herself.

So she waited for one of the crew-cut heads to appear at the hexagonal opening and for one of the expressionless creatures to reach for her. She waited. The only measure of time she had was the frantic beating of her heart. She could still hear them moving about. And then she heard the sound of bodies against mattresses.

They were going to bed. It was hard to believe but they were just going to bed. They didn't know she was there. Bernice waited until her heart slowed before she slipped off her boots, crept down out of her bunk and slipped out of the room.

The lighting was low in the corridors. So was the ceiling. Bernice moved slowly, padding softly on the metal floor, terribly aware that more of the Sunless could appear at any moment. She had just reached an intersection when she glimpsed a flash of purple moving ahead of her. Just for a second and then it was gone. Michael?

She hissed his name under her breath. Nothing. Reluctantly she crept after him. Finally, blinking rapidly as her eyes tried to adjust to the light, she entered what could only be the bridge and caught sight of Michael standing respectfully next to the command chair.

'Ah Benny,' the red-haired woman seated in the chair said. 'I may call you Benny, mayn't I? Jason always did.' Iranda flashed Bernice an impish grin as she delicately crossed her legs. All her earlier nervousness had disappeared to be replaced by smug amusement. 'What kept you so long?'

On a screen behind the command chair, Bernice saw a recording of a grey-suited figure chasing after a truck at the gates of the spaceport. The camera was quite far away and the light-enhanced picture was grainy, but she didn't have any trouble recognizing herself. The tiny Bernice on the screen looked completely ridiculous, hanging on to the back of the truck and making little unsuccessful attempts to hop aboard.

It was humiliating.

'Benny, you look surprised. Did you really think that you and your little friends could have broken into this spaceship if I hadn't planned for it?'

Little friends? Bernice cursed to herself. Iranda had actually referred to Emile and Tameka in those patronizing terms at the collaborators' party and Bernice hadn't picked up on it. Iranda had no reason to know that Bernice hadn't come to Ursu alone. Bernice kicked herself for being so stupid.

'Actually,' Iranda began smugly, 'it was quite an effort on our part to stop several loyal spaceport personnel from raising the alarm.'

Har bloody har. All the woman needed was a one-piece Lycra catsuit.

Bernice watched Iranda nod to a Sunless seated at the helm. The expressionless humanoid began to prepare the craft for takeoff and a few moments later Bernice felt the ship tremble beneath her as it lifted gently away from the planet.

'Going somewhere, are we?' Bernice remarked.

Iranda deliberately ignored her question. It was such an obvious display of power that Bernice almost laughed out loud. In that moment she realized that Iranda was much younger than she first thought. No more than nineteen or twenty.

'Oh *good*, I do like a mystery tour.' She turned to Michael. 'I presume that Scott isn't really on board. Is he dead too?'

'No, he's safe,' Iranda said before Michael got the chance. 'He wouldn't tell us where the visionary was, said he didn't know. But you know, don't you, Benny?'

'You did all of this – killed people – for that bloody lump of rock?'

'Please don't change the subject.'

Bernice gave Iranda a withering look. 'Just tell me about Jason. What have you done with him?'

CONVERSATIONS WITH THE ENEMY

'Don't argue, Kitzinger. Just do it!'

'It won't make any difference. What do think is going to happen? Someone appear out of the floor and hand you this doomsday weapon?'

'Do it!' He was really angry with her now.

She had felt some of her old strength returning since she realized that he was never going to let her go home. She had begun to accept the inevitability of her death and with that came a curious release.

The stone disc was built into the very centre of the large crystal chamber, directly between the two domed shapes of the Blooms. It hadn't taken them long to find the small recess just below the centre of the circle.

'Oh well . . .' She shrugged and placed the small figurine into the small indentation in the floor of the chamber.

Above her the crystal lattice which made up the roof of the cavern lit up like a chandelier. It was dazzling. One half of the chamber, the other side from where they stood, remained in shadow. Beside them, close to the centre of the circle of symbols, the floor dropped away to reveal a large rectangular indentation. Kitzinger took a few steps backward. For a second she imagined a figure rising up with some ghastly gun in its hands. But no one did appear.

Nikolas raised an eyebrow. He tugged his respirator away from his face for a moment. 'Would you like to revise your theories now, Kitzinger?' he said. His voice sounded thin and insubstantial in the rarefied atmosphere.

Kitzinger ignored him. She moved over to the rectangular hole which had appeared in the ground. There was a humanoid-shaped indentation in the base of the pit.

'It really is a grave!' Nikolas gasped from beside her. His voice was muffled by his mask. 'But . . . but who for?'

Kitzinger shrugged, feeling too far out of her depth even to speculate. The walls of the 'grave' – if that's what it really was – were covered in more of the spiky symbols. The translation software in the hut would make swift work of it. Kitzinger began to make a copy of it. Some of the symbols were already familiar to her from her work over the last year. Translating the images had been fairly straightforward. Vision. Light. Future. Power. Sun. Linking these concepts into a coherent sentence was an entirely different task. Placing the symbols in a structure involved entering into a relationship with the images. It was impossible to discover how they related to one another without applying her own frame of reference. It was just so much guesswork.

When she had completed her notes, Nikolas removed the visionary from its niche. The roof of the chamber immediately fell into darkness. Nikolas removed the mask again. 'I told you there was power here,' he said in a husky whisper, his voice filled with awe.

She looked up into the now darkened shadows. She had been so sure that he was wrong, that he was chasing an egotistical fantasy. Until now. Now she wasn't sure of anything. Except that if there was something here, Nikolas was the last person in the universe who ought to have access to it.

He began to move off, still carrying the figurine. 'Nikolas,' she called after him, 'may I keep the figurine – just for a short time?'

He frowned. 'Why? What do you want with it?' he asked, suspiciously.

'I'm not sure. I may be able to progress more quickly with the work if I can examine it in detail.'

There was a long pause. 'Very well.'

She felt his eyes upon him as she walked back to the pressurized hut. When she reached the door, she dropped down on to one knee, pretending to tend to the strap of her boot. She quickly found a lump of crystal which was approximately the same size as the figure she held in her other hand.

Later, after she had eaten, she pulled the crumbling lump of crystal out of her suit and, using her cutlery, began to carve into it.

18

STAND OFF

'Give me the visionary.'

'Where's Jason?'

'Just give me the visionary, Benny.'

'If you mean the figurine, you're out of luck.' She pointed to the metal floor of the bridge. 'It's back on Ursu.'

'Oh come on, Benny, do were really have to go through this? We both know it's in your rucksack.'

'I'm telling you, it's back at the university on Ursu.'

'No,' Iranda said, a little wearily. 'It is in your rucksack.'

'And what exactly makes you think that?'

'Michael saw you put it there earlier this evening.'

'Ah,' Bernice said, rather lamely. Bugger. 'And what if I don't want to give it to you?'

'Then one of the Sunless will come and take it from you. I think you know by now that they are not gentle creatures.'

Bernice had been expecting something like this. In one movement, she swung her rucksack off her back and pulled the figurine out, lifting it high above her head. 'Do that and I'll smash it,' she said, filling her voice with as much certainty as she could manage.

Iranda smiled, but looked unsettled. Again Bernice thought that the woman was not as confident as she tried to suggest with her camp villainess routine. Why was she bothering with the act?

'I'm not sure that you actually could damage the visionary, Bernice.'

'Well, let's see, shall we?' She tossed the artefact between her hands. 'I'm willing to have a bash.'

Bernice knew that this kind of stand-off was unlikely to go in her favour. She wasn't entirely sure what her next move ought to be. Negotiate for all of their freedom or just try to back slowly out of the room? The ship was now in flight – where were the life rafts? Would a Sunless ship have them? Her chances of getting everyone into one and away before the Sunless managed to get their hands on them were pretty low. And then what?

She saw Iranda surreptitiously touch the controls of her chair. 'Don't touch anything!' Bernice snapped, but it was too late. Behind Iranda, a viewscreen flickered and then flared into life, showing an image of the hold where Bernice had left Tameka and Emile. Tameka had climbed out of the crate they had hidden in and was pacing about impatiently. Emile was standing in the crate, his elbows resting on its lip.

Iranda adjusted another control and suddenly the bridge of the ship was filled with their tinny voices.

'I can't believe you won't give me Scott's necklace, 'Meel. It's all I've got to remind myself of him.'

'He said I could have it. It's mine!'

'So! What can it mean to you?'

'What about that Jeillo bloke of yours on Dellah?'

'That is, like, *none* of your business, Emile. Just give me the thing.'

Iranda made a show of listening to the tinny voices argue. 'You profiteers, you just don't stop talking about things, do you?' She activated another control and warning klaxons began to sound deep in the ship.

'What are you doing?' Bernice said, anxiously. The figurine began to feel heavy above her head.

The speakers which had been relaying Emile and Tameka's argument were suddenly full of the whistling screech of depressurization.

The argument stopped abruptly. 'Oh shit,' a voice swore

fearfully over the howl. Bernice glanced up at the screen, unable to tell whether it was Emile or Tameka who had spoken. The two students were hanging on to the lip of the crate. Tameka's long dark hair was suddenly flying around her head.

Bernice moved forward. 'Stop it now or I promise you I'll destroy the artefact,' Bernice yelled. She looked up at the screen: the huge, metre-thick doors of the hold shuddered and began to move apart. 'Oh my God! You'll kill them!'

Iranda just smiled.

'Grab my hand,' Emile shouted. He felt his words sucked out through the thin dark crack in the doors. The hold was suddenly freezing. The air was thin and bit into the walls of his throat when he breathed. The pressure was shocking, pushing him against the side of the crate. It was hard to pull a breath into his lungs.

Tameka had been standing on the other side of the crate when the doors had begun to open. There was nothing between her and the doors. Nothing to stop her from being drawn out.

'I can't hold on,' she howled fearfully. She was clinging on to the smooth metal lip of the crate by her fingers. Emile could see that she wasn't going to be able to maintain her grip for long. Her fingers squeaked as they began to slip.

He grabbed hold of her wrists and held on as tightly as he could. The pressure squeezing him against the side of the crate kept him firmly lodged in place.

Tameka screamed as her feet were pulled out from underneath her and she was suddenly floating horizontally in front of him. Her eyes were wide with fear, staring madly at him. She was cursing repeatedly. And then she lost her grip on the crate.

Emile screamed as he took her whole weight. The pressure on his chest increased, he tried to take a breath but couldn't. His body wasn't used to this – his grip on Tameka's wrists began to falter as his fingers began to ache painfully.

'Emile!' Tameka screamed. 'Don't let go of me!'

Behind her, in the darkened gap between the doors, Emile thought he glimpsed a star.

He lost his purchase on one of her hands. Tameka screamed wordlessly and swung out away from him. He hung on to her remaining arm with both hands. The air in the hold tore around his ears. His fingers were going numb with the cold. He couldn't breathe.

The pressure which pushed him against the wall of the crate increased until he could feel his ribcage begin to flatten. Slowly his body began to slide up, out of the crate. His hands occupied, Emile tried to brace himself against the metal walls with his legs. No good.

They were going to be sucked into space.

Bernice looked away from the screen and turned to Iranda. 'Which controls close the hold doors?'

'Give me the visionary and I will show you.'

'I'll destroy it! Just shut the doors now!'

'Shan't!' Iranda said, with obvious relish. 'Make me.'

Bernice glanced at the screen for a second. The tiny figure of Emile was hanging on to the box with one hand and to Tameka with the other. They looked like a human washing line. The hold doors were almost halfway open. Small boxes and tools hurtled past them, and out through the doors into the darkness. He wasn't going to be able to hold on for more than a few seconds.

'OK, OK, you win.' Bernice dropped the figurine into Iranda's lap. 'For Christ's sake, just get them out of there.'

Iranda lifted the figurine and examined it for a moment, her button nose wrinkling with melodramatic displeasure as she brushed away some imaginary dirt from its crude crystal face.

Bernice glanced at the controls on the arm of the chair. There were many of them and they were complex. There was no way that she would be able to work out which one operated the doors in time. 'Come on, don't play games with me, Iranda,' her voice sounded feeble, childish. 'Please. Close the doors.'

After what felt like an age, Iranda looked up at Bernice. 'No,' she said.

Emile's arms were being pulled out of their sockets. He'd made a lunge for the top of the crate as he'd slid out. Now he was literally hanging by the fingertips of his left hand, Tameka dangling from his right. His eyes were closed and his lungs ached from the lack of air. The pain in his fingertips was so intense that he had a horrible feeling that they were going to just snap.

He had been hanging like this for about five seconds but it felt like a thousand hours. He wasn't going to be able to hold on for more than an instant longer. They were going to die. He was going to die. Sucked out into icy nowhere. Frozen death.

Tameka screamed as her arm slipped a few centimetres in his grip.

The pain in his left hand was so intense that he knew he was going to have to let Tameka go. He was going to need his right hand to climb back into the crate. He was going to have to let her hurtle out into nothing. The pain in his fingers was unbearable, as if they were being bitten or pushed into deadly acid.

Where the hell was Bernice? Didn't she bloody know what was going on? He shouldn't be here! He was fifteen! He shouldn't be having to do this! She was his teacher! Why wasn't she doing something?

The pain was just too much and he lost his grip on the lip of the crate.

In the tiny instant before he was going to be dragged out into space, Emile knew that this was all his fault. If he hadn't lied about his age on the university admissions form, then none of this would have happened. Then he would be still tucked up at home on the relay station. Still disappointing Father. He'd been so glad to run away, so pleased with his ingenuity at conning his way into St Oscar's. And now he was going to die in space and Father would never know what happened to him. Never know why he hadn't even said goodbye.

He would never know.

Bernice landed on the floor of the bridge cracking her head against its metal grating. She tasted blood in her mouth: Iranda had hit her hard. She was struggling to her feet even as the Sunless moved swiftly towards her. She was just in time to see the tiny grey-suited figure of Emile lose his grip, and he and Tameka shot across the hold towards the gaping hole into space.

'No!' she screamed. Grey arms grabbed hold of her roughly. She fought against them but their grip was like metal. '*No!*'

19

A Thin Line Between Love And Crime And Collaboration

Out of the corner of her eye, Iranda saw a purple hand reach down for one of the needle-thin levers on the arm of the command chair. The whistling sound stopped abruptly. She turned to see Michael staring defiantly at her. 'Brother?'

'I've reactivated the field in the hold.'

'I know what you've done,' she sneered. 'Why?'

He just shrugged his thick shoulders. Iranda turned to the screen. The Summerfield woman's friends were lying in a heap, only inches from the open doors. They looked shaken but alive. The stars were still visible beyond the doors, sharp pinpoints of light against the blackness.

'There was no need to kill them,' Michael said. 'You've got what you wanted.'

Iranda sighed. It didn't matter whether they lived or died. Their predicament and Bernice's reaction to it had only served as a distraction from the Ache. Suddenly Iranda just wanted to be on her own.

Michael didn't look surprised when she ordered him to be locked up with the others. He just stood there staring at her, waiting for the Sunless to restrain him.

Iranda fled the bridge and hurried to her quarters. She splashed water over her face and drank some from her cupped hand. She hadn't eaten or drunk anything all day. She felt the cold water carve out an icy path to her stomach. It only served to highlight the Ache. She sighed and collapsed on her bed. The pain was getting stronger all the time. When she had first become aware of it in her early teens, it had felt like an emotion, like grief. In recent years it felt as if it were physically attacking her body, eating her away from the inside. She wanted to sleep but there was no respite there. The Dream would come to torment her or else force her awake, back into the tormenting embrace of the Ache.

She wanted to scream, to try to release the discomfort, but she was all too aware of the Sunless in the rooms and corridors around her. It was dangerous to show distress or emotion of any kind around them. They didn't articulate it, but Iranda could feel their disapproval of emotional outbursts.

Handling the Sunless wasn't easy. Often Iranda suspected that she didn't handle them at all. The reverse in fact. On some occasions they would do exactly as they were told. As if they saw Iranda and Nikolas as their natural superiors. At other times, they simply refused even to acknowledge their presence. As if the two Ursulans didn't exist at all. The Sunless were completely without egos. It was as if they didn't mind following orders when it suited them because they didn't have to prove themselves at all. Only the promise of providing them with the weapon maintained her delicate relationship with them.

At least she would be seeing Nikolas soon. At least there was one person who knew, who understood. Someone who knew the pain. She cradled the small figurine to her stomach as if it might ease the torment. 'Soon,' she moaned into the pillow. 'Let it happen soon.'

'You shit!' Tameka swore when the Sunless had left them alone in the cell together. Tameka was at least a foot and a half shorter than Michael and was as thin as he was wide. This didn't stop her from punching him hard around the face. He buckled over, gasping. The muscular man didn't try to defend himself at all, didn't even cover his face. Tameka brought her knee up under his jaw. Hard.

Bernice heard teeth crack. Michael fell to the floor coughing, blood flooded over his lips and spilt down his purple chin. His broad, round face creased in agony but still he didn't speak.

'Enough!' Bernice yelled, pushing Tameka away. The suddenness of the assault had shocked her. It had taken her a few moments to coordinate her mind and body sufficiently to intervene. 'That is enough!'

'Let ... me ... go ...' Tameka hissed through gritted teeth as she struggled against Bernice.

'Calm down!' Bernice pushed the young woman against the back wall of the dank spaceship cell. She tried to attract Tameka's gaze, but the young woman was staring past her, her stained blue eyes flashing with hatred.

Tameka stabbed a finger at Michael. 'You're dead, do you hear me?' Her husky voice was cracking with anger. 'Dead!'

Bernice put herself in Tameka's line of sight. 'Just shut up! Just shut up! For God's sake.'

'Bernice! What are you trying to protect him for? He killed them. Errol. Jock. Led the bastards right to us!'

'I know, I know. And he saved your life.'

'What?'

'Who do you think saved you back in the hold? Why do you think that he's in here with us?'

'I don't care! He's got to pay for what he's done,' Tameka said, but Bernice felt all of the struggle go out of the young woman. Tameka slumped against the wall and put her head in her hands. 'I just don't understand how he could do that. To us. To his brother.'

Bernice put her arm around Tameka's shoulder and they slid down to the floor together. 'I know, I know.'

Bernice looked over at Michael. He was kneeling on the floor, his hand over his mouth. He met her gaze for a moment and then looked away.

Emile had been standing quietly in the corner throughout the fight. He moved over to where Bernice and Tameka were sitting, joining them on the floor. Bernice pulled him to her, rubbing her hand through his stubbly crew cut.

214

Bernice looked over at Michael. 'Well?' she asked, strangely calm. 'Why did you give us up to them?'

Michael backed away to the far wall. The empty floor was like a metal desert between them. 'Just leave me alone,' he spat, his voice distorted by the painful wound in his mouth. 'What do you know about any of it, anyway?'

'Try me,' Bernice said.

He shook his head bitterly and Bernice suddenly realized how angry he was. Earlier she'd attributed his quietness to shame, but now she could see that she had completely misjudged him. He wasn't guilty or embarrassed: he was furious.

'You dare sit there and judge me,' he snapped suddenly and then had to stop speaking to mop up some blood which escaped from the side of his mouth. He winced at the pain, but he must have wanted to speak more than it hurt. 'You blame me for all that's happened?'

'You think this is somehow all my fault?' Bernice said, genuinely surprised at the accusation.

'Well, who was it who created this situation? Who was it who dragged my brother into this mess?'

'He offered to help. You're the one who sold him out.'

Michael ignored the accusation. 'Of course he wanted to help. You don't know him at all. He's lived in a village all his life. Hardly ever seen the Sunless before you came. Spent his whole life talking politics out of his arse and idolizing Leon and all his long words. Then you dropped out of the sky and suddenly he'd got his noble mission, a cause. He'd got his chance to prove that he's the great Ursulan he always boasted he was. And what do you do? We're in the middle of an invasion here and you stroll around the city like tourists. You may as well have worn a pink neon sign saying "Profiteer: arrest me". And you think your individualism is heroic. But your heroics over your dying friend just got Jock killed.'

'Bernice didn't kill Jock,' Tameka shouted. 'You did!'

Michael laughed coldy. 'He was dead the second you took him out of the hospital. You've seen the Sunless but you don't understand them at all. People have been murdered for far less than leaving their posts. People have been killed for *thinking* about resisting the Sunless. Jock could never have gone back to the hospital. He had nowhere to go. He was a dead man.'

'Then what were you doing by informing on us?' Bernice asked, feeling increasingly uncomfortable but still feeling angry. 'Just making sure?'

'Fourteen people had informed on you within twelve hours of you arriving in the city.'

'What?' Bernice couldn't believe it. 'Who?'

'People in the dorm. People who'd seen you on the street. You stand out. You're loud. You attract attention to yourselves. You egoize. And that's dangerous. No one wanted you around them. No one even wanted you *near* them. They knew that you'd bring the Sunless down upon them.'

'What are you saying? That you didn't inform on us? That you're not a collaborator?'

'Oh I am a collaborator,' Michael said, his voice dangerously low. 'And I did inform on you. Only I asked Iranda to use her influence to allow me to get Scott out of there first. To take him home.'

'Why would she do that?'

'Because despite what has happened to her – what *is* happening to her – Scott is still her brother.' He wiped the blood on his hand on the leg of his plain grey uniform, leaving a dark smear behind. '*Our* brother.'

Emile had tucked himself under Bernice's arm, resting his head on her chest. He only half heard the argument between Michael and Bernice, catching some words and phrases. He couldn't follow much of what was being said and at the moment he didn't really care. He felt safe and warm in Bernice's embrace. He was alive and that was all that mattered.

He cradled his left hand in the palm of his right. His fingers were burning hotly, as if they were being attacked by a war party of chilblains.

In his mind's eye he saw himself hurtling head over heels towards the gaping blackness – and then suddenly he had hit

216

the floor of the hold, coughing and retching and desperately trying to get oxygen back into his burning lungs. His ribcage ached terribly – his whole chest was racking-cough sore.

That wasn't the worst of it though. The most frightening thing of all – the thing he couldn't get out of his mind – was the fact that he had almost died. Once he'd lost his grip on the side of the crate and been sent flying towards open space, he'd been absolutely sure that his life was over. One hundred per cent sure.

Bang bang, Emile's dead.

Despite everything that had happened since he'd left home, he'd somehow never questioned that he was going to make it through this. Until now.

Now he felt very fragile. He was suddenly acutely aware that he was a prisoner on a spaceship full of killers. And that, just because Bernice was an adult and his teacher and everything, it didn't mean that she was a superhero. However cool she tried to be, she was a human being, not invulnerable like Mr Misnomer – the Man of Chrome – or Atoma or Comrade 7. She wasn't necessarily going to be able to keep him alive. Wasn't necessarily going to be able to make everything all right.

Hey, Emile, he told himself, you better take an interest in what's going on around you.

Michael was still sitting curled up on the other side of the cell, talking quietly. Emile pulled his face out of Bernice's embrace, surreptitiously wiping his eyes on her uniform as he did so, and started to listen. Carefully.

'They moved through the city slowly – a few streets at a time. They would set up a camp in the middle of a square or at a crossroads. Just sackfuls of plain grey uniforms and a whole pile of batons. Anywhere where locals might congregate. Then they'd herd the people together under the watchful eye of their armoured cars and tell the crowd to make a choice to cooperate or not. It was made clear that those who wouldn't cooperate would be killed. I was caught with about a hundred others. We were left to decide. Slowly people began to drift apart, not looking at each other. You could smell the fear and recrimination in the air. And then those who had chosen to collaborate were given clubs and told to kill everyone in the other camp.'

'Oh my God!' Emile felt his mouth fall open in horror. Michael met his gaze, his large heavily lidded eyes unreadable.

'What did you do?' Emile whispered.

'I chose to live. So I took up a club, weighed it in my hand, and then I killed seven people.'

Emile swallowed, remembering how he had considered letting go of Tameka's hand in the hold. He had heard her cry out to him, begging him to keep her alive, and still he had known that he would have let her go eventually. If his fingers hadn't slipped he would've let her die in order to try to save himself. Once he'd realized that Bernice wasn't going to save them he would have done anything to stay alive. Anything at all.

Tameka looked over to him and smiled. She'd been all over him in the hold afterwards, hugging him, holding him, thanking him. Words spilling out of her. Calling him her Captain Space Boyee. Way out of character. Completely hysterical, in fact. She'd given him all the attention he had always secretly wanted from her. And it had felt good. He'd felt like a hero. Like the Man of Chrome himself.

He didn't feel like that now. He was going to have to stop reading comics.

'Where is this ship going? Where are they taking us?' he asked, suddenly wanting to be involved.

'Don't you know?' Michael sneered.

'He wouldn't ask, if he knew, dick-for-brains,' Tameka said scornfully.

'We're going to the Sunless's world. We're going to their home.'

20

DOWN AMONG THE DEAD MEN

Extract from the diary of Bernice Summerfield

We sat in an uncomfortable silence as the ship shuddered and lurched through the atmosphere like some poorly maintained theme-park ride, taking us down to where we did not know. I didn't know what else to say to Michael. There was an element of the absurd about the situation. The grotesque. I mean, what do you say to someone who has done something so vile? My anger was just too big, like an avalanche of emotion. If I started to let it out, it would consume me, bury me. And if I did let it out then I knew that I would have to face my part in this.

The ship finally landed after practically shaking my brains out of my ears. My teeth chattered violently and I bit my tongue. The sharp stinging pain distracted me from the presence of the Sunless who led us silently through the dull metal corridors of the ship and into the airlock. Their movements were coordinated, walking in step, but fluid, with none of the jerkiness or rigidity I still associate with androids. What kind of people could they be? They handed us respirators, which I thought did not bode well for the conditions outside. I asked one of them why we needed them but it ignored me.

The outer hatch opened and I gasped as the cold hit us.

A swirl of icy snow was blown in on a wave of arctic air that was so cold that it literally ripped the breath from my lungs. The air was painfully thin. I gratefully pulled the respirator over my head under the dark watchful eye of the Sunless. I realized then why I find them so unsettling: they have the stares of corpses. Flat and unfocused. If it was amused by my distress it didn't show it. I don't think that they can feel amusement. I waited to hear the tiny compressor inside the respirator begin to whine before I stepped out of the ship.

Cold was not the word for it. I would have needed a three-inch-thick thesaurus committed exclusively to describing low temperatures to even begin to describe the planetary conditions. The Sunless didn't seem to be affected by either the low temperature or the rarefied atmosphere, striding calmly out into the blizzard, not even blinking against the hail. I tucked my hands into my armpits and cringed from the attack of scarlet hailstones as I made my way down the ramp and on to the rocky surface.

And then I knew why the Ursulans called them the Sunless. Above the barren landscape hung a bloated pale-pink sun that just about ate up the whole bloody sky. Its outer layers were already beginning to peel away to form a gritty cloud of planetary nebula. Despite its size and the scarlet light which invested the arctic landscape, it gave out little heat. It was dying. Puffing itself up before it collapsed for ever, like a patient with a terminal condition taking one last deep breath before the end.

I stared up at it for a few moments, and I remember thinking that it didn't look real. Its pinkness made it seem almost magical. I was reminded of pantomime and cute students, and all those other things that are best enjoyed from a certain distance. I had just enough time to see a line of ugly black ships resting on pincer-shaped legs, stretching away into the storm, before I was pushed back into line. I meekly followed my captors down through a dark portal in the rocky surface and into blackness. Into their subterranean home.

I wasn't surprised to learn that the Sunless lived beneath

the ground. Their home was dark and cold, and it smelt bad.
Reptile-house bad.

Extract ends

They were led through a series of long spiralling tunnels, and on to ramps which sloped sharply downward. The walls were made of some dark rock, supported by a network of thick metal girders. Rust streaks bled on to the surface of the rock. Low orange glow lamps had been installed along the metal scaffolding. Small vermin scurried in between the lights or dropped down, oily coats glistening, to skid and skitter on the icy floors.

No one in the party screamed at this or did any more than soberly avoid stepping directly on to the ratlike creatures.

We have greater fears to face, Bernice thought.

There were niches cut into the wall, what looked like living quarters of some kind. Bernice thought it curious that while there was much evidence of high-level technology, the actual standards of living were pitiful. She pondered whether they might have been deliberately arranged this way. Like some faiths which require their followers to abandon the comforts of life. It didn't feel deliberate. Their guides moved through the abandoned warren of tunnels, oblivious to their surroundings. She began to suspect that it just never occurred to them that there might be better ways to live.

The underground maze was almost completely abandoned. Only occasionally did Bernice spot human-shaped shadows in the darkness. They didn't approach. How many Sunless were left on this world? Was the invasion complete? Or was this underground nightmare far away from where most of the Sunless on the planet lived?

The journey came wordlessly to an end by a series of black pits in the ground.

'Down,' one of their captors said, its face contorting slightly as it spoke as if struggling to articulate a language not its own. Benny glimpsed its sharp teeth as it spoke and decided to obey.

She walked to the edge of the hole, which was rough and

broken. There was nothing to give an indication of its depth.

Emile and Tameka were looking on in horror. Probably mirroring the expression on her own face. One of the Sunless prodded Michael towards the pit, but he resisted. It slipped its arm around his neck and for a moment Bernice thought it was going to kill him. Instead, it abruptly kicked his legs out from underneath him and he hit the edge of the hole before plummeting down, howling in fear and pain. Almost immediately they heard him hit the bottom and curse.

Somewhat reassured, Bernice lowered herself gingerly over the edge, her feet dangling in blackness for a moment, and then she dropped into nothing.

Her feet hit the ground and skidded on something metal. She ended up sprawled on her backside with a sore ankle. She heard rather than saw Emile and Tameka lower themselves down after her.

Bernice heard them call her name and she reached for their hands in the darkness. She was aware that Michael was somewhere around them.

He'd have to hold his own hand.

'Wait,' a harsh voice commanded from up above them.

There was a long pause. After a few minutes, Bernice thought that she could hear singing or chanting in the distance. Young voices, she decided. She was probably beginning to hallucinate.

'Well this is *real* nice, Bernice,' Tameka said eventually. Her defiant voice brought Bernice's mind back into focus. Tameka's tone was assertive and confident, but still sounded shaky. 'Well, Professor, you want to speculate on the purpose of this construction?'

'At least they want us alive,' Bernice replied. 'We'd be dead if they didn't.'

She heard something move around her. Metal sounded against metal dully. Bernice grabbed hold of their hands more tightly.

Please don't let there be something else down here with us, she pleaded. An image entered her mind unbidden: the large ratlike creatures spilling over the lip of the hole, falling on

222

them, around their feet, piling up around their legs.

Bernice called Michael's name.

'Yeah, it's only me. There's a cup and a bowl here. They're empty. Cutlery too. Someone's been down here before us.'

'A prison!' Emile said suddenly. 'We're in a prison, like solitary confinement or something.'

'Let me see.' She groped the darkness until she touched the cold metal of the cup and bowl. Her hand brushed Michael's. It was warm in the cold. Without consciously having decided to, she asked him if he was OK. He only grunted something in reply.

The items were small. Child-size. Suddenly Bernice could hear the chanting voices clearly. They had been in the background most of the time they had been in the pit, only she hadn't been aware of them. 'It's not a prison,' she said, suddenly realizing exactly where they were. The pits were clearly the Sunless's idea of detention. 'It's a school,' she said.

Tameka listened as Bernice clambered on to Michael's shoulders and scrabbled for the top of the hole. 'No good, can't reach,' Bernice muttered, her voice straining with the effort. Tameka heard her jump back down.

'We could try it with three,' Michael suggested.

'I've always wanted to join the circus,' Tameka said.

'Me too!' Emile piped up, entirely missing her sarcastic tone.

Their first few attempts were disastrous. Tameka could easily stand on Michael's shoulders but Bernice kept toppling the tower when she tried to climb up over them. Finally, with Michael crouching on the floor, Tameka sitting on his shoulders, Bernice was able to clamber up. Tameka felt Michael's body quivering beneath her as he straightened his legs.

'Got it!' Tameka heard Bernice grunt. Bernice's weight disappeared from her shoulders. Tameka dropped down on to the floor, eager not to stay in physical contact with the big man. They heard nothing from Bernice for a couple of minutes. Tameka was beginning to panic when she heard boots crunching on the tunnel floor above her. A green bulb appeared high above. Tameka was forced to blink rapidly a few times before she saw Bernice's head peering over the edge of the pit in the unearthly light.

'Hang on,' Bernice said.

There was a pause and Tameka heard the sound of scuffling for a moment and then a chain-link rope ladder was thrown down. Michael ascended first, his huge feet struggling to find the narrow rungs. Like the prison itself, the ladder was clearly designed for children. Tameka was relieved when he reached the top without breaking the damn thing. She turned, wanting Emile to go up before her.

The boy was standing in the middle of the pit, holding the cup and bowl in his hands. They were battered and filthy, just as he was. In fact, she could easily imagine that Emile was a young Sunless, in his grey uniform and crew-cut head. She wondered if they were thrown down here for missing school or answering back. The same stupid things that got kids a smacked hand back home.

Illuminated by the lamp, Tameka could now see their prison clearly. Puddles of frozen water filled the gaps in the uneven floor. Bits of rag and animal droppings were all over the place. Over in the far corner, a solitary ratlike creature sat on its haunches and stared nervously at her, its eyes blinking rapidly.

These bastards really took being bastards seriously.

'Hey 'Meel,' she said quietly. 'Time to go.'

He put the cup and bowl on the ground carefully, almost reverently, and nodded. She made sure he had a firm grip on the ladder before letting him start to climb. She didn't want him to fall and break his neck.

Emile was like one of those baby sea tortoises in the science holos at school. Just breaking out of his shell and making his first clumsy, chubby-ass steps down to the sea. Oblivious to all the birds and crabs and shit that were out to get him. Not to mention the big fish in the sea. And since they had met Bernice Summerfield they had been swimming

224

with sharks. Boy-eating sharks. But some of those tortoises had to make it past the dark shadows in the water. Emile had got past his dad, who sounded like a right bastard. Got away from that backwater satellite with its tinpot religion. And if he did make it past the predators, she knew that he'd swim a thousand miles, paddling away with his fat flippers until he found his *island*.

She stopped herself suddenly. Exactly when had she started to feel so protective of the boy? She was surprised by the strength of the feelings she had for him. He'd saved her life of course – hung on to her when anyone else she could think of would have let her go. But it was more than that. Maybe she was scared of seeing him get hurt. Scared of hurting him herself if she got it together with Scott. If they ever found the dragon boy again. It was obvious that Emile had a balloon-sized crush on the scaly Ursulan.

Hoo boy.

A voice called to her from above. She looked up to see Emile staring down at her from the top. 'Tameka, are you going to stay down there all day?'

She got hold of the bottom of the ladder and put her boot on the bottom rung.

Emile giggled.

'What's so funny?'

'I was just thinking, if I unhooked this ladder down now . . .'

'As if you would even dare, boyee,' she said coolly, but scrambled up double-quick anyway.

Bernice hadn't really been surprised that they had been left unguarded. Or that they had been abandoned in a pit which was relatively easy to escape from. The Sunless clearly didn't see them as much of a threat. If adulthood was equated with emotional repression for the Sunless, then they probably considered a party of sulky Goths and screaming queens as akin to children. Ineffectual and unimportant. Chuck 'em in a dark hole and get on with more important things.

There were four other pits in the long underground

chamber. Two had been flooded with rank water from a leaking pipe in the ceiling. They were covered in a thick layer of ice. If anyone had been in either of those . . . In the third they found Scott. He had been beaten and was barely conscious. Red weals and bruises ran down his chest. He didn't say much. He couldn't. Tameka busied around him, making a fuss, while trying simultaneously to remain utterly casual.

Bernice left them to it, although as she made her way over to the final pit, she noticed that Michael was keeping his distance. Scott wasn't going to be pleased to see his brother.

She'd left the glow lamp with the others, so she pulled another out of its grip on the wall and knelt down by the edge of the final hole. Before she dared look, she thought of Mum, and whispered a prayer to God or anyone or anything that might be listening. And then she peered over the edge.

A man lay curled up in the far corner of the pit. He was asleep, his head resting on his outstretched arm, like a dog. There was frost in his long stubble.

It was Jason.

For a moment she just stared down at him, taking in every inch of him. He looked tired and ill. There were cuts on his legs and arms. His feet were bare and filthy. Probably had a terminal case of frostbite.

She lowered herself slowly over the side and dropped gently to the floor of the pit. The soft sound woke him, and he pushed himself against the wall, holding his hand over his eyes.

'Please,' he said, his voice cracking. 'Please . . . don't . . .' He looked terrified, like an animal that somehow knew that it was destined for the slaughterhouse. She swallowed. All the things she had thought of saying to him over the last couple of weeks – all the quips and jibes, the jokes at his expense – all faded away. Feeling like she was walking on air, she crossed the room unsteadily and knelt beside him. Initially he tried to push her away, screaming and yelling. Bernice was scared the Sunless might be alerted by his cries.

'Jason, it's me,' she said. 'It's Benny.' She repeated the words over and over again until he stopped struggling and collapsed into her arms.

21

ALL MEN ARE BASTARDS

'Michael, take off your boots.'

'What?'

'Just do it!' Bernice snapped, impatiently. Jason was
having trouble walking on the rough surface. Even in the
strange light, his feet looked blue. The skin was painfully
cracked around his heels and toes. She doubted he was going
to keep all of his toes.

Michael shook his head, sullenly. His round face was
ebony in the low lighting. Bernice was about to start arguing
with him again when the large man stalked over and lifted
Jason effortlessly over his shoulder.

'Hey!' Jason exclaimed, impotently.

'I'll carry him, but I need these shoes as much as he does.'

They hid in a network of smaller holes which perforated
the nearby tunnel walls. They led into cramped sleeping
quarters. Nothing more than cells. The beds were short. This
was still part of what Bernice had decided was some kind of
school or children's quarters. The sound of young voices was
slightly louder now, raised in a flat, toneless song. Bernice
didn't recognize the language. It was both sharp and guttural,
lots of consonants and clucking sounds. The voices sounded
like they were shouting instructions or making demands.
They echoed around the tunnels, grating on her shot nerves.

Michael wasn't happy with her decision to hide there, but
Bernice knew that running blindly through the enemy's lair,

hoping to just bump into the exit, was the easiest way to get caught. The easiest way to get themselves killed. Her idea was to hide out here until the alarm was sounded. Hopefully the Sunless wouldn't think to start looking so close to their prison. And then all she had to do was work out some way of getting off this world.

Easy.

Scott was slipping in and out of consciousness, murmuring words Bernice couldn't make out. His green hair was filthy and plastered to his skull. He was drooling saliva and kept repeating something about the sun.

'Iranda has that dream,' Jason said, quietly from beside her.

'Everyone in our Eight does,' Michael said quietly from the shadows.

Bernice ignored this remark. She turned to Jason. He was sitting up, hugging his scrawny knees. His eyes were clear now; and he looked a little more like the man she knew.

Bernice felt something inside of her break. Suddenly the overwhelming, protective feelings she had experienced towards her ex-husband were replaced by a bitter, jealous anger. 'Actually, Jason, right now I don't need to know about Iranda's sleep patterns, all right?'

She bit her lip. Why was it easier to love him when he was only semiconscious?

For a second he looked shocked. 'I'm sorry,' he said, and then his face cracked into a wry smile. 'I'd forgotten how jealous you can get.'

'And I'd forgotten what kind of git you really are. Jason Kane, you are a git. The king of all gits.' She poked him in the chest. 'Git. Git. Git.'

And then, much to her annoyance, he started to laugh. 'You came all this way to abuse me?'

'No, I came all this way to rescue you, actually. Although, now I'm here, suddenly I'm not at all sure why I bothered. I have been arrested, blown out of the skies, drowned. I have kidnapped people, performed terrible drag – in public – crashed cars, not to mention almost being throttled to death on the roof of a moving vehicle ...' Her anger suddenly abandoned her as she remembered the real cost of their adventure. 'People have died to get me to you. People I liked.'

The smile disappeared from his face. 'I'm sorry, but you –'

'If you're about to tell me that I didn't ask you whether you wanted to be rescued,' she snapped, interrupting him, 'then I shall thump you. So don't, all right?'

'I was going to say that you shouldn't have put yourself in danger for me,' he said, although Bernice suspected that he was lying. Self-sacrifice was not a quality that he had in abundance. Self-pity, yes. Self-sacrifice, no.

'I'm grateful though, Benny. Really, I am.'

Bernice put her head in her hands. 'Oh I didn't come all this way for your gratitude. I . . . I don't know why I came.'

'Well thank you for coming anyway, thank you for saving me.'

'Don't take that for granted. We're not out of this yet.'

'Where's your ship?'

'Ah, you've put your finger on the one small hole in my otherwise watertight plan.'

'No ship?'

'No ship.'

'Bloody hell. How did you get here?'

'We got a lift with your *girlfriend*.'

'Oh.'

'Yes, "Oh".'

'You've met Iranda?' He actually sounded worried.

'Oh, we're old friends.'

'Then you know that she had me kidnapped on Apollox 4.'

'To get that figurine, which she thinks is the key to a weapon – I'm way ahead of you.'

'How do you know that?'

'You said you married me because I'm clever.'

'I did. You are.'

'Not clever enough. Your girlfriend set me up. Had me chase you halfway across the galaxy just to bring that crystal figurine to her.'

'You didn't, though, did you?'

Bernice shrugged. 'Walked straight into it, I'm afraid.'

'Oh Jesus Christ, Benny! We have to get that back.' He began to push himself to his feet, but Bernice shoved him back down on to the bed.

'We are not going anywhere near that woman. We need to steal a ship and get away from here. And that's all.'

'I'm not leaving without that thing.'

'I can't believe you're thinking about yourself at a time like this!'

'Myself? What do you mean?'

'I presume you're planning to sell it.'

'What are you thinking of, Benny? Haven't you been paying attention to anything that's been going on? If Iranda gets both the visionaries then there'll be nothing to stop her. Nothing in the galaxy.'

'Oh behave, Jason. Don't tell me you've swallowed this ancient-powers nonsense.'

'Iranda has been scouring the sector for those pieces. She's completely obsessed with it. The visionaries are the keys to the device. She found the male piece months ago. The female visionary was all that she needed to activate the weapon.'

He sounded evangelical. Bernice was furious that he could have been taken in by Iranda. 'Listen, Jason, this is what I do, remember? There is no fortune and no glory in digging up the past, beyond the occasional press conference and book launch. You're worse than bloody freshers who think they're going to dig up a lost spaceship or a burial chamber filled with gold. Take it from me: ancient artefacts do not possess mystical powers; centuries-dead civilizations do not leave super-weapons lying dormant for others to stumble across.' She was almost shouting now, not caring even if the Sunless heard her. 'And X never – ever – bloody well marks the spot! Trust me on this one, Jason, I know what I'm talking about.'

There was a shocked silence from the others in the room. Bernice was suddenly very aware of all the eyes upon her. Her cheeks were hot and she could feel her scalp prickle with sweat beneath her hair.

'And have you thought about the consequences if you're wrong?' Jason said quietly. 'Well have you? What would happen if a completely ruthless race like the Sunless gained the power to travel across the whole galaxy or to destroy a planet from space?' Bernice was silent. 'You know what would happen, because you've seen it happen before. You and I have seen stuff, stuff that no one else gets to see. We've been witness to Armageddon. Can you take the chance that it's not going to happen here?'

'I can't,' a quiet voice said from the other side of the room. Scott was moving towards them, refusing Tameka's offer of assistance. 'What Jason says is true, Bernice. If my sister thinks the power is here then she is right.'

'What do you know about it?'

'I've seen it in my dreams all of my life. All my family do.' He glanced at Michael for the first time since he had become conscious. His brother looked away. 'A blinding, searing heat that consumes everything. It exists, I know it does. I've felt it. If Iranda has been stupid enough to search it out, then I'm going to try and stop her giving it to the Sunless.'

Jason put a hand on her shoulder. 'If you want to take a ship and go, that's fine.'

'Oh thank you – your permission is *so* important to me.' She shrugged his hand off and moved to the doorway of the room. She felt lost. Why was it so much easier to think clearly when Jason wasn't around? Was she really only refusing to get involved because she was angry with him for falling in love with someone else? Maybe it would have been easier if the woman he had fallen in love with wasn't bloody eighteen. Why did men have to go and do that? she asked herself. You never heard about women doing that sort of thing, did you? She suddenly remembered Doran. Ah, yes, Doran, the student with the floppy fringe. Well she hadn't actually had sex with Doran or fallen in love with him or anything ridiculous like that. Well, not really. And anyway, that was entirely different.

She felt the beginning of a wry smile creep across her face.

She looked across the cavern. Green lamps spotlit the crisscross supports embedded in the rock walls. Although the pits where they had been imprisoned were obscured by the darkness, she could work out where they were. There was no one in sight, which probably meant that their escape hadn't yet been discovered. Which meant that surprise was still on their side.

The only thing that was on their side, mind you.

It was only then that she realized that she wasn't going to abandon Jason and Scott to their heroics. She was going to stay and stop Iranda as well. The realization made her feel slightly giddy.

'Crikey,' she whispered to herself. 'I had only suspected it previously, but Bernice Summerfield, you are certifiably insane.'

The children were kneeling on the floor, facing forward. They were all dressed in identical grey outfits, heads shorn, chanting the same words over and over. They were staring at the far wall. Bernice couldn't see their faces, but she imagined them blinking at the same regular intervals.

There was no teacher or adult in the room. No windows or cameras: no obvious means of surveillance. Her eyes searched the children for some indication of disobedience or individuality, but there was nothing. Just six rows of conformity. From where she stood in the doorway, it was impossible even to tell whether the children were boys or girls.

From the back, if their hair had been half a centimetre longer, any one of them could have been Emile.

She heard a noise from the corridor outside and slipped all the way into the room as quickly and as quietly as she could. It would only take one of the children to glance over their shoulder for the alarm to be raised. Peering through a crack in the door, she glimpsed a flash of grey as a Sunless marched past the door and then was gone. Her heart pounded in her chest. She'd lost her watch at some now forgotten point in the last few days, so she counted slowly to sixty before slipping out of the room.

The corridor was made of rusting metal. The school, if that's what it was, was built into the underground tunnels. Like the spaceship and the tunnels, this part of the Sunless's home was pressurized. Perhaps the children were not as strong as the adults. Perhaps they had to acclimatize to a rarefied atmosphere over time.

There appeared to be few adults in this part of the underground burrow. She presumed that most were on Ursu now. It made sense that the children would be among the last to be transported to the colonized world.

A hand fell heavily on to her shoulder and she gave a little yelp of fear. Her body coursed with adrenaline as she prepared to flee down the corridor. And then she saw that the hand on her shoulder was not pale white but purple.

''S OK, Bernice, it's me.' Michael's round face loomed over her shoulder.

'Bloody hell, Michael! What are you doing here? I thought I told everyone to stay put.'

He shuffled awkwardly. 'I thought you could do with some company, in case you run into trouble.'

'I can take care of myself, thank you. There's at least one of them wandering about around here, so keep your voice down.'

She thought for a moment before turning to appraise him. 'That's not the reason you came, is it?'

'No.'

It was clear that he didn't want to pursue the conversation, but Bernice was too curious to let politeness be her guide. And she couldn't think of any reason to make life more comfortable for the young Jeillo man. 'Scott, is it?'

'He's made it clear that he doesn't want me around him. And anyway, your friend keeps threatening to kill me.'

'Tameka?' Bernice almost laughed. 'I can't say that I blame her.' The large man seemed a little forlorn as he hovered next to her. Which wasn't very surprising. Michael didn't really have anywhere to go. Stuck between hostile camps both here and back on Ursu. His treachery had made him homeless. He had betrayed his brothers, disobeyed his sister. Trapped between vengeful Ursulans on one side and vicious collaborators on the other. Bernice wondered what treatment Michael would face from his comrades back on Ursu. The collaborators would probably kill him, but she didn't know what punishment might exist in a society that didn't have laws. Perhaps they would just blank him as Scott was doing. It seemed a light sentence for a murderer.

'Sometimes I wish I were like them,' he said, indicating the door to the room full of chanting children.

'What do you mean?'

'You don't understand their language, do you?'

Bernice shook her head. 'You do?'

'Iranda speaks their language fluently. I've learnt a little.' He paused for a moment, listening. And then, in time with the chanting he began to translate. 'To be without feeling is to be without fear. In the darkness only the fearless survive. In the cold only the fearless survive.' He paused for a moment. 'There's more but you understand the meaning.'

Bernice nodded. 'Yeah, yeah, I do. And I thought they were learning grammar by rote. I wonder what happened to them to make them like this. Sometimes colonies get cut off . . .'

'Does there have to be a single reason?' Michael said. 'And anyway, this was never a colony. Not like Ursu. This has never been part of human space.' He looked as if he were about to say more and then stopped. 'I don't think this is a good place to stand and talk. I think I hear someone.' He began to back away down the corridor. Bernice followed cautiously. Michael clearly knew more about the Sunless than he was willing to say. She made a note to question him about them further.

And then she promptly forgot all about it when they turned the corner and walked straight into a Sunless female. It didn't show any shock or surprise to find them, but that was only to be expected.

It looked from her to Michael slowly, as if sizing up the threat they posed. Its flat industrial-grey eyes gazed upon her without interest.

It was going to kill her. Bernice realized that she had absolutely no idea what to do. She froze as she remembered the attack on the roof of the car. The Sunless were unstoppable. Far stronger than she was. She couldn't see that there was any point in trying to fight one of them hand to hand.

Michael obviously didn't share her view. He took the opportunity to move first while the Sunless sized them up. He leant on his left leg and then kicked it hard in the groin with his right foot. The Sunless staggered back but didn't fall. Michael followed through quickly, not giving the Sunless female a moment to recover, punching it hard in the face. Bernice heard the soft sound of cartilage tearing. The Sunless doubled over, blood streaming from its nose, but still it didn't fall. It only appeared to be a little uncertain on its feet, and then it reached up for Michael. Its thin pale hands grabbed hold of his head, its thumbs pressing against his heavily lidded eyes.

It was going to push Michael's eyes into his brain. Bernice was just beginning to think about trying to grab hold of its wrists, when she glimpsed a flash of metal in Michael's hand. A knife? Where had he got hold of a knife?

A spray of blood hit him across his face.

He had stabbed the Sunless woman in the eye.

The Sunless tumbled over backward and was still. Its right eye socket flooded with dark-red blood, which spilt over and ran down to pool on the floor.

The knife in his hand was covered in thick dark blood. 'Where did –' she began but then stopped as she realized it wasn't a knife: it was a fork. Part of the battered set of children's cutlery they had found at the bottom of the pit.

Michael wiped his hand on his trouser leg. 'They're strong, but they're not fast. They don't feel fear and they don't feel anger. It slows them up.'

Bernice was speechless.

They dragged the body without a word into the nearest empty room. Michael helped Bernice to strip the Sunless of its uniform. They worked in silence. Bernice didn't want to talk or even to think about what had just taken place in the corridor outside. Removing the uniform from the dead weight of the corpse was hard work and took a long time. It was messy too. The blood got everywhere. Out of its uniform the Sunless appeared more human, and disturbingly, more like a woman. Her skin was pale and hairless, muscular but pasty.

Bernice examined the corpse's arms, squeezing the hard muscle, before pressing her hands against the dead woman's stomach, searching for any indication of augmentation.

'What are you doing?' Michael asked.

Bernice gave up her examination. 'I had wondered whether they were cybernetically altered somehow. You know, part human, part machine. There's a lot of it about in this part of the galaxy. But she's just your basic humanoid who has adapted to her environment.'

'Does it make a difference?'

'I don't know. I think maybe it makes a difference to me. I would just feel better if they had computers for brains or a biomechanoid exoskeleton or something.'

Michael seemed to understand this. 'Something that would make them separate from us.'

'From me, anyway.' He didn't miss the accusation. 'Yeah, but I'm afraid to say that the truth is you don't need a bionic rebuild to put on a uniform or abandon your feelings.' Bernice took one last look at the woman's body.

She clambered to her feet and hugged herself tightly. 'Still, I think her uniform will fit Jason.'

Michael nodded. 'Scott's uniform is striped. He'll need another.'

'The stripes come off. He did it once before,' she added, remembering the night she had crashed on Ursu. That seemed like such a long time ago now. Dragging Errol into a pressure suit and then into the airlock, before scaring the young Ursulan half to death beneath the surface of the lake.

She remembered how hard they had all worked to keep Errol alive.

'What is it?' Michael asked, looking closely at her.

'Nothing,' she replied. She told herself that there wasn't

any point in fighting Michael. They were in enough danger without fighting among themselves. But she didn't want to be too civil to him either. Somehow that felt like dishonouring the memory of her friends.

She began to take an interest in her surroundings for the first time. They were in a storeroom of some kind. Stacks of dull metal boxes and what might have been sporting equipment. Weights, bars, ropes – not the sort of thing she had much time for back on Dellah. A quick trip around the quad on her bicycle was the best she could usually manage. And her bike had a motor fitted to help with the hills.

She pulled out one of the boxes, although she wasn't at all sure what she was looking for. It made a fierce grating sound as it came free. The box was full of children's uniforms. The next one contained hair clippers.

'We'll need these,' she said and threw a couple of pairs of clippers to Michael. He looked at them for a moment before frowning.

'It will take more than short haircuts to pass ourselves off as Sunless. They are humanoid, not human. And anyway, they will spot me straight away: none have Jeillo heritage.'

'I know. But I haven't told you about my secret weapon yet, have I?'

'Secret weapon?'

'Tell me, do they have Goths on Ursu?'

CONVERSATIONS WITH THE ENEMY

Kitzinger tried to appear relaxed as she handed the results of her handiwork to Nikolas. She had never been particularly good with her hands and it showed. The original figurine had a blank expression on its simple face. The one she had fashioned with her cutlery looked like it was scowling. If Nikolas did more than glance at it, she was going to be in trouble.

In her pocket, her hand fingered the shard of crystal she had carved into a sharp point. If Nikolas saw through the deception she would kill him and then make a run for her life.

As always, he had brought two Sunless with him; another had been standing guard over her all day.

She wouldn't get far.

Kitzinger breathed a sigh of relief as the young man impatiently took the figurine from her and tucked it away in one of the pockets of his heavy coat. He hadn't noticed anything. He asked her if she had learnt anything about it, and she shook her head.

She pulled the respirator away from her face and instantly felt the cold winter in the chamber attack her face. 'The other statue – I can't help wondering: has it arrived?' she asked, tentatively, before pulling the mask back in place.

Nikolas was an unpredictable man. This time he didn't take offence at her question. 'The other visionary is on the planet, Kitzinger. My sister is bringing it here. Then the work will be complete.' He gazed around the chamber, staring up at the crystals which shimmered above them.

Sister? But of course he would have a sister. He was an Ursulan, he would have seven brothers and sisters. His Eight. There was a chance that she had been the midwife at his birth, although judging by his age it would have been at least nineteen or twenty years ago, quite possibly more. She had birthed thousands of children since then. An image of his sister appeared in her mind.

Kitzinger caught her breath. No, not an image. A *memory*.

She saw two red-haired children playing among a melting pot of races. Playing alongside a human boy with Saurian scales, a purple Jeillo with tiny, perfect wings sprouting from his shoulder blades, a lanky Saurian with human eyes. Grey eyes. All of them had mercury-coloured eyes.

Sunless eyes.

And then she knew exactly who Nikolas was. Eighteen years ago two extra human children had appeared in the Blooms. Splicing genes. Mixing species. Creating children who were neither fish nor foul. An Eight had become a Ten. No one had known why. There had been theories of course. It had caused quite a stir at the time. Everyone had entertained different ideas and explanations. But it had all been hot air – nothing grounded in hard evidence. Kitzinger herself had always suspected that the Blooms had produced Nikolas and his sister for their own reasons, although she hadn't ever articulated her suspicion for fear of being laughed at or being accused of projecting the concept of agency on to the cloning machines.

And so the two extra humans had been birthed without any explanation for their behaviour. And as time passed people had tired of trying to explain the irregularity.

And the children had grown into adults.

In the entire year she had spent on the planet she had never made the connection before. Perhaps because she hadn't wanted to think about Nikolas having family or friends. She had wanted to keep him as impersonal as possible in her mind. Now it was obvious.

She turned to where Nikolas was examining the symbols on the stone disc. Suddenly, the eighteen-year-old question of why the Blooms had produced two extra children seemed pressing.

Perhaps he knew the answer. 'What will you do if you do obtain this super power?' she asked, trying to keep her voice neutral. 'More war? More invasions? Is that what this is about?'

'I don't know.' He shrugged, still intent on his work. 'That all depends on the nature of the weapon.' He turned to face her, pulling his respirator up, his face was relaxed beneath. The vicious laddish grin that accompanied his lies and brutishness was absent. For a second, she saw a profound weariness in his eyes. It didn't belong to someone as young as he was.

On an impulse, she asked, 'And then you'll kill me, won't you?' Her voice was slightly muffled by her respirator, but the fixed expression on his face told her that he had heard what she had said.

He nodded. 'Probably,' he replied, almost absently. 'You won't be going back to Ursu, that's for sure. But then you must have known that,' he added.

'Yes. Yes, I suppose I always did.'

'You may as well go back to your little hut. There's nothing either of us can do now until Iranda brings the female visionary. All we can do is wait.' And then he turned and walked away.

Kitzinger watched him go, pressing her finger against the edge of the crystal knife in her pocket.

Now that she knew she was never going home she could let go of her life. And anyway, if, as Nikolas said, these creatures had colonized her world then the Ursu she dreamt of returning to no longer really existed. Just in her dreams. For the first time she allowed herself to imagine what the Sunless might have done to her world.

She had lost everything. Her home. Her only friend. Her dreams. Her life.

And possessing nothing, you are free. The old Ursu saying

reassured her. She hadn't lost herself. She smiled ruefully. She was free even to choose whether to live or die.

Kitzinger looked up at the Blooms on either side of her. Their huge curved undersides were now deeply buried beneath the floor of the chamber – only their top halves were visible. Dark ribbed domes rising up from the ground. She had spent her whole life in and around the giant organic devices in their home under the university. No, that wasn't right, the university wasn't their home – this was. This was where they belonged, before the companies had ripped them out of the ground.

And now they were back in their home. Surrounded by the children they had spontaneously spawned.

It hurt her to accept that the whole of Ursulan society was built on a theft. The devices which had allowed her society to be created free of the chains of patriarchy, the tyranny of human reproduction and possessive love, had been based on the greed of the companies.

It was ironic. The people who had designed her world had called the Blooms a gift. Putting their discovery down to serendipitous good fortune, to the existence of magic in the universe. The original Ursu Group, a consortium of people from different worlds and different species, had seen in the Blooms a chance to make a world untouched by the cold heart of profit and oppression. They had been scientists, therapists, healers, politicians, warriors. Their backgrounds had been diverse, but they had been united in their desire to create a society where a person might be truly free. They had been influenced by philosophy, science and art. The name they had chosen for themselves and for their world had reflected their utopian ideas, their love of literature and their humour.

A kiss to a dreamer from the past.

They had been so sure that they had left the evils of the universe behind them. So sure of the purity not only of their ideals, but of their actions. She sensed the conceit of her society, the smugness of her people. How arrogant they had been. She felt a wave of bitterness. And shame. They had tucked themselves away on a forgotten world and pretended that they were untouched by taint of wealth and selfishness, and all the time the foundation of their society had been the pillaging of another's culture, another's heritage.

Perhaps we deserve the Sunless, she thought.

Kitzinger watched as Nikolas reached the two Sunless that had been waiting for him by the entrance to the huge crystal chamber. Moving in unison, they flanked him and escorted him out of the chamber.

Servants or masters? she wondered.

She spent the rest of the day clearing the ice from the flat disc of stone which sat in the very centre of the chamber. Symbols spiralled out from the disc. Kitzinger had translated the account of the visionaries herself. Yesterday they had dug into the ice which packed the surface of the disc and discovered a second niche on the opposite side of the circle. Presumably this was where the female figurine fitted.

Could they really be keys to immense power?

Well if the next few minutes worked out the way she intended, Nikolas was never going to find out.

The Sunless guard began to move towards her, indicating that it was the end of this shift of work. This routine had become so well established over the last year, that usually the Sunless only had to begin to move towards her and she would finish her work and head back to the pressurized hut. However, this time Kitzinger didn't move away, but continued to go through the motions of working.

She heard the Sunless's heavy boots crunching on the ice behind her.

'Finish. Now,' it said. Its accent was thick and harsh as it struggled to say the few words it knew in her language.

Still leaning over her work, Kitzinger nodded and, as she twisted around to face the guard, she pulled the shard of sharpened crystal out of her pocket and in one movement, thrust it upwards, hoping to cut through the soft flesh under the Sunless's ribcage and pierce its heart. However, the Sunless hadn't been quite as close behind her as she had anticipated and she lost some of her momentum as she was forced to stretch her arm awkwardly to complete her attack.

She managed to stab the Sunless, but only with the tip of the crystal dagger. The Sunless looked impassively down at the wound and the makeshift weapon. Kitzinger might have found the scene comical if she hadn't been so scared. And then its eyes lifted and met hers for a second before it launched itself forward. It didn't even bother to pull the dagger from its chest.

Kitzinger tripped as she backed away and fell awkwardly on to her back. The Sunless was on top of her in a moment. It straddled her legs and slipped down on to its knees. Its hands grabbed hold of her neck. Suddenly she couldn't take a breath.

It was going to suffocate her or break her neck. They had killed Aric and now they were going to kill her.

For a moment Kitzinger was resigned to letting it happen. And she felt something hard pressing painfully against her chest. Out of the corner of her eye she spied the shard of crystal protruding at an angle from the Sunless's body. As the guard leant down on her, the blunt end was being pushed against her, forcing its way a little further into the Sunless's body. Dark blood blossomed on its pale-grey uniform, spreading out from the wound. The creature must have been in agony. She had no idea how it was able to tolerate that level of discomfort. It must have registered the pain, because it removed one if its hands from around her throat and began to reach down for the shard.

Kitzinger seized her moment. She pulled up her foot and with all the force in her body kicked its knee out from under it. The Sunless lost its balance and toppled on top of her.

She screamed in agony as the blunt end of the crystal smacked into her, bruising her breastbone. But she felt it slide up into the Sunless, skewering it. The dead weight of the creature was suddenly on top of her. Its head cracked against her skull and suddenly she was looking directly into its dead eyes. They looked no different now from when it had been alive.

She pushed the corpse off her angrily and staggered to her

feet. Her chest hurt. She could feel a deep graze under her clothes. It had almost killed her! She wanted to kick it but she stopped herself. She didn't have much time before they would discover what she had done. She had to leave.

Escape wasn't on her mind. She knew that there was nowhere for her to go on this barren planet. There was only ice, rocks and the Sunless.

She took the male figurine from her pocket. But if she could get a few miles between her and the chamber, she might be able to bury the figurine somewhere where it would never be found.

And then whatever Nikolas hoped to awaken in this room – weapons, power, whatever it might turn out to be – would stay buried for ever. And once it was hidden she would wait until the wind and the ice and the snow ate into her body and sucked the life out of her.

She turned and fled from the cathedral-sized room that had been her prison for the last year.

22

Sunless 'Я' Us

'Hey, dragon boy, your teeth are getting smudged.'

'What?'

'Come here.'

A little reluctantly, Scott bared his teeth and Tameka wiped away the tiny smear from the otherwise perfect triangles she had created by blacking out parts of his front teeth. It was a waste of extremely expensive eyeliner, but she had to admit that it was pretty damn realistic. His teeth looked as dangerous as razors. Vampire sharp.

She had used up all of her pale foundation giving them all Sunless complexions. Almost half of it had been used to whiten Michael's dark, purple face. She'd always found Jeillo boys sexy, with their deep skin tones and muscular bodies. Michael looked really weird ghost-white. His head looked unreal, somehow, like it was made of clay. There were still traces of purple around his eyes, where she hadn't been able to cover his skin completely. Close up he looked as if he hadn't slept in about a thousand years.

And she didn't find him sexy any more.

She stood back and admired her handiwork on Scott. With their freshly shaven heads, uniforms and shark teeth they all looked alarmingly like the real thing. But the brothers' shiny mercury eyes left them actually indistinguishable from the grey men. Tameka was feeling curiously confident. As long as no one got too close she had a sneaking feeling they were going to get away with this.

'Have you finished?' Scott asked, the irritation evident in his voice.

She was a lot less confident about Scott. 'Yeah.'

He went to move away, but she tugged him back. 'Hey, give us a kiss.'

'What?'

'For luck. Yeah, I know luck's a profiteer's concept. But just do it, all right?'

His face broke into a gentle but not wholly easy smile. He leant forward and pressed his colourless lips to hers. 'Be careful,' he said softly. 'I don't want you to smudge my make-up.'

Tameka laughed.

He looked puzzled. 'Have I said something funny?'

She sighed. 'Forget it.' She was about to let him go, when she couldn't stop herself and blurted out, 'I'm really pissing you off, aren't I?'

He looked uncomfortable. 'This isn't the time, Tameka.'

'There might not be another time,' she said and then instantly regretted saying something so clichéd. Particularly as it was probably going to turn out to be true.

'Tameka, what you want of me makes me feel uncomfortable. Since we had sex I feel as if I am standing in a room full of people when I am alone with you.'

It took her a moment to realize what he was saying. She was *crowding* him. Oh shit. 'Right. It's fine,' she said, putting her hands out in front of her. 'It was just sex. I understand.'

'It was good sex. I mean it was kind of strange but I enjoyed it.'

Her heart was sinking faster than an express elevator. 'Thank you. I think.' Suddenly she just wanted the conversation to end. Perversely, Scott seemed to be warming to it.

'Emile said –'

'Never mind what 'Meel says. He doesn't know –'

'– that you were in love with me.'

'– shit.'

There was a pause. The words hung in the air between

them. Tameka swallowed. She was going to kill that boy. To Death. 'Oh yeah? And when exactly did he say that?'

'Back on Ursu, when I asked him why you were behaving so differently.'

'He said that I was in love with you?'

'No, he just said that you had fallen in love.' The way Scott pronounced 'fallen in love' suggested that he hadn't heard those words put together like that before.

'So why did you think it was you?' She was about to tell him exactly what kind of conceited bastard she thought he was when he added, 'Well, because he gave me three guesses.'

Hoo boy! She was going to have to kick that boy's chubby ass good and proper!

She was trying to think of a smart reply when a Sunless appeared around a bend in the rocky tunnel. Tameka was desperately trying to work out whether it would be better to try to bluff it out or just make a run for it, when she realized that it was only Bernice sans hair. Her tutor looked scrawny and much older with a skinhead cut. Tameka ran her hand across her own bare scalp.

Her stylist was going to be furious.

'Are you going to stand around chatting all day?' Bernice demanded. 'Or are you going to come and risk your lives for an insane and improbable cause? On second thoughts don't answer that. Come on, Jason's found a ship.'

Jason Kane crouched close to the entrance of the burrows. The pale red light leaked weakly into the tunnel. From where they had secreted themselves he could see the huge curved supports of the nearest Sunless ship. With its six bowed legs and bulbous nose, the craft reminded him of a giant black housefly. Freezing scarlet mist blocked his view of the other ships, which he knew were out there beyond the first. He took a final deep breath from the respirator and handed it back to Bernice, who had just joined him at his side. Without the benefit of the respirator, the air was thin and chilled his lungs uncomfortably. However, there were six of them including himself and only four respirators. Bernice and he were sharing, and the pretty Mexican girl with the sexy, husky voice – Tameka? – had volunteered to share with Scott. He forced himself to focus on his breathing in the long moments when Bernice was using the respirator. Otherwise it threatened to spiral out of control as he tried hopelessly to take air into his lungs.

He still wasn't absolutely sure why Bernice had brought her students with her on this rescue mission, but he didn't want to appear critical by asking. He was just pleased that she had come for him, and felt a total cad that she had needed to in the first place.

He was worse than a cad. He was a rat. He'd made a mess of everything. As usual. Bernice had risked her life to come and find him and what had she discovered? That he had fallen in love with someone else.

Everything he touched in his life seemed to crumble.

Earlier, when Bernice had gone to search out the two missing members of their party, he had seen Iranda leave with a group of Sunless, heading out into the storm to climb aboard the nearest ship. Their ship.

The months they had spent together had been among the most exciting of his life. He'd enjoyed being her travelling companion as they travelled from system to system, searching out artefacts and negotiating with disreputable dealers as well as some of the most prestigious art historians in the galaxy. Iranda adapted completely to any situation. She was a consummate con artist: they had rarely paid for hotel rooms or travel. Iranda could bluff her way into or out of anywhere. She was only consistent in her steadfast determination to collect the artefacts. They had been like Bonnie and Clyde, Cassidy and Sundance. For a while Jason had felt that he was living the wild, adventurous life of which he had always dreamt.

And then he had begun to piece together the true nature of Iranda's task. Gradually he had learnt about the device she wished to construct, and the more he had learnt the more fearful he had become. Until one night, after a long day when they had failed to negotiate a sale with a stubborn private collector, they had broken into his private museum and stolen the female visionary. That night they had celebrated and Iranda had drunkenly boasted of the power now at her disposal. He had spent a restless night worrying about what he had done, and then in the morning he'd slipped away before she had woken.

And where had he gone?

He glanced at Bernice. Back to the one person in the whole universe who had ever genuinely loved him. And now he had messed that up. Probably irretrievably.

A group of Sunless marched past and strode out into the blizzards. Despite their faces being open to the elements, they didn't even break their stride.

Benny handed him the respirator and nodded her readiness. He took a final breath of oxygen-rich air and then stowed the mask.

It was now or never.

Benny turned to her friends. 'Masks off, everyone. Keep in step and try not to use your hands to cover your face. Try to think like a psychotic alien git.' She turned to look at him. 'Which some of us will find easier than others.'

He frowned.

'Now, by the left . . .' she ordered.

The six ersatz Sunless stepped out from their hiding place and marched in time out of the tunnel, following the group of the genuine article ahead of them.

Iranda stood on the bridge of the ship, waiting for the last of the Sunless to board. The journey would be a short one. It would only be a matter of hours before they reached the target site a few thousand kilometres to the north.

The Ache was stronger than ever today. Like an addiction, it carved out a hollowness inside her body, emphasizing the absence of . . . what? She didn't know. It had been in her life for so long she couldn't imagine being without its nagging presence. Only Nikolas shared the Ache. Only he truly understood.

250

She glanced at a nearby monitor. The main ramp of the ship was still down. There was a Sunless standing there, motionless. She could see a group approaching the ship. She hoped they were the last. She hadn't wanted to wait for the troops, but the Sunless had insisted on a substantial presence and, as ever, there had been no question of negotiation with them.

With nothing else to do she contented herself by watching their progress across the rocky terrain.

The wind had ripped the breath from her lungs as soon as she had stepped out of the protection of the tunnel entrance. Tameka tried to suck the oxygen out of the cold air and had to suppress a strong urge to pull her respirator out of her pocket.

The wind bit into her exposed ears and scalp. Coldness quickly faded into a numbness which threatened to seep into her brain. The storm raged against her. It was as if the planet were trying to force its way inside her body. She had to squint to see the ramp of the ship. It was at least a hundred metres away. And all the while a Sunless stood at the bottom of the ramp, staring at them impassively. Observing their every step with clinical detachment.

She began to feel panicked. *What if they recognize each other by smell or something we didn't think of? What if it knows we're phoneys?*

A little over three-quarters of the way across the plain, Tameka began to feel seriously light-headed. The air around her was so thin that she felt as if she had a plastic bag around her head, and she was just breathing the same breath over and over. She couldn't feel the cold at all now. Her face felt solid, numb.

Ahead of her, in the middle of their party, Emile faltered and stumbled to his knees. His ears had turned an angry red against his pale scalp. His bare hands slipped on the ice as he struggled to his feet, his boots sliding out from under him. He looked like a first-time skater abandoned in the middle of an ice rink.

251

Damn. She'd been so busy thinking of herself that she hadn't spared a thought for the boy. What should she do? What was the *Sunless* thing to do? She was all too aware of the guard ahead of them. Watching them closely.

Helping him was out of the question: they didn't go in for basic human kindness around here. But if she abandoned him to the winter blizzard, he wasn't going to be able to get up on his own. She thought all of this in the few short steps it took for her to catch up with him. Without quite knowing why, she grabbed hold of Emile under his arms, and pulled him roughly to his feet. His large brown eyes were glassy and unfocused. His mouth hung open. The shark teeth she had carved out with eyeliner had already smeared hopelessly. He looked like he'd been chewing on a leaky pen.

She'd never seen him look so young.

Grabbing hold of the collar of his uniform with one hand, so he wouldn't fall, she slapped him hard around the face with the other.

He gave a little cry which was swallowed by the hungry wind.

'Baby, you gotta move,' she begged urgently. And he wobbled slightly, like a string puppet in the hands of a drunk, before nodding vaguely and marching on with new determination.

She didn't take her eyes off him until he reached the ship.

By the time her boots clanked against the metal of the ramp, Tameka was pretty sure that she was suffering serious oxygen starvation. The pressure in her head was so intense that she felt as if she had been holding her breath underwater for a month. The veins must have been standing out on her forehead like worm casts in wet sand.

She was halfway up the slope, when she heard the guard call out.

Damn. She had been beginning to think that they had got away with it. Bernice and the others were on board now. Only Emile was still in view. Just in front of her.

She paused for a second, and then decided to risk walking on.

The voice came again, harsher this time. This was one Sunless who wasn't going to be ignored. She took a deep breath of nothing and fixed her face into a neutral expression before turning to face it.

It marched over to her and pointed at Emile, who like a fool had also stopped, and then started speaking to her in its strange guttural language. It was quite old, tiny wrinkles cut into its angular face. She didn't understand a word it was saying of course, but the meaning wasn't hard to fathom. She shouldn't have slapped Emile out on the rocks. Tameka had no idea whether it thought that she'd been too lenient or too harsh. But the fact remained that it didn't approve.

Emile was standing next to her as still as a statue.

She was wondering exactly how she was going to handle the situation, when the Sunless gave up with words and smacked her around the face.

This was no ordinary smack. The cold only made the pain worse. Like when someone steps on your toe when you've been out in the snow. The blow left her doubled over. For a moment, she thought the bastard had broken her jaw.

She screamed out in outrage, screamed in anger, screamed in pain. Cursed the wrinkly Sunless with all the swearwords she'd ever heard. The vilest and ugliest ones. Then she kicked him in the bollocks and stamped on his head.

But only in her mind. On the outside, in the real world, she just pulled herself upright and averted her eyes. She had to fight an instinct to nurse her face with her hand.

The Sunless said something else and then returned to its post, missing the first whimper which she had been unable to contain. Tameka paused to let the violent trembling in her legs subside before she trusted her ability to walk and could climb the ramp and enter the ship.

On the bridge Iranda watched the violent encounter between the Sunless.

She found it strange that the female hadn't responded to the direct questioning of the other.

Weakness is death. So why had the female helped the

253

child? And that was another thing: why was there an adolescent on board? That was unusual in itself. The Sunless were protective of their young. She had never been permitted to see them, let alone talk to them. The Sunless were private to the point of being completely paranoid.

Nikolas and she had argued long and hard with the Sunless to bring a team of intergalactic experts to the planet to conduct a proper investigation of the Blooms. However, the Sunless treated the Blooms almost reverently and had quietly forbidden it. Bringing Kitzinger and the young man from Ursu had been an uncomfortable compromise.

This Sunless youth might be more open, might well prove a useful source of information and insight into her taciturn allies.

They hid in the hold. Which wasn't ideal considering what had happened to them last time. But Bernice hadn't been able to find anywhere else on the ship which offered a place where they could all stow away together. And she didn't want to risk moving among the Sunless any more than was absolutely necessary.

They tucked themselves behind machinery and crates of equipment. Bernice pulled a heavy machine cover, like a greasy tarpaulin, down over Michael and Scott. She wanted to check on Tameka and Emile before she took up her position with Jason for the journey.

Emile was tucked away under a series of thick black pipes which ran about a metre above the deck for the whole length of the hold. He looked shaken, really upset. The inside of his mouth was black as if it were rotten. Bernice was a little relieved when she realized it was only the eyeliner. Tameka was sitting slumped beside him cradling her head in her hands, looking pissed off.

That was all she needed on top of Jason and everything – the two of them squabbling over something ridiculous.

'Tameka, what's been going on? What's the matter with Emile?'

Tameka must have heard the accusation in her voice,

because she looked up defiantly. 'I . . . did . . . not . . . do . . . shit . . . to . . . him . . .' she answered, the words broken, as if making them into a sentence hurt her somehow.

Bernice suddenly felt that she had misjudged the situation entirely. She wanted to apologize – find out what was really going on. However, at that moment she felt the craft lift away from the surface, and, remembering how turbulent the last journey had been, knew she needed to get back to her own hiding place. Feeling pensive, she smiled apologetically, before slipping away.

They sat in the darkness, waiting. Tameka could only just make out the outline of Emile's smooth, round head opposite her. The fuel feed above them rumbled loudly, reverberating with the noise of the engines. The Sunless's ships were fairly standard scout ships, but they hadn't bothered to fit some of the ordinary features usually installed in a passenger ship, like gravity buffers or interior sound insulation. They probably thought getting thrown around and having your ears blasted was good for the soul. No, they probably didn't have souls.

They must have stolen the design for the ships or copied them using an original as a blueprint, because there was no way that this shit heap was a licensed construction. Tameka had heard that, away from the commercial lanes, this sort of replication happened a lot. And you didn't get much further out of the way than this.

The vibration of the ship rose up through her, setting her teeth on edge and aggravating her bruised jaw. She was just managing to drift off when Emile began to speak.

'Thank you for what you did. For saving me,' he whispered.

'You're lucky, boyee. I almost didn't bother.'

'Huh?'

'After what you did, you little scumbag.'

'What'd I do?' He sounded anxious, as if she might have a thousand things to choose from. She was suddenly very aware of the number of years between them.

'It doesn't really matter now, 'Meel. But I would have kind've *preferred* it if you hadn't said what you did to Scott.'

'What'd I say? I didn't say anything!'

She sighed. 'You told Scott that I was in love with him.'

'Oh.' The word was half a whisper, half a sigh. 'I'm sorry. It just sort of came out. I didn't mean to.'

''S OK. Don't worry 'bout it.' She reached over and squeezed his shoulder. 'Try to get some sleep, OK?'

There was a long pause. Her jaw was really beginning to throb now.

'Why do you like me?' Emile said out of the blue.

She leant forward again and poked him in the ribs. 'Who says I do?'

He pushed her hand away. 'Hey, I'm serious!'

'You really want to know?' She wasn't really sure what to say. It was such an insecure thing to ask. Such a kid thing. She thought back to the time they had first met, on the passenger ship heading to Apollox 4. He had been curled up on the floor, wailing like a baby. 'You want the truth, Emile?'

'Yeah,' he said, uncertainly.

'I like you, 'Meel, because you're such a *child*, and because you believe all the bullshit everybody tells you. And because you'd follow the Grel into Psychos "Я" Us if they promised you ten per cent discount and free bumper stickers. You're like a brand-new toy – batteries fully charged – setting off on your new adventures. And sometimes, sometimes, I wish I was like you.'

'You do?'

'Yeah, I do.' But she could tell he didn't really understand what she meant. Not fully. How could he? 'I do and I don't. I mean, you're *wide* open. Everybody can see it coming. Like they've got a window right into your brain. I mean you're gay and people know it. You're a kid and people know it. Everything about you is just written all over your face.'

She felt Emile sit bolt upright, his legs pushing against hers. 'Who knows I'm gay?'

She laughed. 'You didn't think you were keeping it a secret, did you?'

'Tameka! Oh my God! Does Bernice know?'

'Emile, strangers pass you in the *street* and know.'

'Oh my God!'

'Damn it 'Meel, you sound like you didn't know yourself.'

'Well . . . I did. I mean, I do . . . know that is. I just, well . . .'

'Well what?'

'I just don't usually say it like that.'

'Oh? So how do you usually say it?'

'I . . . well, I don't . . . I mean, I haven't . . . said it. Ever. Not out loud. Not actually *to* anyone else.'

'No kidding?' Suddenly she was so full of affection for him she could have burst. 'You are such an *asshole*, 'Meel.'

There was a pause.

'So why do *you* like *me*?' she asked, half seriously. Well, maybe a little bit more than half.

Emile made a show of sounding nonchalant. 'Who says I do?'

Tameka laughed, throwing him off guard. And then she leant over quickly and tweaked his nipple through his uniform.

Hard.

He yelped.

'Like I said, *wide* open.'

23

IN THE COLD LIGHT OF DAY

Emile woke as a huge clanking sound echoed around the hold. The floor shuddered once beneath him. For a moment there was silence, and he blinked himself properly awake, wondering if the sounds and sensations had been part of his dreams. And then there was the sound of a motor whining and a vertical line of scarlet light appeared in the far wall of the hold. A spray of hard snow chased the light into the room, scattering hailstones the size of marbles across the metal floor. Slowly the main cargo doors opened revealing the now familiar bleak winter landscape. A short distance away, Emile could see part of a huge block of ruby-coloured glass rising out of the ground at a sharp angle. He could see another just beyond it, pushing its way out of the ground. They crossed each other like swords, rising up out of sight.

Tameka had seen them too. They exchanged glances and she shrugged. Clearly she didn't know what they were either. She smiled at him and squeezed his arm.

'You OK?' she asked.

'Yeah, course.' Then he remembered the conversation they'd had before he had slept.

Oh . . . my . . . God . . .

She knew! She had bloody well always known. He felt himself blush and his face was so hot that he was sure it must have shown through the pale foundation.

They all knew! He began to feel light-headed and then he

realized that it was because the wind had swept the oxygen in the room out into the stormy landscape. Fumbling, he reached for his respirator mask and was relieved to hide his face behind it.

He watched through the two round glass eye holes as the interior door to the hold opened and a few Sunless strode into the room in silence and immediately began to unfasten machinery from the floor and carry it out into the snow.

He wanted to wear the mask for ever. They knew he was gay. Bernice. Tameka. All of them. And now he knew too.

He'd always known of course, deep down, but somehow he'd managed to avoid actually admitting it to himself. Somehow he managed to keep his thoughts and feelings apart. He'd fancied boys. Oh he'd *ached* after a couple of boys who lived on the relay station. Fallen into month-long depressions when they'd moved away or met girls. But he'd never thought *about* it consciously. Never let himself acknowledge it.

How the hell had he managed that? How had he lived like that? Was he so screwed up that he didn't even know what he felt?

He'd been such a liar.

Emile was distracted by the Sunless lifting the huge covered cargo crate. His eyes widened as he realized it was the one Scott and Michael had hidden in. From his hiding place beneath the pipes, he saw grey-uniformed figures marching out into the storm, the heavy tarpaulin of the device flapping in the wind.

Where were they taking them?

He had pulled his mask away from his face and mouthed *What do we do?* at Tameka, when Bernice appeared with Jason behind her.

'Come on. And keep your respirators out of sight.'

Emile fell into step beside Tameka and behind Jason. The four of them marched down out of the ship and found themselves at the bottom of the strangest building he'd ever seen.

He'd only glimpsed it from the hold. It was built, if it had been made by people, out of huge ruby-red crystal struts which reached up high into the stormclouds. He couldn't tell if they actually were red or whether it was the strange light which changed everything. He was staring up at the huge glasslike needles, trying to see where they ended, when Tameka kicked him hard in the shin.

He glanced over to her, but kept walking. Her bald head looked as pink as a baby bird in the light.

'Like Sunless, remember,' she hissed. 'Not like bloody tourists.'

Oh yeah! Immediately he looked straight ahead as he marched and tried to look blank, but he couldn't get the huge building out of his mind. Building wasn't the right word, but there wasn't another which fitted. It was as if it had *grown* on the surface of the planet. Like crystal gardens in jars at school or the dark, uneven lesions that had grown on his mother's hands and arms before she had died.

It was cold and getting hard to breathe.

A woman appeared from beneath two of the crossed crystal spears and walked towards the Sunless, who were busy setting down the equipment at the edge of the structure. The woman's hair was almost pink in the strange light. She was wearing a respirator, which covered her face, and a large, heavy fur coat.

Emile glanced at Jason, who was still marching towards the entrance. Was this the woman he had left Bernice for? She would only have to glance in their direction to recognize him! There was no way that a bit of make-up and a haircut was going to fool *her*. This wasn't like Go-Go Girl, who only had to remove her glasses and change the way she parted her hair to fool her boyfriend into thinking she was plain old Maggie Chascarrillo.

A man followed the woman out. He had the same flaming hair and was dressed in similar heavy clothes. They pulled off their respirators to talk. He heard them arguing loudly as his party began to march past. The woman and the man were sheltering next to the equipment the other Sunless had brought out of the ship.

260

'Where can she have gone?' the woman exclaimed, angrily.

'I don't know.' The man glanced across the icy plain. 'It doesn't matter now that we've got the other visionary. We don't need her any more.'

'We still might need her help if we run into problems activating the device.'

Emile was now directly level with them.

'Wait!' the woman said, and planted a hand on his shoulder.

It was shocking to suddenly become involved in the scene he had previously only been observing. Emile ignored her command and tried to walk on. The woman swore to herself and then said, 'I mean . . .' Then she must have translated 'wait' into the Sunless's language because the next few words she spoke sounded like someone coughing up catarrh.

He ground to a halt. He tried to stop his eyes widening in fear, but wasn't very successful. He sensed Tameka hesitate next to him but then she marched on, leaving him alone. Alone and breathless.

The flame-haired man shifted awkwardly. 'I'm sorry, Iranda. I don't know how Kitzinger managed it. She killed a Sunless on her own. Stabbed it through its heart.'

The woman shrugged, facing her companion but still resting her hand heavily on Emile's shoulder, like a teacher who was finishing scolding one student before turning to bawl out the next. 'Then it's just as well I kept Summerfield alive, isn't it?'

'Who?'

'The person I used to bring the visionary here. I didn't want to risk another attempt myself after I snatched Jason. There were Trans-System police sniffing around.'

'Is the visionary on the ship?'

The woman pulled a parcel from her heavy coat. 'It's right here.'

The man nodded, and pulled his mask down before heading inside. Emile watched him go. Bernice, Jason and Tameka reached the entrance and then disappeared inside.

The woman, Iranda, turned to him. 'Now my little friend, what *are* you doing here, hmm?'

He was thinking up a reply that might convince her that might pass as an ordinary Sunless sort of thing to say – but what would? – when he realized that she wasn't speaking their language to him. She wasn't expecting a reply at all. The woman was just talking to herself, as he did sometimes when he thought that no one else was around. 'Your people usually keep their children tucked away, too precious a commodity to be let out in the world. I wonder what makes you so different . . .'

He stared straight past her, trying unsuccessfully not to blink in the harsh wind. He was beginning to feel distinctly unwell. His legs were slowly turning to jelly.

The woman reached out a hand to touch his bruised cheek. Her expression was intense, a frown cut across her delicate brow. Her mercury eyes twinkled with interest and intelligence. 'You look familiar and I'm not absolutely sure why.' She was about to grab hold of his chin to get a better view of his face when there came a crash from behind her.

She turned to the Sunless who had slipped as it had tried to lift the cargo crate. There was the sound of broken glass tinkling from inside the large box. 'There are delicate sensors in there! I need that equipment to measure the power we release.'

The Sunless just stared at her, clearly not understanding a word she was saying. She swore and turned back to Emile.

'Here. Hold this,' she muttered angrily and stuffed the package containing the female visionary into his hands before striding off towards the grey figures standing around the large crate.

Emile stared at the package in his hands, hardly believing his eyes. He had it! The thing they had come all this way for. In his hands! He looked around frantically, forgetting completely about pretending to be a Sunless. Now that he had it he had no idea what he should do with it. Bernice and everyone else had disappeared into the building.

He was running out of options and oxygen.

Emile started to move towards the crystal structure but his legs felt like someone had slipped away with his bones when he wasn't looking. His vision began to blur.

'Emile!' A voice shouted. He looked up to see Scott swing his legs over the edge of the crate and jump down on to the ground. The Sunless and Iranda turned to stare at him. Iranda's expression of disbelief was only exaggerated by the lack of a visible reaction in her companions.

Scott dodged around them and hurtled over to Emile. 'Throw it to me!' he cried.

Emile's experience of ball sports was limited to a holographic volleyball puter game. And he hadn't bothered with that for long because he preferred more fantastical stuff. He hadn't had much practice at ball-throwing – well there wasn't much call for it on an artificial satellite. The idea of getting it wrong terrified him. But he did it anyway. A long underarm shot which went – shit! – a little high.

Scott leapt up into the air and caught it. In return he threw Emile his respirator and sprinted towards the crystal structure.

Michael clambered over the side of the crate after him, but the big man wasn't as fast as Scott. One of the Sunless intercepted him, dragging him violently down to the ice-packed ground. The woman had already set off after Scott.

Emile looked between the two brothers. He wanted to follow Scott, but decided that Michael was in greater need. Emile pulled the respirator on to his face, before realizing that it was too little too late. He managed only a few steps before he stumbled and then crashed head first into the earth.

This time Tameka wasn't there to save him.

Scott's legs were cramping up by the time he reached the dark triangle beneath the two crossed crystal needles. As he passed under the threshold he was temporarily blinded as his eyes tried to adjust to the darkness.

'Scott! Over here!'

He stumbled towards Bernice's voice. She swam into focus and he saw her crouching close to the wall, Tameka and Jason next to her.

'Bloody hell, is that what I think it is?' she exclaimed, staring at the parcel in his hands.

He nodded, trying to catch his breath. 'Iranda . . . behind me. Sunless too.'

Tameka was suddenly at his side. 'Where's Emile? Is he OK?'

'I don't know. Didn't see. They got Michael. I think he's dead.'

'Shit. I gotta go see to the boy.'

Bernice nodded. 'Jason, go with her.'

'What?' he said, surprised.

'Jason. Just do it, all right? Keep the kids safe. Try and slow Iranda down. I'm sure you can think of a few ways to distract her. Tameka, try to get to the ship. Scott, you're with me.'

The two pale figures departed. Bernice handed Scott her respirator. 'You look like you need this,' she said. 'Come on, let's find somewhere to hide the figurine.'

They turned and ran into the crystal building.

Jason sprinted out of the crystal structure and straight into Iranda, who was coming in. They hit each other with such force that they both tumbled to the floor.

Tameka was a few steps behind him. She leapt over them and continued out into the storm looking for Emile. Frozen rain was tumbling fast out of the sky. Sharp diagonal darts that stung where they struck her unprotected scalp and ears.

Two Sunless strode out of the storm. Sheesh, these guys hardly even squinted against the weather. One of them carried Emile, slung over its shoulder as if the boy were a doll. The other was dragging Michael by his legs; the big man's arms flailed behind him.

On seeing her, the Sunless nearest her dropped Michael's feet and began to move in her direction. Tameka put up her fists. She wasn't going to go down without a struggle. But the Sunless ignored her. It moved smoothly past her. Scarcely able to believe her eyes, she swung around and saw it go through the entrance of the structure and pull Jason off Iranda.

264

Tameka didn't want to take a chance on the second Sunless being equally loyal. She headed off at a flat run along the edge of the structure. It didn't follow. She pressed her back against the base of one of the giant needles and waited as long as she dared before heading back.

The Sunless had disappeared. Probably inside. Michael lay where the Sunless had dropped him. His eyes were closed and he wasn't moving. She stood over him for a little while, staring down at his grey face; patches of purple were showing through the make-up.

She was just thinking that he had got what he deserved, when he opened his heavy, sad eyes.

'Help me,' he groaned.

She scowled and looked away. His still being alive was in bad taste. She focused on the ugly black spaceship standing in the near distance. On anywhere but him.

'Tell me about your dream,' Bernice said as they moved quickly down a long tunnel. The only light in the passageway came from the rays of the pale-pink sun which penetrated the frosted crystal walls. It was like running through a bag of strawberry bath salts.

'I didn't think you believed in the Sunless's weapon.'

'I don't. Tell me about the dream anyway,' she panted and gestured for him to hand her the respirator. 'Is it always the same?'

He nodded, passing it to her. 'I'm floating between the stars, falling towards a sun. It explodes burning me up until I'm nothing.'

Bernice took two deep breaths and then returned it. 'And then?'

'Well, then I wake up.'

'Doesn't give us much to go on, does it?'

'No. But it's the most realistic dream I've ever had. That's why I don't doubt that the device exists.'

Bernice sighed. On a whim she said, 'Unwrap our little friend.'

Still hurrying on, he obeyed, holding it out in front of him as they scurried down the corridor.

'Feel anything?'

He shook his head. 'Nothing. Just that it's cold and a bit heavy.'

They turned a corner and ran headlong into a figure coming the other way. Bernice was knocked backward to the ground. For a second she thought that it was a Sunless and she felt the now familiar panic grip hold of her.

It wasn't a Sunless, though. It was a human being. The middle-aged woman stared down at her, looking almost as scared as Bernice felt. The woman was heavy-set, with a serious, hard face and short iron-grey hair.

She was holding a figurine in her hand. The male figurine. The other one of the pair.

'Snap!' Bernice said, brightly.

CONVERSATIONS WITH THE ENEMY?

Kitzinger backed away from the two Sunless. She pulled her home-made knife out of her fur coat, but she knew there was no way she could kill them both. Her escape attempt was over before it had even properly begun.

She stood there waiting for the inevitable.

And waited.

The Sunless didn't spring into action. The female said something Kitzinger didn't understand. A one-syllable word. An order of some kind? The male stood there, hugging something to its chest, staring at her expectantly.

And then the female Sunless did something Kitzinger had thought she would never see a Sunless do.

It smiled.

It was a friendly smile that, absurdly, made Kitzinger want to smile back. At least until she saw the rows of sharp triangular teeth in the Sunless's face. Kitzinger shrank back in fear.

'No, wait,' the Sunless said, its voice strangely full of emotion. 'Oh, I see. No, it's all right. It's only eyeliner pencil.'

The words didn't make any sense. Nothing about the Sunless in front of her did.

The grey-suited figure climbed to its feet. 'Look,' it said and rubbed its front teeth vigorously with its finger for a second. The 'teeth' dissolved into a grey stain. 'It's just pretend. Don't worry.'

This Sunless had the strangest accent Kitzinger had ever heard. She tried to place it and failed completely.

'My name is Bernice Summerfield,' it said, stretching out an empty hand in a gesture that was universal. 'I'm a professor of archaeology. Don't be scared. I'm about as hostile as a Toblerone. Actually, as a cultural reference that probably doesn't help much. But if you're only half as scared of the real Sunless as you are of me, then I suspect that you and I have rather a lot in common.'

Kitzinger took the proffered hand and shook it gently. The woman's hand was cold, but undeniably human. She hadn't touched another woman in more than a year.

'Hey,' the woman said, resting a hand on her shoulder. 'Hey, it's OK. We're friendly.'

Kitzinger looked over the woman's shoulder at the other Sunless: a young attractive lad, who grinned back at her. His teeth were already a little smeared.

'Hello Kitzinger,' he said. Now that accent she did recognize. The young man was an Ursulan. 'Remember me?'

And then he pulled open the collar of his uniform, exposing his shoulder, which was covered in dark-green Saurian scales.

The dragon boy. Iranda's brother. Here. Disguised as a Sunless. What was going on?

The woman who called herself Bernice Summerfield looked just as surprised as Kitzinger was. The bizarre Sunless woman turned to the lad. 'You know this woman?'

'Of course. All my Eight know Kitzinger.' He grinned again. 'All ten of us. She birthed us.'

'Crikey, Scott! Are you telling me this is your *mother*?'

'Don't be silly, Benny, of course not. There aren't any mothers on Ursu. Kitzinger tended the Blooms when I was born.'

Kitzinger was struggling to follow their conversation. The woman was either an idiot or . . . or she wasn't an Ursulan. Kitzinger was distracted by the object in the boy's hand. 'You have the female visionary,' she said, hardly able to believe her eyes.

268

He held it up for her to see. 'Yep.'

'But do you know what it is? What will happen if your brother and sister get hold of them both?'

The woman next to her spoke. 'Ah, that's a rather contested topic at the moment.'

'We have to keep them apart. Apart they are nothing. Together they could give the Sunless the power to spread across the galaxy.'

Scott became serious. 'What do we need to do?'

'Separate. I was trying to get outside to hide or destroy this,' she said, indicating the male figurine. 'But there were too many Sunless around the entrances. I couldn't get out without being seen.'

The woman Bernice shook her head. 'We're safer together.'

Ahead of them, from the direction Scott and the woman had come from, Kitzinger heard the sound of booted feet crunching on the loose rock floor.

'We're not safe anywhere,' Kitzinger snapped, preparing to run. 'Make up your mind, Scott.'

The dragon boy looked between them and then nodded at her before hurtling off. Kitzinger grabbed hold of Bernice's arm and dragged her towards a side passage. 'Come with me. There is so much I need you to tell me and so much I need to know.'

24

REUNION

Scott wasn't at all sure where he was heading. Just away from Kitzinger and Bernice. He needed to find somewhere to hide the little figurine or else find something to smash it to smithereens. He struck the walls of the ice corridors with it as he ran, feeling like a kid trailing a stick against a metal fence, but only succeeded in chipping off splinters of rock from the wall. Whatever material the visionary was made of, it was tough.

He decided to head for the entrance. Kitzinger had spoken of hiding her figurine in the desolate landscape outside. If he kept moving he ought to be able to get two or three kilometres away before the temperature got to him, unless his respirator gave out. The only problem was that he was no longer sure which way led out.

The tunnel he was running down suddenly opened out into a vast circular chamber. Huge ice walls leading up to an enormous glittering crystal canopy. But he was most struck by the two ribbed domes which sat opposing each other, partly submerged in the rocky floor. Clams on the ocean bed.

The Blooms.

He hadn't seen them since he was a child. His heart fluttered when he caught sight of them. He knew it was stupid, but he felt a little awed in their presence. Like every Ursulan, he had sprung from them a half-grown child, ready to grow into an adult among his family of peers. It was shocking to see them here, buried in the ice. He was so overcome by their presence that it was a moment before he realized that he wasn't alone.

Iranda was walking towards him from the dark scarlet shadows on the other side of the room. She was wearing a respirator and a heavy coat. At this distance she looked little more than a bundle of furs, but he still had little trouble recognizing her. She had always exuded confidence and charisma.

He hadn't seen his sister in several years. He had lived most of his life in the country and she had chosen to live in the cities with Nikolas. After the Sunless came he had been shocked to hear that she and Nikolas had been among the first to collaborate. He had never dreamt that one of his family would have sided with the invaders. He had wanted to travel to see them, to confront them, but movement between zones had been forbidden.

Iranda paused when she was standing directly between the two curved shadows and removed her respirator with a flourish. 'Hello, Scott,' she said, smiling. 'Have you got something for me?'

Not bothering to reply, he turned and headed back the way he had come.

Nikolas stepped out of the entrance to the chamber, his arms opened wide as if preparing to embrace him.

'Welcome, brother,' he said.

Sunless moved out of the shadows, flanking him on either side.

Bernice had stared after Scott's retreating back for a moment, before the sound of the approaching Sunless goaded her into action. Kitzinger had led her up through a curved tunnel which opened out to become a gallery, about thirty feet above the ground of a large chamber. They had a clear view of the small figures standing in the centre of the room.

They were just in time to see Jason's girlfriend take the female figurine from Scott.

'I said we should have stayed together,' Bernice hissed.

Kitzinger shrugged. 'Scott might still be free or –'

'Or we might all be down there enjoying my successor's hospitality,' Bernice finished. 'I take your point.'

The older woman turned to her, her weathered face creasing up into a frown. 'Your successor?'

'Oh, don't worry about it.'

She shrugged. 'I'm not worried about it. You look a little distressed, that's all.'

Bernice had forgotten all about Ursulan honesty. 'I'm OK, really.'

'You're a profiteer, aren't you? From the companies.'

Bernice couldn't be bothered to argue. 'Yeah,' she said. 'I am.'

They watched as Iranda moved to a disc of patterned stone in the very centre of the room.

'She's putting Scott's figurine in place.'

Bernice gasped as half of the crystal lattice above them silently blossomed with tiny sparkling lights. It looked like a chandelier, but – and she grinned at the thought – one with only half its lights working. Bernice had to blink rapidly as she adjusted to the change in brightness. A rectangular outline appeared in the stone disc. A section dropped away to reveal a grave-shaped hole in the circle. Bernice recognized it from the images recorded by the survey team which she had brought from the Butler Project back on Apollox 4, but her attention was drawn back to the transformation taking place above them.

The bright lights above her moved in almost regular patterns, like a repeating firework display. She chased individual lights across the ceiling with her eyes, losing them and picking up the trails of others. For a moment, she allowed herself just to enjoy the beauty of it, terribly relieved to be out of the depressing, all-pervasive, pale-pink sunlight.

And then her mood suddenly plummeted like a rock. She had been wrong. There *was* something here. Ever since Jason had first told her that the small statues were part of something ancient and powerful she had scoffed at the idea. She had been so sure that she had known better. Her view was supported by centuries of knowledge. Her view came from a discipline which had spent its long life laughing at all the treasure-seekers and grail-chasers.

She had gone along with Jason and Scott. But she hadn't actually considered the outcome if the Sunless did get their hands on a weapon with power beyond a sun, because, if she were honest with herself, she hadn't really believed them.

The lights reflected on the crystal walls like summer sunlight on a lake. She had been so arrogant, so certain. And, if there was one thing she should have learnt by now, it was that there were no certainties in the universe.

All she did know for sure was that she was going to have to work out a way to prevent the completion of the device.

'Nikolas is putting the male figurine in place now.'

'What?' Bernice exclaimed. 'But I thought you had the other figurine!'

Kitzinger nodded, not taking her eyes from the scene below them. 'That's right. He's only got the replica I carved with my dinner knife.'

Bernice laughed. 'Do you know? That is *exactly* the sort of thing I would have tried to do.'

Kitzinger continued to observe the scene for a moment before turning to grin at Bernice. 'What clever people we are.'

The figurine was in place now, but of course the ceiling above that side of the circle remained in darkness. They heard Nikolas's voice roar in anger. They saw him throw something – presumably the fake statue – against the chamber wall. He cursed Kitzinger venomously.

'He doesn't sound a happy boy, does he?' Bernice said. She was all too aware that Nikolas was likely to take his anger out on Scott, who was standing to one side, surrounded by Sunless.

'What now?'

'I'm not sure. I don't think they're going to take this setback lying down, do you?'

Kitzinger pursed her lips. 'No.'

They didn't have to wait long. Ten minutes later, Sunless

dragged Jason and Emile into the chamber. Bernice winced. Using amplifiers, Iranda issued a series of predictable demands which echoed around the entire cathedral-sized building. At the end of which one of the Sunless grabbed hold of Jason by the throat.

The meaning was clear.

Jason of course shouted for her not to try to save him. 'That is a classic Kane manoeuvre,' Bernice told her new companion. 'Selfless self-sacrifice is the oldest trick in book. He is *so* manipulative. He just *knows* I'm far less likely to abandon him if he tells me to. He is a such a git.'

'Are you sure this man doesn't just mean what he says?'

'Trust me. That man *never* means what he says.'

'Why not?'

'What?'

'Why doesn't he just say what he means?'

'I'm really not sure. I think he just never got into the habit. Or else lost it soon after we married.'

'Married?'

'Yes, you know, weddings and all that. Oh no, of course you don't. Tell me, do you have funerals on Ursu?'

'Yes.'

'Well weddings are like funerals, only you get to smell your own flowers.'

'Bernice, I think you need the respirator.'

'Why? I've just had it. It's your turn.'

'But you're breathing very rapidly, talking nonsense and your face is flushed.'

'It is? Oh dear.'

'What?'

'That isn't oxygen starvation, although it has similar symptoms and one of its effects is to close down the higher functioning of the brain. I should've recognized it myself really. After all, I have been suffering from it for a few years now.'

Kitzinger looked puzzled. 'What are you talking about?'

'Love,' Bernice said quietly. 'I'm in love with him and I can't let him die. I just can't. You'd better give me the figurine.'

Kitzinger shook her head. 'I can't do that.'

She watched as Bernice's face contorted through several emotions in quick succession: surprise, incomprehension, incredulity, and then, finally, predictably, anger.

'Listen,' Kitzinger said, urgently, remembering how Nikolas had tricked her into surrendering herself and then killed Aric anyway. 'We mustn't let them have the device – the consequences for my world would be catastrophic. They will kill this man, Jason, whatever you do.'

'I know. But I can't not try. I just can't.'

'Well I can. And you must learn to.'

'No!'

Emile looked up at the sound of the cry. He searched around the flickering walls of the chamber for a moment, before he caught sight of Bernice standing on a little ledge several metres up the far wall, fighting with a woman he didn't recognize.

Iranda and a few Sunless moved towards the distant figures. She gestured for two of them to leave the chamber, presumably intending to locate the passage which led up to the ledge.

They needn't have bothered. After struggling for a short while, Bernice lost her footing and, pulling the other woman down with her, they tumbled from the gallery they were standing upon. They slid down the sloping ice-covered walls, shrieking all the way, dislodging large chunks of ice, and collapsed in a messy heap at the bottom. A tiny avalanche of snow followed them down more slowly, dusting the two women with its white flakes.

Iranda slowed to a leisurely walk, before casually plucking the artefact from the middle-aged woman's hand. She returned, holding the little figurine triumphantly out in front of her. 'At last!'

Emile didn't know what to do. A female Sunless stood next to him. Another held Jason in its vicelike grip, forcing the man to stand on tiptoes or else be hanged.

Iranda jammed the little statue into a small niche in the floor. 'There!' she yelled. 'Finally, it is done. The device is complete.'

Emile cowered as the entire ceiling lit up with bright white light.

It was over. They had lost. He waited for something bad to happen.

25

BEYOND THE SUN

And waited. And still nothing happened. Silence filled the room. The chamber was now so full of flickering changing lights that it was as if they were all standing inside a kaleidoscope or superimposed against the background of a spangly music promo.

But no one here looked like a pop star. With their shaved heads and vampire complexions, they looked more like death-camp victims. The red-haired woman, Iranda, was looking maniacally around the room as if she might spy her prize at any moment. She had completely lost it. 'Where is it?' she cried. 'I need it!'

From the other side of the room, Emile heard a slow clapping sound. He turned to see Bernice rubbing the ice and snow from her hands as if it were flour. The woman Bernice had been fighting with broke out into a fit of coughing and then started to climb a little uncertainly to her feet. Bernice stopped tidying herself up in order to help the woman.

'You see,' Bernice said to her companion. 'What have I been saying all along?'

'It is here!' Iranda screamed at her. 'I can almost taste it. Come here!'

Bernice rested her hands on her hips and turned to acknowledge Iranda for the first time. 'Release Jason,' she said coolly, 'and we'll talk.'

'Attend to the device! Why does it not function?'

The louder Iranda shouted, the calmer and more controlled Bernice appeared to become. 'Isn't it a bit late for all that? Anyway, why should I? I presume you're going to kill us all anyway?'

However, Bernice walked over to the stone disc. She sat down on the edge of one of the graves, dangling her legs down inside. The light in the chamber rippled over her face in such a way that it looked to Emile as if she was bathing her feet in a tub of luminous water.

'Have you translated the writing in these pits?' Bernice asked Iranda in a chatty voice.

'Yes, I did,' Kitzinger cut in. 'Only on the other grave, though. I haven't seen this one before. I think the message is the same, though. I recognize the order of the symbols.'

'Really? This message was also with the figurine Jason entrusted to me. What does that suggest to you?'

'The repetition, you mean? I don't know,' Kitzinger replied. Emile noticed that she kept glancing nervously at the young red-haired man. Emile wondered if they knew each other.

'It suggests to me that it's all we need to unravel this problem.'

'And do you understand it?' the young man asked, moving to stand beside her.

'Almost,' Bernice said and then paused before adding, 'Hello, I'm Bernice by the way. In all the confusion, I'm afraid formal introductions have been overlooked. You must be Nikolas.' Without looking over to her ex-husband, she said, 'Jason has been without a respirator for about five minutes now. Any longer and he will begin to suffer severely. Much longer and he will die. Call off your dogs and I will tell you what I know.'

Nikolas exchanged glances with Iranda and then gestured to the Sunless. At first the silent creatures didn't respond. And then Nikolas said something in their language – it didn't sound like an order. More like a request. Even a plea. The female Sunless released Jason.

Jason sank slowly to his knees, gasping in the thin

atmosphere. Without thinking about his own safety, Emile hurried over to Jason and fixed his own respirator over the man's face. He knelt by Jason, resting the palm of his hand on the older man's back, which was trembling violently. Emile remembered the first time he had seen Bernice's ex-husband, at the dig on Apollox 4. Jason Kane looked about a hundred years older. Mind you, it felt about a hundred years since then.

'Thank you,' Bernice said very quietly. She smiled gratefully at Emile and he felt her appreciation wash over him in the cold room.

'We've done what you asked. Now tell us!' Nikolas was almost begging now.

'All right, but you won't like it. Kitzinger, what did you make of that section?'

Kitzinger peered at the side of the pit where Bernice was pointing. 'Oh, I *do* recognize that, it says: "The vision of the male and the female will lead us out of the night".'

'And here?'

'Er, oh yes: "The visionaries will give themselves up to release the power beyond the sun".'

'You used a puter, right?'

Kitzinger nodded. 'Yes. Yes, I did. How did you know?'

'Me too. Software must employ similar interpretative strategies. It hasn't got to grips with the syntax at all. It got the words partially right, but the ordering of words is all wrong. I mean anyone can see it doesn't make sense.'

'That's what I thought when Nikolas first suggested that the figurine was the visionary, because how could a statue have a vision?'

Bernice nodded. 'One thing is clear: they are not referring to the crystal representations.'

'Representations?' Iranda snorted.

'That's right.' Bernice nodded, completely ignoring the woman's dismissive tone. 'They aren't the visionaries – only the representations of them.'

Iranda smiled coldly, as if she knew what was coming and didn't like it. 'Then what is?'

'It's obvious, isn't it? You are.'

Iranda swallowed down a wave of nausea. The Ache was so strong, she found it hard to concentrate on what Summerfield was saying. All she knew was that she had to have an end to the pain inside her. Nothing could distract her from the desperate need that every nerve in her body was expressing. A need for *something*.

Bernice's words had stung her. Penetrated her as only truth could. They *were* the visionaries.

The visionaries will lead us out of the night.

And give themselves up for the power beyond the sun.

Give themselves up? No, she couldn't accept that. She wouldn't. Her mouth was dry, there was a roaring in her ears, and she had to shout to be sure that she was speaking at all.

Through the misty glass lenses of her respirator, Bernice watched as Iranda staggered back a few steps as if she had been punched.

'You know nothing about this!' the young woman yelled at her.

I know more than you, Bernice thought. Iranda was wrong. In that moment, she understood it all. She appraised the striking young woman carefully, thinking hard about her next words. Eventually she said, 'I kept wondering why the super-villainess routine was so unconvincing. And now I know. It's because you were just covering up the fact that you really don't have any choice in any of this. You were pretending that you had chosen to search out the Blooms, to come here. You made a melodrama out of it in order to disguise the fact that you've just been following some kind of biological imperative. Just following orders.'

'I'm still an Ursulan!'

'No, but you're not really, are you? You never were. You're a child of the Blooms and the Blooms were programmed to make you years before the Ursu Group had even begun to dream of their world without rules.'

Kitzinger nodded. 'That makes sense. The theft interrupted

the process. If the companies hadn't stolen the Blooms from here, the Ursu Group wouldn't have been able to use them to set up the colony. The Blooms wouldn't have been programmed to breed the Eights in the first place.'

'But the two extra children from Scott's Eight would still have been born. Only they would have been born here. Where they were *intended* to have been born. The visionaries ready to activate the device, and most importantly, to use their vision, the knowledge they had been programmed with, to prepare the civilization which existed then for the momentous moment.'

'Then my family are all visionaries,' Scott said suddenly. 'And the dream is the vision.'

Bernice shrugged. 'The Blooms had been programmed to produce the visionaries, but they were already in use when the programme was activated, so everything got a bit messed up. Genes were mixed. The vision blurred when it was shared. It spilt over into all of your minds.' Bernice sucked on her respirator for a moment, before walking towards Iranda. 'I imagine that it must have been a bit difficult for you growing up in a society where freedom and choice were valued over everything.' Iranda said nothing. 'So here we all are. The device is primed. But the irony is you are going to have to die in order to activate it.'

'I am not a cog in a machine.'

'Well prove it, Iranda. Choose not to activate the device.'

Bernice used the tense silence that followed to think about escape. The two Sunless whom Iranda had ordered away had not returned, which left four. A male next to Jason and a female a little way to the left, standing on its own. And then there were two more by the entrance. She frowned. There wasn't going to be any escape that way.

As far as she was concerned Iranda and Nikolas were no longer really in the equation. Which left four Sunless and five of them. She chewed on her knuckle. They were not good odds.

Movement distracted her. She turned and saw Nikolas

walk across the stone disc to one of the graves. His feet fell heavily on the stone, sending small rocks skittering across the uneven rock floor. He shrugged off his heavy coat and let it fall to the floor. He pulled his mask from his face, keeping his pale head down, not looking at anyone. It was as if he were somehow ashamed of what he was about to do.

Iranda called his name, but he didn't answer. Didn't once look up.

And then he lay down in the open grave. For a moment nothing happened and then his body began to shimmer. He gave a short desperate scream, before the colour drained from his face completely. His hair and clothes dropped away as if they had only ever been delicately resting upon him. All that was left of him was a smooth statue, lying in the recess. Simple, crude features cut into a stone face.

Bernice ran her tongue over her teeth, tasting the foul greasy eyeliner. The atmosphere in the room had changed in the moment that Nikolas had died. As if the tension had been turned up a few notches or they were all suddenly sitting under a pylon.

One down, one to go.

Kitzinger was struggling to understand what Bernice was doing. Why was she trying to persuade them to activate the weapon? Even if Iranda died, the Sunless would still inherit it. It didn't make sense.

Iranda was staring in horror at what remained of Nikolas. Kitzinger reached into the folds of her coat and rested her hand on the crystal dagger. It was clear to her that killing the woman was the best way of preventing the Sunless having access to the weapon.

Iranda looked desperate. She was clutching her stomach protectively as if she were in pain. She kept repeating the same words over and over. 'That's not going to happen to me that's not going to happen to me that's not going to happen to me.'

Kitzinger slowly started to move forward, tightening her

grip on the hilt of her weapon. She stopped in her tracks when Iranda suddenly ordered the Sunless to put Scott into the second grave.

Emile was on his feet even as Bernice was angrily telling Iranda that the substitution wouldn't work. Iranda shook her head, as if she didn't want to hear it. Bernice didn't sound at all confident. The Sunless had moved away from him to snatch Scott. Emile had a clear path to the stone disc. To the hole in the ground. The grave.

Emile ran. He heard Bernice call his name but he didn't look back. He was just certain that he wasn't going to let them put Scott in the ground. Wasn't going to let them turn him into stone. And he could think of only one way to stop them.

Before he had a chance to have second thoughts, Emile slipped around the Sunless holding Scott and jumped into the grave, screwing his eyes up tight.

The boy gave out a high-pitched yell.

'Emile!' Bernice screamed, hardly able to believe what he had done. She skidded to a halt at the top of the grave. The pale-faced figure lying at the bottom of the grave stared back at her.

'Oww,' Emile said, rubbing his elbow. 'I duffed my funny bone.'

Bernice wanted to laugh, cry and smack him all at the same time. Instead she turned to the two Sunless who were holding Scott between them.

'The man you're holding isn't the visionary. I don't know what will happen to him if you place him there. For all I know you may damage the device.' She stared at them for any sign of a change of heart. Any sign that they had heard her at all. They just calmly stared at her, not even bothering to blink.

'Can't you see?' she pleaded, gesturing around the room. 'All this belongs to you. Why risk your legacy to save that woman's life?'

Iranda walked over. 'Nice try, Benny,' she said brightly. She waved over the remaining Sunless who stood at the entrance . They began to move smoothly forward, walking in step. 'Unfortunately for you these Sunless can't understand a word you've just said. Get that child out of there.'

Reluctantly Emile clambered out, kneeling in front of the grave, nursing his bruised arm.

'In a few moments,' Iranda announced to Bernice, 'I'm going to have all the power in this room at my disposal. And then we will see whether or not I am a machine or whether I am free.'

Out of the corner of her eye, Bernice saw Kitzinger pull a shard of blood-stained crystal from her coat and begin to move towards Iranda.

'Kitzinger, don't!' Bernice shouted, but she could see that her words were not going to have any effect on the Ursulan woman.

So Bernice charged forward and slammed her shoulder into Iranda's side. The woman staggered backward and came to a halt at the edge of the grave, just in front of Emile. Without looking behind her Iranda said, 'You don't get rid of me that easily.'

The two Sunless were almost upon them. Bernice saw Emile preparing to climb to his feet.

Last chance.

'Oh no?' Bernice said as she walked forward and pushed Iranda hard in the chest.

The young woman tried to take a step backward to steady herself, but Emile was in the way. She wobbled for a second, wheeling her arms around madly, and then she fell backward over the kneeling boy and slid into the open grave.

There was a scream.

The beautiful lights went out.

Blackness.

The sound began as a whisper and then increased into a whistling hiss.

'Here it comes,' Bernice said to anyone who might have

been able to hear. After the brightness she couldn't see anything more than grey shadows in the familiar pink gloom.

The whistle became a rumble. Distant but growing.

The ground started to tremble. Loose rocks bounced and tumbled painfully against her ankles.

The noise was coming from directly in front of her. The stone disc lit up from beneath like a luminous novelty dinner plate.

The rumble became a roar.

And then a beam of pure white light burst from its centre. A cylinder of energy burning in the very centre of the room. Bernice staggered, fighting to remain standing. The ground was vibrating like the skin of a drum. Ice and grit filled the air, irritating her eyes. Squinting, she saw the beam of light spiral upward and hit the crystal lattice.

The roof became a band of platinum fire. The room was blasted with heat.

She heard a woman – Kitzinger? – cry out next to her. 'We've lost!'

Bernice reached out a hand and felt a clump of short hair. Kitzinger. The older woman was, after all, the only person in the chamber who had any to speak of.

'We have to get out of here!' Bernice screamed over the noise. The chamber was bleached out, but slowly Bernice began to see outlines of shaved, uniformed figures. The light was too bright to distinguish her friends from the Sunless.

Taking Kitzinger's arm, she made her way to the entrance, where she found Jason and Emile sheltering from the brightness.

'Where's Scott?' Emile demanded.

Bernice shook her head. The last time she had seen him he had been in the arms of the Sunless. She closed her eyes for a moment, summoning the courage and determination to go back for him. She was about to set off when she saw a figure moving towards her out of the light. It was silhouetted by the bright pillar, edges blurring. A stick figure against the sun.

Scott.

'What happened to the Sunless?' she demanded.

'I don't know,' he shouted back. 'They just left.'

'I think we should follow their example.'

They ran out on to a different world. The pale pinkness which had drenched the entire landscape was gone. The blood-red glaciers were gleaming white. And the patches of rock were no longer maroon but light brown.

And a new yellow sun blazed in the sky above them, shining down on the landscape. A thread of light burnt between the highest point of the structure and the new star.

Grey figures stood in the plain staring up at their new sun. There were about forty of them, the crew of the ship and Iranda and Nikolas's personal guard. The Sunless were shielding their eyes from the brightness around them. Bernice saw the nearest one to her turn to its neighbour. And for a moment she thought she might have seen an expression cross its face. It looked almost . . . uncertain.

A large shadow fell across them as a black ship swung down to greet them. It carved a passage through the new blue sky, its six legs curled below it like pincers. It hovered a few feet above the ground, sending up a spray of ice.

It wobbled dangerously as if it might drop out of the sky at any moment. A hatch in its side opened and Michael appeared as the ramp extended. His face was mostly back to its natural purple now, but it was still streaked with white. He waved them aboard.

The ramp ended three feet up in the air. Bernice gave Emile a leg up to the shaking platform and then clambered on herself. She turned to help Kitzinger. Their eyes met and she grinned.

'You knew didn't you?' Kitzinger asked.

Bernice nodded. 'Well, I did what archaeologists do best. I made an informed guess.' Her good humour faded as she saw Scott refuse Michael's outstretched hand and he climbed unaided on to the bottom of the ramp.

'Is Tameka flying this thing?' Bernice asked Michael, who was now looking a little troubled.

He nodded.

Bernice turned to Kitzinger. 'Now we really are in trouble.'

The black ship headed off through the heavens. After a little while, the beam of platinum energy stretching between the planet and the star faded, almost as suddenly as it had flared into life. But the rejuvenated sun continued to shine on the planet, investing the huge crystal structure which grew on its surface with golden light.

At the base of the structure sat two ribbed, clam-shaped objects.

One gurgled quietly for a moment before falling back into a restful silence.

'J'VAIS LE DIRE A MON PAPA . . .'

From the diary of Bernice Summerfield

I didn't feel completely relaxed until the ship had shrugged off the planet's pull and we were safely in space. I collapsed on the floor of the bridge, my legs splayed ungraciously out in front of me. I ran my hand over the fine stubble on my head. I needed hair extensions, a bath, a posh frock, and a large glass of red wine.

Although not necessarily in that order.

Emile came and sat next to me. 'So tell me, Professor S, does that sort of thing happen on every field trip?'

'Good heavens, no!' I exclaimed and then thought about this for a moment. 'Well, not on *every* trip.'

Kitzinger joined us, still wearing her heavy coat. Her short hair was full of grit and flakes of ice. 'There is just one thing I don't understand,' she said after a moment's contemplation.

Jason caught my eye and grinned privately.

'How did you know what the device was?' Kitzinger asked.

'Well I had the advantage of not believing in any of that tosh about weapons in the first place. I have said this before but I do feel that it is worth reiterating, if only for the benefit of those of you who are about to embark on archaeology degrees. Ancient and powerful civilizations do not leave dangerous weapons lying around on the off chance that their descendants should ever find themselves in a tight squeeze and need them. The whole idea is silly nonsense. But once I realized that I had been wrong to think that there wasn't anything there at all, I went back to first principles and tried to work out what kind of device an ancient civilization *might* leave for its descendants.

When I looked at the inscription again I realized the mistake the puter had made. It wasn't power beyond the sun, which is quite an awkward description anyway. It was to power the sun beyond its natural life. The puter couldn't get to grips with the syntax of the language and missed a couple of words, that's all.'

Jason scratched his chin. 'You got all that from a single sentence?' he said, obviously impressed with my genius.

'Oh yes,' I said, beaming.

Kitzinger sat down on the floor next to me and I brushed the grit out of her hair. 'That's why I had to stop you killing Iranda. Because otherwise the Sunless wouldn't have ever got what they wanted and would have taken out their frustrations on us.'

She asked me what I thought would happen to them. And I told her that I wasn't sure. 'We need to send a message to Earth about Ursu's plight. But I doubt it will prove too difficult to drive the Sunless from the planet, particularly not now that their own world has been given a reprieve.'

'We will still have to rejoin the rest of the galaxy. Ursu will never be as I remembered it.'

'Without the Blooms to make Eights? No,' I said, 'I suppose it won't.'

Extract ends

Jason was content to listen to the two women as they spent a couple of hours animatedly discussing their theories about the origin of the device. Despite her deathly make-up, blackened teeth and bald head, he had never seen Bernice look so radiant. So alive.

Bernice and Kitzinger offered their differing theories with a great deal of enthusiasm, interruptions and hand gestures.

Kitzinger believed that the Blooms had been created by the ancestors of the Sunless before their society collapsed. It was a classic pattern, she said, repeated throughout the universe. Bernice disagreed, suspecting that the Sunless were actually the servants of the Bloom-makers, and had, at least originally, been artificially grown from the Blooms themselves. This made sense to Jason, as it accounted for their eyes being similar to Iranda's.

Jason somehow doubted that the companies had really not known of the presence of the Sunless before they had begun their 'salvage operation'. And their theft of the cloning machines had left the Sunless to scratch out a meagre existence on their increasingly inhospitable world. The Sunless had given up everything in order to stay alive. He thought about his own youth, hanging about Piccadilly and later in grubby interstellar terminals. He remembered the things he'd done just to get by, just to stay a few steps ahead of starvation or hypothermia. He felt a little sympathy for the ashen-faced creatures for the first time.

On the way to her cabin Bernice came across Tameka, who had tucked herself away in the medical bay. The young woman was hunched over Iranda's puter. A medical program flickered blue light over her face. When she saw Bernice she quickly suspended the screen. Bernice backed away. 'Sorry, I didn't mean to intrude.'

'Hey, it's OK. Wait up,' Tameka exclaimed, calling her back.

Bernice sat down beside her on the examination couch. Tameka had washed the pale foundation from her face. Her skinhead haircut only served to make her face more angular. Her thick eyebrows stood out further. Her eyes looked a little puffy. Bernice wondered if she had been crying.

'What is it?'

Tameka reactivated the screen she had tried to hide. 'I just discovered that I'm pregnant.'

'What?' Bernice exclaimed. 'Who? Not Emile, surely?'

'Oh give me a break! Scott.'

'Oh.'

'Yeah, "Oh".'

'Didn't you –'

'I didn't think I needed to! You were the one who told me that they used bloody giant clams to make babies!'

'Yeah, I was, wasn't I?' Benny slipped her arm around her. 'Ursulans can't have children with each other.' She shrugged. 'Perhaps only the women are infertile. Perhaps ... well perhaps after the blooms were taken life found a way. Who knows? How do you feel about it?'

'Dunno. A bit shocked really.'

'Yeah, I can imagine. Do you still want to come back to Dellah?'

'Well, I'm not about to set up home with the dragon boy am I?'

'No?'

'No. Well for starters I've already got a boyfriend.' She winced suddenly. 'Oh shit, how am I going to explain *scales* to Porl? But mostly because "falling in love" is yet another of those profiteering concepts Scott claims not to understand.'

'Ah. But shagging indiscriminately is no doubt a well-respected Ursulan tradition.'

'You guessed it.'

'They really do think and feel very differently to us.'

'What? Men?'

Bernice laughed. 'Well, I was thinking about Ursulans actually. Growing up in their Eight provides a template for their adult relationships, which are also non-possessive and group-orientated. They don't have that early experience of focusing completely on another individual. Fascinating really.'

'I don't need another tutorial, Benny.'

'No. No, of course you don't.' Bernice frowned, suddenly uneasy.

Tameka noticed. 'What is it?'

'I just hate the idea of the price of complete freedom being not falling in love, that's all. It feels mean, somehow. Does ... well, does Emile understand about this?'

291

'What? That Scott's a promiscuous shitbag? I don't know. I guess he'll just have to find out for himself.'

Bernice winced. 'Ouch.'

Emile was curled up in one of the Sunless's honeycomb bunks when Scott found him.

'Hi,' the Ursulan said. 'I just wanted to thank you for what you did back there.'

'You're welcome.' Emile slid out of the bunk and stood awkwardly in front of Scott, in his underclothes.

'And I also wanted to ask if you wanted to come back to Ursu with me.'

'With you?' Emile's heart skipped a beat. 'Why?' he added, more cautiously.

'Because I think Ursu needs people like you. To help us to try and remember what our lives are all about.'

'Oh. Right.' *Ursu needed him.* It was sort of what he'd expected to hear. But he wasn't going to lie to himself and pretend that it was what he *wanted* to hear. 'Thanks for the offer, but I've got to get home. I left without saying goodbye and I need to see my dad.'

'I understand.' Scott made to leave.

Emile called him back. He *had* to know. He couldn't let it just end like this. 'Back at the dormitory, you know where Michael lived . . .'

'I do, yes.'

'You . . . well, you asked me if I wanted to, you know, to have sex with you.'

'Uh-huh.'

'I was just thinking. Well, that meant that *you* wanted to, didn't it?'

'Wanted what?'

This was agony. 'To have . . . you know . . . to have sex with *me.*'

Scott smiled. It was a nice smile. 'Emile, I wasn't trying to keep it a secret.'

'Well I wanted to too . . . I just couldn't say it. Then.'

'I know.'

'You do? You did?' Was he just an open book which anyone could scroll through whenever they felt like it? 'Well, I just wanted to tell you personally, that's all,' he said, feeling a bit huffy.

'Ah.' Scott walked over and kissed him lightly on the lips. 'Well, I'm glad you did, Emile.'

'Oh?'

Scott only smiled and began to tug off Emile's vest.

'Scott!' he squealed, panicking.

'What?'

'Don't. I'm really fat. Can't we . . . can't I keep it on.'

Scott looked serious for a moment and shook his head. He pulled off his own shirt.

Oh my God! Scott had the sort of pecs that could give a non-smoking, vegetarian, fifteen-year-old closet case *cardiac arrest*.

'I think that there are far too many *things* between you and the rest of the world as it is, young profiteer,' Scott whispered. 'Too many things between you and me.' He tossed his own shirt on to the floor. Reluctantly, Emile allowed Scott to remove his vest and stood uncomfortably as Scott appraised his naked body.

Scott ran his fingertips down over Emile's plump chest and traced the bulge of his round belly.

'Yes, you are quite fat. What difference does it make?'

Emile was learning to hate Ursulan honesty. 'I was kind of hoping you were going to disagree with me, you big git.'

Scott laughed easily. 'Then you are speaking to the wrong man.'

The young Ursulan's skin was cool and smooth. His tiny green scales were dry, just like Emile thought they would be.

'Emile,' he whispered, 'beauty is just a decorated box with nothing but dust inside.'

'That's easy for you to say. No one tells you that you've got a *chubby ass*. And besides, you're the most beautiful person I've ever met!'

'Ursulans aren't beautiful. Not on the outside.' Scott prodded Emile lightly in his puppy-fat stomach. 'But inside

– inside we *shine*.'

Emile felt a wave of sadness over him. The same feeling of hopelessness he had experienced when he had first been told that his mother wasn't going to recover from her long illness. 'I don't shine. I've been so full of lies and shit for so long.'

'Emile!' Scott exclaimed, exasperated. 'Emile, you are such a complete *asshole*, you know that?'

Emile burst out laughing despite himself. Tameka's insult sounded so strange and funny coming from Scott's mouth. Like he was trying to swear in a foreign language.

And, Emile considered, maybe he was.

From the diary of Bernice Summerfield

After all that I tucked myself away in Iranda's cabin and shamelessly rifled through her belongings. I was lying on her bunk, staring at the ceiling, when Jason came in. He sat quietly on the edge of the bunk and didn't look at me.

After a long time he coughed and asked me what I intended to do next.

I sighed. 'Go back to work. I'm way behind schedule on *Down Among The Dead Men Again* or whatever I end up calling it. I spent the advance ages ago. I daren't pick up my office phone half the time for fear it's my publisher. Plus a million and one other things that are no doubt pressing for my professorial attention.'

'You really like it there, don't you?'

'Dellah?'

'St Oscar's.'

'Yes. Yes I do. It's my home. I like having somewhere to miss when I'm away.'

'I was wondering whether . . .'

'What?' I sat up on one elbow and appraised him closely.

'Well, whether you might want to have dinner with me or a drink or something?'

I told him that I didn't know. He looked rather crestfallen. Actually, crestfallen is generous: he looked as if he were dangerously close to sulking.

Which, I believe, is where we came in.

'Jason,' I started, not really knowing what I was going to say next. 'Asking me if we can start seeing each other again, I mean, it's like asking me if after having had one car crash I want another.'

He looked a bit wounded by that. He got up and started fiddling with something on the nearby desk. It was the necklace Jock had given to me on Ursu. I explained to Jason about the Ursulan tradition of articulating their personal beliefs. Writing down their code of ethics. He asked to read it and I shrugged, barely remembering what I had written.

This is what it said:

Bernice Summerfield is a human being. And as such she is all too capable of being cruel and cowardly. And yet, while she is often caught up in violent events, she endeavours to remain a woman of peace.

Extract ends

COMING SOON
IN
THE NEW ADVENTURES

SHIP OF FOOLS
by Dave Stone
ISBN: 0 426 20510 3
Publication date: 21 August 1997

No hard-up archaeologist could resist the perks of working for the fabulously wealthy Krytell. Benny is given an unlimited expense account, an entire new wardrobe and all the jewels and pearls she could ever need. Also, her job, unofficial and shady though it is, requires her presence on the famed space cruise-liner, the *Titanian Queen*. But, as usual, there is a catch: those on board are being systematically bumped off, and the great detective, Emil Dupont, hasn't got a clue what's going on.

DOWN
By Lawrence Miles
ISBN: 0 426 20512 X
Publication date: 18 September 1997

If the authorities on Tyler's Folly didn't expect to drag an off-world professor out of the ocean in a forbidden 'quake zone, they certainly weren't ready for her story. According to Benny the planet is hollow, its interior inhabited by warring tribes, rubber-clad Nazis and unconvincing prehistoric monsters. Has something stolen Benny's reason? Or is the planet the sole exception to the more mundane laws of physics? And what is the involvement of the utterly amoral alien known only as !X.

DEADFALL
By Gary Russell
ISBN: 0 426 20513 8
Publication date: 16 October 1997

Jason Kane has stolen the location of the legendary planet of Ardethe from his ex-wife Bernice, and, as usual, it's all gone terribly wrong. In no time at all, he finds himself trapped on an isolated rock, pursued by brain-consuming aliens, and at the mercy of a shipload of female convicts. Unsurprisingly, he calls for help. However, when his old friend Christopher Cwej turns up, he can't even remember his own name.